TO GINA COVERT!!!

IT'S THE STUFF THAT DREAMS ARE MADE OF!!!

# PAINLESS

**BILL POJE**

Library of Congress Control Number:        2008908270
ISBN:            Hardcover              978-1-4363-7049-3
                 Softcover              978-1-4363-7048-6

To order additional copies of this book, contact:
Xlibris Corporation
1-888-795-4274
www.Xlibris.com
Orders@Xlibris.com
52636

# CONTENTS

## PART I: THE ATLANTIC COAST

## PART II: THE GULF COAST

## PART III: THE LANTERN OF DIOGENES

PAINLESS is dedicated to

# Dr. Fred Bernard

Who taught me what the art of the Word is all about

## A Poem to Fred

Whose Woods He Is in The Speaker Doth Know
To Speak To The World These Lines They Do Go
A Teacher And Friend My Wish Is To Crow

Twas More Than My Mind That Fred He Did Bend
My Thought Processes Too The Man He Did Rend
I'll Argue With You Again In My End

The Author wishes to acknowledge the PAINLESS influence and support certain individuals had in bringing the book to life:

Mom
Tom Poje

Rich Martin
Mark Wallace
Robert McRae
Jennifer McRae
Claudia
Jim Pierson
Elizabeth
The Professional
Swirl
Michael
Keith & Keith
Mr. Yes Yes

And . . . of course . . . the staff at Xlibris!

# Killer Beez

# PART I

## THE ATLANTIC COAST

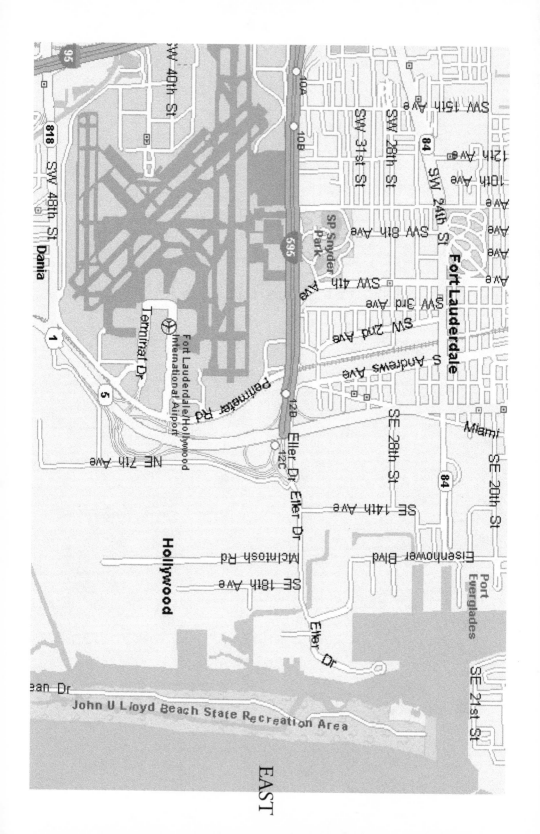

# CHAPTER 1

## AUGUSTUS VALENTINE

Icky Vicky was not icky. This was evident by the light beeps from the horns of the hi-los driven by the hombres at the Trove Import-Export Company as they passed by her. The men liked to see her big smile, and it was natural for Ms. Chavez to oblige. But then again, this was Vicky's style. Even when asking pointed questions, she would smile. Rare anger was the only emotion that sometimes took her grin away.

Her age was half past the hour, and she still fit snugly into jeans accentuating voluptuous hips. This made her feel good about herself. Her hips helped keep her lips pointed upward. Daily artistry on upturned lips made the cheeks go higher. Rouging the cheeks made the blue eyes smile brighter. The eyes would see how tight the clothes adhered to the skin, and the lips would swell a little. It was her version of the "knee bone connected to the hip bone" game. The difference was that the points of interest were not linearly connected, and the end bone was not in the skeleton song.

The start of this week was nice in that the Vickster was allowed to wear jeans today. The standard dress of US Customs Department inspectors is not normally so relaxed, especially so when at an import-export-company site. This day was to be spent in the warehouse of Trove Import-Export, looking over the opening of various container shipments that had arrived in the United States. This made today dress-down Monday.

Vicky's coworker companions were Julio Rios and Cameron. They were the grunt and the second pair of eyes and nose, respectively. They added legitimacy and protection on this visit. The legitimacy was added to make the trip look official and protected because one just never does know what one will actually find when one isn't looking for anything. At times in life, when one doesn't look for anything, one finds everything.

Vicky and Julio had paperwork on clipboards and various tools in hand and pocket. Accompanying them were Mr. Augustus Valentine and Mr. Francisco Garbey. Augustus was president of Trove Import-Export (which neatly acronyms to TIE). Cameron walked around on all fours and possessed a biological tool. Francisco, well, he may run the day-to-day operations at Trove, but some would just consider him to be a plain tool. Today they could work together and tie all things up.

US Customs normally does inspections at their own site for the x-raying or the opening of ocean containers. If there is to be a container inspection, then the inspection is usually only of one individual container. The single-container inspection will cover all the paperwork tying to all the goods in the container, tying out every single detail. If every detail ties up, then the customer is good to go for years. Fail any part of this compliance inspection and then Customs descends on the customer like a swarm of flies descending on a fresh cow patty. For today, US Customs made a decision to visit Trove and "eyeball" operations to get to know the company better. US Customs was legitimizing to make sure that TIE was on the up-and-up. The TIE employees were loving it. The eyeballs were on the operation they wanted to get to know better. With Vicky around, the employees were definitely on the up-and-up.

The customer is the end recipient who contracts with companies such as TIE to broker the receipt of the goods being shipped into the USA. The broker must, in fact, get power of attorney to be able to do this (a funny situation since most brokers are nothing shysterish like a normal attorney is). But if the broker fails to make sure the customer has their house in order for international transportation activity, then the broker and the customer get to have more fun with US Customs. No broker or customer wants that. This is the beauty of signaling theory. Since customs cannot inspect everything, they detail spot check. The signal has been sent that a failure of any part of the spot detail check means life becomes difficult for the broker and the customer. Today was not a spot-detail-check day. Today was a day not to find anything out of the ordinary so that it could be said that nothing out of the ordinary was found.

TIE's operation is located outside of the gate at Port Everglades. TIE is a two-minute drive from the port gate. When exiting the terminal, it is a short drive up Eller near where Highway 1 has NE Seventh Avenue curve off it. Fifteen years ago, Aug and Trove had opened up as a small brokerage. TIE now was one hundred thousand square feet for bringing goods in and out of the country.

Spending a day in a warehouse this size is why Vicky was dressed down. July in South Florida is always hot and working in a pole-barn-style building can be even hotter. Fans blow but not much else cools the facility. The day starts muggy from the muggy night before. The heat sticks to the skin. The skin breathes cooling sweat, making the heat stick to both the clothes and the skin. Modern makeup may not run or smudge as poorly as in the past, but it can still break down over the pores. The pores want to breathe, but they are filled. All pores get filled with dust and dirt. And there was so much hot air to deal with too, like plenty of whistles from the floor workers who don't get to see attractive females in the warehouse that often. There is nothing like a building of baying wolves held in check to make a confident female smile. Vicky's dressing down delivered dingolike dalliances.

Bay doors open at the start of the morning, and heat and dirt start rolling in. Semi and hi-lo wheels kick it up. The rigs are covered in it. Even rigs with seemingly clean insides bring in their share. As containers are opened, dirt goes everywhere. At the end of the day, it is always time to sweep up only to start again the next day. Dirt is even blown out of nostrils into Kleenex. Yuck!

Much of what comes into TIE are perishables like various fruits and vegetables and loads of bananas. Those perishables containers get opened and closed early in the day to get them on their way. Next up are loads of apparels: menswear, women's wear, and infant wear. Vicky and Julio snooped and poked and prodded at the items. The apparels came from Latin America and China. Those Latin Americans and Chinese can be tricky, and one never knows what may be found hidden inside some underwear.

After the clothing, Vicky and Julio checked out containers of furnishings and electronics for a real estate development in the Florida Panhandle. Then the inspection turned to skids of bar stock metals shipped from Russia and destined for a manufacturing plant in Cocoa. After the silver and pewter inspection came inspections of containers of personal goods of people changing their lives and moving their personal effects to the United States. Also included were expensive home furnishings for rich people who could afford to build dream homes and furnish them however expensively they see fit with globally purchased wares. Then came raw materials such as chemicals consolidated in the Bahamas or elsewhere for shipment into the United States. It's all the industry of industry influencing industrious individuals in innumerable idiosyncratic manners.

The day was long as it took time to look inside crates or to open shrink-wrap around skids. They took poking and prodding tools and devices out of back pockets or from tool kits to rend open goods to look for contraband. Hi-los moved more goods in while completed containers were driven away. In the meantime, export loads were being packed for shipment out. Ghetto blasters were blasting, mechanical engines were revving, phones were ringing, the PA system was speaking, people were talking. So much noise to be followed at night by so much *silencio*.

Francisco Garbey owned the title of operations manager at Trove. He had arrived at TIE's inception in the year of some people's Lord 1990. Things were small and more chaotic back then (like fifteen years is really "back then"). Now TIE was much larger, and business was a more controlled chaos. Frank sported a thin mustache and a TIE shirt with his name printed in script in the fabric. His Spanish skin was a little wrinkled and darkened with age. Was he ten years from retirement? Fifteen years had been a long time, and so had the preceding forty years. Older and wiser, he smilingly directed *la niños* wheeling goods around while spending hours on the phone receiving and making calls for transportation arrangements—or maybe for box seats to a Marlins game or a J.Lo appearance. Transportation companies in the United States are one of the best places to get great complimentary tickets to all events. Frank's peerage had its rewards.

During the day, Vicky evaluated not only goods but also the men around TIE. When one is waiting for the next semi to back up to the docks, one has to do something! It had been a few years since she booted out her lazy ex-*marido*, and she still kept a sharp eye out. Eduardo had been college educated, but he had no drive to build a career. He used her to do the work to generate the *dinero* that they lived off on. Here she saw men who at least appeared to show up for work every day. But they would not amount to much. They would love to have her pull their chain. Then they could go back to their *esposa legitima* and yell at her for being something other than what they wanted.

Francisco was older and wiser; he was not what Icky considered a good catch. Frank was a little shorter than she was, but at twenty years difference, he did not fit her classification scale of ranking candidates. Aug was a different tale altogether. Aug had built Trove, and by luck, today, he even happened to be around to go through the shipments. He'd be a great deal. Aug was tall, slender, possessed a tanned whiteness and hazel green eyes, with intelligence that would simultaneously smile and seem devious. There was almost always a smile on his lips. His curly hair was cut short and nicely layered. Even after a day of poking through containers, it seemed as if his shirt color was still an unblemished white with black cuff links beaconing. No sweat seemed to appear. He wore such a cool tie. The tie was blue and black with a clef note design. A blue note! His seductive cologne seemed as fresh at the end of the day as it was at the beginning of the day. The background music pulsated beats that unconsciously moved her body. It was time to freshen up.

Augustus Valentine was on his cell phone when Vicky came back. "Yes, well, I am sure that there is some present for you that came back with me." Pause. "Baby, it's a surprise. It won't be much of a surprise if I spoil it by telling you what the surprise is!" Pause. "Yes, well, I gotta go." He turned and winked at Vicky. "That Icky government agent of ours is calling, so I need to wind things up here." Pause. "HEY! You be nice! I'll call you later. Love you! Bye!"

Vicky looked at Aug somewhat lasciviously. "Hmmph! Who's that? Your hag from up the coast? The one that leaves you alone at night while she goes out and plays?"

Aug beamed. "Now, now, now, be nice. Jocelyn is a nice girl. I think you would like her if you ever got to know her better."

Vicky angrily retorted, "Is she Latino? No? Then I don't like her, and I don't want to get to know her better! She is no good for you! You could do so much better. You need a good warm-blooded Hispanic from down here in your home area to take care of your affairs!" Vicky paused a second. "And furthermore, I wish you wouldn't call me Icky!" She posed with a wonderful smile for him. "Just what is so icky about Vicky? Hmmm?"

They both laughed on that one. His loud voice was always dominant. "First off, there is definitely nothing icky about Vicky. The words just rhyme nicely. Second, I may live here, but this is not my home area. There's never any snow on the ground here, and you never ever see your breath in the air. The place I remember as home is a place where one could make snow angels and go sledding down hills in the winter. Heck, we used to make ice hills and try to stand up on them while going down the hills. It's kinda dangerous 'cuz if you fall backward and crack your head, you can do some serious damage, but that made it fun too. Ya know, another thing we used to do as kids was we used to break icicles off the eaves of houses and eat them. Then again, in the summer, the weather would sometimes get hotter and muggier than it is here today. But here? Here, there is always heat and wet. No, I may live here, but it has never become home. Now come on, here is the next container ready to go. Let's get this over with. It's getting late."

Vicky replied, "See? That is just what I am talking about. If you had a good woman, you wouldn't feel that way about living here. There is beauty that you have not seen or tasted. You should enjoy the heat and the wet rather than reject it. Besides, listen to you, Mr. 'It's getting late.' Where are you going tonight? Anywhere? Maybe out to dinner and some wine and dancing somewhere? Hmmm? No?"

Aug laughed and parried, "No, I am not going out anywhere. I've been gone away for a few weeks. I need to work late tonight to catch up on things around here." Aug eyed Vicky. "And I'm thinking of eating Oriental for dinner tonight."

Vicky was indignant. "Well," she fumed, "you can just . . . ," and Vicky let off an angry Spanish torrent of words that Aug did not fully understand. Her meaning was not lost on him. To accentuate her point, she hit him with her clipboard. Vicky ended with a "So there!"

Aug stared at Vicky with a large grin. He said nothing. Vicky started up again, "And another thing!" She smiled. "You should eat Mexican instead!"

Aug could not let that go. "Hey," he quietly asked her, "what do the sharks in the Gulf of Mexico call Mexicans?"

Vicky suspiciously eyed Aug. "What?"

"Junk food" was his reply. After that quip, it did not take long for Vicky to break her clipboard beating him about the head and arms while he laughed at her.

The shipping office was next to the loading docks. They found a replacement clipboard for her among the utility tools and paperwork on and around the desk. Vicky had calmed down, and she was reorganizing her paperwork on an unbroken clipboard. "You know," she told Aug, "you picked a very good time to be away. You missed Tropical Storm Anna."

Aug replied, "Yes, after last year with Charlie and Frances and Ivan and Jeanne, we hardly need more storms. Man, that made a mess of shipping last year. Half my crew is still trying to work out paying for housing repairs. I think they all owe the company money. I'm very glad to finally miss one."

Aug thought about upcoming events. He thought about the lies to come. Softly and aimlessly, he sang to himself a Stone Temple Pilots song lyric, "And I feel so much depends on the weather, so is it raining in your bedroom?"

Vicky heard him. "What is that all about? 'Is it raining in your bedroom?' See, what did I tell you? You need a new woman. One who is sunny. Not one who is stormy. You know, I might just happen to know some attractive, charming, happy female who is bright who just might be interested. Hmmm?"

Aug was amused. "Well, eagle ears! You are quite the word parser, aren't you? Didn't I just get done saying I liked wintry weather?"

Vicky chided him, "Wintry weather is not always stormy weather. I have been around, you know. I have been in snow and ice." She shivered. "Rent-a-winter is nice, but I'd much rather be warm and tan all over—warm from shedding clothes to get a tan rather than warm from putting clothes on-wouldn't you?"

Aug laughed. "You do got a point there!" He eyed her over and smiled. "You have plenty of points there!" They laughed. He said, "C'mon, we need to get this show on the road. Time's a wasted go."

Vicky flipped to her clipboard. "What's next? This is a twenty-footer from . . . Grand Cayman Island. After what Ivan did there last year, I'm amazed that they are even exporting anything yet! Let's see, what it says, we have . . . ten skids of Big Black Dick cigars, alcohol, clothes, towels, playing cards, shot glasses, hot sauce, and novelties? OK. This stuff has to be illegal. Let's pull a skid out and take a look." She smiled at Aug. "I've never seen a Big Black Dick before!"

The skid that was forked out had boxes of torpedoes on the top of it. Vicky called Cameron over for a quick sniff of the tobacco while Aug cut open the shrink-wrap and opened a box of cigars. Aug smiled at Ms. Chavez and said, "Here you go, Vicky. You can suck on a Big Black Dick for a while!" Even she had to laugh on that one. So did everyone within earshot.

Vicky picked up a random cigar and smilingly looked at the men around. "You know," she said as she smelled the stogie, "I'm sure that this cigar is like all the men around here." Vicky snapped the cigar in two and looked inside at the leaf and then at the men. "It's broken in two and dried up with nothing inside!" She sniffed the tobacco and wrinkled her nose. "PU! It doesn't even smell good either!" Satisfied that there was no contraband in the cigars, she placed the broken one back in the box and closed it.

They went through the rest of the skids. Upon clearing the goods, the contents of the containers were stashed on racks inside the building for various pickups later. The next container was a forty-foot-high cube container with a killer game inside. Vicky checked her paperwork and looked at Aug. "The Killer Beez game?" she quizzically asked. "One back cabinet, one front cabinet, eight lawn mower motors, boxes of parts? Lawn mower motors to go after killer beez? Wow! I didn't realize that the Brazilian superswarm had made it to Florida! What, are you going to go mow beehives?"

Aug undid the door locks and swung open the container. "Sorry, you don't wear your hair up! Anyway, well, I picked some old amusement games up in Italy to be fixed up at Refurbishments." Aug came close to Vicky and discreetly told her, "As for the bees, hey, you've never felt anything 'til you've felt their big sting!" Aug then told Frank, "We'll need all the boys to help get this back cabinet out. There's some bars inside for rolling the back piece out. But you know what yer doin'. We've handled these before, and they are a pain in the—"

Vicky cut him off, "Julio let's have Cameron sniff this stuff before Frank takes them off." She smiled at Aug. "Considering the source, I know there has to be something illegal in there!" Cameron sniffed around, but the dog did not confirm her suspicions.

This particular Killer Beez game was a sixteen-player game (sometimes it is made for fewer players). When fully assembled, players stand at the front cabinet and aim a plastic gun that looks like a WWII fighter plane—mounted machine gun with a two-handled firing mechanism. Plastic balls automatically cannon out fired by the lawn mower motors. In the back cabinet are both drone bee and queen bee targets. Hit the drones and the queen drops down. As in real life, the first player to kill the queen wins the prize.

The boxes of skids and motors were forked out. Then it was time to tackle the front cabinet. The cabinet weighed one thousand pounds, which made it easy enough for eight men to maneuver. By pushing the cabinet upward, the fork truck teeth could be slid underneath without tearing up the side laminate. Bars to roll the cabinet forward out of the container to the warehouse could then be placed underneath. The cabinet could then be easily rolled out. After getting the cabinet out of the container and onto the warehouse floor, then fork teeth could be used to hold each cabinet end up so that the rollers could be removed, and then the cabinet was set on the floor. It would be loaded into a moving van the next day for reshipment locally.

The back cabinet was much harder to deal with. It was thirty feet long and weighed five thousand pounds of wood and metal. The frame was covered in laminate, and the unit was wedged into the back corner of the ocean container. It was too heavy to lift, but there was no way to stick the hi-lo forks underneath without tearing up the wood and laminate. To move the cabinet out of the ocean container, they had to get started by first pushing the cabinet out from the back corner of the container.

Five men bent down and moved inside the cabinet to help start pushing the cabinet forward. They repeatedly slammed their bodies against the wooden pillars inside the cabinet frame—a semi-self-defeating task as they were standing on the flooring of the item they were trying to push forward. But since no one could get behind the cabinet to push, it was the only option available to get the cabinet started moving forward. By slamming their bodies into the uprights while workers outside tried to push and pull any way they could—all at the count of three—the cabinet moved inch by inch forward. Fifteen minutes and hundreds of swear words later, they had enough clearance where all of them could actually push upward, and the cabinet tilted back enough to get a starter roller underneath. Sweat of hard labor formed Lake TIE on the floor. They eventually got the cabinet to the floor and chocked the rollers in front of the loading dock so that the cabinet could be reloaded the next day.

The Killer Beez game and the games in the next and final container of the day were all redemption games that had been brought back to the United States. The containers had shipped from Salerno to Port Everglades. They were on their way to a small local business that Aug had a hand in named Refurbishments. Refurbishments did just that. They take broken things and make them look and work like new.

The Vickster was amused by the amusement games that were on the manifest for the last container: the Fireman's Ladder, a Whack-a-Mole, the Slam-n-Jam, the Wacky Duck, and many more. There were about thirty games listed on the manifest. Undoubtedly, they were strategically packed to maximize space and minimize damage.

The container doors opened. The first thing everyone's eyes went to were five giant white plush bunny rabbits sitting on top of Wacky Gator and Dino Spin games. The bunnies were three feet tall and smiling and oh so cute. The first thing to hit Vicky was emotion. The rabbits were lovely and wonderful. Then the customs agent kicked in. Where was the plush merchandise on the manifest?

"Aug?" she questioned slowly. "These . . . animals . . . aren't on my paperwork. Where are they? These aren't supposed to be in that container."

Vicky's paperwork problems did not matter to the TIE staff. Chum had been thrown in the water. It was a feeding frenzy to try and grab the plush and lay claim to whatever could be stolen. The laborers could get lucky for a day or a week with a cool plush present for a spouse, girlfriend, or child.

Frank bitched at the men to calm down and go clean the warehouse since it was the end of the day and getting toward time to go. Frank would personally see to unloading this container, and all employees would get their due.

Aug gave Vicky a look of surprise. "They aren't on your paperwork? They're on mine. What do you show for this container?"

Aug and Vicky matched up documents while Frank directed one hi-lo driver to move skids and animals out. Giant plush Popeye, Stewie, and Betty Boop came out on top of games. Smaller dogs and rabbits came out as well as teddy bears. Then there were a handful of six-foot pink flamingos in the back. A six-foot-tall panda bear came out.

When they matched up paperwork, they realized that they were looking at different documents. Aug tried explaining to Vicky what had occurred. "Well, what happened is that at the end of the trip, I was able to get the animals thrown in for free. Someone in Italy must have screwed up and prepared the paperwork based upon the wrong list. We can resubmit with everything corrected."

Vicky was not amused. "Aug, this is not supposed to happen like this! And you know better! This is going to cost you." She looked around at the plush material. A smaller dog about a foot and half tall caught her eye. He was Droopyish. Droopy was not outlandish like the other large plush. Puppy had a green body with a white chest patch and pink ears. Above all, puppy was a very cuddly smaller item. "I want this one," she said and grabbed the animal. Cameron, who had been busy sniffing the plush, growled at her in jealousy.

"What?" Aug replied, smiling away as he took the canine from her. "I suppose you also want a Tiffany Case too? Talk about breaking rules! I can't give you a present! That is definitely against the law. That's worse than the paperwork being bad! Two wrongs don't make a right, you know." Aug paused and thought about that as he scanned the other plush. "And what would Cameron think about you having another dog? Besides, a giant flamingo would suit you better. C'mon. Let's go up front and get the paperwork corrected and let people finish back here. That was the last load today anyway."

Vicky directed Jose to take Cameron out for a walk and to leave for the day. She would wind things up with Aug. Augustus and Vicky started walking to the front office with Ms. Chavez playfully grabbing at the dog under Aug's arm. "Awww, Aug, this one is soooooooooo cute! I can't cuddle a flamingo when I am sleeping! Gimme gimme gimme GIMME!"

Aug held the dog behind his back while she pressed against him for the animal. "Hey, now stop that! Now, it just so happens that puppy here is spoken for. You're just going to have to settle for something else!"

They had reached the door to the office. Vicky smiled at Aug. "Oh, I'm just going to have to settle for something else, am I? And so, mister, just what is that something else that you had in mind? Hmmm?"

"I told you. I think a flamingo is better for you." Aug gave Vicky a smile. "You never know. It could be the key to your happiness!"

Vicky rolled her eyes on that one. "Hmmph. A flamingo being the key to my happiness? That'll be the day. Now you tell me. Just who is my puppy for? Some crooked car saleswoman perhaps?"

"No no no. A friend of mine wanted something small like this to give to his niece, so I promised a puppy to them already." Aug stopped. "Hey! Jocelyn is not a crooked car salesperson!"

"Really! That's funny. I never heard of a car dealer who wasn't crooked." Vicky stepped back a bit to show her profile. "At least the only place I am crooked," she said with a big knowing smile, "is in all the right places!"

It was Aug's turn to roll his eyes. Vicky continued, "So that's the way it is, eh? Well, if you want to clear up this shipping issue, then you have to answer a question for me."

Aug replied, "Vicky, you know I always cooperate with the government. What is it you want to know?"

Vicky queried, "Aug, how come you never remarried?"

This did catch Aug by surprise. "I . . . uh . . . now where did this question come from?"

Vicky chidingly lay onto him. "You agreed to answer my question, not for me to answer your question. You want no paperwork problems with the plush? Then you answer my question! So tell me why."

Aug paused. They looked into each other's eyes; their pupils moved like rapid elevators up and down as an assessment process was occurring between two adults.

Aug explained, "Vicky, I like you a lot, and I would love to take you out sometime. But I can't do that, at least not right now. Trust me when I tell you it just wouldn't work." Another brief pause as he chose his words. "Ya know, when Laurie left, a lot of things changed for me. A lot of things changed me from when we first met years ago." Pause. "What I personally want out of life changed for me. It's hard to explain. Maybe it is a religious thing. Ya know," he philosophized, "some religions believe when you marry someone that is it, that you are married for life." Aug unconsciously felt his empty ring finger. "Maybe . . . maybe I still feel married. Maybe I am just not ready yet to take that step and move on." Aug paused. "Maybe . . . someday . . . we can go somewhere and talk about it. I . . . I think I would like that. But the time is not now, and this building is not the place."

Vicky saw a painful tiredness in his green eyes. The happy and in-control man she knew was suddenly somewhat defeated in nature. He had energy and was tired all at the same time. His tall, slender frame drooped a bit at the shoulder. She snorted at him, "Hmmph. I've never known you to be very religious at all, and I sure as hell don't still feel married to that lazy bastard who was my husband. But if you are thinking about it, then maybe you should not wait too long 'cuz maybe, just maybe, when you do decide to move on, at least this puppy dog may have left the kennel."

Aug softly and happily said, "If I have a change of heart, you'll be the first to know. I'll be the puppy returning to the kennel." He sang again, "'When the dogs do find her, got time, time, to wait for tomorrow.'" He held up the puppy and looked in the plush eyes. "Who knows? Maybe tomorrow things will be different, and this dog will find her. I'll be like Abel in the Bible, you know, the prodigal son who returned home?"

Vicky's retort was swift. "I should punch you!" Vicky followed through on her threat. "Abel? The prodigal son? HELLO! You dummy! Abel wasn't the prodigal son! Abel was killed by his brother Cain!" She thought a second. "Heck, the prodigal son didn't have a name! He was a character in a parable. That's it, mister! You're coming to church with me this weekend! You do need some religion!"

Aug embarrassedly laughed. "Oh. My bad. Show's you what I don't know. You're right. I guess I am not very religious after all!" He thought a second. "So you mean to tell me that the prodigal son was like a John Doe? That he was just another unknown nobody in the world? I guess that doesn't sound too appealing a person to be to me." Aug thought further. "That's funny. Cain kills someone and you know his name. Abel gets killed and you know his name. But the guy who finds his way in life is a John Doe. Nobody knows who he is. Doesn't seem like much of a way to make your name in the world, does it?"

Vicky placed a hand on Aug's chest. "Aug," she said, "that's why we go to church. Those are mysteries for the minister to explain." Vicky sighed. "It sounds like to me you still have a broken heart." Aug brought his left hand up to hold Vicky's hand. She once again noticed the large scar in the palm of his hand. The scar had always made her curious. It had to be another broken Aug thing.

"It was not my heart that was broken" was Aug's reply. "And I don't think any preacher is going to tell me how to think or what to do." He opened the door and beckoned her in to the front office.

"Well," Vicky said as she stopped before crossing through the threshold of the door, "you may be right. You may not have been the person with the broken heart." She paused a few seconds. "But I can't agree that your heart was not broken." With that, she crossed the threshold to the front office.

Yin 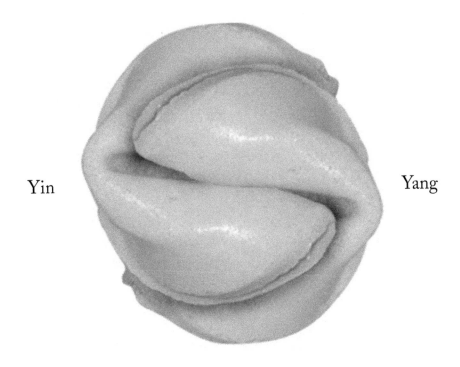 Yang

# CHAPTER 2

## WORKING LATE

Vicky and Aug wound things up after that. It was now evening, and everyone but Frank and Aug had left. Frank and Aug were there discussing the future of Trove, where things were headed.

The plush had secondarily been a deal for the employees to give to friends and families. Aug always looked for deals for his staff. Some deals buy long-term loyalty. Some deals are rewards for a job well done. Some deals are just bad deals that one can't do anything about. Both of them were dealing at the moment, and they both understood that it was both a good and bad deal. That made this a somewhat sad deal.

Many days when the warehouse closes for the night, semi-trailers are left locked up at the loading docks. This makes it easy for the crew to start working right away in the morning. Frank's final deal of this night before he left was to load a skid of Big Black Dick goods into one of these semis and park the rig in the yard and lock it up. Aug had been out of the United States for a couple of weeks. He had paperwork and phone calls and e-mails to catch up on. He would stay and lock up.

The Wild East Asian Bistro was called for food delivery. Yummy Oriental food always does a condemned man good, and Aug was condemned to a night of work. But eating crab rangoon and happy family does take some time. This means break time, a chance to catch up on the activities of the state. To occupy himself while eating his food, Aug perused copies of *Florida Today* that Maria had dutifully left for him.

The back pages of a week-old paper contained a Pensacola byline story that caught his eye. Some poor banker was in the wrong place at the wrong time and was caught in a drive-by shooting. The poor man took it right in the skull among other places. It was the second tragedy in a week to hit the White Sands Bank. The paper noted that the White Sands Bank president had also died in the last week of a heart attack.

Aug thought about how funny this story was. What a difference a region makes. If this murder had happened in South Florida, then this story would undoubtedly be front-page news. The death would be number X in a series of annual drive-by events. For Pensacola, a drive-by murder was a back-page item.

The story of the deaths activated Aug's brain cells. He thought about how only a small percentage of the population really want to consciously kill themselves. The rest of us all die by the hand of some fate. Some people die by an unfortunate deal of the cards. Depending on the game being played, some people are dealt a royal flush and are trumped by a lowly spade. Or maybe it was a heart or a diamond or both that clubbed these men. The banker's life of money had disappeared in an instant, although an instant may not always be as quick as it seems to be.

Aug's musings were interrupted as some bamboo shoots and snow peas became stuck in his throat. He was choking on his happy family meal. It took a minute to get his throat clear.

As Aug choked, his arms flailed about while he looked through the delivery bags for napkins to shoot shoots into. When he finished clearing his throat, he noticed then that he had received two fortune cookies with his dinner. Aug was curious. It was time to see what fate had in store for him. He cracked open the first cookie and read the fortune while eating the dessert. The first fortune read,

Your present plans are going to succeed.
Lucky # 7, 18, 32, 40, 48, 50

The fortune surprised Aug. He looked around his office. Was this a good omen? Was this a sign from God or maybe Buddha or Confucius? Now he was really curious. What did the other fortune cookie say? He cracked it open and read the paper.

Beware of lightning that strikes.
Lucky # 4, 11, 21, 30, 32, 46

This fortune disturbed him. Unease filled his body, and he involuntarily shuddered.

Aug stared at the fortunes. They mesmerized him. After a fashion, he folded them up and put the prognostications in his wallet. He thought, *I'd better not mess with fortune. If fate is giving me lucky numbers, then I better buy some lottery tickets.*

He looked at his watch. The time was about nine-thirty. It was time for a floor walk.

No matter the business, every good manager makes periodic floor walks. The eyes see so much more than what the ears hear. In the computer room, he saw the security cameras rolling. At the doors, he saw that the alarm was set. He walked through the door into the warehouse. He walked down the aisles in the warehouse. The warehouse was looking good. The aisles were swept clean. The racks looked organized. He saw about half the plush left on the shelves. He saw drums of HCL that had been brought in for shipment consolidation. He saw skids of metals for the Upper Terra Mint.

Aug stopped and looked at the skids. They were an odd item to come through. There were twelve skids in all. There were five skids of pewter. Each skid had a thousand pounds of pewter ingots. There were five skids of silver. Each skid had a thousand pounds of silver ingots. There was a small skid each of gold and platinum ingots. Each skid carried fifty pounds of precious metal.

A good businessman knows his customers. Mr. Valentine did not recall ever having processed anything for Upper Terra before. Nor did he recall having received or shipped metals before. *Well,* he thought, *new business is always welcome.* Aug continued on his way.

Trove was silent. The ghetto blasters were shut off. The phones were not ringing. No hi-los and semis were revving. No voices were over the PA. No one was yelling at each other to do something.

Aug turned off the alarm and opened up a bay door. He looked at the trucks in the yard. A smile crossed his face. His eyes gazed upon the sky, and he felt that they were violet, more violet. The stars were so bright. He was reminded of The Kinks song *Stormy Sky*. His baritone voice loudly sang Ray Davie's lyrics to no one,

"Oh-oh, oh darling,
Little darling,
Did you ever see such a stormy sky?
It's never been like this before.

I see it,
Can't you see it?
Do you see it?
Feels like we're in for a stormy night
But I can't see a cloud in sight."

His voice cracked a bit at the end, and tears welled up in his eyes as he saw the image of Laurie in the heavens. The past was remembered, and he wished he could have it back. A wounded puppy face graced his visage. Deep breaths were taken to restore his composure as he closed the bay door, reset the alarm, and turned his attention inward.

His destination was known, and it was reached. He was at the shipping office by the docks. He picked up a flashlight out of a wall holder, and then he walked out of the office over to the back cabinet of the Killer Beez game. Although the rollers were chocked, he was a little concerned about them giving way as he bent down to enter. The torch was activated.

The cabinet entrance was about five and a half feet high. Aug stood a little over six feet, so it meant walking in kinda bent over. About midcabinet, he found the spot he was looking for. It was a two-foot section of paneling in the cabinet that was set into the rest of the frame. He reached his hand over the top ledge and found a release. He activated the release. The paneling opened from the top out toward him. The two-foot section contained the treasure trove inside Trove.

Nine plastic bags were inside a very large bag. Each individual bag contained gemstones. The gemstones were inside paper containers. The paper containers were labeled with the weight and type of stone contained. Three of the bags had one thousand individual papers. These were to be the one-carat diamonds, sapphires, and rubies. Three bags had five hundred small paper containers in them. These were to be the two-carat diamonds, sapphires, and rubies. Last were the bags with seventy-five papers. These were to be the five-carat or larger diamonds, sapphires, and rubies.

Aug opened up a couple of the large ruby packets and looked at the contents in the flashlight. They looked good, they were a good deal. They were a dream of reality. They were a reality that was hotter than Hades. The supposed market value was forty million, but because they were stolen, they cost a lot less. Aug did not know the final price that had been paid. He had not made that deal. His deal was to move the goods into the USA, and then a commission would be deposited into his Bahamian bank account.

What were these stones really worth? Did he even care? Aug thought it was a funny thing, or a funny tingum. One day a stock like Enron is worth a hundred dollars a share, and then months later, the stock has no value. Yet the way that the Enron management operated had not changed fundamentally from when the value of the stock had value. People will believe that something that has no value is worth investing billions of dollars on. Then, when their God fails them, they place the blame elsewhere for their own investment judgment. Same as the management of the failed corporation places the blame for the collapse of the company on something other than greed or bad management decisions.

Would these stones perhaps have no value someday? Like Enron, how much would this handful be worth tomorrow or the next day or maybe even a month or two from now? Aug smiled and closed up the packages and bags and prepared to exit the cabinet. Exiting the cabinet proved to be difficult.

## WHOOSH.

Aug's head and right arm had come out of the cabinet first. The rest of his body did not exit by his own volition. He heard the quick *whoosh* of air but did not see the blackjack device that struck. He sure did feel it though.

The first strike upon his skull did not knock him out. It knocked him woozy. He struggled for a couple of seconds, trying to get his balance. His body bounced off the wooden cabinet like a pachinko ball dropping through a game. The bag and flashlight dropped out of his left hand to the floor.

## WHOOSH.

The second blow took him out completely. It was "destination ground" for him. His time travel to teen trauma took place before his body hit the cement.

# Laurel Park Place

## Now Open For Your Shopping Convenience

160 Ahhh....Cashmere
280 American Eagle Outfitters
660 Ann Taylor
290 Benetton
510 The Bombay Company
200 Chami's Menswear
175 Charisma Salons
360 The Coffee Beanery
690 Compagnie International Express
485 Coopersmith Books
MC Courtyard by Marriott Hotel
100 D. Dennison's
230 Dara Michelle
240 Eddie Bauer
130 Fannie May Candies
350 Footlocker
490 Gantos
680 The Gap
670 The Gap Kids
630 i Natural Cosmetics
J Jacobson's
190 Jos. A. Bank Clothiers
370 Leo's Coney Island

385 Little Caesars Delicatezza
MH Marriott Hotel & Convention Center
205 Mastercraft Jewelers
110 Max & Erma's
460 Meyer Jewelers
580 Musicland
NBD National Bank of Detroit
400 Olga's Kitchen
170 Optiks
550 THe Poster Shop
640 Rigorno Sunglass
340 Rivalry
540 Russell's Tuxedos
210 Sherman Shoes
195 Status Faux
150 Tobacco & Gifts
405 Unique Leather
140 United Health Spa
220 Victoria's Secret
270 Williams-Sonoma
470 Winkelman's
390 Y Not Yogurt

**Office Building**
AAA Michigan
AMC Theatres
Pro Tailor & Shoe
McElhaney Photography
Market Street Florist
SKF Office World

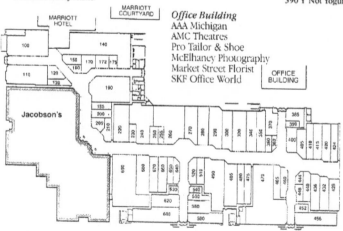

**Laurel Park Place**

HOURS
Monday thru Saturday
10:00 a.m. to 9:00 p.m.
Sunday
12 noon to 5:00 p.m.

(Including Jacobson's)
Restaurant, Theatre
and Health Spa
hours are extended.

# Chapter 3

## Summer Vacation

The Laurel Park Place Mall was hopping. It was late afternoon on a Friday. School was out for the summer. Big and little kids were everywhere. Women flocked to the newly opened Jacobson's to shop at the largest store in the chain to buy wonderful clothing such as furs on sale or expensive summer dresses or maybe even a Pablo Picasso sweater. The mall was an enclosed building catering to Livonia and beyond. It had opened the prior year, and there was still a newness buzz about it despite only having one anchor store. It was day 250 for the diplomats held in Iran, but no one at this mecca minded.

The mall had another draw. Across a fifteen-foot walk outside was an office building that also housed a new ten-screen movie theater.

Valerie and Augustus Valentine had gone to the mall for dinner and a movie. Mom was forcing Olga's Kitchen on Aug. Aug wanted either Leo's Coney Island or Little Sleazer's Delicatezza. Valerie had also forced shopping on her son. She had taken a long time to slowly wander through Jakes, Gantos and Winkleman's, all the while asking Augustus what he thought about a ton of clothes that he could care less about.

Valerie's hair and clothes were radical for her. Her Farrah hair was now cropped into a short pert coif. It was an acknowledgment of growth. The shorter and more discreetly styled the hair meant that the larger the growth to maturity as a human had occurred. It was a summer Friday night with her son. She had chosen blue jean wear that was discreet if not a bit baggy on her petite size. For now, formfitting Friday felt unnecessary. For now the need for nonverbal flattery from men was gone.

Val finally decided it was time for them to eat. The line for Olga's extended out into the mall. Valerie fidgeted with her son's hair while they waited in line. It was too thick for her liking. Many things were too thick for her liking. It was time to thin them out.

"Auggie, dear," she opined, "you need a haircut. We should get that taken care of soon."

"Awww, Mom, cut it out. I like it this way. I like having my hair thick" was his reply as he pushed her hand away. This whole evening out was annoying to him. Aug's friends were out causing trouble, and he wanted to join them. He did not want to waste Friday at the mall and a movie with Mom. If nothing else, one of them should be home with Dad—although the Tigers were on tonight, and Dad had a bootleg view of them on PASS. But here she was, buzz-killing his Friday night. His teen angst was blooming. Aug was torn between the onus of family obligation versus the desire to party.

Both mother and son had acquaintances who said hello to them while they slowly moved forward in line. They were perfunctory hellos that let Valerie look at purchases her neighbors had made at stores and which also allowed for brief chitchat. Obligatory questions of how Vitellius was progressing were asked. Would he ever walk again? And how was the court case proceeding? Had the News and Free Press really been correct in what they reported in the papers? What did Valerie think about the other woman? These were reconnaissance questions designed for information gathering for dissemination throughout the local housewives' guild. Valerie's answers were carefully guarded.

The answers to the questions that the neighbors asked changed Aug's life in the last year. The way he was looked at in school by his peers had changed. He was now the son of a juicy-gossip family. Before the car crash, he had been the son of a seemingly crazy but at least respectable family. The family was respectable in the fact that they had a nice house near the golf course and, therefore, that meant money. The family was crazy because Vi hardly ever seemed to be at his union job and the hot mother didn't work. That left them time to play.

Before the accident, other parents welcomed Aug into their houses. After the accident, parents would still allow him through their threshold with the offspring, but the reception was chilled. Mothers certainly did not want their daughters to have him as a friend. This was a "no future" child in their eyes, and mothers know best about such matters.

The true answers to the questions were what Valerie's life was, and she was not about to share the answers. Youth, beauty, and fertility were still possessed. It was time to get away from the rumors that had chased her for years. The past would always haunt her to some degree, and maybe she had not always learned from her mistakes. But that did not mean she had to face today over and over the rest of her life.

They were close to entering Olga's when Aug suddenly lurched forward a couple of steps. He was propelled by two hands on his back. The propelling was courtesy of Steve Champion.

"Auggie, buddy," Steve said. He proceeded to grab Aug in a headlock and give him a noogie. Aug fought back, and soon they were playfully slapping at each other. Mike Champion joined in, and the six arms flailing bothered everyone in line. Aug was still shorter than Steve and Mike, which gave them the upper hand.

"BOYS! Quit that! Honestly! This is no place for that behavior. Where are you manners?" Valerie started apologizing to the other people in line while the boys backed down.

"Awww, hello, Mrs. Valentine," Mike replied. "We're just funning around." Mike grabbed Aug's head and started knuckling Aug's skull again. Aug broke free and started another round of hand slapping.

Mike was the older of the brothers. They were a couple of grade C spartans at Adlai Stevenson. Mike was a senior, and Steve was a junior. Together they made a happy-go-lucky Mutt and Jeff sort, although some suggested that they were a white Amos and Andy. They dressed the part. They wore cutoff blue jeans and T-shirts that said Led Zeppelin and AC/DC. Steve was also sporting broken eye capillaries.

"STOP IT!" Valerie stepped in and broke them up with a display of disapproval. She looked at Steve. "Well, it's obvious to see that you've been in some other fights, Steve. Where did you get the black eye?"

Aug chimed in with a snorting laugh, "He got his ass kicked at the drive-in the other night!"

"Did not! I whupped his ass! That was a good fight!" Steve was grinning ear to ear.

Mike chimed in, "You got yer ass kicked, and you know it!" The Three Stooges routine started again. Valerie had endured enough.

# SLAP! SLAP! 🖐

Valerie tagged the two brothers and then turned her attention to her son. Valerie sternly berated her child. "Aug! Is that what you've been up to! Getting in fights at the drive-in? I hope you haven't been drinking there or doing anything else!"

Aug protested. "M-o-ah-o-m! I didn't do nothing. I was in the car, and we was watchin' the movie. All of a sudden, there was a huge crowd outside; and when we went to check it out, Steve was dukin' it out with some other dude. Honest, I wasn't doing nuthin' wrong!"

The perpetually grinning Steve and Mike chimed in, "Aww, he's right, Mrs. Val. Little Auggie wasn't doing anything wrong. He's too fragile. He's too scared. He was hiding under the car seat. He's just a little sissy boy."

It was then that the line mercifully let Valerie usher Aug in for dinner while the Champions went off to chase schoolgirls or something around the mall. The Valentines took a barstool table for two at the perimeter of Olga's. The restaurant was separated from the mall pathway by a four-foot wooden rectangle that kept the patrons in. Olivia Neutron Bomb was in "Xanadu" on the restaurant speakers.

Aug sat and idly looked around the mall. Unique Leather was behind him. The Coffee Beanery was in front of him, and Meyer Jewelers was across the way. His gaze came back from the jewelry store and stopped at the attractive young blond chickie working the sunglass kiosk. The kiosk was next to the gumball-machine area. The mall had an oblong setup of fifteen different gumball machines with all sorts of different flavors.

The chickie thought young Aug was kind of cute. She smiled at him as she drank from a Big Gulp and played with her display of shades and other jewelry baubles like cheap earrings and bracelets.

Mom found her son's eyeball flirtation amusing as she fidgeted with her wedding ring. "Aug, you really need some different friends than people like those two hoodlums."

Aug tried arguing. "Mom, Steve and Mike aren't hoodlums! They're just a lot of fun to hang out with. Besides, you and Dad really should talk about hanging out with hoodlums!"

Valerie snapped at her son, "Aug! Stop that. I won't have you talking about your parents in such a manner." Her tone softened. "Honey, what I meant was that, well, like, what are Steve and Mike going to do with themselves after they get out of high school? I mean, you're getting older now. You're going to have to think about your future at some point. What are you going to do? *Hang out* with the Champion brothers all your life?"

Aug answered, "Aw, Steve and Mike are going to go into the army. They signed up for the Delayed Entry Program. They'll be all right."

Valerie came back with "And you? What do you think you are going to do? Go into the army too? Don't you have more ambition than that? Dear, you have to do well in school and get a degree and go into business if you want to make it somewhere. You know, if this last year should have taught you anything, it should be that your dad and I won't be around forever, you know." She looked down a moment and then at her next generation. She grabbed his hands and, sighing, spoke. "Honey, I love you, and I don't want you to make the same mistakes that your—" She caught her voice a second and resolutely continued, "I don't want you to make the same mistakes that your parents made."

Augustus was not amused. "Geez, Mom, I'll be all right. What's yer worry? It's not like I'm a total screwup or somethin', ya know."

Valerie gave her child a motherly look, and she looked at her watch. "Dear, it's getting near showtime. What do you want to see, *The Shining* or *The Empire Strikes Back*?"

Aug made his play. "Aww, Mom, let's not go to the flicks. I don't wantta see either of those. Let's go home and see how Dad is doing. He shouldn't be there all alone. One of us should be with him in case he needs some help with something."

Valerie silently looked down. Emotion welled up inside her. She looked at her son drink his soda. She remembered his birth. She remembered him running around the house as a toddler. She remembered so many things prior to that. Quietly, she inhaled deeply and gathered herself. "Aug, dear, there is something we need to talk about." She took a deep breath. "Aug, we're leaving your father."

The soda went down the wrong throat. Aug chokingly got out a "What? What are you talking about? What do you mean?"

Valerie answered. "I mean exactly what I said. You and I are leaving your father. We're moving. Next week. We're moving in with your Uncle Mark in Philly." She paused as Aug looked at her. "Aug, dear, it's a done deal."

Aug protested, "But, Mom! What will Dad do?"

Valerie replied, "Aug, your"—she momentarily choked up—"your father will be all right. I'm sure he will be taken care of. But you know, there are a lot of things I've put up with over the years, and, Aug, I know how hard this is for you to understand. You are so young still. But . . . well . . . your father never needed anyone but himself. I used to love him, and in a way, I still do . . . but . . . over the years, he has taken advantage of me, and I have had to put up with it, but I can't do this anymore. You know, I wasn't much older than you are now when I became pregnant with you, and I was so young, and things were . . . well . . . things were different than they are now. But he has never really been straight with me, and now . . . now he has made us outcasts, and I can't do this anymore."

There was a truly pregnant pause. Valerie looked off, and tears came to her eyes. "Aug, I'm pregnant, and it will start showing soon. The baby is not your father's, and I can't go through all the . . . all the things that I'll go through with all the people who used to be my friends and stuff. I need to go, and, honey, you need a change too! You can go to a new school where people don't know what has happened here, and you can get a new start on things. Your uncle loves you and will be happy to have you around, and he's got other family too that you like. It'll be fun, and you'll be much happier, trust me. And you'll have a baby brother or sister to enjoy too."

That was it, she thought. The bomb was exploded. Mother and son silently stared at each other. Valerie averted her gaze to the front counter.

Val started talking again. "Honey, it's almost showtime. We need to get moving. I'll pay the bill, and we can talk about this on the walk over to the theater. You think about it, and I'll be right back."

Aug was floored. He was speechless as the recognition of her plan slowly sank in. Mom had made up their minds, and Dad did not know. The whole shopping trip had been a ruse. From his point of view, all he could see was that Mom was going to screw Dad over. He had made the journey from T-Ball to Little League a long time ago. Now he was getting a taste of a bigger league. Bigger leagues mean bigger costs, and now it was time to pay the bill and go to the movies.

Aug sat on his stool looking at the people in the mall. Ma had gone to pay the bill. He saw many people talking and laughing and people with bags walking around. They did not exist to him. The sunglass salesgirl smiled sweetly at him. He dumbly looked ahead. This would all be gone soon. Everything and everyone would be gone. When they had walked into Olga's, he had been focused on how to get out and party with his friends for the evening. Now he was going to be rapidly reduced to farewells. It was a youthful taste of surrealism.

Aug's numbed gaze saw Mike Champion walking across the mall floors by the park benches opposite the kiosks. Mike's gait was rapid. He barely could control his own laughter. Mike was coming from the direction of Meyer's jewelry store. He saw Aug seated at Olga's. Mike winked at Aug and rapidly turned the corner.

Aug's head rotated ninety degrees. Mike was up to something. This meant that Steve was up to something. Steve had to be somewhere. Aug's eyes found him on the far side of the jewelry store. Steve was hanging out near a mall map that was near empty stores that would be opening soon. He had a devious grin on his face. The construction cut down Steve's view of what was coming around the corner. To Aug's eyes, the situation moved in slow motion. Steve was down one exit leg of the mall. Hidden to his view was a security guard lazily walking up the center aisle of the mall. The guard was clearing by Coopersmith Books and Y Not Yogurt. A lady in Meyer's was being presented some watches to look at. Steve couldn't see it, but Aug knew what was coming.

Steve ran into Meyer's and busted into the shopper. He shoved her aside. Her grabbed the watches and took off. The reflexive screams caught the attention of everyone who was within earshot. Sunglass girlie stood up with drink in hand and stepped around from her kiosk to see what the hubbub was. She found out face-first as she stepped into Steve's path.

# SPLASH!

Steve barreled into her. The Big Gulp went flying and covered the chickie. Steve was stunned—but not from the physical contact. His view was of a hot wet girl lying on the floor in front of him with her legs opened. Her shirt was very wet. Steve forgot that he had just robbed a store fifteen feet away. He had to smile and apologize and try to help her up and to brush the liquid off her. Ms. Sales Girlie was in no mood for his help. "Get your hands off me, you . . . !" she screamed and started swinging at Steve. Steve started laughing as he parried her swings at his head.

Mall security was less chivalrous. Steve was in mid-apology after helping her to her feet when he realized that he was about to be tackled by a rather large male. Steve toreadored aside and reached over to the glasses and jewelry display. He pulled it down on the guard and the salesgirl. Merchandise flew everywhere.

Steve spun and looked to run out. The security man grabbed his ankle and tripped him. Steve fell forward into the gumball display. The security guard hopped up and unhooked his flashlight from his belt. He started cursing at Steve during this motion. The guard violently swung the flashlight at Steve's head. Steve managed to get his skull out of the way, but the Atomic Fireball gumball case was not so fortunate. The flashlight smashed the glass, and gumballs spilled out everywhere. Steve's eyes got big as he realized that the dude meant business. He was caught off guard, and he caught a shoe to the gut. A hand grabbed his shirt and lifted Steve. "Your ass is mine" entered his ears.

Aug hopped over the wooden barrier at Olga's. The security man picked Steve up by his shirt and laid him on the gumball machines. He raised the flashlight to deliver a big blow only to find he had Aug on his back holding his arm from swinging. The security guard tried flinging Aug off his back. Steve saw the opportunity to punch the security man in the nads as hard as he could. The blow glanced into the thigh and nothing happened. So Steve reached both hands out and grabbed more jewels and squeezed as hard as he could. The scream scared everyone in the mall, and the security guard collapsed, grabbing his family heirlooms.

Aug and Steve looked at each other and knew it was time to go. Steve hopped up and gave the security guard a kick in the ass before running down the exit aisle. They hightailed it to the exit facing the movie theater. Some men followed. Steve and Aug reached the doors and exited. Across the walk, security was coming through the door from the movie theater building. A green Skylark's tires squealed and pulled up between the groups. Steve yelled, "Shotgun!" and both he and Aug barely made it into the vehicle. Mike was not waiting around, and as soon as the car doors were opened, he took off while the boys scrambled to get in.

They blew across 6 Mile down Bloomfield heading toward Greenwood Park. The roads worm all over the place, and it is easy to get hidden. Such is life in the white flight suburb of Livonia where the middle class escaped the morass that the city of Detroit had become.

Steve gave high fives to Mike and Aug. He let out whoops of joy. "Oh man," he exclaimed. "I about peed my pants back there!" He turned and looked at Aug. "Auggie! Dude! You saved my ass back there! Oh man!"

Mike looked at Steve and Aug. He asked Steve, "What the hell happened back there? I thought you got nailed. I kept waiting and waiting in the car. I thought sure I was going to have to try and bail you out of jail tonight."

Steve informed Mike, "Brother, man, I shoulda been nailed." He reached back and started rubbing Aug through his hair. "Our adopted brother here saved my ass. If it weren't for him, I woulda been nailed!" Steve leaned back in his seat and then raised the upper half of his body out the window and let out a "Woo-hoo!" exclamation. He fell back in the seat and continued explaining to Mike. "Man, I grabbed the watches, and I was running out and that hot chick with the big ol' titties that sells sunglasses like stepped right in my way. Oh man, I tagged her. And she had like a Big Gulp that went all over her." Steve used his arms and legs to give the visual. "An' it was like she was lying there on the ground with her legs just wide open, and her shirt was all wet. It was . . . it was like allova sudden I was checking out Frank Zappa's 'Charming Mary from Canoga

Park in her bid' to win the fifty dollars!" Mike and Steve started laughing real hard. Aug didn't get it.

Aug pointed to Steve's right cheek. "Hey, you've got blood on your cheek."

Steve wiped the back of his right hand across his right cheek. There was a little bit of blood on his hand. He cranked the rearview mirror around to look at his cheek. There was a slight scratch visible. Steve said, "I guess I must have scratched it on the gumball machine."

While Steve was occupied with the mirror, Mike cranked up the stereo a bit in honor of his "Problem Child" brother. Mike then grabbed back control of the rearview mirror and asked, "Gumball machine? So what happened?"

Aug cut in, "Oh man, your brother nearly got brained!"

Steve grinned and said, "Yeh, but I got a couple watches outta the deal!" With that he reached in his jean jacket pocket and pulled out three women's watches that looked kinda nice to the boys.

Aug asked, "So what are they worth?"

Steve answered, "Hell if I know! Mike dared me to snatch whatever they were looking at. He didn't think I had the balls to do it! WOO-HOO!" They shared a round of high fives.

Aug was stunned. He slapped Steve across the head. "You stupid shit! Oh man, if you'da gotten busted, wouldn't that fuck with your army deal?"

Steve and Mike looked at each other and at Aug. Steve answered, "Yeah, sooooo, and your point is?"

Aug sat back. He knew they were crazy, but wow, this seemed a little too much. "Man, you got more balls than I do." He thought about it. "Hell, you got more balls than that security guard!"

Mike looked at Steve and Aug. "What's that supposed to mean? Hey, you need to finish the story!"

Steve said, "Oh yeah, well, like this chick was just all wet, an' I helped her up and was wiping the pop off her titties and such, and she starts swingin' at me, an' I forgot what I was doin' and just started laughin'. And this rent-a-pig came flyin' at me from nowhere."

Aug butted in, "He didn't come from nowhere. He was there the whole time. You just did a shit job of casin' the area."

Mike laughed. Steve continued, "Whatever, dude. Anyway, piggie kinda tripped, and then he tried to fuckin' brain me with his flashlight. That's when he tagged the gumball machine, and shit went flyin' everywhere." He looked at Mike. "Oh man, you shoulda seen it. And then I thought he was gonna brain me, and Auggie here comes flyin' in on his back and saves the day!" Steve high-fived Aug. The car started pulling into the Livonia Cemetary. Mike found a secluded parking spot while Steve continued. "That's when I grabbed the security dude by the balls and squeezed as hard as I could."

Mike's eyes got big. "You WHAT?"

Steve grinned and laughed. "Yep! I copped me a man feel! Man, it was weird feelin' too. It was like I was squeezin' his nads through his pants, but I could feel mine like shrivel when he screamed. It was totally not good. Oh man, I wouldn't want anyone to do that to me."

Steve turned to look at Aug. "Dude! That was awesome. That was great the way you took out the security guard. Grab that Frisbee out from under the seat and clean us a bowlful. This calls for celebratin'!"

Aug reached under the seat and pulled the Frisbee out. The disk was a 165-gram disc that had a few additional grams of weight added to it. There was some primo Hawaiian on a massive stalk inside a baggy. Aug opened the bag, and a very skunky odor was released. The buds were exceedingly sticky. Aug peeled a bud apart and produced a clean pile. Steve produced a glass tube pipe from the glove box. There was an open end near the bowl to use as a shotgun. Steve and Mike looked at each other, and the pipe was handed to Aug.

Steve said, "Dude, in honor of bailing my ass out, you get the first hit. Fill it up and fire it up!"

Aug obliged. He placed his mouth over the tube. The tube acted as a toilet-paper-sized funnel to the lungs. Steve lit the bowl for him. The smoke filled the tube, and Aug released the shotgun. Aug half-spoke and half-coughed. "You guys . . . *hack hack* . . . are . . . *hack hack* . . . fucking crazy." You're never going back to that mall again. Mall security is gonna be looking for your ass."

Mike took the pipe for his hit. Steve and Mike looked at each other and laughed. "Those rent-a-pigs are too stupid to remember me! Besides, they change people anyway in that job all the time. I bet that dude won't even be working there next month." The toking continued. "But I don't think your ma is gonna be too happy with you!"

Aug's surreality came back. He pounded his fist on the car window. "Fuck, oh man, Mom. She's gonna kill me. Oh man, crank down the windows. I can't come in reeking of weed. Fuck. FUCK! Oh man, you guys have just really made this day."

"Yeah, well," Steve laughed, "she ain't gonna be too happy of your taking out that rent-a-cop at the mall either. I don't see you heading to the mall anytime soon yourself there, Auggie. You better hope they don't stop her and ask her about you flying in to the security guard."

Aug's buzz started to worsen. "Yeah, well, I guess I don't gotta worry about being busted at the mall anytime soon. Ma said we're moving to Philly next week to live with my uncle."

The Champion brothers looked at Aug and then at each other and then back at Aug. "WHAT? What are you talking about, little brother?"

Aug nodded. "Yep. That's what Ma was telling me at the mall. She's leaving Dad, and she said I am going with her."

Steve and Mike both spoke in unison. "Oh man, don't go! Are you serious? Move in at our house. Our 'rents won't care. Damn, what will your dad do? Oh man, that's some fucked-up shit! What the hell is going on?" It was a buzz kill that the brothers could understand.

Aug told them, "I don't know what's going on. Mom just laid this shit on me while we were eating. It's really messed up. Man, I don't know what I'm gonna do."

Mike asked Aug, "What does your dad think?"

Aug looked at both of them. "Fuck. Dad don't even know." He paused a sec. "Dudes, I gotta go. You gotta take me home."

Mike resolutely nodded. He fired up the car, and they were off. The car windows were rolled down to aerate the vehicle as best as possible. They wormed their way through side streets to Fairway Street where the Valentine residence was. When they arrived, Aug opened the car door to leave the vehicle. Steve stopped him. "Hey, Aug. Thanks again. You saved my ass today. I owe you big-time. You need anything or any help with what's shakin', me and Mike 'll be there for ya." Steve reached in a shirt pocket and pulled out an Atomic Fireball and handed it to Aug. "Here, for your breath!" Aug popped the ball of gum in his mouth, and the brothers sped off.

Aug started up the front walk. His emotional state was high. He was in turmoil. Besides that, he reeked of marijuana, and he was quite high himself.

There was a quiet in the neighborhood. Somehow, the ranch house looked different. The garage door was down. The walkway lined with younger pines looked like a gauntlet. The three sparty green awnings that covered windows in the front of the house somehow looked ominous. All the shades and drapes were drawn. The chimney stack looked like it had wisps of smoke exiting it. He looked around at the street and saw a couple cars parked on the road that he had never seen before.

Aug came up the walk to the front door and tried opening it. It was locked. This was a surprise. Dad was home, so why was the door locked? The spare key was hidden in a flower vase off to the side of the porch. The key was retrieved, and the house was entered. He crossed the door threshold into the house and took a left turn into the living room. Halfway into the room, it registered to Aug what he was seeing. The day of surprises continued.

Vitellius had been a tall, strong man. He had stood six-five, but now he sat as a cripple in a wheelchair. His legs had been crushed when the steering wheel, dash, and door exploded on him. The air crash system was defective, and it exploded instead of inflated.

Standing next to Vitellius was a shorter man in black clothing and a black ski mask. Five and a half feet still looks tall next to a wheelchair. Dad was gagged; his arms were tied to the wheelchair. The man in the ski mask wielded a hunting knife. Aug's old man had been sliced up real good through his torso.

The man in the ski mask spoke. "Well, well, look who's here. Now ain't that a surprise? Just in time for the fun!" With that, the man in black sliced through Vitellius's right wrist. Dad's open artery spurted a blood mural on the wall. The Johnny Cash wannabe looked at Aug. "Now it's your turn."

Aug was blind with shock and rage. He screamed, "DAD!" Aug and the knife wielder ran at each other. They met in the middle of the room. Aug's right hand and the assailant's left hand locked together. Aug's left hand and the knife met. The blade dug into Aug's hand, but he paid it no mind. His dad was bleeding to death.

The males were locked in an embrace. They were not moving, but the masked man was stronger. The adult would shortly wear down the youth. Aug spit his gum in the masked man's face. He followed this up by spitting in the eye of the masked man. The hooded one wavered a bit. The spittle attack caught him by the surprise. An opportunity presented itself to Aug. He brought his knee up to try and get the jewels, but he caught thigh. The knifeman turned the blade in Aug's hand. Aug felt severe pain. He dropped to his knees. His right hand reached to his left hand. A knee came up and caught him flush in the mouth. It stunned him. A hand grabbed his thick hair and held his head. Another knee caught him in the jaw. His teeth bit his tongue and blood filled his mouth. Aug was out on his knees.

The hand pulled his head back. Aug was powerless to do anything about it. He could see the downward sweeping motion of the knife coming down at his throat. He barely heard his mom scream, "NO!" as she ran into both Aug and his attacker. Aug found himself bowled over, and he flew sideways and cracked his head on the fireplace hearth. He was out.

# CHAPTER 4

## PLUSH

Just like twenty-five years ago, Aug was awakened by someone shaking his body. Just like twenty-five years ago, his head hurt just as bad.

The police and paramedics had awakened him back then. He was still in his living room. The EMTs were checking him out. Was he OK? His head was bloody. There was a massive knot on it, and he had a blackened eye. His tongue needed stitching. A knife cut that ran across his throat was bleeding.

The medics were also working on his left hand. The knife blade had pierced his palm. He would recover the full use of the hand, but a nasty scar stayed with him.

There were also paramedics working on his dad, but Vitellius was long dead. His blood covered the wall and floor.

His mother was also gone. She had been brought to St. Mary Mercy by some unidentified man with her stomach gashed by a forceful knife wound. The blade ripped through her uterus. She spent hours in surgery before expiring. Too much internal damage had been done.

After the murder of his parents, Aug moved to the Philadelphia area to live with his Uncle Mark and his family. That part of Valerie's plan worked. Financially, though, his parents had not planned for Aug. Lawyers ate up any money the estate had left the young boy. Uncle Mark helped Aug get a management degree from Villanova, and later, he also helped Aug get set up starting Trove.

Twenty-five years later, he was awakened by Frank shaking his body. He was on the floor of Trove. His face was not bloodied, but there were a couple of welts on his head. One protrusion was across his right temple, and another was across the back of his head. Augustus did not yet know this. All he knew was that his head hurt and that the lights above him and the activity around him only made his head hurt more.

He was physically awakened, but mentally, he was having a hard time piecing together where he was. The overhead lights were so bright, and everyone was asking him questions, and he had visions of the past, and he crawled forward to the edge of the dock and had a good case of the heaves. His stomach was emptying a lot of bad things.

Maria had come out into the warehouse. He could hear her and Frank talk in a blistering staccato, but it was all Spanish gibberish to his ears. On a normal day, it was hard enough to understand them when they spoke Spanish very slowly to him. Today, all he heard was noise that made his head hurt. They were bending over him and moving him around to check out his physical condition. Maria was doting like a mother hen. She was very concerned for her boss man's condition. Aug rolled to his back and asked them to "Please just shut up. I'm all right."

A sense of reality kicked in. Aug looked around but saw no bags of papers around. He saw no one with anything in their hands. It appeared he was now a figurative eunuch. His jewels were gone.

Frank had taken charge of the situation. He directed the crew to not load or unload anything. He handed the new inventory list off the shipping desk to the warehouse staff and directed them to start checking the aisles to see if anything was missing. He directed Maria to make an ice pack for Aug. Frank would take care of checking the yard and the security tapes in a little while. First, they needed to get Aug to a chair in the break room.

The stumble across the floor wasn't too bad. The help that Frank provided wasn't really needed as Aug could function. While making the walk, Aug realized that he had a sore upper back leg. He emitted an "Ow" upon sitting down. It felt like his butt was bruised. His rear felt like someone had literally kicked him in the ass.

Phrenologist Frank was more concerned about the cranial calamities he was inspecting. "Hmmm, the right side of your head took a good shot. You are lucky That is a good swelling of the eyebrow, and the eye will probably turn black-and-blue with the swelling, but they do not appear to have damaged anything. Let me see the back of your head here. Ahhh, that is a nice bump here. Let me see. How does it feel when I do this?" Frank proceeded to give Aug a noogie right over where the skull was bruised.

Aug screamed in pain and reflexively moved his head and body out of the way. His body hit table legs, and he tipped over his chair as he fell to the floor. "GODDAMMIT, FRANK! WHAT THE HELL ARE YOU DOING! GODDAMN, THAT HURT! MOTHERFUCKER!"

The agitated response made Frank laugh. "Now you is awake! You got coshed pretty good, but you will be all right."

Aug was not amused. "Yeah, right. Tell me something I don't know." He climbed back into his chair. Aug thought a second. "I've been 'coshed' pretty good? 'Coshed'? What the hell is that?"

Frank informed him, "Coshed? That means hit with a blackjack. You do not know this? Well, I am not responsible for your illiteracy. You know, you make me laugh. You may not know Spanish, but sometimes, I think I know English better than you do! And I guess I already have told you something you did not know!" Frank thought about it a minute. "But I will tell you something I bet you did not know."

Aug wryly peered through his good eye at Frank. The tone of voice made him wonder. "OK, so tell me something I don't know."

Frank asked Aug, "What do a cue ball and a Mexican have in common?"

Aug was ready to answer when Maria came in with the ice bag. She rushed in and started pressure with the bag against his head. "Oh, Señor Aug, this is so terrible. We need to get you to the hospital. We need to get you to the doctor. We need to—"

Frank cut Maria off. "Maria, what we need to have you do is just keep quiet and baby his head for him. Señor Aug will be fine. We've got enough to do around here without sending him off to the hospital."

Aug yelped, "Ouch!" to Maria. "Not so hard, please! I've already been brained once today." He looked up at Frank. "And you! You're not my doctor. What makes you think I'm OK? You go to med school too?"

Frank beamed. "Ah, Señor Aug, I went to better than med school! I went to spic school! You know, you remind me of the crazy white boy I met a couple weeks ago who asked me if I had watched the Gatti Mayweather fight. Of course I watched the Gatti Mayweather fight! Who ever heard of a Mexican not watching a fight? Besides, you think I never had a bottle smashed over my head? I was not born either this stupid or this ugly."

Maria gave Aug some aspirin and water. "Don't listen to him, Señor Aug! He doesn't know anything. You need proper medical care. We need to get you to the hospital now. They know best. They can take care of—"

It was Aug's turn to cut Maria off. "Maria! Please. I think I'll be fine. I think this may be one of the few times Frank is actually right about something. Besides, I want to know what happened here, and I can't do that so easy from the hospital."

Frank walked to the door. "I am going to call the police and Mr. Kelly. I will also check the security tape and see what happened there. But I have three things to tell you before I go. The first is you need to take a punch better than you are taking this. After a fight, the boxers are up and about. Look at you. You are still down for the count. The second thing is you need to know when it is time to take a dive. That's why they hit you two times. You did not go down the first time." He opened the door to leave.

Aug had to ask, "And the third thing?"

"The third thing?" Frank looked at Aug and then Maria and smiled. "I am not looking at your ass for you to see if it is bruised!" Frank laughed and started to close the door.

Aug yelled, "WAIT!"

Frank stopped, suspecting that he knew what was going to be asked. "Yes, Señor Aug?"

Aug needed to know. "So what's the answer."

Frank's grin grew bigger as he said, "The answer is that I get to keep a moron in suspense!" With that, he left the room.

Maria quizzically looked at Aug. "Señor Aug, what was that about? What did he mean by that? He is not a very nice man, you know. And I still say you need a real doctor. You need to let me drive you to the hospital. Maria knows about these things. I'll get my car to the front door and—"

Aug cut her off again. "Maria, I love you. You are so sweet. And I want you to know that I greatly appreciate your concern. But I am not going to the hospital. The only place I am going is up front to the bathroom. And then I will go lay down in my office until the police arrive. I want to be here to deal with them. I'll be all right. I am all right."

Aug went up front into the restroom and entered a stall and gingerly sat on the throne. He left his pants up and thought about his reality. The robbery had occurred. What was his story to tell his Uncle Mark? Moving around had made him woozy again, and he laid his head against the stall wall. This lasted a couple hours until Frank rousted him again to let him know that naptime was over. The police were there, and it was time to meet them.

Aug washed his face and checked his image in the mirror. He had a good Frankenstein going with a bulbous eyebrow. The bump on his head was tender. He did feel quite a bit better. The fog in his mind was dissipating.

Detectives Joe Ortiz and Derrick Williams were with Frank and Jim Kelly. Jim was Trove's property insurance agent. They greeted Augustus in the warehouse. They reviewed where Aug had been found on the loading dock. They discussed that the alarm system had not been tampered with. Whoever had assaulted Aug had evidently turned off the alarm system via the current access code. The security tape system had been smashed. All existing tapes stopped short of showing the assault. The inventory had been checked over, and it looked like two things were missing. The missing items were the loads of metal for the Upper Terra Mint and a skid of Big Black Dick goods. The metal ingots appeared to be what the criminals had been interested in stealing. The commercial invoice valued the goods at five hundred thousand dollars. In relative value, the Big Black Dick was worthless.

They all adjourned to Aug's front office to review the situation. The chairs had to be emptied of the plush panda and flamingo sitting in them for the policemen to claim a seat.

Joe Ortiz started first. "I must tell you that this is one of the more unusual robberies I've ever seen. You just happened to be working late, get bashed on the head by some unseen assailant who knows the security system, and this assailant makes off with a half million in gold and platinum, and some Big Black Dick rum and cigars? So they had to back up a semi and load it up all while you don't hear anything? This is a most unusual thief. Most crooks that we run into wouldn't be so smooth. What do you really think happened here?"

The insinuation was incensing to Aug. "What do you mean 'What happened here?' I got beat up the side of the head! That's what happened here! I was taking a walk through the building. I was taking a break from dealing with the things that have built up since I have been in Europe. The next thing I know, Frank here is waking me up."

After a deep breath, a little calmer, Aug continued, "Now, this seems as strange to me as it does to you. I don't know what happened, and I don't know what someone would do with skids of pewter. My guess is that they came for the gold and platinum and silver and took the rest. But yeah, duh, someone obviously knew what they were doing."

Detective Joe looked at his partner Derrick and then back at Aug. He continued, "So these metals, they were for a business up in Cocoa? The Upper Terra Mint? Do you do a lot of business with Upper Terra? Do you have a lot of metals come through like this come through Trove?"

Aug looked over the shipping paperwork. "No, in all the years we've been in business here, I've never seen anything like this come through. It was kinda an odd duck. The guy who runs Upper Terra, Mr. Joseph Khan, contacted me about this shipment a few weeks ago. It was a couple of days before I took off. Anyway, I guess Joe usually buys his raw material in the US, but he got a deal lined up for these goods to come out of Russia. One of my other customers put them in contact with us to handle the shipping and clearance and Upper Terra passed a credit check so, sure, they seemed like a good new customer to me."

Derrick Williams chimed in, "You look like you got hit upside the head pretty good. How come you aren't at the hospital getting checked out?"

Aug replied, "Ya know, I think I'll be fine, and I can go to the doctor later on. Look, put yourself in my shoes. First, I gotta call up the Upper Terra Mint. You know how fun that call is gonna be to make? I gotta call Mr. Kahn up and say, 'Sorry, those metals you got out of Russia? They were stolen from my warehouse.' I don't think he's going to be very happy about that. And besides that, we're now going to be a day behind on all other shipping. The fricking trucking companies are gonna hate us too 'cuz all the trucks we have lined up to load today are pushed back. Then there are the containers to be loaded for ships that are leaving. We're gonna have a lot of pissed-off customers and vendors. I got a lotta logistical work to take care of, ya know?"

Joe asked, "And you have no idea who did this? No suspicious staff members come to mind? No enemies who might want to cause you trouble?"

Aug answered, "No, sir. No one comes to mind."

Detective Derrick chimed back in, "Russia? Do you handle a lot of Russian shipments? Is that where you were the last week? You said you were in Europe?"

Aug replied, "Well, we deal with goods from all over the globe. From Europe, South America, Central America, China, Africa, Japan, South Korea. But I can't think of any shipment that we've had come from Russia before. As for me? I was over in Italy. I was meeting with some other brokers and vacationing a little. I got in some diving and some R & R. I worked on my golf game a lot. My driving accuracy sucked, and it needed fixing. It's been quite busy around here lately. Business has been good. Now I am happy to answer any more questions, but if there is nothing else or if Frank here can handle anything else, I do have a lot of calls to make and a business to run at the moment and some insurance issues to discuss with Jim here soooooooooo . . ."

The detectives acceded to the request to move on for the moment. Their stated intent was to come back and review personnel files and interview more staff in the next day.

By the time Aug was through with the police and phone calls and normal business, it was the end of the day. There were plenty of messages to attend to, but two particular calls were necessary. He need to call his Uncle Mark and explain that something had gone wrong; someone inside had robbed him. He also needed to touch base with Jocelyn. Aug closed the door to his office and reclined in his chair.

The office was nice. It had oaken furniture and piles of paper. On the desk and wall were pictures and a diploma and awards from civic activities. There were pictures of Laurie and Mom and Dad and Uncle Mark and Uncle Mark's family and also of Jocelyn. These were the proof of a life that had been lived. The flamingo and panda had been placed back in the chairs. The puppy dog was now on Aug's desk. The plush smiled at him as he picked up the phone. Aug felt his left palm itch over the scar tissue while he waited for the call to be connected.

Mark Kledas passed his semicentennial a year ago. He enjoyed a wonderful fiftieth year. Life was good. Two sons graduated from college and they both had started both careers and families. His daughter, his princess, attended high school. For a parent, watching your progeny grow and be successful is much more important than any other consideration. Well, most days, it is.

Mark had also watched his adopted nephew grow under his tutelage. That was not the actual plan. The actual plan had been that Mark helps in getting Sis out of a bad situation. This was to appease his mother. Mother's wish was a mistake helping a mistake helping a mistake.

For years, Mark operated in the background of the development of certain family operations. This rewarded him well. He owned a residence in Bala Cynwyd. He owned a cottage along the Jersey Shore. He owned a lovely wife. He owned the ability to pay for his children's college in cash. He owned the connections so that he did not have to pay for his children's college in cash. He owned washed money in foreign accounts. And he felt he had a chance to stash a few million more away for his children as well as the opportunity to close some accounts. It was too good a deal to pass up.

At seven o'clock, Uncle Mark was enjoying cocktails in King of Prussia before enjoying dinner. He was with his bosses, discussing some unpleasant activity that had occurred in the last week when the cell phone rang. Mark recognized the caller ID. Aug's call was not expected, and so a request was made to be excused to take the call outside. He was not fully expecting Aug's story.

Mark answered the phone, "Aug! Welcome back to the USA! How's everything going? Were your travels were OK? Were they successful?"

Aug answered back, "Hello Unk, it *is* great to be home. Those extended trips outside the US get a little long, but Italy was nice. I made it back OK. And the trip was a successful trip. Where are you now?"

Mark informed, "Glad to hear that. I'm having some drinks with Mr. Vitale and Mr. Rossini. We are dining at Morton's tonight. I told them it was you on the phone, and they send you their regards. And where are you now?"

Aug informed, "I'm at Trove still tonight. It's been a long day. Actually it's been a long couple of days."

Mark queried, "Oh? A long couple of days? How so? What's going on?"

Aug relayed, "There was a break-in here last night, at Trove, while I was here, working by myself. Trove was robbed." There was silence at the other end.

Mark digested the news. His voice was very sober. "Are you telling me you were robbed last night? Am I understanding you correctly? Why don't you tell me what happened?"

Aug continued, "Well, I can't tell you exactly what happened because right now I don't know what happened. I was in the building last night working away, and then I woke up this morning laid out on the loading docks. Someone coldcocked me. I'm sitting in my office right now with two big lumps on my head and a black eye coming on. Anyway, between dealing with cops and insurance and keeping things running today, this is the first chance I've had to call."

Mark thought a minute. "Aug, I assume that you mean that this is not a good situation, or you wouldn't be calling me. Am I right? What can you tell me? Who did this? What's going on down there?"

Aug concurred, "Oh, you are right all right in your assumption. It had to be an inside job. Someone who knew what was going on. Whoever broke in knew the security code. They also knew how to destroy the surveillance tapes. There's no digital record of the assault or robbery. Someone knew exactly what they were looking for."

Mark paused and thought about what Aug said. The statement did not make sense. He asked, "Wait a sec. Aug, you said cops and insurance. What do you mean cops? What happened with the police? What was the insurance man there for?"

Aug informed him, "Well, there are a couple of things that were stolen out of here that we got insurance claims issues on. There was a skid of things from the Cayman Islands. It was a skid of various Big Black Dick things. Things like Big Black Dick rum and cigars and beach towels. And then there were twelve skids of like steel and silver that had come in. They were going up to a place in Cocoa. I kinda think someone came in for those skids, and they were surprised I was in the building. The thing that gets me is, who here did this? I mean, I know most of my crew pretty good. Good enough to know that they probably aren't hauling away a truckload of steel or metals. Or so I thought."

Mark closed his eyes. He didn't believe he heard that last one. "Aug, please tell me that you aren't talking about some skids of goods to go to the Upper Terra Mint. You aren't, are you?"

It was time for Aug to show surprise. "HEY! That's exactly what I am talking about. How do you know about that?"

Mark answered, "Uh, that's a separate story for later. Is that all? Is there anything else? Anything else you need to tell me?"

Aug reclined in the chair and felt the bumps on his head. "Ooooohhhhhh yeahhhhhh, we have a lot to talk about. Those car parts I was bringing in? They're also gone. All of them. Someone knew what they were doing."

Aug waited. He could almost hear the wheels of injustice spinning. He stared at the plush puppy dog in his office. The dog's face leered at him, even if the puppy face really couldn't leer. Aug asked, "Unk, are you still with me?"

Mark answered, "Yeah. Yeah, I'm still here. Hey, Aug, I need to run. I got some things I need to take care of. You take care of yourself and see what you can find out. I'll be back in touch real soon. You hear? Real soon. Keep your phone with you. OK?"

Aug wound up the call. "Sure, Unk. No problem. I'll be looking for your call. Have a good night, OK?"

Mark finished, "You have a good night, Aug. I'll be in touch. Bye for now."

Aug was grinning. He expected that the metal mishap surprised Uncle Mark. He had a feeling something was up. It probably meant a visitor shortly. Now it was time to call Jocelyn and check in with her. Her number had popped up on his cell phone last night, this morning, and this afternoon. Her messages were the typical "Where are you?" messages. What could he say? Oh, the lies and the lying. Why? Why? Why? Everything was built on lies, and he didn't like it. He wanted to be honest with her, but it could not be.

Jocelyn answered the call, "OH! Well, look who finally decided to return my call!"

Aug's said, "Hey, baby! You have no idea how nice it is to hear your voice. How's yer day going?"

Jocelyn said, "Don't you *baby* me, mister! I thought you were going to call last night? What happened? I thought after a couple weeks out of the country you'd be happy to seriously talk to me. Did you go out drinking or something? You couldn't have been that busy today to not talk to me. Trove isn't that busy. Maybe I'll just hang up on you! What do you think of that?"

Aug pleaded, "Awww, J, now don't be like that. I've had a rough day, and I have a very good reason for not calling last night."

Her bitter voice replied, "*What*ever, Pinaugio. Your reason better be good. You're on my shit list, ya know."

The process made Aug grin. "Trove was robbed last night. I've had a lot on my head the last twenty-four hours, so you just need to calm down and cut me some slack."

Jocelyn excitedly spoke. "WHAT! You were robbed? What happened? Are you all right? Details, details. Tell me what happened? Who broke in? Are you all right? Baby, I'm sorry I was mad with you. What's going on? What was stolen? Details. Tell me, tell me."

God, Aug thought. This is just like listening to Maria babble on in Spanish except worse. He could unfortunately understand this. "Now, baby, just calm down. Everything's OK. I'm fine. Except for a couple of bumps on the head. I was—" Cut off, that's what he was.

Jocelyn interrupted, "WHAT? Bumps on the head? Aug! What do you mean bumps on the head? What the hell happened? What are you talking about?"

Aug calmly spoke. "Jocelyn, if you'll calm down and let me finish, I'll tell you what happened. I was working late last night, and someone came in and sapped me across the head. I woke up this morning out on the loading dock with a pretty big headache. So I think I have a pretty good reason for not calling last night. Anyway, the crooks made off with some skids of goods, but everything is insured, so we should be OK. It's just going to take a couple days to figure out what happened."

They talked about the incident a bit more, and then it was on to the obligatory small talk about friends and acquaintances and cooing and innuendo and how they missed each other. They talked about the typical things that couples talk about when they have nothing to say, but they are apart and have been apart and want to keep saying things anyway. It wasn't pointless. It did serve a purpose. It served the purpose of familiarity. It was the same familiarity as going to a religious service at a specified time interval. And like a religious service, a mass was set. He would drive up to Cocoa Friday night and take her out.

The time was near eight when he was done on the phone. Everyone else had left. Like last night, Aug was all alone at TIE. He had the new security code, but it was not activated yet. Aug stiffly walked the giant panda bear and pink flamingo out to his nice blue DeVille. The plush filled both his front and rear seats. He heard the rumble of a sixty-nine GTO coming from the road. The Champion brothers had arrived.

Steve hopped out and said, "Dude, sweet eye ya got going there! Been to the drive-in recently?" Handshake greetings were exchanged. Mike and Steve then looked at each other, and the fight was on. Mike rushed Aug and grabbed him by the waist. Aug put his arms around Mike and started to rassle with him. Steve came behind Aug and gave him a noogie on the bumps on his head. That hurt Aug a lot, and he yelped unflattering comments with expressions of pain and started flailing his arms back at Steve. A flailing knuckle caught Steve squarely in the nose. This caused Steve to back off. He tripped over his feet and fell backward. Mike now had leverage on Aug as Aug had been fighting backward, and he proceeded to pile-drive Aug to the somewhat cushioned ground. The ground was somewhat cushioned by Steve's body as his face received a full Aug butt treatment as it fell on him.

This led to arguing and bantering and eventually laughing. After a while, they entered the front office. Mike brought in a man purse of goods. Aug locked the doors. He went into his office and grabbed a bottle of Jack Daniel's from a desk drawer and the plush puppy that had been Vicki's fancy. They adjourned to the warehouse. Swigs of lovely Lynchburg liquor were lapped from the bottle, and time was caught up on.

They were so many years different. Aug was now taller than the two of them. All of them had enjoyed the fortune of business travel. Aug's business travel had been through Trove. Mike and Steve's business travel had been through the army. Despite engaging in much nefarious activity, they had somehow managed an honorable discharge after a career in munitions. Aug wasn't sure exactly how they had survived and made money over the years. He didn't want to be privy to the details. He just knew they were trustworthy.

They looked so much the same except they were so tan from being in Florida for years. They were still wiry, and their hair was still jet black, maybe a bit more stringy. But they were still as happy-go-lucky as ever. AC/DC and Led Zeppelin had been traded for Alice in Chains and Nonpoint on their shirts. The brothers had been to Europe and Asia and the Middle East through a few tours of duty, but had settled down in Indian Rocks years ago. They had a nice thirty-five-foot Sea Ray that they would charter out or use for other activities. The Champions were champions of making friends with other current and ex-grunts, and there always seemed to be odd ways of making cash while enjoying a life of leisure. Not big cash, not all of it IRS cash, but not bad cash.

After a warehouse tour, Aug bade them to the desk near the bay doors. The dog and bags were deposited there. Aug opened up four of the bays to expose that semi-trailers were backed up to them. The trailer doors were opened, revealing loads of furniture and electronics and other miscellany for filling a bar restaurant.

Aug told them, "Gentlemen, and I use that term loosely, these are the final furnishings for Poseidon's. This is what we have to work with. Now let's see what you brought."

Steve and Mike looked at each other and smiled. The man purse Mike had brought in was maybe thirty inches long with a single zipper and a shoulder strap. Mike opened the bag and started pulling tools out: various tape rolls, utility knives, hammers, screwdrivers, drills, insulation. Then he pulled out the real goods: a time-delay firing device, explosives material, and two splatter grenades.

Aug pointed to the grenades and asked, "What are those things? I wasn't planning on hand grenades."

The devilishly grinning Steve picked one of them up. "These babies are cool. These aren't hand grenades. These are splatter grenades. There are a hundred little metal balls inside that shoot out. You don't want to get hit with these. They will hurt. They use them in prisons to, like, stun the inmates when there's a riot goin' on."

Aug picked one up and looked at it. It was a small round cylinder with some markings on it. He set it back down. "Well, you guys are the demolition experts.

God knows you've destroyed enough crap in your life." He paused a minute. "Are we all set for Sunday?"

The boys looked at each other and then at Aug. "Mike's gonna take the boat up tomorrow. I'll drive the Mustang up Sunday AM. The plan is that you'll meet us sometime late Sunday at the Sunshine Café. Right?"

Aug nodded. "Right. You got my grenade simulators and keys already?"

Mike replied, "Yepper! The noose is ready to go too. We figured out a quick install plan." He looked down a second and then looked back at Aug. "You sure you want to do this? I mean, I understand why, but this is nuttier than I think any stunt we've pulled in our life."

Aug laughed at Mike. "Look who's talking about nutty stuff! The man who likes to flash his nuts at people during parties! I don't see how this is any crazier than pulling your unit out for a crowd full of people. Besides, I owe some sort of payback."

Mike smiled at Aug, stating, "Hey, whatever gets ya off, right? It's all good! And speaking of being paid and showing things, we showed you ours, now you show us yours."

Aug obliged. He picked up a large knife that the brothers brought, and he laid the plush animal out in front of himself. He inserted the knife into the throat area and drew an opening. Using his hands, he pulled open the neck and started removing stuffing. Inside the stuffing were nine bags. These bags contained the real diamonds and rubies and sapphires. The prior night's haul had been replicas created to buy some time. The bags were removed. "Look at 'em and weep, boys." The whistles were long and loud as Mike and Steve checked the bags out.

Aug removed a couple of five-carat stones and gave one each to Steve and Mike. "Here ya go, you can each buy yourself a neat new toy. These aren't the replacement players. They are the real thing. And now let's get to work."

# Chapter 5

## Suzy's

Ed Amerozo was breaking Rocks. Rolling Rocks. He was also busting up over the Scab Eagles. "These guys are terrible. I'm glad this is the last weekend for replacement games. Man, it's gonna be fun when the Cowboys come to town. I gotta go to that game. There's gonna be tons of fights at the Vet, for that Buddy's gonna have them ready to commit murder! Too Tall's gonna be Too Small after they break his scab-fucking legs! Man oh man, that's gonna be a fun one!"

Mark Kledas was less amused. He had been sitting all day at the bar at Suzy's watching the Eagles play. The place was a hole. It was a pasty bar, and the only things working there this Sunday were old. There were only a couple of girls working. More like mature women beyond their prime who could only get a stint at a run-down dive like where he was at. They bothered him when they asked for dollars or drinks. They bothered him because it just wasn't what he liked.

There were less than ten people in the bar. Mark told Donald Vitale that he needed to talk to him, but why Donald had suggested this dump was beyond him. Donald had been adamant he wanted to watch the football game here. Mark found the suggested destination odd. He didn't think pasty bars opened on Sunday. It must have been a football game special. But it was so far away from the city.

He was really drunk now. The game was nearing the end, but the Packers had a field goal attempt to tie it. They had been there since the pregame, and along the way, this drunkard Ed had wandered over and started yapping at them about football. Mark was silent. He was still trying to get the nerve up to talk to Donald about what he needed to say.

Donald had drunk quite a few beers. "Oh my god. They're gonna tie this fucking thing. Can you believe that?" He watched as the field goal went through the uprights. "A fuckin' forty-six yarder by a scab." Mark was drinking more beer, so Donald slapped him in the back in middrink. "Whaddaya think about that? A scab coming up big. Fucking A. They say these games are gonna count in the standings, and the fucking Eagles will have lost everyone. Hell, they shoulda put Guido back in as quarterback. He wasn't any more a stiff than Tinsley is."

Ed chimed in, "These guys are terrible. It's another fuckin' year of nothin' for the Eagles. Fuckin' Cowboys. Fuckin' union breakers. I can't wait 'til they're here in a couple weeks. I bet I'll see a minimum of twenty fights in the stands." He finished his beer. "MISSY!" He raised his bottle, and the bartendress nodded. Ed turned and faced Mark and Donald. "Ya know, the last game I saw at the Vet, there were these two guys, see, and one was walking up the stairwell and the other down. Not another person around. And these guys, see, they gotta bump into each other and start brawlin' on the staircase. The fuckin' staircase has gotta be fifteen feet wide and these two guys can't miss walkin' into each other. An' it ain't like either one had a Giants jersey or anything. Fucking unbelievable. Ya gotta love it." Ed drank beer. "Man, I can't wait for the Cowboys game. I betcha Buddy will pay to have Dorsett's legs broken for crossing that line and playing. Oh man, I bet everyone wearing a Cowboys jersey will get their ass kicked. The Vet jail will be full that night."

"Markie, whaddaya think of that?" Donald took some beer in. "Ya wanna go to that game? Maybe my nephews can come along and see the fights. Whaddaya think?"

Mark quietly said, "Yes. Yeah, that would be nice."

Donald started in on him. "Mark, yer awful quiet today. You were the one who wanted to talk about somethin'. Well? Time's a-wasting. OT is about ready to start, and I ain't got room for too much more beer." Donald looked around at the working women. His glassy eyes and mouth smiled at Mark. "Or has my sister been giving you blue balls lately? Maybe you're seeing somethin' you like to have a go with?" He slapped Mark on the back.

The brunette that had been trying to work them all day came by. She ran her fingers through the hair of the men as she wandered past them. "Hey, boys, got a tip for me? Buy me a drink maybe?" She jiggled herself at them.

Mark noticed that she did look better than when he first saw her. She had big boobies, but they were a bit stretched and starting to sag. The face was covered in makeup, and the front teeth had gaps. Like most hustlers, she smoked cigarettes. Her mouth and body had probably ingested a lot of substances in her life.

Donald put his arm around her waist and gave her a fleshy hug. He looked at Mark. "Mark, brother-in-law, whaddya think? Got a tip for . . . what was yer name?" He bent his head back and looked at her. "Star? That's right. It was Star. Got a tip for Star here?"

She laughed. "Sure, big boy. Even if my name weren't Star, it would be for you!" They laughed.

Mark quietly said, "Sure." He pulled a dollar off the bar in front of him and placed it in her G-string.

Donald and Star looked at each other and then at Mark. "Well, ain't you the big tipper! I hope ya treat my sister better than that!" Donald looked at Star. "That's a thing I don't geddabout this guy. He loves playing with money, but give a nice tip? Gamble in a casino? Nope. He's too cheap for that!" They turned and looked at Ed. "It's Ed, ain't it? Ed. Why don'tcha help the lassie here out. Give the hard-working lady a tip. Why don'tcha show 'er what a tip is."

Ed turned his body and eyed her up and down. "Suppose I do give her a tip? What do I get in return? Maybe some sugar perhaps?" He gave her a dirty old man look.

Star smiled and walked over to him. She rubbed her hands and chest against his chest. "Well, who knows there, Ed? Make the tip big enough and maybe you will get some, ah, sugar?" She rubbed a hand through his hair. She leered. "Make the tip big enough and maybe I'll get some sugar!" They laughed.

Ed reached in his shirt pocket and pulled out a variety of smaller bills. He put a ten spot in her G-string. She smiled at him and said, "Well, that will buy me a drink, but I'm not so sure that will buy you much else." She walked back over to Donald. "And what about you? Are you the big spender of the group?"

Donald inserted Ulysses Grant in her G-string. Star smiled and gave him a big hug and a bit of a rub. "Mmmmm. Thank you! I bet you're also the big boy of the group, ain'tcha? Why don't you and I take a walk and leave these other big spenders behind? Hmmm?"

Donald laughed. "Maybe after the fucking Eagles lose this thing." He looked at Mark. "Hey, whaddaya thinkin' there? I thought you wanted to talk about somethin' today. It's getting late. What's on yer mind?"

Mark had been trying to discreetly bring up the business at hand all day, but he had gagged on every word when he tried to speak. He was fucked, and he knew it. He had done it to himself. And now he was out of time, but this was not the company to speak in front of. Not in front of strangers, and not in front of some drunk and some working girl. His head hurt, and his bladder was full. "I have to go to the bathroom," he quietly said.

Donald laughed and said, "Hey, don't let me stop ya."

Mark ambled off from his barstool to the bathroom. The door was flimsy, and so was the stall room. The sink was dirty. The sit-down needed cleaning. The urinal looked backed up. The basin bottom was filled with liquid and cigarette butts. He started filling it. It did not overflow. There must have been enough that pushed through as more came in to keep it from overflowing. As he relieved himself, he could tell how drunk he was from the beer. He morosely stared down at his stream and thought about how his bad news was going to sound worse now that they were drunk.

## *WHAM! WHAM!*

Mark had been so caught up in his misery that he had not noticed anyone enter the john. His hair was grabbed, and his head was slammed forward two times into the stainless flushing piping. The nose exploded in blood, and cuts appeared in his face and forehead, but he was too stunned by the savage blows to notice. He was out on his feet.

His legs were kicked out from under him, and his head was directed to the clogged basin. He felt a front tooth chip as he was given a nasty face wash. He tasted piss on his tongue and smelled it in his nostrils, and he started gagging. His head was pulled out, and he heard Donald say, "You stupid SON OF A

BITCH!" The face was dunked again. "How fucking stupid do you think I am? How fucking stupid do you think any of us are?"

Mark was babbling while gagging and puking and spitting, going, "What?" The thing was, he already knew what. Obviously, someone else did too.

## Kick! Kick!

Donald was enraged. "What did you say?" He dropped Mark down and gave him two hard kicks in the midsection. Mark then found his head lifted up a bit as Donald bent down at him. "Did you just say 'What?' Don't fucking insult me, asshole!" Mark was released, and his midsection was stomped a couple times by Donald's foot. "I can't believe you! Where did we go wrong? Where did I go wrong? Let's see. You marry my fucking sister so I get you set up to manage a bunch of funds in the market, and what do you do? You lose a few million on deals you shouldn't be making! Ya know, it'd be one thing if you lost money stupidly and came clean about it, but what do you do? You give me phony financial statements saying yer making money!"

## Kick! Kick!

The stomps happened again. "Do ya think I don't keep tabs on what's going on? I know why you needed to talk to me today. You sold a bunch of stock short, and the bill is due next Friday, and you need the cash to cover the bets! You just don't have the fucking balls to be able to tell me!"

Mark lay on the floor, trying to breathe through his blood and puke and taste in his mouth and nose. He wheezed out a "You knew?"

Donald walked over to the sink and washed the piss off his hands. He looked at the crumpled Mark. "Of course, I know. You're playing with damn near a value fifty million of family cash! You think the people you sold short with aren't going to want some assurances that the sale is good? You're fucking lucky that the stocks you bet on went down this last week. If the market had kept rising like it had been, your ass would be in even worse shape than it is now. You might even make a little money back against your losses, but I bet you ain't making up all that you lied about losing. Hell, it took me a shitload of time working with my brokers, arranging things so that I have the cash free to bail you out of this. I had to dump a bunch of blue chip stock this last week just to be prepared to cover your ass.

Donald walked over and put his foot on Mark's chest. "But what do you think happens in twelve days at month end? When the family finds out you've lied and that you haven't made money but that you have been losing it? I ain't lying for your ass about that! I ain't lyin' to my sister when you disappear and you're put away in a room somewhere where people keep you alive and awake as they cut out your organs so that they can be sold to make some money back. It'd be one thing if you lost money and didn't lie about it. It'd be another thing if you made money and lied about it. But you were told from the beginning. Don't lose money doing things you shouldn't be doing! Invest wisely and conservatively, and opportunities will come. And what do you do? You let gambling fever go to your head! Mr. 'I can't drop fifty dollars in a casino' bets millions on CBOT futures and loses it. And then you risk more millions selling stocks short!"

# Kick! Kick! Kick! Kick! Kick! Kick!

Donald furiously kicked Mark repeatedly.

When his anger abated, Donald bent down. "Mark, I tell ya what we're gonna do. You're gonna give Rebecca the week off. And you're gonna sit in your office all week long and do nothing. And we are gonna see how this plays out. And if you're lucky, all that'll happen is you lose the business and you can go hustle for someone else. You'd need a miracle to survive this."

Donald stood up. "I'll talk to you in a couple days. *Don't* do anything stupid! I'd rather not have a widow for a sister and end up inheriting your kids." He left Mark to lie in his own stink.

# CHAPTER 6

## MARK KLEDAS

Mark Kledas stood five-five and still had thick black hair. He carried a paunch that had steadily grown over the years. Baggage has a tendency to do that. His baggage was being added to while he was reducing it. Mark was once again relieving himself. This time the WC was clean.

The eighteenth anniversary of the replacement football game was approaching. Mark had never lost that baggage. He carried it with him every day. It was the day before he had gotten away with his own murder.

Mark remembered stealing money back then. He was looking to steal money now. He was formulating plans to steal even more money than he had originally planned on stealing. The business in hand finished, he washed up and went out to enjoy his lunch.

Lunch was at a Peruvian seafood and karaoke restaurant in Hollywood. It was such an odd mix as advertised that he had to try it. As he enjoyed his *chupa de camarones*, he also read the *Florida Sun Sentinel*. There was a story about two dead visitors to South Florida. Two men had been found shot in the head in their hotel room at the South Beach Courtyard. The story discussed how it was assumed to be a drug-related hit. Mark knew better than that. The dead men were in Miami at his behest.

The dead men were in Miami because Jack Dough was created, and he came to Mark with a great plan. Become involved in the development of Destin and Sandestin, Florida, by opening the Destin Dreams Management Company. Destin Dreams could line up the development of homes and businesses using dirty money. Open the White Sands Bank and they could launder dirty cash in any manner Destin Dreams saw fit. Open Trove Import-Export to help shuttle goods or cash in and out of the country.

For years, the scheme had worked to perfection. The Destin and Sandestin areas developed nicely. The many developments of mega-million-dollar homes all needed construction crews and exotic furnishings as well as affiliated support businesses in the area. They all used cash that was funneled through the White Sands Bank after a turn of hands or two. Who cared about a sleepy little bank where the wealthy people reside? So what if there were large funds transferred out of the country? Rich people and rich businesses do that with money. This was just the rich at play. Sometimes, the cash would be used to buy things that could be brought into or shipped out of the United States. Trove took care of the importing and exporting. And since the Florida real estate market boomed in the meantime, everyone made more money, making everyone happier with the investment.

It was the damn Arabs who spoiled everything. They had intended to disrupt global society, and in an odd way, they had. They changed the rules of engagement. After 9/11, the White Sands money transfers came under closer scrutiny. Just where was the money going? It took a couple years, but too many people started asking too many questions. The money wasn't feeding terrorists, but something about it generated suspicious activities reports. The family had friends within the treasury department who had told them it was time to stop operations. Not an abrupt halt. Just sell off the assets and cash out and quietly go away into a new deal somewhere else before the feds busted things up.

The issue was that when shutdown would occur, then someone needs to go to jail. There would be a public bust to show that the feds were doing their job. It would be akin to busting the middlemen in a drug deal while the ring leaders go free. Or maybe akin to having lower political lackeys sacrifice themselves for the good of the bosses by falling on their sword. The idea was that Jack Dough and the White Sands Bank management would be the group to take the fall.

But then a delay occurred. Jack came up with two last deals that were too good not to do. Jack had come up with black market purchases of both gemstones and gold and platinum at prices too low to be ignored. Stones are small. If something befell them before they were delivered, then who would be the wiser? And while he did like his nephew—hey, if he were hung out to dry for getting robbed while Mark profited nicely from the deal, then so be it. Mark's mother had passed away, and she would not know. And Mark's sons could take over Trove.

This was why there were two stiffs at the hotel. They were supposed to go rob Aug of the stones, but they wound up with bullets instead. The voice on the phone had told him to look for the story to confirm it. Now Mark was going to have to pay more to buy back the stones he wanted to steal for himself in the first place. And the metals that Aug had said were stolen? There was no mention of them. The muffled voice said Mark would be called Friday afternoon for details on arrangements.

Someone he knew had set the robberies up. It had to be someone inside who knew about both deals, and that left one primary candidate. There was also the issue of the dead men from the bank. They were supposed to go to jail, and now they were in the ground. This was all very disconcerting.

It was time to walk down to the children's park and meet his nephew. Mark paid his bill and exited the restaurant. The July heat blasted him upon exiting. It was an immediate offset to the AC in the eatery. The children's park in Hollywood was a short walk down Harrison Street past a variety of local specialty shops. A tree-lined promenade adorned the sidewalk to the park. He walked past bushes sculpted into figures like horn men or trumpeters. The arboreal walk provided pleasing relief from the sun, but by the end of the block, his Tommy shirt was already becoming soaked with sweat. The sweat made the print come to life.

Auggie had come to his care many years ago. It was after his parent's death that the bitter young man had arrived. He was so much like his parents at first—very rash. Mark's sister had been rash in her behavior. That's how she had gotten knocked up at an early age by a man ten years her senior. At the time it happened, Mark was too young to really understand just what his older sister had done. Then she ran off to another state to have her child rather than face the realities of her family and friends. Later he realized that Sis was a victim of her own rash decisions all the way to her death.

Aug didn't want to be in Philly. It was only after it dawned on the boy that he had nothing without Mark that the boy came around. His parents had ultimately left him nothing. There was no plan for life after death, and without cash, one can't do anything. Mark convinced Aug to be a good student in his senior year in high school. Aug did well enough in school to convince Mark to financially help him with college. Aug proved willing to learn business, and this led to his involvement setting up Trove. That was a matter of luck and timing for Aug more than anything else. The family wanted and needed someone who could be trusted just at the time that Aug exited college and got married. The family felt he was trustworthy enough to be set up in business.

Mark and Aug had met a few times before at the park over the years. The park's circular design made for a nice walk that allowed for a "public" private discussion. The last time they had met here, it was Fat Tuesday Saturday. They laid out the plan for the smuggling of over four thousand carats of stones. The park was extremely busy that day. Cheesy vendors were there selling T-shirts or beads or other trinkets or food to throngs of parents and kids. Skits were being performed on the park stage. There were even two portable two-floor boxes that were caged stages. Each box held a dancing girl in Mardi Gras wear. They found it amusing. It isn't every day that they had a one-stop stage, shopping, showgirl, and smuggling.

The money would be transferred out in a couple months. The goods were stolen, so the cost was low. It wasn't the first thing Aug had been requested to bring in, but it was to be the last. Of course, like the actual purchase price, Aug was not to know this.

Mark saw his nephew ahead. The old kid was standing at the stones that lined the north end of the park. The stones looked like the Atlas stones. The stones looked like they were staged for the world's strongest man contestants to come along and lift them onto a platform.

The view of his nephew made Mark internally chuckle. Here Mark was profusely sweating in a pair of khaki shorts, and there was Aug in light yellow dress pants with a silk dress shirt and looking as cool as December. Aug's back was turned to him. Mark could see the head welts as he approached. Something across the park by the baobab trees seemed to have Aug's undivided attention. Mark wondered what it was.

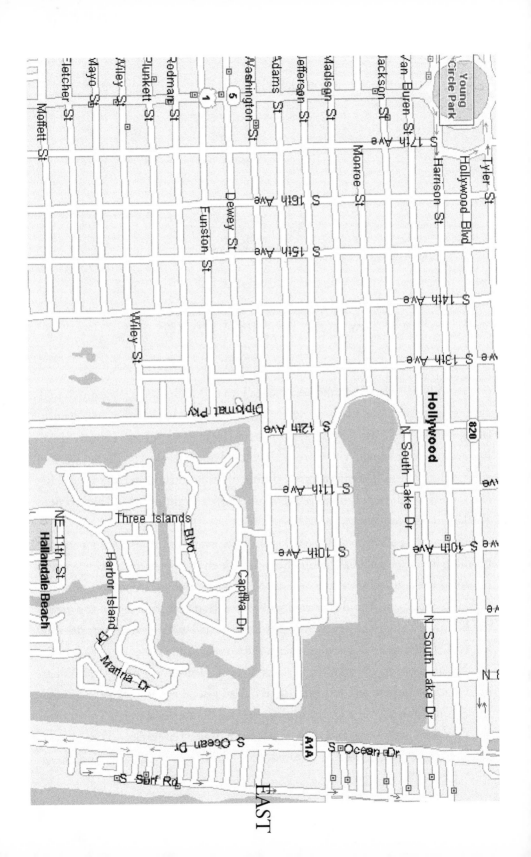

# Chapter 7

## A Jog in the Park

Aug's house was on South/North Lake Drive. Both he and Laurie purchased the residence back when they moved to Hollywood, back when they had dreams of a family. The house was a short distance from Trove for his evening drive home. Aug took the big curve from Fort Lauderdale down 1 to A1A past the signs telling of the streetlights being dimmed during turtle-breeding time. The Intracoastal Waterway ran along the road. Then a turn on and off Hollywood Boulevard past residences, and he was home.

Now that Laurie had departed, time was available to go jogging in the morning just after daybreak before the sun made the day even hotter. Some days, he would make the quick curve around North Lake and jog around the country club. Other days, he would go across Hollywood Boulevard and jog up and down the Boardwalk along the beach. Another route he had was to go the opposite way west on Hollywood and to run through the Young Circle Park.

He did not see any stars as he jogged along Hollywood Boulevard. What he did see were new and old intermixed. Some houses were not kept up and some were. Mercedes and Dodges lined the road. Some yards were nicely mown with proper flower beds, and some yards were in need of weeks of weed work. Like humanity, the path was covered with those who progressed and those who stood still.

Hollywood Boulevard comes out to the children's park. The park provided a nice circle to run around and then loop back home. The area is older and sometimes dumpy looking. It is especially dumpy after a Saturday night when bottles and fast-food trash are littered across the various lots across from the park. Some of the buildings that circle the park are decrepit-looking older local buildings and businesses. Other businesses that arc the park are newer Subways and Walgreens. Aug enjoyed the dichotomy of old and new.

The jog was taking him past the statue of the Madonna and child when he caught the whiff on the air. Aug's curiosity was aroused. Someone was having a naughty early-morning smoke, but he saw no one was around.

He continued jogging around the park to the Atlas stones, and then he turned down the center path of the park. He saw her sitting against the biggest baobab tree at the back of the park. He could see raven hair extend below exposed shoulders. Her hair appeared to have waves cut through it. The eyes were covered by aviator sunglasses. She was looking California. The right hand was bringing a joint to a beautiful full face. The facial contours looked European? Maybe kind of Slavic? Or maybe it was just a mixture of mutt that was beautiful to see.

The feature that struck him most was the relaxed repose. Her back was against the tree, and her black dress barely draped down to her thighs. A lot of olive skin was exposed. She sat with her legs apart and with her left arm draped down, almost as if she were casually tickling herself. It was hard to tell as there was a sheer black wrap that was discreetly adjusted when she saw him approaching.

This bore investigating. He jogged up and parked himself by a tree branch, making sure to breathe as tired as a jogger can breathe. He offered a "Hi there."

Her response was less than enthusiastic. She slowly rotated her head to look at him. A big drag was inhaled. The dragoness blew smoke out of her nose. No emotion was showing. Her arm extended, and she silently offered the joint to him for a hit. Aug raised his hand up and waved the offer off with a smile. "Sorry, never touch the stuff."

Olive skin shrugged her shoulders. "Suit yourself." There was a brief pause followed by another drag, followed by a "Loser." Her head turned away.

He queried, "So what's your name?" She ignored him. It was decision time for Aug, but he wanted to stay more than he wanted to go. "All right, if I take a hit, will you tell me your name?"

She took a drag and said, "I thought you never touch the stuff. Are you saying you are a liar?" Aviator glasses turned and looked at him. The reefer was extended. Aug bent down and picked it out of the offered hand and obliged and took a hit. He properly held his hit in. Then he handed the unit back to her while he blew smoke through his nostrils at the same time.

She leaned forward to take the joint. "Hmmph. Never touch the stuff, huh? That doesn't look like that is your first hit ever." She leaned back and took another drag, holding in her hit. Her shades eyeballed him.

Aug asked, "Soooooo, what is your name?"

Her parried reply was "I don't know that my name is any of your business." The joint was offered back, and he accepted again.

"Well, OK then." Aug took a hit and looked around thinking about what next to say. "Maybe . . . well . . . do you smoke joints here often?"

Olive skin sarcastically replied. "Why? Care to join me? Oh, I forgot, you don't touch the stuff, Pinocchio!"

Aug returned the sarcasm. "M-a-n, yer tough! You need to smoke more pot. It might help unsour your personality! I bet you just do what you want to do, don't you? I bet you are one of those people who don't listen to what you are told to do." He passed the reefer back.

She took the joint and leaned back against the tree. "I don't do what I am told to do." She sang to him a Hole-y line, "'When I get what I want, I never want it again.'" There was a pause. "But I might do what I am asked to do. And I already smoke a lot weed. I like getting stoned. It makes me horny. See?" With joint in one hand, she used the other hand to rub around her breasts through her dress, taking care to pinch her fingers off at an erect nipple. "And for your information, I am very happy with my personality, thank you!"

The vixen stood up, rubbing her back against the tree as she arose. Aug was impressed. She was more voluptuous than brick house! This one was mighty mighty, and as much as the tube dress held it in, she was letting it all hang out.

The brunette walked over by Aug, eyeing him up and down through the shades while lightly rubbing her fingers over his chest and nipples. He guessed her height was maybe five foot seven. It was getting think to hard, and Mr. Cool was perspiring after the run. "Doesn't getting stoned make you horny, Mr . . . . ah . . . 'I don't like your personality' or whatever your name is?"

It took quite a few seconds for Aug to shake the webs being spun out of his brain. Good sense started to take over the fantasy. "Aug. My name is Aug. Augustus. Augustus Valentine. And I just want you to know that I was told if you don't do what you are told, then that means you are engaging in self-destructive behavior. At least, that's what I was told. But I must ask, do you always sit in the park early on a Sunday morning smoking joints with strangers, Ms . . . . ?

She laughed and turned away. The jezebel works were turned off. "Sure, I always hang out in a park, getting lit with strange men on Sunday morning." She stopped and thought a second and lightly thought to herself the refrain of "Sunday Morning." The air was still. Where was the breeze?

Raven hair continued, "No. No, I was down at Snatch for a bachelorette party with some people I know. Ms. Goody Two-shoes daddy's girl is getting married, and all the girls had to do stupid bachelorette things to celebrate."

Aug expressed his confusion. "Um, you were down at Snatch? Do you mean like at her snatch? Uh, is that what you do for a girl when she is getting married?"

She wheeled around and kicked him hard in the leg with a shoeless foot. "No, dumbass. Snatch is a Miami Beach club. Ya know, dancing? To a lot of shitty new techno mixed with oldie crap?" Her body shimmied a bit while talking to make her point. "It was so stupid. It was what this girl from North Carolina whose daddy owns a car dealership wanted to do to have a crazy fling before her matrimonial bliss. Playing lots of stupid-girl bachelorette games around a bunch of fags and girls who think they know how to dance but really can't. All on 'glorious' South Beach so that years later, when she is getting divorced, her ego can be stroked by the memory of her lead up to the wedding. Anyway, it was all right, but kinda a waste of time." There was a thoughtful pause.

"Ya know, you can thank Paris Hilton for this joint here." She stuck her tongue out and got her fingertip wet and extinguished the roach. "She and her 'entourage' were there looking oh so cool dancing this way and smoking that way." She slunk her body one way with her arms out and then brought her body back the other way, bringing her hand to her mouth as if getting stoned while dancing. "I was so bored, I decided to steal their weed."

Aug was like, "And?"

The vixen answered, "And so I did. It was great. I figured out which purse of which friend of hers there had their stash. Then I got the biggest beers I could buy and dumped them all over this chick." She placed the palm of her hand over her forehead. "Oh! The horror." The sarcasm made her smile. "Anyway, I got her into a stall to help clean her up 'cuz I was like 'Oh, I am soooooooo sorry.' Then I robbed her ass and got the hell outta there before someone figured out what had happened!"

Aug stared at her in thought. In his mind, things didn't click. "Sounds like you're just a BFF for everyone you meet. Didn't your girlfriends wonder about you ditching out on the party? Yer quite the friend."

The thief of joints replied, "Ooooooouuuuuuuuuuu, a *BFF* reference. How modern of you! Anyway, I never said she was my friend. I just came along for the ride. I sell cars for a living, and that got me invited. The more the merrier, ya know?. Besides, they all probably figured I was out getting laid somewhere. I can tell them I met some hot guy and that we did it out on the beach somewhere, and they'll all be superimpressed and superjealous."

Aug's mind was racing slowly. It had been quite a few years since he had been stoned, and his tolerance level was waaaaaaayyyyyyy low. He was trying to decide whether she was telling the truth. The story was too far-fetched to be real. "You lie."

That warranted a kick from the other leg. "Oh fuck you, Mr. Aug. I lie? You lie, Mr. 'I never smoked pot in my life.' What? You've never stolen anything in your life?" A snort followed. "You're so full of shit. You lie like all the rest of the men in the world. You lie like a dog. Pinocchio? Your name should be Pin-*Aug*-io! That's what your name should be!"

She turned and made a move to walk away. He didn't like the thought of that. A couple of quick steps forward were taken and her upper arm was grabbed. "Hey, hey, don't be like that. I'm sorry . . . I . . . ah . . . I didn't mean to be insulting. So what's your name anyway?"

She looked at him disparagingly and shook his hand off her arm. "My name? Let's see, last night I was Ginger, even though Mary Ann had the black hair." She worked her fingers through her hair to accentuate the point. "And we had Cinnamon and Spice and Marilyn and Jayne." She thought a second and turned and faced him with a smile. "But there was no Tarzan. There was also plenty of wine, but there was no vine."

She came close again. He was feeling his response again, but she was the one who spoke. "Maybe for you my name should be Yellow Pages. Maybe you should let my fingers do the walking." Her fingers slowly started walking all over his torso and legs. Aug was frozen. "Well, well, Tarzan, that is an impressive amount of vine you do have down there!" She moved in closer rubbing her thigh up and down against his.

"And what's your story, Mr. Aug? Aug the Dog? Is that what you are? Auggie the Doggie?" She put her arms around his neck while her thigh continued working him. "Where's your doggie tags? Had your shots recently?" She thought a second and lasciviously laughed. "Aug the Dog? Mmmm, more like Aug the Horse! Maybe, just maybe, I won't be lying about how the bachelorette party turned out after all!" He had lost all ability to either think or speak. She pressed up against him and spoke into his ear. "I didn't lie about one thing. Getting stoned does make me ohhhhh sooooooo horny!"

# CHAPTER 8

## A WALK IN THE PARK

Her name was Jocelyn Lockwood. Aug found the last name to be apropos.

Aug's journey to the past was interrupted by Mark's hand on his shoulder. Reality replaced an unreality.

"Aug, how ya doin'?" Uncle and nephew shook hands. Mark eyeballed Aug's discolored eye and bulbous skull. It was hilarious to see such a well-dressed man so bumped and bruised. They had the look of an odd couple. He reached a hand up and moved Aug's head around, taking a good look at the damage. "You got smacked pretty good, didn't ya?" There was a pause. "Well I'm glad to see my nephew is all right. Glad you could make it here today."

"Hello, Uncle. It's good to see you again." Aug looked around and then back at Mark. "It wasn't too hard to break away. Cops are all over Trove today interviewing the whole staff." Aug pointed to his head. "They're too busy to bother with me since I'm not implicated in anything." Aug looked around and smelled the fresh air and then looked at Uncle Mark. "It's kinda nice to get out of TIE for a little while. Too much monkey business going on there." There was a pause. "How are you doing? How are Joan and the kids?"

Mark informed him, "Joan is fine. She sends a hello and kisses. Joe and Robert are now over in Atlantic City. They both started in casino management trainee programs. Joe is at Bally's, and Robert's at Trumps. And Eileen is enjoying summer vacation. She's working as a lifeguard this summer at the country club, so that keeps her busy. Ya know, I'm sure they are all curious what you have to say, what you are up to. When was the last time you spoke to any of them?"

Aug answered, "Oh, I guess it's been a couple years now. What, Joe graduated from St. Joe's two years ago?" He thought a second. "Heck, I guess it was three years ago now. That was the last time I saw them." He paused. "Wow. Three years. That's a long time."

They started to walk around the park. A smattering of people occupied the park this midday. Parents had children climbing on monkey bars. Kids were swinging on swings. Park lunches were being eaten by people on lunch break. Aug and Mark looked at everyone. They looked at every car parked and at every car that passed by. Their bodies may have been made from atoms on the periodic chart, but trust was an element that was missing.

The walk did Aug some good. His head was still smarting, but the periodic throbbing had decreased dramatically in the last day. His leg and glutes were stiff, but the walk loosened them up as they went along.

Mark told Aug, "You know, you really should visit sometime. At least give them a call. I know they all really miss you."

Aug answered, "Well, I miss them too. I'll just have to do that." He looked at his uncle. "You got down here really fast."

Mark answered, "I caught the early US Air flight out of Philly this morning. After your call last night, I figured I better get down here." Mark patted his hand on his nephew's shoulder. "The situation didn't sound good, and it sounded like my nephew may need some help." There was a sighed pause. "And we obviously couldn't really talk about this over the phone." He stopped walking and looked at Aug's eyes. "Why don't you tell me what happened?"

Aug started walking. "Well, there really isn't much to say. I brought the jewels in like I said I would. They were inside the Killer Beez game. I had just pulled the packages out and was leaving the back cabinet when—**_BOOM!_**—the lights went out. The next thing I know, people are waking me up, I've got some welts on my head, and the stones are gone. And that's that."

Aug paused for a little. "What gets me is—why steal all that pewter and silver? I mean, jewels I can understand. But twelve skids of metals? I mean, yeah, they're worth a bit—five hundred g's on the commercial invoice—but nothing like what the stones are worth. That's a hell of a lot of work to come in for jewels and then decide to back up a truck and steal a bunch of skids of metal. No crook I know is going to steal millions in gems and then think, *Hey, there's a few hundred g's in silver here. Let's go find a truck and steal skids of that!* Sooooo, I'm thinkin' someone came in for the metals, knocked me out, and got lucky finding the jewels when they knocked me out. On impulse, they decided to grab what they saw was in my hands, and now they're probably shittin' bricks now trying to figure out what to do. Once they figure out what they got, I bet someone's gonna be in contact with me, trying to work something out. I mean, where are they gonna go with the stuff? It's too much to fence. Who's gonna wanna touch it?" Another pause occurred. "Of course, I can't explain how the robbers knew the alarm system. Somebody knew something when they came in.

Aug stopped a step and looked at Mark. "Unk, what was up with that Upper Terra shipment? How did you know about it? I never talked to you about it. You never mentioned anything about it to me, and then last night, you indicated you knew what was shipped. I just thought Upper Terra was a new customer. What's really going on here?"

Mark looked away and then back at Aug. "Well, Aug, you know Jack Dough who runs Destin Dreams?

Aug answered, "Yeah."

Mark told him, "His brother runs Upper Terra."

Aug looked surprised. "You mean, Joe Kahn is Jack Dough's brother? That's odd. Their last names are a little different, ya know."

Mark replied, "Well, yeah." They started walking again while Mark told his tale. "Joe had an extended vacation for some, uh, legal indiscretions in his past. Jack cut some deals to get his brother out of the stir and then set him up with the shop in Cocoa. Joe's real name was David, but he changed his name so that there would be less chance of any legal headaches arising 'cuz of his name. Anyway, recently, Jack lined up another deal. He was contacted by some people in Russia about some gold and platinum that they had stolen and were willing to sell at a severely discounted price. To get the goods out of Russia, what they did was have a thousand pounds of each smelted into ingots, and then they were thinly covered with pewter and silver so that the shipment looked like pewter and silver. Sooooo, buried in the five thousand pounds each of pewter and silver you brought in were a thousand pounds each of gold and platinum. And being the good smuggler that you are, you graciously brought it in for us. It was an odd special deal."

Aug stopped walking. He looked at Uncle Mark in seeming disbelief. His voice quietly seethed. "Wait a second. You're telling me I smuggled in a load of goods that I didn't get a cut of? That's my ass on the line! If that shipment got found out by US Customs, I'm in big trouble." He paused for a second and glared into the eyes of his uncle. They sized each other up. "Just how many more of these odd special deals have you been pulling off under my nose!"

Mark raised his arms out and placed them on Aug's arms. "Now, calm down there, Aug. This was a onetime deal. I haven't been jacking you around. But this all cropped up rather suddenly, and you were busy making arrangements with the stones. All of the arrangements to bring the metals in were already made. Everything just needed to come through a broker house. If this hadn't at all cropped up, you wouldn't even be concerned about those goods anyway."

Aug disengaged their arms and pointed a finger at Mark's chest. "What the hell are you talking about? Smuggling anything through Trove is my risk, and for me, there should be some reward. That's my money you're talking about! I'm taking the risk of prison time and fines if the shipment gets found out about, so I get some reward! That's the deal!" He paused a minute. "Just what should have been my take on that deal anyway? How much was it worth? What are we talking about?"

Mark angrily replied, "Will you forget about that now? Haven't you been well taken care of over the years? C'mon! Get your head out of your ass. We've got a real problem here, and we need to figure out what we are going to do about it."

Aug was incensed. "*We've* got a problem? What I hear you telling me is that you set up a smuggle that I knew nothing about to come through at the same time as I'm bringing in a load of diamonds, and the people that came in to steal your deal just happen to be in to rob my deal? Where's this *we* come in? How did I screw up? You're the one who timed the two deals together! You're starting to sound like an *unk unk*, Unk."

83

Mark was indignant, furious. "Aug, I'll tell ya how the *we* comes in. The *we* comes in 'cuz not a goddamn person who put fifteen mil for metal and thirty mil for stones is gonna give a shit about who did what with what deal if their goods aren't delivered to them! Do you understand what I'm sayin'? The only cut for both of us is gonna be a cut through our throats! Pardon my pun, but this is a real test of our mettle!"

The men glared into each other's eyes. Mark broke off and started the walk again, looking around, his voice a bit more conciliatory. "What do you mean I sound like an *unk unk*?"

Aug just stared off. "Oh, it's nothing. I just need a good night's sleep, that's all. Anyway."

Mark went on, "Anyway is right. Aug, ya know, I raised you since you were fourteen, since your parents died. I helped you get set up this business, and I have always looked out for your best interest. Sure, we haven't always seen eye to eye, but we've both done well over the years. I wasn't looking to jack you around. It's just that things worked out . . . differently this time. I'm sorry about that." A few steps were taken in silence. "Now let's get back to the business at hand. Do you have any idea how to proceed? Do you have any clue who robbed us?"

Aug thought about it for a little while. "Well, let's see. Assuming that whoever pulled off the robbery came in for the platinum and gold and lucked into the jewels, then that means that someone who knew about the metals is responsible. Right now that makes three people that I am aware of: Mr. Destin, Mr. Cocoa, and you. Who else was in on the deal?"

Mark replied, "Well, that's about it from my end. I don't know much about the sellers. Jack lined all that up. And I don't know who else they brought in on this. What about the guys who work at Trove? What's the possibility that someone working at TIE stole everything? That they just got lucky on what they stole?"

Aug stated, "Maybe, but I doubt it. That just doesn't add up. The cops think that may be what happened. I mean, you read and hear about things like copper wire and such being stolen and sold for the value of the wire, and a take of half a million in metal would make a lot of people happy to get that kind of take. I'm keeping an eye toward the people in the warehouse, but right now, the cops are all over the place. They're digging up that route and that may flush someone out or make them nervous enough to fess up to the robbery. But I don't think that is what happened."

Aug continued, "I don't think anyone working at Trove is big-time enough to handle what we're looking at. If they did it, I doubt they're gonna want a piece of this action once they realize what they have done. I guess that's assuming that they ever even realize what they have." Aug thought further. "What the heck were you gonna do with a ton of gold and platinum? I mean, the stones are small enough to fit in a safety deposit box or somewhere safe. That part I get. I mean, we've moved them in the past. Never so many as this time, but this was nothing new. But ingots of gold or platinum? What is someone gonna do? Ditch 'em in a vault somewhere? Ya gotta move 'em." Aug looked at Mark. "What were you going to do with them?"

Mark smiled. "Oh, it was a beautiful plan. The idea was to resmelt the gold and platinum that could be, um, shall we say, 'naturally' stored for use when needed. Up at Upper Terra, they have a furnace set up, and they are doing a run of gold- and platinum-plated plates and goblets. You know, kinda medieval-looking-like. Well, instead of making all the plates and goblets plated, the plan was to make full gold and platinum plates and goblets. The manufacturing process works the same. The same molds can be used. Who would ever know that these supposedly decorative items were actually worth a bunch of money? It's a good hedge to have, and the price was right. Plus, they would now be, in some ways, more easily transportable. I mean, the weight is the same, but no one gets too excited over some shipments plated goods. But wave a bar of platinum in their face and they go gaga."

They had made it back to the Atlas stones. Mark went on, "Sooooo, that's what the deal was." The men looked at each other. Mark continued, "All right, Aug, where do you suggest we go from here?"

Aug mused a bit. "Well, I am off to meet with Mr. Kahn tomorrow. I made the appointment to see him to talk about what had to be done because I just had his shipment stolen. You know, insurance and replacement material issues. Now . . . now I don't know what I'm going to tell him. I'm going to have to think about that."

Mark nodded his head. "I can imagine. Look, I'm staying at the Wyndham in Hollywood. I'm going to be snooping around Trove tomorrow, and I'll also be making some calls to see what I can find out. Maybe we can meet tomorrow night? You find out what Joe has to say. I'll talk to Jack Dough and see what I can find out from his end, and we can compare notes and match up from there. How does that sound?"

Augustus begged off. "Uh, no, I was planning to take Jocelyn out tomorrow night. I haven't seen her in nearly a month. She'll kill me if I don't spend the night. I expect to come back Saturday. Let me get a hold of you then and we can see where we stand. I've got a couple feelers out on this, and maybe I'll know something by then."

Mark smiled. "Jocelyn. The lovely Jocelyn. And just how is Jocelyn these days? Still as big a sex bomb as ever? Like she is missing seeing you! Hardly! I bet! I bet you were missing tapping into that while you were gone!"

Aug smiled back. "Aww, she's all right. I've been so busy the last few months I haven't seen her a lot recently, and she's none too happy about that. I was hopeful that after this latest deal was done, we could take a trip somewhere nice for a while. It looks like, for the moment at least, this changes everything." He looked off in the distance back at the baobab. "I guess we have some things to, uh, iron out."

# CHAPTER 9

## UPPER TERRA

The drive to Cocoa from Hollywood can primarily be made via three different roads. It all depends on how much time one has to kill. The slowest drive is up the ocean path of A1A. The ocean route provides a scenic view of the coastline, coastal cities, and tourist traps that dot the way. The middle of the road method is Highway 1. Once a primary artery, it is now a secondary path. Many hucksters are on this road. There are tons of pawnshops changing past treasures to cash for not much money.

The fastest way is the interstate. The stores are bypassed for speed. The drive up from Hollywood is a couple hours long. For Aug to be at Upper Terra at ten, he had to leave Hollywood fairly early, and the interstate was the best route north. He wondered if he could "live through this" un-Hole-ly CD in his disc player for the drive.

Augustus subscribed to the theory that a condemned man should dress his finest for the execution. The finest gold pinstriped suit was worn. A refined purplish black paisley tie was worn. Black cufflinks and polished wingtips completed the ensemble. Well, sort of. The black eye and bumped head were the final complement to the wear. Well, sort of. The final complement was the giant black-and-white panda bear completely filling up the passenger seat. Mr. Panda elicited hoots and honks from many passing vehicles enamored with their brief view of his charm.

Up to this point, all of the dealings between Aug and Joe Kahn had been by remote. Now they were to meet. Augustus was steeling himself for the meeting. No niceties were really expected. While driving, a continuous mental review of the intended script for today occurred.

The billboards along the way amused Aug. Every few miles, the Ron Jon Surf Shop advertisements kept announcing the countdown in miles to the store at Cocoa Beach. Twenty-four-hours-a-day sales of surfing merchandise. There were attractive women in bathing suits adorning each ad. How Aug wished he could walk into this dream of unreality. The billboards said fifty, then thirty-two, then eighteen miles. Finally, there was an off-ramp advertising that the beach mecca was ten miles away. His eyes drifted to the dash, and he noticed it was a steamy ninety degrees outside.

I-95 exits at 520. The 520 runs across to 1. Just off 1 South is Factory Street, so appropriately named. On the north side of the street is a small factory, thirty thousand square feet, the Upper Terra Mint. The company operated as a job shop making specialty runs of goods. Inside the walls, small presses operated, forming metals and plastic into various decorative or commemorative products. From what Aug had gathered, it was a sleepy company that laid low. To Aug, this meant that illegal things went on behind closed doors.

When he pulled into the parking lot, he was presented with glass doors framed by large glass panes. There was fairly new lettering above the glass, announcing:

# UPPER TERRA MINT

Smaller panes of glass were on the sides of the building, shaping the office area. Venetian blinds were down. So much glass created to let the sun in only for the sun to be blinded by the blinds.

The parking lot was fairly empty. There were a Cadillac and an Alero parked up front and a couple of pickup trucks parked at the side parking area of the building. The loading docks were on the side of the building, and one of three bays had a moderate-size truck parked against it. It looked like some steam was coming out the roof at the back end, but he couldn't be sure. What he could be sure of was that there was little sign of life showing. The place looked and sounded dead.

A pretty little blond named Gayle acted as the receptionist. Undoubtedly, she was a graduate from the local high school up the road. Gayle was the only person in the front office. She bounced up and down in her chair, swinging one leg while chewing gum and talking on her cell phone and twirling a finger through her hair. Aug found this impressive. She could do four things at once.

Gayle saw Aug approaching, and she rapidly finished her call. Aug entered the front reception area that was glassed off from the rest of the office. Her head rapidly turned to check her desk mirror, and then she smilingly stood to greet Aug. "Hi there, Mr. Valentine!" she said in a perky voice. "Welcome to the Upper Terra Mint."

Aug was amused by the late teen's greeting. He took a long look at the strategically placed name tag. "Hello, Gayle. It is my pleasure to be here."

Gayle tried to be adult, but she came off as a youngster who got big thrills with sneaking into bars and drinking. She giggled at Aug. "You look cute there, mister," she said as she pointed at his eye.

Aug told her, "You don't look so bad yourself, sister."

Gayle giggled some more, and her eyes got big. She was getting a big thrill from checking him out. Her mind immediately thought of deeds of great importance. She had to get on her cell phone and call her girlfriends and talk about the arrival. But first she had to let Aug in. The door was opened into the office area. "Please come in, Mr. Valentine. Mr. Khan is expecting you."

There were a half a dozen cubicles in the office area that were empty. The PC monitors were darkened. Gayle led Aug to a modest-sized office with nice mahogany furniture and wooden chairs with thick leather coverings. He also saw that Saint Andrews and the Island Green adorned a couple of walls. Drawn blinds covered the windows. Joe Khan occupied this office. Aug took a seat, and the door was closed.

"Mr. Joseph Kahn," Aug said with arm extended, "Augustus Valentine. It is a pleasure to finally make your acquaintance. I wish we were making our acquaintance under a different circumstance, that the situation was not so knotty." They shook hands. Each man exerted a firm grip.

Joe Khan was shorter than Aug, coming in at five foot seven. He looked mean. Tinted Cazal glasses covered his eyes and prevented Aug from seeing clearly into Joe's glaze. Joe's hair was thick. His jaw was set. His skin had the look of someone who golfed every day. The short-sleeved shirt was a solid green that must have cost thirty dollars at Sears. Aug mentally envisioned where the "Love Mom" tattoo was.

Joe eyed him over. "Nice shiner. I guess that's where you claim they hit you when you lost my goods, eh?" He paused. "Now! Cut the crap. You lost my goods, and now I got a factory shut down because you fucked up. I want to know. What are you doing about getting me my goods back?"

Aug relaxed back. "Well, the insurance claim is being processed, but I am not sure how long it will take to get a claim through." He leaned forward and bent his head down for a second—momentarily noticing that the carpet was quite old—before turning his head back up and looking at Joe. "But the insurance really isn't the issue here, is it? And neither is idling the factory, is it? I had a little chat with my uncle before coming up here, and he told me what the issue is. The issue is the disappearance of what was surreptitiously inserted in the stolen shipment. That's what the issue is, isn't it? The insurance money will cover some things, but I don't think it will cover what we are talking about here now, will it?" He leaned back.

Joe leaned back in his chair. "Yer right. The insurance won't cover what was stolen." He leaned forward and opened a desk drawer and produced a handgun. Joe shut the drawer. He pointed the gun at Aug's head. "But I was lined up with people and places and a schedule to do something with those goods, and now all of our plans are messed up. And the people who put up the money are none too happy about your fuck-up. Now, I think either someone at Trove or, maybe, maybe even you stole everything. And I want to make it clear to you that I expect my goods back ASAP." He pulled the trigger.

# Click!

The hammer came down on an empty chamber. Aug's sphincter loosened up very slightly.

Aug looked deliberately at Joe. "Me? You think maybe I stole everything? Hey! I didn't even know what was hidden until yesterday. Heck, I just got back in the US. I've been away for a couple of weeks." He paused. "Are you looking to hang this around my neck?" Augustus could see the wheels turning.

The line of questioning from Joe began. "Let's get this straight. You run an import business. Correct?"

Aug had his eyes on the pistol as he answered, "Yes."

The next logical question came. "And you brought in a shipment of goods destined for this building. Correct?"

Again Aug answered, "Yes."

Joe concluded, "Then as far as I am concerned, it's your job to get me those goods!" He slowly opened the desk drawer again and pulled out a bullet and a thin tip white paint marker. Joe proceeded to write the letters *A-U-G* on the .38 caliber projectile. Then he inserted the bullet into the waiting repository in the pistol. The gun was pointed back at Aug's head. "Now, Mr. Valentine, this gun truly has a bullet with your name on it."

## BANG!

The pistol moved sideways. A shot fired past Aug's head into the wall behind him. Joe opened the drawer and procured another bullet while he spoke. "Now, let me make this clear. I don't give a shit what you knew or when you knew it. What I want you to tell me is, when are you going to quit screwing around and deliver me my goods?"

Aug stirred after being shaken and rapidly stated, "One week from now."

Joe shook his head no. "That's not good enough," he said.

## BANG!

The shot went by Aug's head again. Joe procured another bullet and loaded the revolver.

Aug blurted out, "OK, next Monday. Monday. I'll have you the goods next Monday."

## Click!

The gun was fired again, but on an empty chamber. Joe pointed the gun upward and addressed Aug. "Let me repeat this to you so that we are both clear on this. Next Monday you are going to deliver to me a truck carrying my stolen property. Is that right? Is that what you are promising me?"

Aug answered Joe, "Yes. That is a promise."

Joe stated, "Mister, that is a promise that you better deliver on, or I will personally blow your fucking head off. You understand me?"

"Yes, sir" was Aug's reply. "Yes, sir, I do. Deliver the metals or it'll be a lynch mob for me."

The comment left Joe looking at Aug rather suspiciously. Aug looked around the room. He looked back at the holes in the wall and then back at Joe. "Um," he said, "if there is nothing else, I will show myself out the door. I think I can remember the way." With that, Aug rapidly took his leave. He quickly paced by Gayle who was sitting there with her mouth agape. The gum she was chewing almost seemed visible from the roof of her mouth to her tongue like she had frozen in mid-bubble blow inside her mouth. The cell phone was held in the palm of her hand.

"Don't worry," he advised her as he strode past. "People shoot at me all the time!" Aug thought as he left that maybe he had overestimated Gayle. Right now she couldn't do one thing at the same time.

Aug entered his blue DeVille. When he backed the Caddy out of the parking lot, he noticed a bullet hole in the front window. One of the bullets had evidently come through the office through the window. No wonder Gayle was freaked! Well, better a hole in the pane than pain in his hole. The thought going through his mind was that he had just met a type A personality. That was type A with a capital *A*. Capital *A* for capital Asshole. He did not doubt that Joe had done time for aggravated assault with intent to kill. Too bad he hadn't yet been jailed for more than intent.

He drove out of the Upper Terra parking lot down to Highway 1 and headed north the couple of blocks to where 1 and 520 meet. He took a right down 520 past the Hyundai dealership on the hill. There were two political placards positioned on the lawn. One read, "Jaclyn Colon for Tax Collector," and the other sign said, "Elect Judge Butts." Aug mused a "no wonder J lives in Cocoa!" He turned the corner and pulled into the parking lot of Norman's Raw Bar and Grill. It was time to regain his composure. He knew that there was no way he was going to be shot in daylight in the office back there, so the show wasn't completely scary. But no matter what, having bullets fly by one's head does have a rattling effect.

After Aug calmed down, he took the drive across 520 toward Cocoa Beach. He crossed the Hubert H. Humphrey Bridge. Plenty of boats adorned the waterway. Then there was the Merritt Island stretch. Traffic was heavy. The mall was on the right, and many chain and local stores dotted both sides of the way. The sun was shining brightly. The day was cloudless. The meeting had been brief, the time was now about eleven. At Banana River Road, he turned left into Island Lincoln Mercury. The time was ripe to see what Jocelyn was up to.

The windows to the car dealership were fronted by shrubs and lawn. The glare of the sun made the glass more reflecting than transparent. After squinting a bit and cupping his eyes, he could see her with some clients. He walked into the anteroom of the front doors. He saw that Jocelyn was with what looked like a father-and-son duo. Her specialty was luxury. She was selling the latest XK8.

Jocelyn's walk was never fast and was certainly not slow. Her movements always swung naturally. Today she was, for a car dealership saleswoman, outrageously dressed in black knee-length boots. Her bottom was framed by a short black leather skirt. Her walk was the sensation of a happy-Slash-sexy riff. It was very bouncy and alluring, yet very sinuous like a snake slithering. She knew her clientele well. Aug enjoyed watching her walk. Her callipygian curvosity kindled cravings.

The Jaguar was a red convertible model. She requested the boys to sit in the car. This allowed her to show off a view of all features.

Junior sat behind the wheel. Aug thought maybe he was a college graduate and daddy was going to treat his son? The males in the car were thrilled as she leaned all over the vehicle, explaining the various features of the ride. Her blouse barely contained her breasts, and they could read the lace stitching on the brassiere. The customers were enthralled, delighting in the statements phrased that surely the graduate knew how to "drive a stick."

The potential customers who came in to the dealership may not all have been capable of purchasing such a vehicle, but in the four years since she had shown up, the humans had flocked in anyway. She was one of those women who ooze sensuality out of every pore. Every word seemed to convey not just a sense of sex, but a sense of hours of sex. It's a great talent to possess for selling expensive automobiles. And sell she did, so much so that she had earned the right to operate in her own style. Vehicles went out the door, so who cared?

It is said that "people talk," and this is certainly true of men and women. One could use Anne Frank's hiding place or the Jeepers Creepers cellar, place a beautiful woman inside away from any contact, and somehow people will find a way to talk about her. Place her around showy automobiles and a wildfire of gossip is started.

Florida is a land of attractive females. They love to parade around in clothing dictated by heat, which means short, shorter, and shortest. Quite a few are bisexual. Jocelyn was a queen in this land of flesh. She didn't have competition. She had a succession of male and female sexual suitors to choose from. She enjoyed the luxury of choice.

Today she was with a cosmetic surgeon and junior. The doctor was going to buy his son a graduation present, and it was going to cost eighty grand. It was only a matter of time before he asked how much for the extra to make the deal happen, and she wondered if she could make it a double sale. Thinking about the possibilities made it that much easier to enjoy, and she really did like thinking that way. Her motor was already in high gear, but as enjoyable as the sale of a couple of Jag's might be, she doubted this would slake her excitement.

Aug could see what was going on. He didn't mind. The reality did not threaten his ego. We all have to make a living somehow, and nothing lasts forever. So he happened to see this particular display. If he wasn't so early, he would never know, and then who would really care? If a hot babe fell in the woods and there was no soul mate there to see it, did it ever really happen?

For a flash, his rearview mirror morphed into a vision of Ms. America replete with gown and tiara and high heels and roses. The wood was beginning to float. Then Ms. America morphed into a petite blond replete with lush curly hair and a noose around her neck, the cut rope end hanging down the back. His enjoyment disappeared.

He did hate to blow a sale of hers. His presence would not help. What to do? He stepped back out to his car and wrestled out the panda bear. It was time for him to address his business. What better way to be early than with a big bear?

From the parking lot to the door to inside, every head turned to see the spectacle of a pinstripe-suited man with a protruding black eye carrying a cute six-foot white-and-black plush Ling Ling. Inside the dealership, everyone momentarily stopped whatever they were doing and turned and looked before going back to their activities.

Jocelyn had her torso leaning over Dr. Brian Blower as he sat in the passenger seat while she pointed out features in the car. The good doctor and his son Nathan were in gentlemen's club heaven when the commotion of Aug's entrance drew her attention. Various emotions ran through her electrochemical neural paths. Jocelyn was furious because Aug was not supposed to be around until the evening. Jocelyn was confused because Aug never made plans to show up at a specific time and then change those plans. This was out of character. Jocelyn was already excited, and the sudden appearance of her lover gave her a thrill. Jocelyn was extra excited because she was in love with the panda. It was such a killer present. As far as doctor and graduate Blower, she could care less. She was confident that the sale was under her thumb.

"Will you gentlemen excuse me a minute, please, mmm?" She stood up and leaned against the hood of the car, folding her arms and raising her right leg a little to keep the young boys occupied. As old as the father was, he still impressed her as a young boy who happened to be rich enough to buy a luxury vehicle. She could keep their attention without any difficulty while she dealt with the new situation. When Aug got close, she also walked toward him. She was mad, but she couldn't help but smile. He was bringing her such a cuddly, cute big present, he looked so good in the beautiful suit, and he looked so wounded with a black eye. He also seemed to be walking a little stiffly. As they came together, he said, "Happy Valentines Day!" and extended the bear.

She accepted the bear. The panda filled her arms and seemingly dwarfed her. She wanted to give Aug the obligatory and perfunctory hug and peck on the cheek, but the panda was just too big! The plush prevented her from having that reach. With a smile and a seethe, she quietly fired at him, "Thank you, baby! Aug, what are you doing here? I wasn't expecting you until this evening! And it is *not* Valentine's day!" She extended her arms to check out the panda; her smile increased. "But he is soooo cute! He gets a kiss, but you don't!" With that she gave the bear a light buss, making sure not to get him lipstick stained.

Aug said, "Hello, J!" Her look made him smile just because he was happy to see Jocelyn. He looked into her emerald green eyes. The imperfection in her right eye, a jagged white strip, was pulsing. "Uh-oh, your lightning bolt is flashing," he said.

"I've told you before," she replied in a quiet seethe, "lightning at the eye of the hurricane is the worst lightning there is!" She gave him a mean, pouty, Charmed Ones look. "Now, just what are you doing here?"

Aug tried to be as charming and disarming as he could be. "Hey, what can I say? I had a meeting up the road that I thought would take all day, but it ended rather abruptly. So I decided to come over and see what you were doing. It's been so long since I have seen you, and I thought maybe we could do lunch or you might be able to get away for the rest of the day. Besides, you were mad at me the other night for disappearing on you. And here I really thought you would be happy to see me early! But if you'd rather I drive back to Hollywood and come back later . . ." Aug gave her a pause. "Or maybe you would prefer I go to some place local like the Inner Room or Cheater's and hang out."

Jocelyn smilingly pounced on his remark. "Hmmph! If you hang it out there, you sure as hell ain't hanging it out here tonight!" Her eyes lowered and rose up to accentuate her meaning. They laughed.

Jocy serioused up. "You know, you've said that I'm the one who doesn't do what I'm told to do, and yet here you are hours early. So who's calling the pot black?"

Aug replied, "I just said that I would be here later. I was never told to be anywhere at a specific time. My not doing what I said I would do is not the same as your proclivity for not doing what you are supposed to do."

Jocelyn gave him a bemused look. "WOW! Check out Mr. Vocabulary! *Proclivity!* Well, suppose my proclivity to not do what I am told to do is based upon someone else's proclivity for telling me to do things that means there is a conflict of interest between my doing all the things that everyone tells me to do, which leaves me with the unenviable dilemma of making decisions that make it appear as if I have a proclivity for not doing what I am told to do. Isn't that the same as you not doing what you say you will do?"

Aug grinned. "I don't know. I guess that makes my head hurt is what it means."

She cradled the bear as best as she could in her left arm so that she could use her right arm to show attention to his injuries. "Oh my god, is that where they hit you?" With mutual concern and sarcasm she said, "You poor thing. Are you sure you're all right?"

He held her hand as she tried caressing his face. "Baby, I'm fine. I'm just a little sore, that's all."

Jocelyn said, "Well, Aug, I'm kinda busy with some customers right now, and I had lunch plans. Why don't you get a coffee or something or check out the movie in the lounge for a little while and let me see what I can do about getting free. OK?"

Aug agreed, "OK, OK. I understand. But you better get free, or I'm not responsible for what showgirl and I end up with!" He smiled and gave her a peck on the cheek. Then he turned and walked away.

Jocelyn watched Augustus stride off. She liked his walk. It was very direct, very efficient, and the slight hitch really gave her a big playful smile. She held the panda in front of her and smiled. The panda *was* super cuddly!

Now it was time to complete the sale. She seductively walked back to the Jag where daddy and son were engaging in a conversation that she was sure she knew about. She carefully laid the panda down on the hood of the car and slowly laid herself down on top of panda. She squeezed him and rubbed on him and then turned her smiling red lips to the boys, saying, "Don't you just like my new plaything? Isn't he so cute and cuddly? Pandas need love too." With that, she slightly but noticeably gyrated her hips on the plush. In her mind, she saw titles to two vehicles appear like magic above their heads. Her lascivious smile grew, knowing that commissions for the upcoming end of July had just increased by two fully loaded Jaguars. This life of rebirth was much better than her life before her death and resurrection.

# CHAPTER 10

## JOCELYN

Jocelyn could see her breath forming in the night air as she stepped to the door of the older house off Lee Road that she was renting. The crisp air enhanced her feeling of life. The oxygen did not feel cold. The crisp air tasted fresh. Her lungs felt fresh from the chill. She was bouncing to herself while singing "Black Leather." She loved black leather.

It wasn't the toot that she had done or the beer she had drank or the smoke that she had inhaled that was exciting her so much. The need for the use of a privy helped her bounce a bit, but that was not the main reason for the bounce in her gait. The thrill of theft emotionally charged her. Jocelyn's black leather purse was filled with booty. She needed release. She was commando beneath her leather skirt, so that would make things easier. It wouldn't be long before relief would be achieved.

She opened the door to the lower-middle-class two-bedroom house. The time was three in the morning, and the living room was dark. The heat had kicked on. It provided an initial feeling of warmth. The light was turned on, and she immediately knew there was trouble ahead. Mo the Bo was standing across the room.

Their eyes met, and they closed to slits as the two females angrily eyed each other. A man stood on each side of Jocelyn. She was so focused on Mo and so intoxicated that she did not notice them in the room. Her purse was yanked off her shoulder by one man. She turned to protest, and then her other shoulder was grabbed and she was turned.

# POW!

A fist impacted her jaw. The punch staggered her, and she reeled, but she did not fall. The skinny young man who had hit her was surprised by this. He loaded up harder for a second blow.

# POW!

The next punch was a little higher up and caught her across the cheek. Jocelyn fell back against the door of the house. The men grabbed her arms and threw her down on the couch in the room. Her purse was thrown to Mo. The men then went to the couch, and each one grabbed one of Jocelyn's arms. They painfully pinned her facedown on the sofa.

Mo said, "Check her coat. Let's see what Ms. Five Fingers has in the pockets." The men forced her coat off Jocelyn. A white short-sleeve blouse was revealed. The coat was searched. A set of keys and a cell phone came out. There was nothing else.

Mo opened the purse and started emptying the contents. A compact came out. Mo threw the compact as hard as she could at Jocelyn's head. She did the same thing with the lipsticks she pulled out. A pillbox came out and was hurled. Pens were taken out and thrown. The wallet was removed, and the small amount of cash was removed, and that was thrown at Jocelyn. Tampax were removed and hurled at Jocelyn.

Mo then said, "Well, look here!" She pulled out a ziplock baggie of powder and rocks. The men whistled. Mo walked to the couch and bent down and waved it under Jocelyn's nose. "What's this?" she said sarcastically. "Maybe a couple ounces of some blow? Maybe freshly stolen from someone?"

Jocelyn raised her head and spat in Mo's face. Mo stood up and wiped her face off with her hand. She stared at the snot. Anger welled up.

# Boot!

Mo kicked Jocelyn in the mouth with her boot. Jocelyn's lips split open. She spit blood at Mo's boot. Mo swung her foot up to kick Jocelyn, but Jocelyn moved her head aside. The kick caught air, and Mo had to steady herself from falling. The two men started laughing. Jocelyn started laughing with them.

Mo screamed at all of them, "SHUT THE FUCK UP!" She put the coke back in the purse. She pulled out a rubber-banded wad of cash. She threw it to the closest male. The male released his hold on Jocelyn and opened the wad and flipped through it. There was a mixture of hundreds, fifties, and twenties. He nodded his head at Mo and then pocketed the cash. Mo looked at Jocelyn and said, "Well, well, well! Been a little busy robbing someone else tonight?"

Jocelyn replied with a "FUCK YOU, YA FUCKING DYKE!" As she spoke, she tried to lunge free and get at the purse. The male holding her arm twisted it as severely as possible while the other kicked her in the abdomen. Jocelyn screamed in pain, and the other male grabbed her flailing arm. Jocelyn started kicking at the men, but she had no angle. They twisted her arms hard, which made her scream in pain again. She quit struggling.

Mo laughed. She said to Jocelyn, "Lovin' every minute of it!" She went back to the purse. "Is this what you wanted?" she said as she pulled out a handgun.

Jocelyn looked up at her and spat more blood. She said, "Yeah, well, why don't you try that revolver on yourself? God knows ya can't get off with the other kind. Who knows? If you pull the trigger, you even might like how the bullet feels!"

Mo threw the purse aside. She screamed, "BITCH!" and jumped on Jocelyn. The men released Jocelyn's arms, and the two women went at it. The guys were laughing with each other as they watched the catfight. Arms were flailing. Mo was not a professional fighter, and her swings had nails exposed so that the swings were half-scratch, half-swing. One swing of nails caught Jocelyn below the elbow and scratched down her arm to the wrist, digging up flesh along the way. Skin curled under the nails and blood streamed from the marks. This attack surprised and angered Jocelyn. She knew that Mo kept no nails for ease of personal pleasure. Mo now had nails for a single intent. Mo was intent on scratching Jocelyn. Jocelyn parried the rest of the flails and lined up her opening.

# POP!

Jocelyn caught her in the nose. There wasn't enough room to get off more than a blow to stun, but it did stun Mo. Her flails slowed down, and Jocelyn grabbed a hold of Mo's sweater near her neck.

# POP! POP!

Jocelyn doubled up and nailed the nose and lips. Mo's lips split. Mo was out on her feet. The guys knew it was time to break it up. They jumped back on Jocelyn and grabbed her arms, which allowed Mo to dazedly fall back to the floor. One of them spoke. "Sorry, babe, but it's time for us to enjoy you. It's time for you to pay for your sins." The guys looked at each other as Jocelyn struggled to get free. "Let's take her to the bedroom."

There was a short hallway to the right with a bathroom off it and a bedroom beyond. The men dragged the struggling, protesting Jocelyn to the room. The lights were out, but they could see the bed from the light coming in from the living room. They threw her down on the bed. A bed-stand light was turned on.

Jocelyn lay on the bed while the men looked at her. She needed an edge. She opened her body as wide as possible to give the men as good a view as possible. She smiled at them and told them, "Hey, fellas, let's have a little fun while we're all here, hmmm? I betcha Mo didn't getcha off." Jocelyn slowly raised a leg toward the crotch of the nearest male. "If you want to enjoy me, I could make it real enjoyable."

The nearest male produced a switchblade and opened it. He came down on the bed next to Jocelyn and grabbed her head by the hair and pressed the knife blade against her cheek. She could feel the edge of the blade prick her. It felt like an edge of broken glass running against her cheek. The man spoke softly. "Sorry, love, but I'm a queer myself. That's why Mo hired us. She knew you would try the charm trick. And she specifically told us what to do when you did that." He moved her head around up and down in a nod. "You know what she told me to do? She told me to slowly stick this knife blade right through that pretty cheek of yours. She wants your pretty face sliced up real good."

The man started to slowly exert pressure on Jocelyn's cheek with the blade. Jocelyn experienced a sensation she had never really felt before. It was the sensation of fear. The fear that she might not get out of what she had gotten herself into. The fear her past had caught her. She'd made her bed; she would have to lie in it. Her eyes involuntarily widened. Jocelyn struggled to break free, but the other male hopped on the bed and held her arms and head. The blade wielder yelled, "MO! Get in here! You wanted to watch!"

Mo entered the room. She flicked a wall switch, and the light in the room went on. Mo screamed. There were two other men in the room. Each man had a small solid metal rod in their hands. The men occupied with Jocelyn had no idea of the other occupants until they heard Mo scream. They turned to look at what made Mo scream.

# Smack! Smack! Smack!
# thud    thud    thud

They saw the rods coming at their heads, and that was the last they saw. The rod wielders delivered three blows to each head to make sure the men were out. Jocelyn was stunned by the rapid destructive damage the blows had done. Broken teeth and noses and skulls bloodied the bed while she looked at the damaged faces. The bloody air bubbles from difficult breathing were the only way she could tell that the men were not dead yet.

They rod men turned and looked at Mo. Mo trembled in fear as she saw the blood drip from the metal. She turned and ran to the living room. One man ran out, and he swung the rod and hit Mo in the back. Mo flew forward onto the couch. A knee was placed in her back. The rod was placed on the front of her throat and pulled back, causing her to choke. Mo struggled. She heard the following in her ear. "Now, BITCH! I'm gonna tell you something. I'm gonna tell you what we are going to do here! I'm gonna let you and your faggity boyfriends live. I'm even gonna let you have the coke and the money that you found as payment for what was stolen from you. And you're gonna consider any debts paid in full, and you're gonna forget this other bitch in here ever existed. Do you understand me?"

Mo choked out a meek, "Yes."

The rod was pulled even harder against Mo's throat. "DO YOU UNDERSTAND ME?"

The rod was loosened, and Mo screamed, "YES! YES! I GET IT!"

The man eased on his knee in the back, and he slowly pulled her over to her back. Mo felt a little more at ease when he started to stand up. That was when he swung back down and hit her in the temple with his fist while it held the rod. Mo checked out of consciousness.

In the bedroom, Jocelyn smiled at the man who was her rescuer. He looked to be maybe fifty years old and was tall and broad shouldered. He smiled back. That was when he swung back down and hit her in the temple with his fist while it held the rod. Jocelyn checked out of consciousness.

There was the light of day but no sun when she awoke. Her head and jaw hurt so did her abdomen. She tried to move an arm up, but she could not. After a couple tries of opening her eyes, she realized she was restrained in a chair. She was roped like a head of cattle.

Being tied up infuriated Jocelyn, and she attempted screaming, but she was gagged. Only muffled noises came out. Blood and snot came out of her nose. The cocaine postnasal drip mixed well with the aftereffects of the beating she had taken.

She struggled violently with the restraints. The chair she was in bounced up and down, and eventually the chair fell over to the floor. She kept at it. There were some legs in pants that she could see, but she could barely see them because all she could see was red.

She felt the chair lifted up from behind into the air. She was a couple feet off the ground, still furiously struggling. She heard a pleasant but stern voice say in her right ear, "Calm down." This enraged her even more, and she struggled harder. The chair was set on its feet on the floor, and she immediately toppled it again. She heard a voice say, "Suit yourself." This was followed by a "C'mon, let's go have a smoke."

Jocelyn struggled and struggled and got nowhere. She looked around as she wriggled on the floor. She decided she was in a hotel room. Maybe it was a suite as this seemed to be a denlike area. There had been some cooler air entering the room a couple times. Maybe some people walking out on a balcony opening and closing a sliding door? A lot of time seemed to pass. She was getting nowhere. She quit fighting.

Eventually the chair was picked up again and set down on its feet. Jocelyn started fighting again. The voice said, "Calm down." She continued to resist. The voice barked, "HEY! WISE UP! YOU'RE NOT GOING ANYWHERE. NOW! CALM DOWN!"

Jocelyn seethed. She quit fighting, but her body was tense. Her breathing was excessive through her nostrils. She noticed the desk in front of her. There was a man sitting at the desk. The man had on a Ronald Reagan mask so she could not see his face. The voice behind her spoke. "Listen to me and pay attention. If you calm down, we will remove your gag, and Mr. Reagan here will talk to you. If you scream or do anything stupid, we'll gag you again and send you back to the people you ripped off for that coke and cash the other night. It is that simple. Now the choice is yours to make. Are you going to make the stupid choice or the smart choice? Nod your head." Her head and hair were grabbed. They were moved up and down and then side to side while the voice said, "Yes for smart or no for stupid. What is it going to be? Calm down or go back to the people you ripped off. Smart or stupid?" Her head and hair were released.

Jocelyn let her head drop. She stared at the ground. Her breathing rate slowed, and she thought about her environment. She decided to be inert. She decided to do nothing. The voice behind her said, "Boss?" She raised her eyes and saw Ronald Reagan shrug his shoulders. The voice behind her said, "OK, I guess that means you chose stupid." Broad-shouldered man walked around in front of her and cocked his right arm while putting his left arm to raise her head. Jocelyn furiously started shaking her head yes and was saying such through the gag. Broad Shoulders looked back at Reagan. Ronald waved him away.

The voice said, "Now why did you have to make that choice so hard?" The gag started to be loosened, and the voice continued, "Remember, you do anything stupid like scream or anything stupid and you're going back out to the street. Nod you head yes if you understand me." Jocelyn furiously nodded her head. The gag was removed.

A voice muffled by the Reagan mask spoke. "You're pretty hardheaded, aren't you? You also aren't in very good control of your emotions, are you? That's why you struggle so hard here today. Rather than calm down and assess the situation and realize the opportunity in front of you, you decide to waste energy fighting bonds you can't possibly hope to break away from."

Jocelyn's retort was short and swift. "Fuck you."

Reagan chuckled. "See? There ya go. Always fighting."

Reagan spoke to the other people in the room, "Boys, would you mind stepping out for a bit? I'd like to speak alone to Ms. Anger Management here." The two men who had been in the house exited the room.

When they had left, Reagan continued, "Now, Jocelyn, I'd like you to take a minute and think about where all this fighting has gotten you. It got ya divorced after a year of marriage. It got you disowned by your father. It's pissed off your mother." Reagan walked around to the front of the desk and sat on the desk in front of her and spoke with his arms as much as his mouth. "You've burned most of the bridges with the friends you had. Hell, no one can trust you! You steal from everyone. I mean, gee whiz, if we hadn't a bailed ya out last night, I think the beating you got would have been quite a bit worse. My men tell me you'da had a knife run through your cheek. Now, Jocelyn, I ask you. Is that what you want out of life? To be a cheap thief who burns through people all the time? To get beat up periodically? That sounds like a hell of a career you've got going! You're twenty-four years old now. You won't see thirty at the rate you're going."

Jocelyn's rage welled up again. She wanted to yell and scream at the man, but she knew some of what the man said was true. She had realized as she had moved into her twenty-second year that she was going nowhere, and that the only way out of it was painful. Reagan was espousing the rite of passage she had learned that had fueled her death wish. The only other ways out were to marry rich or go to college, and either case meant years of no fun and the sacrifice of years of life. It was a sacrifice she was not prepared to make. She had decided to die from burnout instead.

Her retort came out vehemently. "Screw you, you ass. I've taken punches before, and I would have gotten myself out whatever the hell that lesbo bitch was going to have those guys do." Jocelyn spat on the floor. "They punched like sissies anyway."

Reagan laughed. "Sure. Sure, Jocelyn. Sure they punched liked sissies." Reagan's hand came across and caressed Jocelyn's slightly cut cheek. "But even these sissies could have slashed you bad just the same."

Ronnie stood up and started walking around in front of her. "Jocelyn, I wish you could see what your face looks like right now. All puffy lipped and swelling and bloody. You have such a beautiful face too! It seems like such a wasteful thing to do to have it mashed in, to have it scarred and marred. But if that is what you really want out of your life, well, the choice is yours. But you know, maybe, just maybe, maybe the next person will think to hire my friends to come work you over. Would you like that? Hmmm? Some nice metal pipe bashing against that still pretty head of yours? You like to lay pipe don't you? Maybe someday that's the kind of pipe you will lay? Did you like what you saw happened to those other men in your bed? I understand you got a good look at their rearranged faces. What do you think about that? Is that what you want?"

Jocelyn angrily moved her head away from the hand. She derisively said, "At least I don't need a bag over my head when getting it on. Is that how you get your kick? Some bondage and S & M and some voyeurism? Oooooooo, Mr. Big Man here hiding behind the mask. Screw you!"

Reagan looked down and shook his head. "You don't get it, do you. I'm here to try and help you get out of the shitty life you have built for yourself, and all you want to do is fight. That's too bad." He sighed. He pointed to the mask. "If you must know, the reason for the mask is this. This is a onetime offer. You can take it and move on to a life that I think you would really enjoy. Or you can leave it and fulfill your death wish. But if you choose the latter and you change your mind later on, you won't be able to track me down and beg for a second chance. You won't know who I am."

Jocelyn caught herself and stated it more resolutely. "Fuck you. Why don't you be a man and tell me who you are anyway? How do you know about my past? What the hell do you care about my past? Why don't you take that mask off and let me see who you are?"

The mask chuckled. "There, that is much better. This time you are using your brain." There was a thoughtful pause. "Well, using it a little. Maybe I'd like you to consider me a distant relative whom you have never met before. Someone who cares about your future well-being. And the mask stays on until I am confident that we have a deal."

"Whatever!" was Jocelyn's sarcastic reply.

The mask looked at her and eventually said, "Tell you what. I'll make you a deal. You calm down and agree to come work for me, in a job that will pay you quite handsomely, and I will show you who I am. Otherwise, you can go back to the life that we drug you out of. The only thing I will warn you is this: You agree to work for me and I will see that you are well taken care of. But if you agree, then you are agreeing to do exactly what I tell you to do. Fuck with me and I guarantee you that you will learn more about getting beat up than anything that you have ever experienced in your life. The choice is yours." Reagan went back and sat at the desk and looked at her. "Now what do think?"

Jocelyn thought about her situation. She needed to collect her thoughts and perform some analytical work. "I have to go to the bathroom."

Reagan thought for a second and then nodded his head. He walked to her and started to undo her binding, cautioning her, "*Don't* do anything stupid." The binds were loosed.

Jocelyn went to the bathroom. She took care of business and then searched the room for anything that would give her a clue to her captor, but there was nothing in the room except hotel amenities. When she was done, she looked at herself in the mirror and tried to fix her face and hair as best as possible with the tools in the room. She cleaned and looked at the scratch marks down her arm. She checked out her split, puffy lips, jaw, and temple. She lifted up her blouse and looked at the bruising from the kick to her ribs. She sat back on the queen's throne. She thought about her past and future.

Getting brutalized was nothing new. She expected it. She was actually surprised that she had no visible facial scarring at this point in her life. Her arm and ribs had been broken, and sometimes she felt her spine was out of whack. But the injuries had been internal. Jocelyn bore no scars from mutilating surgery.

The aging process had exerted its evolutionary power over her. She had reached an age where the realization of going nowhere had set in. She had intelligence. She had already put together how she had arrived at her current condition. She had never put together how she would evolve from her current position.

Dad was in the insurance business. Her father always seemed to resent her. Jocelyn never understood why. Mom worked as a receptionist/office manager for a complex of doctors. Mom loved her daughter, but Mom loved men too, and her appetite was large. Jocelyn was only allowed quality Mom time when other men didn't have her time, and that meant events like no visiting Mom at work because an elder child meant people would know how old Mother was. Mom would not stand for that.

The dawns of impressions of consciousness she had when growing up were of being shuttled off somewhere while Mom and Dad partied or, if she couldn't be passed off, listening to Mom and Dad argue or being told to go play in a room somewhere while one parent or the other engaged in some behavior that they were to lie to the other parent about.

She remembered her fourteenth birthday. Her parents actually tried to put aside their own personal differences for an evening to do something nice for the birthday girl. She had a nice new dress. Dinner was at the Hyde Park Prime restaurant with her choice of her girlfriends. It was a Pandora present. Mom was sure Dad was scoping out his daughter's schoolmates because there was some young flesh on the horizon. Dad could tell Mom was bitter over the fact that she had a fourteen-year-old daughter. Mom's time was slipping away. All Jocelyn really wanted was to find a way to have her perfect birthday trifecta: beer, pot, and sex.

She had never left it behind. And since she had never left it behind, she had never moved forward. As smart as she was, she had never learned forward planning. And since she had never moved forward in the past, she never would move forward in the future. This was where her death wish came from.

Now she was older, but what were her options? Go to college and kiss off the partying life for years of college while holding down a job? Could she actually gut out four years or more of college while working and eating crow to get a degree? Maybe she should find some wealthy ass to marry? She hadn't lasted a year in the marriage she had gone through. She hadn't met anyone she felt she could trust that she would enjoy spending years with anyway. And she sure as hell wasn't about to put up with some male ordering her around. Could she really actually last long enough in a fake marriage for money?

She added it up. Her problem now was, who was Ronald Reagan, and could she trust him?

Jocelyn exited the bathroom. Her walk was one of determination across the room to the chair. She noticed the Cleveland skyline as she crossed the room. From the amenities in the bathroom, she had figured out she was at the downtown Marriott. They were on the top floor. The room had to cost very good money. She sat down and spoke. "Tell me more about this proposal of yours."

# Chapter 11

## Meet John Doe

Aug beamed as he walked/limped across the showroom floor. He smiled at the salespeople and staff that he knew. The salespeople and staff out on the floor smiled back. The salespeople knew and liked him. Aug came off as a stable and mature offset to some of Jocelyn's antics. Well, normally stable. Any decked-out male who had been decked in the eye doesn't appear as stable.

The staff really didn't care that much about J's antics. In fact, they kind of welcomed them. What else would one expect from car salespeople? The antics also drew in customers to see both the sow and the show, and the hardest part of selling a new car is getting customers into the showroom. Jocy did her part, and she helped, instead of hindering, their sales. She was happy to help other salespeople increase their commission. The male and female customers were either thrilled or shocked by her activities in the showroom. If the customers were turned off by what they saw, their eyes were averted to the product at hand ("Just ignore it"). If they were turned on by it, they ate it up and wanted more.

Aug made it to the coffee area. He poured himself a cup of joe and also procured a chocolate-covered donut. The receptionist could barely look him in the eye. Her youth and immaturity made seeing a relationship such as Aug and Jocelyn shared a source of titillation beyond compare for her.

Island car dealership pulls out all the stops for the customers. Discount on haircuts are offered. Customers can buy gasoline at a discount from the dealership. A gym for pumping iron has been built for customers to work out in while waiting for vehicles to be fixed. And a small theater exists where classic movies are shown to keep other customers entertained while they wait.

Aug happened to enter the theater as *Meet John Doe* started. He groaned. The start of the movie dismayed him because the film was a black-and-white movie. Aug had a distaste for black-and-white films. This distaste had been fostered by seeing *It's A Wonderful Life* every Christmas when he was younger. It was not a "wonderful life." All the angels in the world cannot appease the loneliness a parentless child feels during the whole holiday period when the child has no direct family to celebrate with.

The more he watched though, the more he became engrossed in the flick. Parallels and opposites relative to his current situation appeared in his mind.

John Doe was a fictional character who was going to commit suicide on Christmas Eve to protest the love gone out of the world. He was created by a fake letter to the editor of a newspaper by a female reporter who had just been axed. The reporter was Ann although she could have been named And. Ann was a modern woman for the Depression era, and she struggled with the concept of "anding." The letter dealt with how love and neighborliness had gone out of the world. How the state of civilization had fallen. How we live in a modern world of social and political injustice. The letter was signed, "John Doe." The fake letter was published.

The public bought into the con. The struggling newspaper found they were playing with dynamite. Fireworks were provided for all. Unto them a savior was born. The savior was John Doeism. It is always so easy for the public to find personal relief trying to save a single person versus saving mass quantities of people. It is always so easy to find personal belief in a single person versus belief in oneself. Belief is abdication and absolution from responsibility.

The John Doe con expanded into John Doe societies. John Doe societies expressed a philosophy that all we need to do is to change how we act toward one another and the problems of the world will go away. Except that there ultimately needs to be a powerful person with the vision of salvation for all John Does to follow. The John Doe con surreptitiously expanded into John Doe societies organized to ultimately elect a wealthy industrialist to the office of president of the United States.

The industrialist headed a cabal of the wealthy. The cabal observed the charisma that John Doe possessed over the public. Media charisma is a conniving tool that can be used to an advantage. The charisma of John Doe both could not and could be purchased. The initial love of John Doe by the public could not be purchased. But the manipulation of the love and the personality of John Doe could be purchased. The purchase price is the price of belief.

Gary Cooper played the out-of-work nobody hired to be John Doe. He was warned by his friend the Colonel not to play along with the game. That playing the con game will eventually chew him up and spit him out. If you play the game, you become a helot. A helot is a person with a bank account. Once you have a bank account, then your heels need a lot and a lotta heels come after you. And that is what happens to John Doe. John Doe is the world's greatest stooge.

All John Doe wanted was a loving wife and a good life and a family. But he had a decision to make. He could sell his principles and accept that path as the only life he has to live, or he can do what he believes to be right. Accepting one path means a fine home and money to live in public happiness. Public happiness did not mean personal happiness. He could not happily live with himself as a tool for others. His choice was to expose the con. But in exposing the con, he exposes himself as a fraud, and the public turns on him. He decided to do what is right. He decided to commit suicide on Christmas Eve as John Doe had originally said he would do.

All John Doe had ever wanted to be was a good family man. For this prodigal son, it had not worked. Life got in the way.

Aug aspired to have a happy family life. His parents had not been too close to each other, and his cousins had all viewed him as the kid whose parents were killed. Year after year, he watched family get-togethers by seemingly everyone else while he did not get to enjoy this feeling. He was a mutt. He was a John Doe in the world.

The attempt to start a family tragically failed. He met Laurie during his senior year in college. She was modeling for promotional photos for local advertising campaigns when they met. She thought he was cute, and he was knocked out by her wit and charm. Their marriage and move to Florida and the start of Trove had been the happiest of times for him.

Laurie's blackouts began shortly after that. Her heart would not speed up when physical exertion began. Her head would lay limp on her shoulder during her waking periods. Despite this, they tried to have children. They were unsuccessful. Life got in the way.

Besides the failure to have a family, to further his life, he bought into the con. He enjoyed the life it had brought him, but the con came with a price. The price was Jack Dough.

Aug thought he had escaped the political and social injustice of the world. He played the game and was rewarded. He enjoyed the lifestyle. And now he was to be rewarded again by being set up to take a fall. Some people who play the game end up on top, and some are made to fall on their swords. He had escaped nothing.

Well, Aug was not going to fall on his sword for nothing. Maybe he was planning to commit suicide like John Doe planned to. Maybe he wouldn't get the wealthy industrialist. But he wouldn't go down alone.

He now realized that no one could ever have a simple life. He was deluded by himself. It was a delusion like all the other *ism* delusions. Capitalism, socialism, fascism, communism, Catholicism, Buddhism, Islamism, and all the other *isms* in the world are necessary delusions in the process of evolution toward individualism. There is always an "I" in every *ism*. The *ism* promoted feeds the benefit of the individuals promoting their *ism*. A proclivity for following other *isms* leaves one vulnerable to the schism of *ism* through myopism. Aug knew that every other *ism* but individualism was jism.

*Jack Dough*, he thought. He realized now that the nom de plume was a play on the name of John Doe. How phony but how fitting a con for a con man? Aug felt that he personally was more of a John Doe than Jack Dough ever would be. Yet he knew that in the end, both of their strings were ultimately pulled by wealthy industrialists. And he had to accept that they were both being told to take the terrible tumble.

Aug watched and waited and wondered to himself. Just what could be keeping Jocelyn so busy? He was also more curious than ever: would the doughboys ever meet?

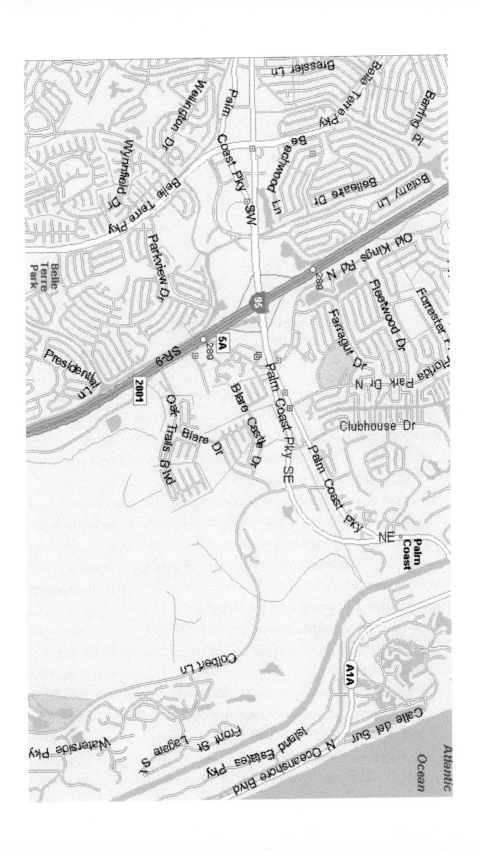

# CHAPTER 12

## WEEKEND GETAWAY

The thrust of the Caddy's car engine directed north. They were on their way to Sawgrass for the weekend. The hour of the daytime would be ending soon, but the sky ahead was already darkening. Storm clouds could be seen forming in front of them. A heat storm was brewing, and they were heading for it. Periodic flashes of lightning could be seen in their future.

She left work early. First, they stopped at her residence. She lived on a Cocoa Beach canal on Bimini Road. It was an older four-bedroom house on the Banana River. Upon her extrication from all of the obligations of the day, they drove straight there, and then they dove straight into the swimming pool. The fountain of youth was found there. Ponce de León should have been so lucky. Rejuvenation to being a teenager occurred. This caused a delay in leaving town. It had been weeks since they had physically seen each other, and there was a lot of pent-up emotion to release.

They had last been together the second of July. That Saturday evening all the residents along the canals were engaging in a Fourth of July fireworks competition. Some of his associates had built a fireworks launcher out of some metal tubes, and they were in stiff competition for winning the battle of the blasts. Explosions and oohs and aahs could be heard all across the canals as mortar after mortar were sent to the sky. Then he unleashed his secret weapon: grenade simulators. The simulators threw up a wall of water in the canal and created an explosion heard all around the canal. Silence was heard, followed by a roar of cheers from all points unseen. They won the fireworks war. It was the kind of event that excited her a lot.

They were now casually dressed and on the road. He now wore yellow silk dress shorts and a solid black silk dress shirt. She had opted for a tennis skirt and a sundrop yellow ribbon—trimmed georgette cami-doll. When she came out dressed in this manner for the car ride, two thoughts filled his mind. The thoughts were *uh-oh* and *WOW*.

The car was now passing Daytona. The traffic was heavy. Friday evening on I-95 can get that way. It had been an interesting drive so far. She was in an excited state. He always felt she was a bit insatiable, but this was something new.

A favorite compact disc of hers played, and she started dancing all over the car seat. She lit up. He had no choice in the matter. She was karaoke'ing to Axl singing Johansen. She urged him to join in. She sang that all he needed was "a plastic doll with a fresh coat of paint" and that he needed a "drag of that cigarette." She had taught him well enough that he knew to chime in that she "didn't blow it all on million dollar bet." "'I'm a human being!'" She let out a throaty rock-and-roll yell.

She wanted to play. She was "Buick Makane." She wanted "Big Dumb Sex." It really didn't surprise him when she crawled across his body to reach the power seat controls. He generally drove with the seat far back as he had long legs but she wanted more room. The seat moved so far back he could barely touch the pedals with the tips of his toes. This concerned him, and he expressed his concern. Her reply was to punch him in the thigh and to sing what she was "gonna do."

The three lanes of interstate north of Daytona were congested. To complicate matters, they reached the storms. It started pouring, and Aug was forced to first turn the wipers on high and then to regular continuously as they passed the threshold of the storm. Lightning followed closely by thunder was surrounding the interstate.

He was trying to stay in the right lane, but there were so many slower semi trucks coming on from the weigh station that he found himself weaving in and out of the right and center lanes. Using the cruise control was not viable. He moved the seat back up a little so that he could use the gas and brake better. This prompted another punch in the leg. His mind was going in three directions. He was trying to drive and negotiate traffic. He was dealing with physical sensations and effects of her playfulness. He had visions of the result of his father's car accident searing through his brain. He did not want to end up a cripple in a wheelchair.

"Aug," she said, "you know I like it better when you pack it down the right side! It's so much easier for me to get at it!" She lightly bit him as punishment for his being a bad boy. It was not a bite to leave teeth marks. It was a bite to activate his senses even more. Her bite caused him to yelp, and the car swerved on the shoulder. Other drivers on the road were getting concerned by the erratic behavior of the Cadillac. He was not getting concerned. He *was* concerned. He knew. There was no stopping her now.

But he was not concerned. She had the evidence in the palms of her hands.

She turned over and started rolling her head, her hair, up and down his thigh, laughing lasciviously the whole time. She sexily told him that she loved him. She loved him from the waist down.

It really was impossible for him to drive. He was stuck in the center lane. He looked for an exit ramp, but he did not see one. The car was boxed in the by semi and pickup trucks. They were boxed in. "Auggie dear," she said. He looked down at her, and she offered a "peekaboo" followed by a lewd laugh and a lifting of her skirt. Her clean tuft showed. "Aug," she said, "how do you like my shave?" She took her hand and showed him. He momentarily lost vehicular and mental control, and the automobile swerved right and then left. The car came close to scraping a semi truck running alongside. The swerve left meant a near sideswipe of a Tundra. Horns blared at them.

She then took his right hand off the wheel. She held his hand in her hands, and she pulled their hands to her busting out flesh. Aug was distracted, and the vehicle drifted right. He nearly sideswiped the semi in the right lane. He yanked his hand back and put both hands on the wheel and swerved the transport back.

He barked, "JOCELYN! GODDAMMIT! Are you crazy? Are you trying to kill us? Are you trying to make me wreck the car? Jesus Christ, what if a cop pulls us over?"

She made a smirking noise. She coyly smiled. She artfully rolled up onto her knees facing him. She raised her arms above her head and crossed her wrists. She pressed the button to open the sunroof, letting rain into the vehicle. Keeping her hands raised together, she leaned her mouth over and sensually kissed his mouth.

She moved her mouth and tongue toward his ear so she could lustfully speak into it. She said, "Well, dear, if they do pull us over, I guess the cops will just have to handcuff me, and you'll just have to share!" She lustily smiled at him. It struck him that maybe this cuffing scenario had played out before. He looked at her wetting hair, face, and body. He knew. There was no stopping her now.

A sign noted it was two miles to the Palm Coast exit. Her right hand was quite busy with his third leg, and she had regained control of his right hand with her left hand. She pulled their hands underneath her skirt and inside of her. He was trying to get over and make the exit. His concentration was lacking. Her mouth was licking and kissing him. She was rubbing herself all over his body and making such sounds.

His heart was racing. Blood was pumping throughout his veins and arteries. The oxygen pumping made him too high.

His mind was racing. The thoughts were *traffic, semis, rain, dash, speed, lane, control, sixty-five miles per hour, rain, brake, speed up,* etc. But it was no use. She had taken control of his brain. His brain had taken control of the gray matter in his skull. The wet was taking control. His sense of survival was overwhelmed by his sense of lust.

Aug started forcing the Caddy into the right lane. He had just missed the start of the exit when—

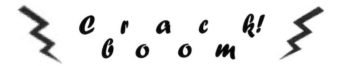

The lightning bolt and thunder clap were simultaneous. A long leaf pine tree fronting his exit from the interstate was struck. The tree exploded in sparks and flame. The reverberation shook the vehicles on the interstate. Drivers were scared by the proximity of the sudden strike.

Aug lost control of the car as he cut off a semi on the right that had been slowing down to let him in. The semi swerved left, and the right front of the semi nudged his DeVille in the left rear as the car tried to clear by. The Caddy shot across the shoulder and low brush across toward the exit ramp. The interstate and exit ramp created a V shape with trees filling the V. The V of the trees was burning like the V of she. The Cadillac was spinning across the shoulder and toward the trees. Cars behind them were locking up and sliding on the wet pavement. Angry horns from the semi and other vehicles blared.

They were moving in slow motion. The burning one pin pine loomed ahead, and it looked like they would bowl a strike. Her call seemed to be requesting them to crash as if she wanted them to end it together. He floored the gas, spinning the car faster. The vehicle sped up fast enough to miss the wooded section and continued twirling across the off-ramp. The vehicles that had been exiting scattered and slammed on brakes and bailed right and left. More trees on the far side of the off-ramp loomed ahead.

He furiously worked the wheel with his one free hand as best he could. She would not release his other hand. She was screaming in ecstasy. All three of them lost control. His left leg and foot uncontrollably went forward as he slid down the seat. His spasming leg slammed on the brake. He released. The donuts turned into fishtails. The car rocked as if it might tip. Then there was one final spin, and the car came to a halt inches from the copse. They were facing the interstate.

He sat there panting. He was drenched in more than sweat. The rain came down in sheets, pouring into the car. Earth to Aug started to sink in. He slowly looked at her in a combination of lust comedown and disbelief. She removed their hands and seductively rubbed their fingertips over her lips. Then she gave him a passionate kiss. "Mmmmm, baby, now that was a ride." She draped his body. She rubbed her hands all over. "Ooooooooooo, Aug," she said, "you *are* all wet!" She reached in the backseat and found the drenched Bahamian spring-break-style beach towel she had put there so she could wipe him off.

He realized where they were. His breathing became regulated. He wanted to be mad. He wanted to kill her as she had nearly killed them. But he couldn't. He loved the thrill and he loved her. They speechlessly gazed into each other's eyes. He reached up and closed the sun roof and then wheeled the car around and got the heck out of there.

---

Their arrival in Ponte Vedra was from the north. Aug made the mistake of noting that they passed Mosquito Control Road and that this road was where she should live because she was such a pest. That she sucked blood like a mosquito. The comment set her off again, and it was an interesting scene when they shortly pulled up to the valet service at the Marriott resort at Sawgrass. He made her wait in the car until he had checked in at the front desk, and the bellhop came and got their luggage out of the trunk. Valet service was very appreciative.

The staff and guests were surprised by his wet appearance and facial discoloration when he procured the room. They were more surprised and were either aghast or aroused by their exhibitionist walk through the lobby to the elevator to get to their room.

He rented a suite for Friday and Saturday. She walked in, saw the king-size four-poster bed, and fell in love with it. She promptly hopped onto one of the posts and gave the bellhop a show while the servant deposited their clothing in the bedroom. He was very happy that other than for room service, this was the last that anyone saw of them that evening.

---

They were walking to the elevator to take it downstairs to the pool for lounging and sleeping. Aug had on black swim trunks and a cotton white ruffled button-up shirt. Jocelyn's purple-and-black half-moon bandeau swimsuit was covered by a light jean shirt and a pair of white satin gym-style shorts. Aug looked at the shorts as she walked in front of him. He was trying to read the shorts as they swung from side to side. The clothing sported Greek-style lettering like shorts that have college or fashion label names. Jocelyn's letters swayingly said, "Callipygian."

Aug tried pronouncing what he saw. "Cali . . . Cali . . . Cali-pie-gean?"

Jocelyn heard him and started laughing. She turned and hugged him. "You silly boy! It's pronounced 'cal-e-pih-g-ann'! Don't you know what that means?"

The playful look in her eyes told him that he had probably opened his mouth and inserted his foot. He should have known better, considering the source! "Um . . . NO! . . . I don't know what cal-e-pih-g-ann means."

She turned around to face him. She grabbed his hands in hers and pulled them to her waist. She pulled their bodies close. "Well, my ignorant Auggie, I am not responsible for your illiteracy. Anyway, the word has a Greek etymology, if you know what that means. It is in tribute of the goddess Calliope. The dictionary defines *callipygian* as having 'fine buttocks.'" Jocelyn held her head back and looked up at his eyes. Her smile was as broad as could be. She scrunched her face a little and squeezed his hands. "What it means, mister, is that I've got a great ass!" The elevator door dinged, and the door opened. She said, "You, of all people, should know that I love being a Greek goddess." Jocelyn turned and entered the elevator. She looked at him standing there. Aug was speechless. She knowingly asked him, "Are you coming, dear?"

They lounged and slept by the pool until it was time for her spa treatment. This afforded him the time to slip up to the room and to slide a small jewelry box under the mattress. When he reached under the mattress, his hand touched something. He lifted the mattress up higher and laughed. There were a couple adult magazines underneath—undoubtedly left by a prior visitor and thrown underneath by a maid not wishing to be seen hauling the magazines around on her cart. Well, he thought as he flipped through, these may come in handy. It wasn't that she needed any help, but she certainly had no objections to some porn. He stashed the mags under the couch pillows and went back down by the pool and slept.

They ate dinner at Café Italiano. She ordered veal saltimbocca, and he was boring, ordering filet mignon. Mandolins played in the background, and they could see the evening rounds of golf on the Player's course wind up. Here, there, and everywhere, Aug was asked about his black eye; and he felt obliged to have a creative lie each time about how Jocelyn had given it to him. ("She shot a champagne cork in my eye," "she strategically placed the bar of soap to be slipped on," "she closed her legs too fast," etc.)

They made an elegant couple. He was dressed in fine Zanella and sported a black eye and no longer walked with a gimp. She wore a black-belted stretch dress with white piping and killer pumps. Their existence seemed to touch everyone who saw them. Women found it especially exciting to see such an attractive couple happily sharing moments together. Men just found her physically stimulating. The couples may have ended up physically having sex with each other that night, but mentally . . .

After dinner, they found a place named Aphrodite's for some drinks, music, chatting, and dancing. The place was fairly empty because the band was not hip enough for the taste of current adults. The songs were not music for women to dance on bar tops or for the vacuous clubbing set. She wasn't a *Hollaback Girl*, and he didn't want to *Drop It Like Its Hot*. But the songs sounded strangely melodic, and that worked for Jocelyn and Aug.

Live music was provided by an odd group fronted by Enyal Yelats and Christy Phletam. The band name was the Tokers. The songs were sung by voices that sounded gravelly from too many cigarettes and too much whiskey and too many late nights. Their voices were offset by a wailing saxophone as well as electric guitar and a rhythm section.

They danced together to songs sung by both the male and female singers. Their dancing was both slow and up-tempo, but it was also lithe and full of coupling. They enjoyed the togetherness and the smell of each other. She enjoyed his sweat and the smell of man it created for her to inhale. He enjoyed her smoothness. She was not there to be a rump shaker, and they were not there to seek foreign flesh. Ionic bonding occurred as they came close and then broke as they danced apart.

Her *Words* fell like *Rain* and gave him *Fever*. *Would* her *Confusion* make her *Got Me Wrong? Because* she was *On Your Side*, she could lose her heart in the *Dance of Love. Can You Hear Me?* he asked, and he would *Never Let You Down*, and they would *Never Grow Old*. Mixed in was the obligatory *Woo Hoo Woo Hoo Hoo* song as well as strange original compositions:

Beware of her lightning
She's oh so delighting
I centered in her eye
Lovely hurricane Di
She flung her bolts at me
Igniting manly tree

Oil and water will never mix
Our wood and water make phoenix

My trunk swam in her waves
Tree ring to her I gave
Her bolts ignited me
Her charge she set me free
From all material things
Beware, beware, lightning

Her wind a massive gale
Her cry a banshee wail
She struck me to my bone
Inside her storm I'm prone
I love my hurricane
To see her rage I came

Our bird flew in the storm
It was the phoenix born
The ashes oh so warm
This lovely bird I mourn

The bird it came from two
Lovely bird I love you
The bird the bird no longer two
My bird to the sky she flew
Phoenix bird you flew from view

After leaving the club, they stopped and purchased champagne to take back to their room. Their visit made the store manager's evening. Jocelyn just had to have the Piper-Heidsieck magnum dressed by Gaultier. The store manager was glad to finally sell it. By this time, she was in overdrive; but with the day's sleep, he had regained composure and was in control.

In the room, he declared he had a surprise for her. The champagne was opened, and they each took some. She gleefully giggled in anticipation of her surprise. He pulled out the magazines from under the cushions of the full-length sofa. She laughed in enjoyment at receiving them. Where did he come up with these? He lied and said that he had brought them along. Aug suggested she enjoy some reading time while he changed and prepped for "bed." Jocelyn was happy to do so.

He retired to the bathroom and undressed. He eyeballed himself in the mirror. He cleaned his mouth and reshaved as close as possible. He mentally steeled himself for things to come. He changed his attire to blue silk pajamas. He anointed himself with Fahrenheit. He exited the loo.

She had already hung her dress and changed. She wore an open red satin mesh chemise that draped over her body. She wore it with no string attached. She was thoroughly enjoying her reading material.

He entered the room. She was excited and wanted to rub her hands all over him. He grabbed her hands, saying she was not to act in such a manner. He told her to lie facedown on the bed and to close her eyes and relax. Aug threw on "Touch" for her enjoyment. Jocelyn found the saxophone thrilling and relaxing. She wondered where he was. She heard a ding from a microwave, and she started to rise up to see what was going on. His strong hand pushed her head back down. "Relax," he whispered in her ear.

Her enjoyment was enhanced when he started massaging her neck and shoulders with warm fragrant oil. There was a rose smell that thrilled her. His soft strong hands felt so good. His fingers were under her ears and all over neck and spine and shoulders. They worked under her shoulder blades. They found knots that her early spa treatment had not addressed. He worked and worked the knots to get the muscles to release. He was kissing and licking her neck. She loved tongue, and that excited her. His body felt so good. She could silkily feel him against her derriere, and she loved that. She was ready. She tried to raise her body up.

He did not let her get up. He laid his whole body on top of her, forcing her back down. "Relax," he said. "Breathe deep. Breathe with me. Deeply. In and out and relax. Let it go." She didn't want to, but she complied. Her breathing became long and deep, and then all her muscles became noodleish. She felt invertebrate.

When he felt her melt, he went back to work. She felt him working underneath her chemise. She felt him working down her back. His hands worked down her back and spine. He found her spot in her lower back that was like a button to her extremities. As he massaged and kissed her lowest back, he could feel the steam rising from her. She felt him work his way back up and down her spine. Up to the neck and back down. Her body involuntarily curled a bit, and she mewed like a kitten.

He moved to her feet. She no longer felt his pressure, and that was disappointing, but she was so relaxed she didn't care. The warm oil felt so good on her soles after a night of heels and dancing. The calves were worked next. Then he spread her legs wider, and he started working each thigh while he sat on her calf. His knuckles kneaded up and down the backs of her thighs. She exhaled deeper and deeper as her body liquefied even more.

His hands went up and down her thigh, and his thumbs dropped down inside. Each pass, his thumbs teased higher and higher. Then he lifted the lower drape of her lingerie and began spanking her. Enough to make it sting, and then he rubbed the sting out. He blew warm and cool air inside her as he worked her. She yelped and wriggled in delight. When he finished, he lay back on top of her, and he started on her neck again.

She felt his weight. It was so strong. It was not drug induced. It was all natural and long lasting. She felt him breathe in and out in long breaths, and she matched him again. She was incredibly excited and yet so at peace. He told her it was time to turn over. She had no control to do anything but what he told her.

The music ended, and the program had changed to "Erotica." She sang along, "'Bad girl, drunk by sex.'" They had more champagne. Aug pulled a couple of silk ties from his pajama pockets. They smiled as he tied her wrists to the bedposts. He buried his head and hands in her top. She could barely keep her legs still from the heat. He worked her front side all the way down. He worked the fronts of her legs as he had the backs. He eventually massaged her thighs up and down; his thumbs slipping higher and higher each pass up the legs. She was in delight she never felt before. He kissed and licked and sucked on her skin in her upper thigh outside of her. She was bouncing on the bed from excitement. He thought she may break the posts.

Now it was time for him to commit suicide. He moved up to her face and kissed her. Aug looked at her and said, "OK, bad girl, I know why you bashed me in the head, and I am OK with that. But did you have to kick me so hard in the ass?"

Jocelyn had been completely disarmed. She had not seen it coming. Her emotional state was so high at the moment. His words weren't sinking in. Her drunken eyes looked at him in a glaze. She was confused. She could not speak. "I had another camera set up that no one knew about," he said. "It was in the rafters. It was away from all eyes. I have the tape. I saw you."

Jocelyn realized what he was saying. She was being accused of robbing Trove. By Aug. By her lover. She exploded in fury. "WHAT? What are you talking about? Is that what this is about? Is that what you brought me up for this weekend?" She let out a roar of rage that made Aug think that this must be what a lioness sounds like.

Jocelyn wanted to beat him, but she couldn't. He had tied her arms too well. Her legs started flying at him, but he was strong enough to hold them down while he moved out of the way. His look was stern and resolute. She screamed at him, "Let me loose, you—," with volume and a variety of various vernacular vituperations. He stated that he would not do so until she calmed down. To pass the time, he walked to the couch and started idly flipping through the magazines.

Jocelyn fumed. Fire expelled from her lungs. She tried to break free from the ties that bound her, but she could not. She tried to concentrate, but her anger was all consuming. It took time for her to regain any composure. Think, think, think. What could she say to such an accusation? "If you have such a tape, then you know it wasn't me BECAUSE I WASN'T THERE!"

She spat out, "What do you mean 'yes and no'! Can't you give me a straight answer? Jesus fucking Christ, what the fuck is with you?"

He tried to explain. "Well, the yes is that occasionally at Trove, we will bring in things . . . for other people. Didn't you ever wonder why we went over to Nassau and I had to meet with the bank over there? It's 'cuz that's where my cut goes. It keeps it out of the US and away from the IRS, and no one is the wiser." Aug paused. "But the no is that no I didn't bring in these metals. I mean, Trove brought in a shipment of metals that had stuff in them. But I didn't know about it. I only know about it 'cuz the stuff got stolen. And now people think that I had them stolen, when I didn't even know they were there! And if the goods aren't produced soon . . . well . . . there's a bullet with my name on it."

She stared at him in disbelief and then rolled her eyes. Her body fell back on the bed, and she stared at the ceiling. "Oh, and *I'm* the crook around here? I'M THE CROOK AROUND HERE?" She thought about it, and her indignation started to turn to concern. She raised her body up on the bed to look at him. "Aug, baby, what are you going to do about it? Did you steal everything? You aren't gonna get shot are you?" She stared at him. "Are you?"

Aug sighed. "Well, it's a little more complicated than that."

She was incredulous. She grasped her hair in her hands. "More complicated than that? MORE COMPLICATED THAN THAT? You're telling me someone stole fifty million dollars, and they're shooting bullets past your head, and there are more bullets with your name on it, and that it is more complicated than that? How the hell could it be more complicated than that? What could be more complicated than that?"

Another major sigh was heaved. He looked around at the ceiling and then back at her as he spoke. "Well I . . . uh . . . I . . . uh . . . well, you see, there was also some jewels that I was smuggling. They got stolen too."

Jocelyn's teary, drunken red eyes bugged out. Her hands and arms went intensely up in the air as if she was pushing the oxygen away. "You're joking, right? I'm not hearing this, right? You had some jewels stolen too? And what kind of jewels were stolen? Just how much were these jewels worth?"

He said, "Oh . . . I guess . . . I reckon . . . oh . . . twice as much as the gold and platinum."

She started to do the math. "Twice as much as the—one hundred million dollars? Did I just hear you right? That you had one hundred million dollars of gems stolen from you?"

Aug stared off at the wall and then back at her. "Yeah, I reckon that's about right."

She held her arms up, palms forward, then held her head, staring at him. "I don't believe I am hearing this. I can't believe you! You just had like hundreds of millions of . . . smuggled . . . smuggled goods stolen from you and you're here? With me? Accusing me? Good fucking god! I may have stolen something in my life, but millions and millions and millions of dollars worth of stuff? Your fucking crazy. Who the fuck are you? I . . . arrrrgggggggghhhhhhhh."

She threw the pillows off the bed at him. Then she launched herself at him and started swinging punches at his head and body. He sat there and took the blows. She was strong, and she pounded him with rights and lefts. She was screaming, "I HATE YOU!" as she hit him. She hit him in the head. In his nose. In his mouth. In his jaw. The blow to the jaw popped her knuckles, and she screamed in pain and rolled off to the floor. She was screaming until she could scream no more. Exhausted, she rolled on the floor, sobbing.

Aug reached under the mattress and removed the small jewelry box he had placed there earlier. He laid it on the floor where she could see it.

"What's this?" she asked.

Aug replied, "It was to be for you."

She took the case and opened it. It was empty. She stared blankly at him. "I don't get it."

Aug pulled both of them up from the floor to the bed. He gave her a panda bear hug and then a light kiss. "There had been a ring inside. I was waiting to give it to you. I was going to ask you to marry me, but now . . ."

Her eyes widened. She had not been expecting this! The full rush of all emotion in her body welled up—the anger, sorrow and pent-up passion. Her body and mind felt electric. She pushed him to the bed and climbed on top of him. "Aug, baby, listen to me. Let's leave. Let's go. Tonight. Far away from here. Now. Before anyone finds out where we are. We can go away, we can hide, start over. Yeah, that's what we'll do! You've got money saved. I've got some money saved too. We can go away somewhere where they won't find us. I don't care what you've done. I love you, baby. We can do this. Trust me. You and me, as a team."

He rolled his fingers lovingly through her hair. He half-smiled. "And just how much money do you think you and I have saved up? Enough to last a lifetime? I doubt it. The money won't last. And sometimes, things aren't what they seem. Besides, for this kind of cash, no one's gonna just let me 'disappear.' We'd probably end up being John and Jane Doe on a morgue slab somewhere. No. No, I don't think running is the answer."

He raised up and reversed their positions. He examined every facet of her face and hair. "I love running my hands through your hair. I love your beautiful emerald eyes and that funky nose, and I love kissing your lips." He bent down and gave her a passionate kiss. "But most of all, Jocelyn, I love you. I don't want to lose you. I want to marry you." Augustus passionately kissed Jocelyn again.

Her eyes grew big. She wasn't sure what she had just heard. "Aug, are you proposing to me?" They looked into each other.

"Jocelyn," he said, "I want to, but I can't. Not until this is cleared up. A storm has started. The storm needs to pass." He rolled over and laid on the bed beside her. "I just hope I survive the eye of the hurricane." He turned his head to her. "I love you, baby, and I don't want to hurt you, and I don't want to lose you. I need you to trust me now."

"I love you too, baby!" was her reply. They kissed. She looked at him. "You trust me and I'll trust you. OK?" They kissed again. "Sooooo, what are you going to do? Aug, don't these people want to kill you? Just who are these people anyway? What is your plan? How can I help?"

There was a grim determination on his face as he turned and looked at the ceiling. "Yes, I suppose. Yes, someone wants me dead. Who it is, who is behind all this, I am obviously not sure right now. The funny things is . . . the funny thing is that it's not for anything that I have done. But I can't change that. The dice have been cast. Time will tell whether it was a hard ten or snake eyes or some other roll." He raised her up and looked at her and kissed her. "And there is nothing you can do to help right now but to trust me. I will find a way out of this, and then we can go away together. As a team." They kissed. "But now I need to get some sleep. There are things that will be set in motion tomorrow, and I need to be ready for them." He walked over to the champagne and guzzled all he could straight from the bottle, letting out a healthy belch when he was done. "We'll talk further tomorrow. Good night baby. Tonight, I will sleep on the couch, alone."

He took a bow. The night and the masquerade were over.

She watched as he walked around and shut off the lights in the room. Then he went and stretched out on the couch while she lay in the bed. They stared in opposite directions. Neither one accomplished much sleep.

When morning came, they packed, had breakfast, and left. They went to the beach, where sleep actually occurred. The day wore on, and they left, taking the long scenic drive down A1A to Cocoa Beach. They did not talk much the whole time. Their only conversations were about points of interest passed along the way and how to both best dry the car and to get rid of the odor. Their personalities were subdued by the moment. They hid behind sunglasses.

They were passing the Cape Canaveral port area when Jocelyn's cell phone rang. She answered the phone. "Hello?" A look of concern came on her face. "Yes, this is she?" A pause. "What! What happened? Who did you say you are?" There was a pause. "When did all this happen?" A pause. "Is he all right?" A pause. "WHAT? Oh my god." A pause. "Yes . . . yes . . . yes . . . I'll come up right away. I'll . . . is this number a good number to reach you at? Ask for Doctor Eastman? Eastman. Got it. Let me call you back in half an hour. Thank you. I'll talk to you in half an hour. Goodbye."

Jocelyn leaned back in the car seat and exhaled. She removed her shades. She looked at Aug. Her eyes were welling and tears started to form and roll from the edges. "Aug, it's my father. He's . . . he's suffered a stroke. That was the hospital. They've taken him to South Pointe. I'm going to need to go home to Cleveland." She turned and looked straight out the passenger window. "DAMN! I can't believe this!"

Aug pulled her close. "How bad is he?" he asked.

She replied, "They don't know right now. The doctor said the hospital was running tests, and they would let me know." She looked at him and spoke. "I'm gonna get a flight up there and see him."

Aug looked forward while driving. He was fidgeting. Finally, he asked, "You want me to come with you?"

Jocelyn looked at him in stunned amazement. "AUG! You can't do that! What's gonna happen with all the stolen goods? If you don't find them, they're gonna kill you! I can't let that happen, baby!"

Aug looked at her and grimly smiled. "You're right. But I figured I should offer." He drove on and looked forward. "Damn! And I was so looking forward to meeting your father someday soon." He looked back at her and hugged her again. "Hey, everything's gonna be all right. You go take care of Dad, and I'll take care of things here, and when we meet again, everything will be different. Everything will be better. I promise. OK?"

Jocelyn nodded in agreement. She nestled closer to him and spoke. "I love you, Aug."

When they arrived at Jocelyn's, it was becoming dark outside. Aug went in and changed clothes from shorts to black pants and a black shirt. She inquired where he was going, and he said back down to Fort Lauderdale to check out some leads. They hugged and kissed. She made him promise that he would see her again. He wished her father well and asked her to call him and keep him informed of his condition. As he shut the car door, he could see her on the porch waving goodbye and blowing kisses. He could see the cell phone in hand, waiting for him to leave so that she could begin making calls.

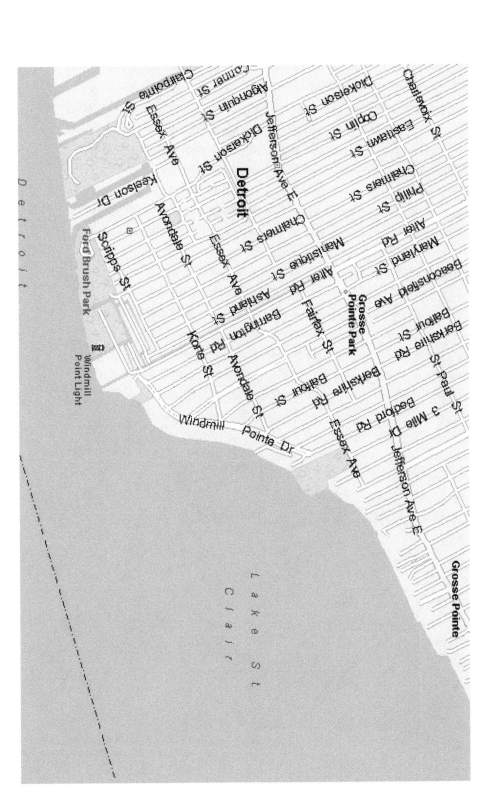

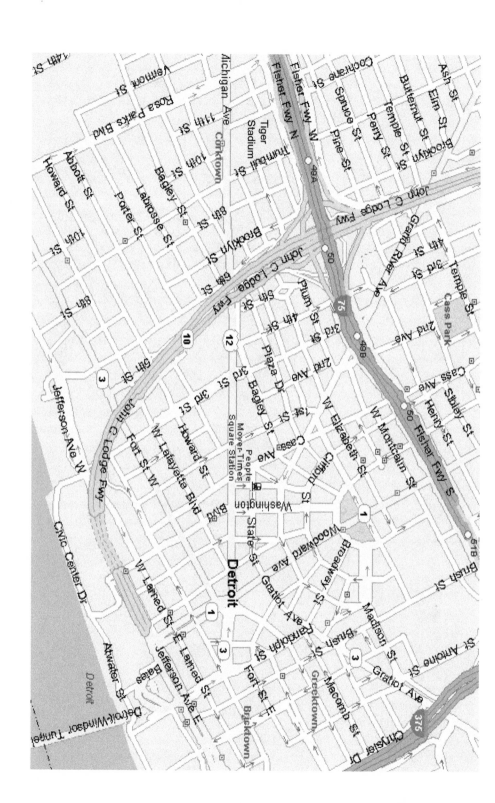

# CHAPTER 13

## TERMINUS

Ginger said, "Hey, open the door, dumb ass. Let me get up there." Vitellius leaned over across the passenger seat and opened the passenger door on the Caddy. Ginger folded the seat forward and climbed out to take over the passenger seat. Upon settling in, she leaned over and gave Vitellius a peck on the cheek. Her hands made their way for denim delight. "There now, isn't that much better?"

Vitellius leaned back to enjoy her handiwork. "Ohhhh yeahhhh! That is much better." He relaxed a bit and then asked, "Hey, what are you doing here anyway? I thought we were going to pick you up in a little when we got done here?"

Ginger smiled. "Well, that's what John wanted to do, but I told him I didn't want to sit around while you guys got drunk before game time." She looked around at the car. "I can't believe you don't have any Stroh's in here! Anyway, John didn't tell me you guys had . . . uh . . . other plans this morning." She looked around more at the car they were in and the house whose driveway the car was in. "Nice ride," she said. "I love the candy red color. Wheredya get it?"

Vi answered, "Rob lined it up. It's an El Dorado, you know." With that, they both looked at each other and said, "Terminus!" The mutual laughter made tears come to their eyes.

Ginger bounced on the seat and sang in a high girlie voice, "Well, maybe he got it for me!"

Vitellius snorted, "Yeah, right. I don't think so. It's probably another one of his clients who wants a later model. This one's got some things wearing out on it." He put his hand to the driver-side, convertible-top release. "Look, this thing's broken."

Ginger looked around at the vehicle. "Yeah, and it's got an eight-track instead of a cassette player! No wonder they want to get rid of this!" Ginger started the eight-track tape. It was Blondie. She reached over and turned the ignition key forward to power the tape. "Oooohhhh, I like this," she said and started singing along to "Rip Her to Shreds."

The car was a bit chilly. Vitally was wearing a blue jean ensemble—a jean coat and jean pants. Ginger joined in the blue jeans, but she was a sweater girl. "Can you turn on some heat?" she said. "It is a little chilly out." Vitellius obliged by starting the car and blowing the heat on full. Ginger started looking around the vehicle some more. "Damn, it's chilly in here. I wonder what the temperature is like today. It's gonna be brisk at the ball park." She pointed a finger at the dash. "You know what would be cool? A temperature gauge in the dash. Now that would be cool." She looked around further and pointed at the wheel. "Is that an air crash system? Wow. This car is loaded! No wonder there's no seat belts."

Vi perked up a little. His face became covered in curiosity. "Ya know, that's funny, now that you say that. I thought every Caddy but the El Dorado had an air crash system as an option." He shrugged and grabbed her hands. "Ooooooooh, you are cold. Here, let me put those hands somewhere warm." He put Ginger back to work, and he adjusted the vents to blow down on her activities. "How's that? Much better?"

Ginger smiled at him. She looked out the back at a sign posted on the roadside that read, "Neighborhood Protected by Magnum Security."

She looked back at Vi. "Aren't you a little worried about security seeing what's going on?"

Vitally had his eyes half-closed, thoroughly enjoying her dexterity. His jeans were really cramped, but the heat and pressure felt good. "Hmm? Oh. It's an inside job. The family here is taking a bus to the game from the yacht club. Grosse Pointe does it right, ya know? C'mon, the whole city is partying downtown for the Tigers home opener. You know how the home opener is always a citywide holiday for Detroit. It's one of the best days for pulling a caper. The cops and security crews are all busy with the game, and they wanna party too. Rob set this one up. It's an insurance scam. We get the jewels and the homeowners collect on the insurance. Rob also took care of getting this car. He had John steal it from somewhere. My ride's down at the stadium. We'll pick it up when we head down there and ditch this one." He paused for a second. "Hell, we might even make it in time to see Soleman throughout the first pitch!"

Ginger looked at Lake St. Clair showing behind the house. Her attention then came back to closer surroundings. The residence was fronted by a three-foot wall that had some sculptures of lions at the driveway gate. There was another weird sculpture she saw of an eel-like creature with a gargoyle head and fins or gills that looked sail-like as they protruded from the neck.

Vitellius opened his eyes toward the manse. "I wonder what is taking him so long. He shouldn't have to go through every room in the house."

Ginger looked at Vi and asked, "Do you think he knows?"

Vi spread his legs wider and snorted, "After that incident at the golf course last year? Um, yeah! Yeah, I'd say he knows."

She laughed and slapped him across the chest. The knowing smile was large. "No, silly, you know what I mean!" Her eyes widened a little, and she cocked her head a bit to indicate "Get it." Her mouth gave out an "Hmmm?"

Vi rubbed his hand along her thigh. His hand was huge; it covered nearly half of her leg. "Oh. Ya know, I dunno? Damn, I hope not." He paused a minute, looking at the house. "Ya know, it's not like he's a saint anyway." He relaxed a bit more, enjoying the moment.

Ginger reached her second hand over to assist the first. "I swear I don't know how you fit into these jeans!"

Vitellius looked at the house. "Better be careful. John should be done about now. I don't think he'd be too happy about you jacking me off here."

## BANG! BANG!

Two gunshots were heard from inside the house. Vitellius and Ginger snapped to attention. They looked at each other and then at the house in wide-eyed surprise.

Two men came running out from behind the house. In their hands were sidearms. The men were raising the guns to point them at the car. Vi let out a "Fuck this," and he started the car. He threw the El Dorado into reverse and peeled back onto Windmill Pointe.

## BANG! BANG!

Vi heard the reports but didn't notice any hits anywhere. He sped north on Windmill Pointe. He saw three Magnum Security cars peel around the corner from Berkshire at a high speed. They were hard-charging at the Cadillac. He asked aloud, "Where did these guys come from?" Vi decided south would be better. He drove across the six-foot-wide grassy median separating the lanes of the wealthy neighborhood and headed south on Windmill. Then he turned west onto Middlesex. The other three cars followed. Two of the cars followed behind Vitellius. The third car went past the ten-foot-wide median and drove up Middlesex the wrong way. The vehicles rapidly reached a speed of fifty. Vehicles on both lanes dodged traffic and parked cars, bouncing up curbs to the sidewalks and back down.

## BANG! BANG!

Vi and Ginger heard the reports but didn't see any results. Vitally told Ginger, "Keep your eye on those cars back there."

Ginger turned in her seat and looked. "Where the hell did these guys come from? Why are they shooting at us? I thought you said this was an inside job?"

Vi replied, "It was an inside job! Hell if I know where they came from. They are not supposed to be here!"

The cars were going over sixty when they ran the stop signs at Korte and Avondale. There was a crossover between the lanes, and the wrong-way car pulled across, aiming to cut Vi off. He yelled, "Hang on," and he bounced his vehicle across the grass and around the oak trees and ended up in the wrong way. Vi bounced the vehicle farther up on the far sidewalk to avoid oncoming traffic. Horns from the nearing traffic were blaring. Vi angled back onto the street and blew through the stop sign at Essex. The pursuit vehicles were not far behind.

Crossing Essex was a zag, and the road name changed to Beaconsfield. The street narrowed. Trombley Elementary was on the right. The school was letting kids out at noon in honor of the Tigers home opener. Ginger screamed. There were a half-dozen kids on bikes in the middle of the road, chatting. Vitellius pulled left as far as he could while braking to avoid plowing into the children. Two Magnum cars went left with him. The El Dorado slid sideways into a parked car on the street. The Magnum vehicles slid into the El Dorado. Vitellius floored it to pull away from the vehicles. The Caddy scraped paint and metal as it took off.

## BANG! BANG!

More reports were heard. Vi and Ginger didn't notice any hits.

The third Magnum car went right to avoid the crash and children in the road, but this took the vehicle at more schoolkids in front of the school. The kids screamed and started running. The car fishtailed to avoid hitting youngsters and drove straight into the side of the school. Parents in cars in the school parking lot hopped out in horror, screaming their heads off and running to see if their offspring were OK. Ginger had been looking back and saw what happened. "One down," she quipped as the Cadillac sped away.

Vitellius couldn't worry about that. Jefferson was up ahead. He was looking to make it to Jefferson. They approached the stop sign at a speed over fifty.

He blew through the stop sign at Beaconsfield and Jefferson. There was another median to cross to go left. Vi headed along Jefferson toward downtown. The first Magnum car blew the stop sign and followed. The second Magnum vehicle went left to avoid a Gremlin that was coming across Jefferson. The Magnum car hit the cement curbing for the median square, and the car steering broke. The driver lost control and went straight over the median, clipping a tree before clipping the rear end of the first Magnum car that had turned up Jefferson. Car number 1 kept control and continued the chase while car number 2 crashed into a red brick wall gating an apartment complex.

Ginger quipped to Vi, "Two down."

The chase down Jefferson went on for miles at speeds reaching ninety miles per hour. Traffic was fortunately light as they used all six lanes, crossing back and forth around traffic in both directions. Traffic heading toward Detroit could see the commotion coming and was pulling over out of the way. Traffic lights were irrelevant to them. They flew by the pawnshops dotting the way that bought and sold cheap remnants of lives. Decrepit liquor stores catering to lowest common denominators were passed. The chase had gone from wealth to poverty as they passed the Jefferson Chrysler plant and the road turned to being lined by bombed and burned-out buildings.

Waterworks Park was passed. Henderson Park was passed. Owen Park was passed. The Detroit River appeared on the left. The city sewage plant was passed. The silver circular towers of the Renaissance Center came into view in the far distance as well as the Stroh's Brewery sign. Gabriel Richard Park came up on the right. Belle Isle was approaching.

Vitellius told Ginger, "Hold on!" He sped up even more toward the light at E Grand Boulevard. A bus of revelers from the Lake St. Clair Yacht Club on their way to Tiger Stadium tried to get out the way by moving right, but the bus accidentally cut Vitellius off. He had to slow down, but the pursuit car sped up and got on his rear bumper.

Another center median approached. Vitellius went the wrong direction. The pursuit car followed behind. Traffic would be coming at them in each lane. The light at Grand turned red. A gravel truck started through the intersection. Vitellius hit the gas and pulled right as hard as he could. He bounced over the median and cut in front of the bus and headed up Grand. He never knew how the Magnum vehicle lost control, but it turned sideways as it tried to brake.

## CRASH! CRASH! CRASH! CRASH!

The Magnum vehicle fishtailed back and hit the gravel truck head-on. Other vehicles lost control and struck the truck as it tried to veer away. Ginger saw vehicles piled up in a spectacular four-car crash. Shattered glass spread everywhere. The Belle Isle Grand Prix met Terminus El Dorado. Vitellius kept going to the right up Grand.

Ginger screamed in exhilaration at seeing the spectacular car crash. She grabbed and kissed Vitellius on his cheek. He turned left at Lafayette and drove down past Martin Luther King High School. Elmwood Cemetery was on the right. He maneuvered the El Dorado past the Calvary Baptist Church and into the graveyard.

Vitellius drove slowly around the winding paths through the tombstones. There were graves hundreds of years old. Statues of humans and saints dotted landscape as well as massive spires of death. In ten years of crime with his buddies, nothing had ever gone wrong. They had never had a bad setup before. What had happened? What was he to do now? He found a lower tier and parked by the T. B. Rayl underground crypt across from the cemetery's pond. He needed to think.

Reality hit Ginger. She started to cry and go into shock. "John's dead! He's dead. He's . . . he's dead. He's dead." She crumpled into Vitellius. He hugged her tightly, comforting her as best as he could.

"Shhhh, shhhh, calm down, everything'll be OK. Hey, we don't know what happened to John. Maybe he's OK." He pulled her face back to make her look at him. "I'm sure he's OK. John wouldn't get hurt in some fool robbery like this. They probably shot at him, and he ran out another exit. We'll probably see him at the ball game later." He pulled her close, hugging her again.

Vitally thought about the situation they were in. They needed to get rid of the car now. It was now marked by dents. Vi noticed that his door was loose. The crash must have broken the locking mechanism. His Camaro was at a parking lot near Tiger Stadium. They could ditch the Caddy in the parking lot down there and pick his car up. The cops would be busy with crowd control. It was the Tiger's home opener. The streets would be packed with people. Even with a 1-7 record to start the season, the home opener was always a citywide holiday. They could blend in and disappear. There's no way the cops would be looking for them down at the game. The police would be too busy with crowd control.

He pushed Ginger back again. "Hey, hey, look at me." She looked up at him. She didn't look good. Her eyeliner and mascara were all over her face. A vacancy sign had been hung at the door of her eyes. He needed to extract her mind back to reality. "Ginger, Ginger, listen to me. I know this looks bad, but things are not always what they seem. Now, we can't stay here. We need to get rid of this car. Here's what we're going to do. We're gonna go down to where I have my car parked at the ball park and switch cars. OK? Are you with me? We need to do this now, and then we'll figure out what we will do after that. OK?" Ginger nodded an assent. "Now remember. We haven't done anything wrong. I picked you up at your house, and we were out driving, and these cars started chasing us and shooting at us. Don't worry about this car. I stole it, and you didn't know that. OK? If we find out later on that they have John, then we'll change our story. OK? Remember, if something happens and the cops take us, don't say anything without a lawyer. OK? ANYTHING!" Ginger nodded again.

Vitellius drove the car out of the cemetery. Concern over being on a main thoroughfare sent him from Elwood to Chene to Antietam. He was working his way through neighborhoods. The slow drive helped calm him down. Some of the adrenaline jag wore off. He came down Gratiot to Monroe to Michigan, heading to Trumbull.

They passed the statue of Thaddeus Kosciuszko. Vi idly wondered who he was. To him, he was just another John Doe in the world who had been lucky enough to have a statue made of him. It made him think of Augustus. Augustus, named for a Roman Emperor. Maybe Auggie would have a statue made of him someday and be famous like a Roman emperor or Mr. Polack here. But probably not. He would probably be another person who lived and died and left nothing but a headstone behind.

The car crossed the lodge, and the road turned to red brick. It certainly wasn't yellow brick. Nemo's was on the right, and it was teeming with people. They were in Corktown, Detroit's oldest neighborhood. It wasn't even the oldest neighborhood. It was just the neighborhood that had survived the longest to be known as a specific area.

The road was wall-to-wall with vehicles. Horns were honking, and people with drinks were walking all around. The bars and beer tents and street vendors were hopping. It was a brisk fifty outside, and there was a slight breeze, but the sun was peeking through clouds, and the home opener is a day that marks the upcoming spring. After months of colder weather, fifty degrees and sunshine makes people cut loose. Vi sunk down a bit in his seat. He pulled Ginger down with his hand. The last thing he wanted was for the two of them to be seen together in this car right now.

Cops were everywhere directing traffic. It was a nerve-racking fifteen minutes, inching past police and people. Traffic cops directed all traffic flow. They passed by Tiger Stadium. The marquee at Michigan and Trumbull stated.

He wanted to get by to Harrison just a couple blocks ahead. His Camaro was in a lot up there. He turned onto Harrison and proceeded to shit bricks. Squad cars were in the parking lot. Cops were looking at his car. He kept going down the road, but as he reached Cherry, he was spotted. Flashers were hit, and vehicles started. It was time to go. The chase was on.

He peeled around Cherry. He wanted to head north on Rosa Parks to get to 75, but there were policemen in the road. He turned south on Rosa Parks. He clipped a Charger, making the turn onto Rosa, denting both vehicles significantly in the rear quarter panels. It was back to weaving around vehicles. Cops were in pursuit.

Ginger started wailing. He looked over at her, and his eye was drawn to the seat floor. The crash appeared to have dislodged a White Owl box. It was partially exposed from under the seat. He yelled at Ginger, "GRAB THAT." She dully looked at him. "THE BOX, GRAB THAT!" he yelled, pointing a finger at the box.

She jostled around in the vehicle as the car lurched from side to side. Slowly she pulled the box up. She opened the box and didn't understand what she was looking at. She opened the box to where she could show Vitellius. He saw what looked like fifty small bags containing a light brownish powder. His eyes bugged as he ran the light at Fort where Rosa turned into Jefferson. Vitellius knew now why things had gone wrong. It was all a setup. One of his partners had sold him out. His guess was that he was looking at heroin. He shut the box. He didn't want to look at it. That bastard Rob had set the whole thing up. John got nailed in the house stealing ice, and he was to be nailed with skag. Well, fuck him. He'd get away and then show him who would fuck who.

He had hit the gas pedal hard, and the car accelerated to seventy. A patrol car entered Jefferson from Tenth; they sideswiped. Vitally wanted to make it to 375. If he could get on the interstate, he could think a minute and decide where to go. He needed to get the horse out of the car, but he couldn't do it while the cops could see it. On the interstate, he might be able to dump the baggies if he could get a lead or get off somewhere. Was there anything more in the vehicle? Had something else been planted in the Camaro? That's why they were waiting for him at his car. They knew he had this particular El Dorado, and they were waiting.

Another cop car entered the chase at Sixth. The cop attempted to hit him in the front end, but Vitellius slowed up enough and entered the oncoming traffic lane to avoid him. Ginger screamed and lurched at the wheel. He threw her off and moved the car back over to the other side of the road. Third Street came up, and he pulled right, turning down the road. Multiple cop cars were in pursuit.

Joe Louis Arena was on the left. The road veered left. A pedestrian was crossing the road. Vitellius veered left around the jaywalker. One cop car went right when the driver saw the citizen. The cop car drove straight into one of the massive red pillars that dotted the sidewalk in front of the park. The cop car behind missed his partners crash and continued right across the grassy knolled park, sending picnickers scrambling. The cop crashed through the fence that fronted the Detroit River, and the vehicle flew into the water.

Cobo Hall came up on the left. Placards on the pillars on the right advertised the upcoming Van Halen Party 'Til You Die Tour and a separate Journey concert. More cops were in pursuit. The cars passed through a tunnel and over the Detroit Windsor Tunnel. Vi veered farther right on Atwater. They were going between fifty and sixty.

The Renaissance Center came up on the left. Banners announcing the Republican Party Convention later in the year hung from the streetlights. Japanese tourists and more picnickers were all over the place, including the center of the road. Ginger screamed when she saw that it looked like the Caddy would plow through a group of people. In a panic, she lunged over and yanked the wheel to the right. The car careened right across the cement plaza that fronted the river. Vitellius grabbed the wheel and yanked it left. The Cadillac went airborne from the five-step drop to the second cement level of the plaza.

The car landed with a crash on the left side. Car parts and hubcaps flew off as metal crunched cement. The air crash restraint system exploded. The damaged door blew off. The jolt from the crash and the explosion of the airbag knocked Vitellius one way and then the next. His legs were momentarily pinned against the steering column, and bones in his legs and spinal column broke. As the vehicle moved forward, both the door and Vi broke from the car, and he rolled unconscious along the cement.

The El Dorado continued forward and crashed into and through the metal barrier separating the plaza from the Detroit River. Ginger and the cigar box exited the Cadillac through the front window. Shards of glass impaled her cheeks as her face crashed into the window. Her neck snapped upon impact with the water.

Police boats and cars descended upon the scene to try and effect a rescue, but they came too late. Between the chilly water and the broken neck, her death was rapid. The box of evidence stayed shut and flew into the river. The current took it downriver before the police could recover it. It was lost forever.

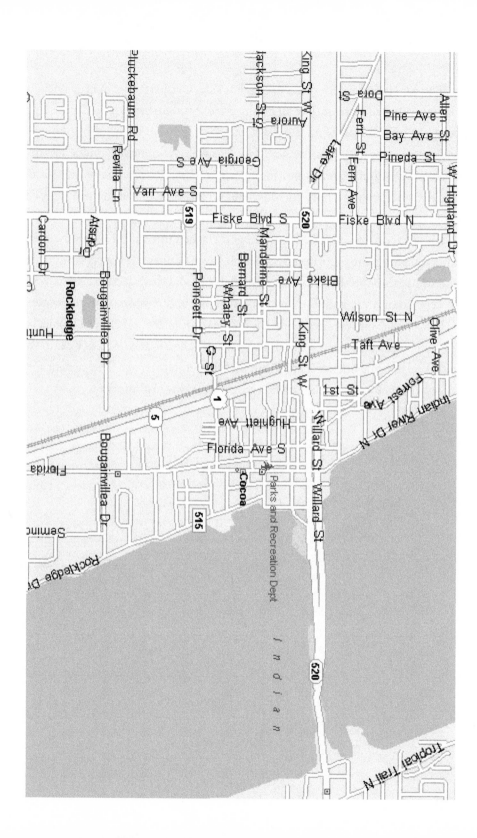

# Chapter 14

## Plates

The headlights on the black convertible Mustang were turned off when the vehicle turned onto Factory Drive. Aug had met the brothers and swapped cars. If anything happened, he didn't want his vehicle involved. Plus, the Mustang could give more sudden acceleration power than the Cadillac.

The brothers were given a head start. As Aug parked in the Upper Terra lot, he spotted the DeVille in the Almost Antiques parking lot beyond the post office parking lot. The streets and lots were empty this Sunday evening. There was also a Windstar parked on the street, and that was it for vehicles.

The car was backed up as quietly as possible toward the front door of the building, and he shut off the engine. He looked around as he pulled in. A Cadillac was still in the parking lot. So were the other trucks. There was still a larger truck at the loading dock. There was still steam exiting to the clear sky. He could see some light in the factory through a small window. Something was being brewed. It was time to open Upper Terra for business.

The first order of business was to tape the grenade simulators and remote exploders to the front windowpanes. He placed one on each side. Practice made perfect. The double tape side was activated, and Aug pressed the devices against the windows. Then he grabbed a flashlight, CD, and keys from the Ford. He flashed a light on the alarm system. The alarm panel showed green. The alarm was off.

Aug's gloved hand inserted the master key into the front door lock. The key worked beautifully. The second key opened the door to the office. The office door to the factory had a small diamond window in it. Light from the factory came through the diamond. Aug went the other way. His destination was Joe's office.

Aug entered Joe's office, and he positioned himself in Joe's chair. The flashlight was set at his feet. The computer mouse was wiggled. No life appeared on the screen. He looked at the desktop box. It was turned off. The power switch was tripped. At boot up, Aug opened the CD drive and inserted the disk he had brought. While the PC went through boot up, he thought of checking the desk drawers. He did not find a revolver. The monitor came to life. The display came up:

## LOGIN SUPERVISOR

Aug logged in and proceeded to activate program COPY. COPY was a discreet name for a virus designed to destroy all data and to infect the server and any other networked PCs. Aug sat back in the chair to let the program run. He was resting there when he heard, "Whatcha doin' there, sonny boy?"

Joseph Khan was standing in the doorway. Joe turned on the light switch. The pistol was in his hands.

Aug pushed the chair back a little and put his feet up on the desk. "Me? I'm not doin' much. Just thinkin' bout copyin' some files from your PC. Just lookin' to see what I might find."

Joe looked at him sternly and pointed the gun at Aug's head. "Ain't you supposed to be finding me my goods?"

Aug smiled at him. "Joe," he said in a drawn-out manner. "I found yer goods. They're out back in the factory. Back where yer smelting them."

Joe grinned back. He waited a moment before speaking, the two men eyeing each other. Joe kept the gun in his right hand and poked a finger into the bullet holes in the wall. "I thought you had an idea the other day. You just seemed too unnerved, and there was no way you could agree to deliver me tomorrow something I already had." He thought a little more. "So, smarty, that being the case, would you mind telling me, just what are you doing here?" His face had a

and he may have some use for me." He looked at both the workers at the end of the line. "Maybe you better shut things down for a minute."

One of the two men man packaging took the gun into his work gloves. "Aww, boss, we're already runnin' tight on time. We can't stop now, we've got another new batch o' metal comin' out of the furnace. I'll keep an eye on him. He ain't going nowhere." The packager set the gun down on his far side on a stack of boxes.

Joe turned toward the loading dock area. "Don't fuck up," he said as he walked away.

Aug discreetly slid his shirtsleeve back and looked at his wristwatch. The time was nine-forty-five. He tensed up a bit in anticipation of things to come. It was time to evaluate the room. There was a furnace at the back wall of the factory. This was where the steam had come from. Ingots of gold were on a small skid by the furnace. The furnace was being used to melt the ingots.

A rail track entered the furnace. An overhead lift system was used to lower a cauldron up and down from the track. The lift system moved the cauldron between two assembly lines. One line molded plates and the other line molded goblets. The cauldron would be tilted forward, and liquid metal poured into the molds.

The molds looked like large pie tins stacked on top of each other, with tubes running through the tins. The tubes brought water in to cool the molten metal. When the molds were opened, they revealed either golden goblets or golden plates. One of the men would grab the newly fashioned item out of the mold and would trim the flash from the product. Then he would hand the newly minted product to the packager.

The last men were packaging the goods. They were putting two plates and two goblets to a box. The box was then taped shut. The packagers were not having fun with the taping process. It looked like the autotaper was broken, and the packagers were struggling with a tape gun to make a neat and effective tape strip.

Aug smirked to himself as he watched. They were trying to work as fast as they could. No OSHA here! It looked like no lockouts were in place for pouring metal or opening and closing molds.

Because of the heat from the manufacturing process, everyone was wearing short-sleeved shirts. Large fans were circulating air as best as possible. Aug realized that this was a skeleton crew to minimize the people in on the deal. A classic-rock station was playing in the background. "Love Is Like Oxygen." Time wasn't on Aug's side. He did not have it at all.

Aug concentrated on determining who was in the building. The packagers at the end of the line kinda looked Art Carney and Marty Feldman. There were three other men working the molds, flash, and cauldron. Aug decided to call them Joe Piscopo, John Candy, and Groucho Marx. There was another guy driving a hi-lo; that would be Curly Fine. Aug couldn't see anyone else around, and he did not see Joe Khan anymore. Joe had disappeared behind racks of goods.

There were also sets of stand-alone presses and other machines on the far side of the assembly lines. It looked to Aug like Upper Terra was a job shop that had suddenly had the assembly lines cobbled together.

He closed his eyes and exhaled, pressing his head against the back wall. He thought about the situation. Six men formed a pack that he would have to deal with. He needed a weapon. What was available? There were many shop tools at the stand-alone stations, but most were probably locked up. And they were far away. The scissors for trimming would be more likely to use. He opened his eyes to look around some more. The cauldron was coming across with more molten metal to pour.

## Crash! Crash!
## BOOM    BOOM

The Champion brothers set off the grenade simulators. Amongst the explosions, glass could be heard shattering. Upper Terra was now paneless.

Everyone but Aug reflexively turned toward the source of the explosions. Aug sprung up and charged at Marty Feldman. Marty reached across the lines for the pistol. He grabbed it. Aug grabbed a tape gun from the end of the line. Marty swung his arm around to fire at Aug. Aug beat him to the punch. He swung the tape gun down onto Marty's arm just below the elbow. It was a direct hit. The teeth of the tape gun dug deep into the flesh. Aug grabbed the arm and yanked the tape gun toward the wrist. The skin peeled up like paint from a scraper. Marty screamed and dropped the gun as blood started spurting out from the wound. The gun fell on the pallet of boxes. Marty grabbed at his arm with his other hand to cover the wound to keep the spurting down. Marty's concern for his own life took over, and he was out of the picture.

Groucho had been packaging at the end of the second assembly line. Aug swung at his neck with the tape gun, but Groucho leaned back. Aug's swing missed. Groucho lunged for the handgun. Groucho got a hand on the gun. Aug grabbed Groucho's wrist with his free hand before Groucho could cleanly handle the gun. They wrestled. Aug swung the tape gun down on Groucho's hand. Groucho screamed in pain and threw his arm up in the air. He let go of the gun. The gun flew through the air and landed on one of the assembly lines near the molds. Groucho watched the gun and his hand. Aug watched the tape gun smack into Groucho's head, causing the Marx brother great discomfort. Aug's adrenaline rush was high. He hit Grouch again in the head. The tape gun broke, and the toothed wheel stuck in his skull. Aug threw the stunned Grouch aside and made a beeline for the gun.

Joe Piscopo raced Aug for the gun. They both reached the gun at the same time and struggled for it. Aug pushed their hands over the mold. They both looked up. The full cauldron of molten gold was above their arms. Joe looked back at Aug and furiously pushed his left hand in Aug's face. Aug's leg rapidly came up and struck Joe's groin. He scored. Joe momentarily lost a sense of where he was. Aug kicked him again. Joe's hand moved out of Aug's face. Aug leaned down with his head at Joe's right forearm. He bit into the arm as deep as he could. Aug tasted blood.

Joe screamed and let go of his grip on the gun. The weapon fell to the far side of the assembly line. Aug kicked him again and grabbed Joe's right arm at the elbow. He pinned Joe's arm against the mold and hit the cauldron release. A stream of molten gold came down on the wrist area. Both Joe and Aug pulled away from the liquid. Joe rolled away screaming and trying to wipe the liquid metal off his skin. The cauldron pulled back up, having made its pour. Aug hopped over the assembly line and picked up the gun. He looked around, assessing the situation. He held the gun with both hands in a forward firing position and moved his arms from side to side.

Two men were injured and were crawling around, trying to address their wounds with whatever bandaging material they could find. Groucho was behind him in between the manufacturing lines. The other three men were on the far side of the assembly line looking at him. Joe had returned to see what the explosions were about. Aug wheeled back and looked at Groucho, barking for him to drag Marty away to a wall and to dress his wounds with whatever he could. Groucho obliged. Aug wheeled back to look at the others.

Aug started speaking, "Listen up, everyone! I don't want to cause trouble or hurt anyone else. I just came here for one reason, for one person." He pointed the gun at Joe. "I want him." Everyone looked at Joe. "It's your choice, Joe. Either come here, or I start emptying slugs into people." No one moved or said anything.

# BANG!

Aug put a round by Joe's head. Angrily he yelled, "I'M NOT FUCKING AROUND, EVERYONE. THE NEXT SHOT IS GOING INTO SOMEONE'S BODY!" All eyes turned to Joe. Slowly, reluctantly, he started walking toward Aug.

Joe and Aug came together. Aug got behind Joe and put the gun to the back of Joe's head. Joe spoke. "You're a fucking dead man. I'll fucking kill you," he seethed.

Aug told him, "You won't do anything unless you want a fucking bullet in your brain. And believe me, Joe, when I tell you that right now this gun has a bullet in it with your name on it." He then yelled out to everyone, "Now listen up, everyone! Joe here is going to walk to the front office with me. Don't follow us. I've got the door wired to go off like the other bombs that just went off. Follow us and you'll have a very unpleasant death." Aug pressed the gun harder against Joe's head. "Now let's go, asshole."

Aug walked back to the office door pulling Joe with him. He took a look into the front office through the portal in the door. The Champion brothers had staged things for him while the fight was going on. Aug backed them through the door and turned the bolt lock on the door.

Joe let out a "What the hell?" at what befell his sight. Glass was everywhere. A warm evening breeze came through the empty building front. Two table chairs were positioned beneath a noose that had been hung through a pulley mechanism that the Champions had installed in the doorway. Aug hustled him to the chairs, all the while keeping the gun to Joe's head.

"The choice is yours, Joe. Take a bullet in the brain or climb up on the chair and put your head through the noose." Aug looked back at the door to the factory;

Curly's face was in the window. Joe had balked at anything. Aug emphasized the point by pressing the gun harder at Joe's skull as he barked, "NOW!" Joe obliged. He slowly stood up on the chair directly below the noose. He slowly put the noose around his neck.

Aug followed Joe. He stood up on the open chair and pulled the noose tight. He put the gun against Joe's head and spoke with rage in Joe's ear. "Yes, Joe, I *do* know the truth. How I know doesn't matter, but I know what happened. It's time for you to pay the price."

Aug then stepped down to the ground and looked in Joe's eyes. "This is for Laurie." With that, he yanked the chair out. Aug ran outside to the Mustang. As he entered the car, his last vision of Joe Kahn was of him struggling to get free from the rope, struggling for air, swinging above the ground. A sensation of satisfaction overtook him.

Aug threw the revolver to the seat. He peeled the Mustang out of the factory parking lot and down to the corner of Factory and 1. As he wheeled the car around the corner and onto 1, he noticed in the rearview mirror that the Windstar had started up. At the corner of 1 and 520, he turned right into the parking lot of the Cocoa Hyundai dealership. He pulled around the dealership building past a giant inflated purple gorilla and parked. From here, Aug could see the intersection, but he felt obscured from the road by the new vehicles in the lot fronting the hillside along 520 and 1. No one driving by could see him.

The Windstar drove by, heading north on 1. Aug waited. He saw one of the pickup trucks speed by and head west on 520 toward 95. Behind it was another of the pickup trucks. It turned east on 520. They were looking for him. It was time to lay low.

Aug waited fifteen minutes and called Mike on his cell phone. Mike answered his phone by saying, "What's shakin'?"

"I'm shakin', that's what! But I'm all right," Aug replied. "I'm sitting in the lot of the Hyundai dealership. I saw a couple of the pickups from the parking lot go by a while ago. They're out looking for me. Where are you?"

Mike replied, "We're back at Sunset. Did everything go OK?"

Aug answered, "Okeydokey. I got everything I wanted. I haven't seen any sign of the trucks in a little while, so I'm just about to leave." He fired up the engine.

"Looks like a clean getaway. Hang on the phone while I get outta here." Aug threw the phone on the passenger seat. He backed the vehicle up and cleared the building. "Oh shit!"

# C r a s h!
# BOOM

A shotgun blast took out his rear window. Art Carney was in one of the trucks blocking the exit. A bloodied Groucho was standing next to the truck, and he had fired a shotgun. Aug peeled forward to the back end of the building and immediately slammed on the brakes. John Candy and Curly Fine pulled up in another truck. They were blocking the other exit. He was trapped.

Mike was screaming on the phone, "AUG! AUG! Are you there, man? What the hell was that?"

The trucks pulled closer around the corners of the car dealership building. They were boxing him in. Groucho had walked around the building and was pointing the shotgun. He yelled, "Stay in the car and shut the engine off, or I'll blow your fucking head off!"

Aug saw a hole. He dropped down and floored it in reverse and crashed into the front of Art's truck. The truck lurched forward and popped the gorilla.

# C r a s h!
# BOOM

Groucho let go a blast. The car stereo exploded. Shotgun pellets hit the hood of the car.

Aug wheeled left, crashing through two new Santa Fe's parked at angles to each other at the edge of the lot. The car bounced across the lawn and flew upward over a small hill. As Aug crested before bouncing down the hill, he saw the Windstar parked in a raised parking lot across the street. That's how they knew where he was. The Windstar had spotted him. Whoever was in there was no guardian angel.

The Mustang bounced down the hill. Groucho hopped into Art's truck, and the truck bounced across the lawn and down the hill after him. They took out the political ads. Aug saw this in his rearview and thought this was fitting. *Some ass for some asses.*

Candy wheeled his pickup out of the lot after them. Aug floored the car as he ran the lights at Forrest and Florida and Brevard. Streetlights lit up the sign, saying, "Historic District Cocoa Village." The trucks were in pursuit. Aug had the left lane, and the trucks had the right two lanes.

They ran the light at Delannoy. A car pulled out at the light at Riveredge. Aug went through the red in front of the vehicle. Art and Groucho switched to Aug's lane and came in front of the vehicle. Candy and Fine thought they would beat the car to the rear side, but the car had slammed on its brakes to avoid the other two vehicles. The momentum was lost. Candy's pickup crashed into the rear end of the car and spun left into the guardrail. The car bounced off the metal and careened back right across the road into a thicket of brushes and trees off the road. They were out of the way.

The other two cars started up the HHH Bridge. They were moving over sixty miles per hour. Aug pulled forward and moved right in front of the pickup. His wheel turned with difficulty at first and then suddenly went free. A surprised Aug momentarily lost control of the Ford.

## CRASH! WHAM!

The right side slammed the eighteen-inch cement curb and went up onto the sidewalk across the bridge. The right side of the Mustang scraped the cement wall of the bridge. The convertible lost momentum as Aug slowed down from fear since he had two tires on the bridge and two tires spinning in air. The pickup sped up and pinned Aug against the wall as they crossed the bridge. Sparks were flying from under the vehicle and along the side of the vehicle. Aug looked over at the pickup. Art was ready to fire. Aug slammed on the brakes.

## BOOM!

Art's blast missed. The pickup truck shot past.

Mike's voice was screaming through the cell phone. Aug reached over and grabbed the phone. He switched the phone to speaker mode. "I'm in trouble. I need some help here!"

Mike yelled, "What's going on? Where are you?"

Aug yelled, "We just crossed the bridge, and I got one pissed pickup truck to deal with!" He glanced in the rearview. He saw flashers in the distance. "And the cops aren't far behind. I think the power steering is messed up. The Mustang ain't gonna make it far. Hang on"

The pickup had slowed up, and Aug wrestled right and left with the steering to try and get by. The truck was turning with him, trying to take him out. They weaved across the three lanes, smacking the cement center median on the left and the guardrail on the right. They passed a billboard stating that Ron Jon's was four miles ahead.

Mike asked, "Can you make it here?"

Aug yelled, "Maybe. But then what? Between the cops and the truck, we ain't goin' anywhere."

They had reached Merritt Island, and there was traffic. Aug swerved into the oncoming traffic lanes and swerved back. The pickup took the sidewalk and weaved around trees and signs that dotted the way. They both made it back to proper lanes before the light at Mcloud. Both vehicles were moving between sixty to seventy miles per hour in a forty-five and were blowing around and by the traffic. They caught a green light here and at Courtney. They passed a large lit sign that said, "Psychic Readings by Tina." Aug briefly thought, *Yeah, psychic this!*

He yelled at the phone, "Need a little help here!" He moved to the far right lane. The pickup broadsided him. Aug yelled, "WHOA!" and the car flew up over a curb and bushes and in between palm trees and heading directly at cars parked in the lot of a TGI Friday's that fronted the Merritt Island Mall. He regained control of the Mustang and continued on the sidewalk and cut over in front of the mall and back on the road. The cops were back in the distance still, but somehow, it seemed like they were getting closer.

He heard Mike's voice, "Where are you now?"

Aug yelled, "Passing the mall."

Mike's voice said, "Here's what I need you to do. Dump the car in the river. Drive it into the Banana River."

Aug let out a "WHAT? ARE YOU OUTTA YOUR MIND?"

Mike answered, "I'm pulling the boat out now. I'll pick you up at the bridge area. Ditch the car in the water and get out and get to the boat. It's so dark out no one will see you."

Aug was incredulous. "No one will see me? Hell, I won't see anything. I'll crash into a wall."

Mike replied, "Listen to me. Steve has gone to find a spot that will work. He's gonna park the DeVille along the road with the flashers on at a spot that will work. Just do it! Trust me!"

The light at Sykes was red. Aug saw the Hooters sign off to the left as he ran the red and avoided cars. He momentarily dreamed of fluffy pillows. He prayed he might see some again.

The traffic and pickup forced him left. The left lane was filled. Both vehicles had to slow down. Cops were getting closer. Aug pulled into the grassy center median, narrowly missing cement electrical poles that dotted the way. The center was grass and then turned into three-foot-high brush. The Mustang bounced violently.

The road opened up to the Banana River business district. The center median gave way to a third lane. He wanted to blow a kiss as they passed Jocy's car dealership. The truck pinned him against the cement center median, creating another spark shower. The median disappeared, and Aug swung into the oncoming traffic lane. He narrowly missed a head-on, and he swung back far right. Turning the vehicle now required maximum effort. The pickup and the Mustang were playing Chinese fire lane drill, swinging back and forth across the lanes. They continued this over the Banana River bridge. Aug could see the Cape Canaveral Hospital in the distance.

Aug took the Mustang to the barren dirt center median. The median grew three-foot-high brush that the Mustang bounced over. He slowed up a bit and let the pickup truck pull alongside. He could see Art trying to line up a shot. He saw the guardrails ending along the ocean. He saw a vehicle with flashers on stopped along the side of the road beyond the guardrails. Looking ahead in the dark, he could make out that square hedge formations with palm trees in the center were coming up.

# BOOM!

He heard the blast but saw no damage. He crossed to drive in the wrong direction on the far side of the center hedges. The police were not far behind in the rearview. He now heard sirens. A lane change break came in where his Caddy was parked, and then the center median started again. He looked left and couldn't see a thing, going toward the water, but there was no way he could make a ninety-degree left. He would have to swing around for another pass. He yelled at the phone, "I gotta come back through. Tell Steve to wait. WHOA!"

# BOOM!

Aug heard the blast. He felt a shot hit the vehicle. Damage had to have occurred but where? He yelled to Mike, "I'm still with ya!" The hospital was closer ahead.

He crossed back over the center section, narrowly missing one of the intermittent hedge sculptures and ran the Mustang side by side against the Ford. They barreled along to the hospital side by side. The pickup was in the left lane. The Mustang was in the center between the traffic lanes. Art was motioning to Groucho as they lined up a shot. They passed the "right lane continuous green" sign. Groucho leaned down to give Art a shot. Aug braked and then pulled behind the truck and gunned the convertible forward. He got on the bumper of the truck. The left lane was red. An ambulance was coming out of the hospital. Groucho saw it and jumped up to try and gain control of the truck. He tried to pull into the left-turn lane to avoid the ambulance. Art jerked the shotgun back and caught the trigger.

# BOOM!

Groucho caught the blast in his chin. Aug floored the Mustang right. The truck started swerving and control was lost. The back end of the ambulance was caught, and the truck turned over and spectacularly started rolling down the center and then the far road. Aug sped by on the right and barely missed getting caught up in the car carnage.

Four squad cars were now the problem. A small bridge was crossed and
A1A came up. Aug fought the wheel as he sped up and turned right on A1A,
but then he veered left over a small cement divider. There was no longer any
power steering. He narrowly missed the four-foot-high hedges in the divider. He
narrowly missed more vehicles and palm trees as he crossed over into the wrong
lane. A billboard flashed in his mind that said, "Ron Jon's—Ten Feet Ahead." One
oncoming car swerved to avoid him and crashed into the six-foot stone Easter
Island heads that adorned the lawn at Ron Jon's. Two trailing motorcycles went
right around the crashed car. The hog riders crashed their bikes into the circular
statue display of surfers that fronted the building. The bikers went flying into
the statue of the surfers.

Aug turned left down the road between the two Ron Jon's buildings. He
reached up and undid the convertible top lever above his head. He pulled left
into the store parking lot and drove through. Pedestrians in the lot scattered.
He reached over and unlatched the convertible top lever at the top right of the
vehicle. He pulled a quick right and left and left and came down Dixie Lane.
He came right onto A1A and then turned left back 520. He picked up cop cars
that had just made it to A1A from 520. They were now right behind him. He
activated the button to lower the convertible top.

The road ahead was dark except for two things a mile ahead. Aug floored
it. The hospital could be seen on the right, and the road appeared to be blocked
by cops and the crashed ambulance and the turned-over pickup truck. It was
decision time. Aug sped up as fast as possible and chose a point between the
back of the pickup and a parked cop car. He insanely screamed as the Mustang
crashed through the barrier. The truck went spinning on its hood. The parked
cop car did a three-quarter turn. Dash lights came on the Mustang. There was
not much life left in the car. The patrol cars in pursuit slowed down to make a
slow turn around the vehicles in the road.

Aug saw the Caddy ahead. He had no choice. He was now committed. The
Mustang lurched a bit and then refired. Aug screamed as he angled right below
the blinking hazard lights on the DeVille. He couldn't see what was in front of
him. The car bounced on dirt and then shot upward in the air tumbling end to end
and side to side. It was slow motion for him. He saw himself with Jocelyn in the

Cadillac careening to the trees and heard her screaming yes in ecstasy. His laughing was maniacal as he realized he had truly lost his mind and was insane.

Officer Larry Medendorp could not believe his eyes. The psycho had crashed through the vehicles in the road and looked to be heading directly at a car with flashers on that was parked at the side of the road. A traveler with a flat tire was about to be rear-ended when the whole road was open. The Mustang barely missed the parked car on the right and barreled toward the water. He saw lights in the air as the car shot off a little berm and some rocks that the tires struck. This started the vehicle tumbling through the air. The headlights looked like out-of-control lighthouse beacons as the car circled around through the air. The vehicle crashed upside down and went dark. It took a minute to get up to park the patrol car. He ran across the water's edge, flashing his torch across the water. It was pitch-black. Even with the flashlight, it was very difficult to see anything. The only other illumination came from a couple boats in the river. He never saw anyone, but rescue services never recovered a body.

# Chapter 15

## Phoenix

The parking garage across from the Wyndham in Hollywood is very right brain/left brain in design. One must drive to the fourth floor on the right and cross over to the left to complete a descending exit. Aug had been here before. The garage design had always made him wonder if this was a form of intelligent design or if it was just an act of creationism?

The car was parked on the second tier of the right side. Before walking across to the hotel, he placed a call to an attorney associate, one Mr. Bradley Frohman, to arrange a meeting sometime that day when Aug was done at the hotel. Then he walked across the bridge that ran over A1A. He paused for a moment to look in both directions at the buildings alongside A1A and the cars passing below. The cars and buildings were irrelevant to each other, and a sense of the irrelevance of others around himself flowed through him. His individuality from his surroundings had taken control. He moved on.

The Wyndham lobby looked beautiful. The atrium was as spacious as a football field. Palm trees created a T within the lobby, framing off the sectional areas. Rectangular black marble sculptures facilitated even flowing water that flowed from one level to another at a slow, constant stream to a pool at the base. The waters seemed to say, "Join our placidness." A decent crowd was milling about, but it was a late morning, so the bustle of guests leaving early had already passed.

It was Tuesday, so the weekend crowd had already passed. It was the downtime before the afternoon rush.

Mark was not available. He was out on an errand. Instructions had been left with hotel security for Aug to be allowed to the pool area that fronted the beach. Aug chose the upper-level pool area. The pool created a T pointing out to the beach and the ocean. It was a slow morning with only a couple dozen adults and children lying out or swimming in the pool. The level below had quite a few more people at the pool down under. Aug leaned back and found a quiet corner of the deck to relax and soak in the sun. His preparation had been Bahama shorts and a Caribbean-style dress shirt and loafers. Aug discarded the shirt and shoes. The Oakley's stayed on.

The walk over helped alleviate the whiplash his body had been traumatized with. The sun felt warm on his skin and relaxing for his muscles. Sol helped calm his mind from all the events of the last week. It helped calm his mind from all the events of the last year. It helped calm his mind from all the events of the last few years. He felt warm. The rush of his near death from when the Mustang hit the water was starting to ebb and flow out of his mind and body. The children in the pool were noisy, but the water sculpture he had seen was so placid that it dominated his mind as he drifted off.

The Mustang twirled and flipped. Aug crashed down into the water. The car landed upside down in the river. The force of the impact stunned him into unconsciousness. The force of the airbag inflation stunned him more. The head of Augustus was underwater, and he did not realize it. It was when the airbag deflated and his body moved forward and impacted the horn that he awakened and realized his lungs were filled with water. There was no oxygen. He was going to die.

Panic set in. All around him was watery black, and he was drowning. He flailed his arms about. Was it the guiding hand of destiny that released the seat belt? It felt like someone or something took a hold of his right arm and directed him to the catch release.

After releasing the belt, he did a uey and came back up inside the body of the vehicle gasping and spitting water. An air bubble had formed inside the inverted vehicle, but Aug was not aware of this. All he knew was that he could breathe. Everything was black, but he could breathe.

Where was he? What had happened? What was he to do? He flailed his arms about to try and figure out where he was. Once again, the guiding hand of fate intervened. The guiding hand guided his hand to the interior lights on the rearview mirror of the car. There was very little illumination, but at least, there was some. There was enough to figure out who and where he was. Enough time to realize that he was inside a car that was coming down on top of him. Aug completed an escape just before the vehicle pinned him down.

There was suddenly light above the water. The light filtered down, and it was as if Aug were swimming in the clearest of oceans. Something large swam by him, creating a long stream of bubbles. Another large entity swam by him, creating more bubbles. The entities were feminine in form, and they swam all around him in a spherical pattern, creating an air bubble for him to breathe inside. It looked like one animal was chasing the other, or was it the other chasing the one? The speed of their movement made it impossible to tell.

When the air bubble finished forming around Aug, the creatures stopped swimming, and Aug could see what they were. They were mermaids. Each one took hold of one of his hands. He was suspended in the Jesus Christ pose inside the bubble. The mermaids were outside in the water.

These mermaids did not have scales or fish tails. They looked like women who swam with graceful force just by the movement of their hips. They were clothed in teddies that gave the illusion of a jellyfish cover. They were blonde and brunette. They were Mermaid Laurie and Mermaid Jocelyn. They smiled at Aug and tugged at his arms, each one trying to pull him their own way. The pulling was initially slight and playful, and then it became more forceful.

Mermaid Jocelyn produced a pistol from somewhere inside her dress. With one free hand, she fired. Aug could see the projectile lazily move through the water at almost no speed at all. The bullet bisected the water, and then the air bubble and then the water. The bullet created a visible shock wave the whole path. The bullet slowly passed in front of his eyes and eventually struck Mermaid Laurie in the neck. The water turned red to his left, and Mermaid Laurie's still-smiling face slowly disappeared behind a wall of blood. Aug didn't want to let go of her hand, yet at the same time, he wanted to swim with Mermaid Jocelyn.

Aug and Mermaid Jocelyn started physically grokking. Their bodies joined into the shape of the phoenix bird. A brilliant light beam blasted from heaven, and they soared up into the path of the warm sunlight. They could see a rectangular variegated coral structure on the beach below. The ocean swelled up and rushed over the reef. The phoenix shot a lightning bolt from each eye. The bolts struck the coral. The structure exploded into rubble and flames.

A lightning bolt came down from the heavens and struck the phoenix. The bird split into two and suddenly Aug felt himself plummeting to the ocean. He saw Mermaid Jocelyn ascend into heaven and disappear as he struck the water.

Water hit Aug in the face. The water was thrown by Mark Kledas. The torpor Aug was in was broken. He found himself swimming back to reality. He jumped forward from the recliner he had been dormant in. His shades went flying. There was laughter in the air as he gathered his wits. More water was thrown. This time, the water soaked his shorts. "That's quite the dream you were having, Aug. The women around here must have loved watching you sleep." There was more laughter.

Aug began to realize where he was and what was going on. He laid back on the recliner. "I was dreaming about Laurie," he said.

A somber Mark replied, "Oh." He sat down in a chaise lounge next to Aug. "Aug, that was a bad deal, and I am sorry about that. If I'da known what was gonna happen, I'da never asked ya ta go to Costa Rica. Hell, I don't know what to say. If Joan . . . if Joan took her own life, I'd be pretty freaked out by it. I can't imagine . . . I can't imagine it." Mark paused and sighed and then laughed again. "But from the size of that tent you were pitching, I'd say it was a good dream nonetheless!"

Aug cocked his head with a wry grin. "Costa Rica. How I wish I had never gone on that trip." He paused a minute and then looked at Mark. "But you know, Uncle, the thing that has never made sense to me? The next time I went to do laundry, there were her . . . intimates . . . in the washer. I mean, you tell me, what woman puts her underwear in the washer and then hangs herself? That just never made any sense to me."

Mark thought about it. "And now?"

Aug looked at the sky. "Now? Now, it doesn't matter anymore. There's nothing I could do about it anyway." Aug paused for a second and then looked at his watch. It was after noon. He looked at Mark. "Where were you today?"

Mark replied, "Aug, ya know, I could ask you the same question. Where were you this last weekend? I thought we were going to get together and go over this situation and figure out what to do. Instead, you disappear. Where the hell have you been? I've been calling your cell phone and went by your place all weekend, and you were nowhere to be found. What the hell? I know you had to have seen my calls. I think this is hardly the time to be playing hide-and-seek with me."

Aug found his sunglasses and put them back on. "I was off following some leads." He paused. "The metals ended up at Upper Terra. Joe Kahn must have stolen them. He was smelting them according to the original plan. I was there Sunday night and saw the operation taking place." Another pause and then a grim turn toward Mark. "It nearly cost me my life."

Mark was data processing. "WHAT? What are you talking about?"

Aug relaxed back. "The more I thought about it after we talked last week, the more some things made both more and less sense all at the same time. Someone who knew what was going on had to be involved in the robbery. It made no sense to me that someone who worked for me was involved. My guys just aren't that bright or that dumb to pull off a stunt like that. And after talking to Joe Kahn on Friday, his story didn't add up to me. So I stayed in Cocoa and camped out and watched the factory all weekend. It looked like there was some activity going on inside. It looked like production was going on. Soooo, Sunday night, I broke in and checked things out. Unfortunately, I'm not as smart as I thought I was, and they caught me snooping around. While they were holding me, I got a good look at what they were doin'. It looked like they were on their final skids of making gold plates and goblets. I'm willing to bet that the platinum was taken care of first. Anyway, there was a fight, and I managed to get away. I stole a car from the parking lot and ended up crashing it in the Banana River. I nearly drowned in the water. I got lucky to get away and that the cops don't have me in jail." He paused to let the anger build up. "This goddamn little deal of yours nearly killed me!"

A flabbergasted Mark looked at him. "Jesus Christ, Aug! Why didn't you let me know what was going on? I'da come up and helped! Hell, I'da rounded up some muscle and torn the place down!"

Aug spoke vehemently. "Uh-huh. Let's suppose you did that. And let's suppose I was wrong and I dragged you and other people up there and we accuse your partner on the deal of ripping you off and then find out there is nothing going on, then what? No thank you! I had to see what was going on inside the building before accusing anyone."

Aug paused and then started again. "Ya know, I made a couple phone calls about Mr. Joseph Khan after you told me that his brother is Mr. Destin Dreams." Aug turned his head to Mark. "Extended vacation? For extortion and taking metal bars to people's heads? You know what else he did? He put a couple bullets beside the side of my head Friday when I was in his office. While people were working there! That fucker is nuts! I don't know how he got out of the can, but that's where someone that insane belongs! Jesus Fucking Christ!"

Aug turned back to lazing and looking forward. After a pause, he continued, "Anyway, that's the person who was responsible for the robbery. That's who you want to go after. That's your mess to clean up."

Mark's reply was "Aug . . . don't you mean . . . our mess to clean up?"

Aug was indignant at the comment. "Our mess? What the hell is this 'our mess' crap? My deal was to bring in gemstones for cash. I did that. It's your partners on a side deal who decided to steal things for themselves. It's you who decided to time everything so that they could rob both shipments at once. I didn't set that up. They were your partners and your deal . . . not mine."

Mark thought about it. "Can you prove that Upper Terra was smelting everything? I can't. What, am I supposed to go back to the family and say, 'Well this is what my nephew Aug says happened.' And what happens when the denials come in? And what about the gems? Where are they? Like it or not, you're in this to the end." The men turned and looked at each other through their sunglasses.

It was Aug's turn to think. "Unk, where were you this morning? You weren't at Trove, and it doesn't sound like you were in Cocoa. What's keeping you so busy down here?"

It was Mark's turn to laze back and look forward. "Let me tell you where I was. I was sweating my ass off in a vehicle, waiting for someone to come by and show me the missing jewels. I've received some calls from someone claiming to have them and wanting to sell them back to me. Naturally this is of interest to find out what is going on. I'd have let you know this, but you disappeared. Anyway, we set a rendezvous time, but it was a wild-goose chase. No one showed." Mark paused and looked at Aug closely. "You wouldn't happen to have known anything about this now, would you?"

Aug exhibited surprise. "Me? I don't know a goddamn thing about what you're talkin' about. I've been sleeping here waiting to talk to you. Who the hell called you? Was it a man, a woman? What did they say? What was the deal?"

It was Mark's turn to lean back and close his eyes. "I can't tell if it was a man or a woman who has called. I can't even tell if it was the same person for each call. Whoever it is did a good job of garbling the voice. The cell phone number had been different each time it has shown up on my phone. There's been three calls so far, and each call has had an area code for Alaska. Anyway, they wanted to talk a price, and I wanted to see some goods before I talk a price on anything. No one will be happy about paying for the same goods two times. Hell, the original purchase cost was so low, that's what's made this a good deal. I figured that if I could get a view of who showed up, there might be a lead there. But I waited for hours, and no one showed, and there was no contact, so I left to come back here and see you." There was a pause. "This was kinda bizarre, so I don't know what was up, whether it was someone yanking my chain or what."

There was a contemplative silence between the two of them. The overtures had been played. The orchestra pit boss had yet to signal an aria.

Aug soloed. "So let me get this straight. My ass is grass unless the goods are recovered. But so is your ass too. Now, the goods were taken to Cocoa, but I doubt they stopped there. When they figure out I'm alive and that I know what happened, someone's going to come gunning for me." He turned and looked at Mark. "They gotta figure I'll have talked to you." A brief pause followed. "But all of this is not due to my fault. They probably came to steal the gold and platinum and lucked into the jewels. You're at least willing to talk to someone about buying back the stones for a price. And for me, the price is my life if I find the goods."

Aug pulled off the shades and looked Mark in the eye. "That's not good enough. I want a cut of anything I recover."

Mark was surprised to hear this. "Not good enough? Not good enough? Your life is not enough?"

Aug continued, "That's right. You heard me. Not good enough! You see, I didn't set this whole eff'ing deal up, and it already nearly killed me the other night. I didn't like that. I had someone shoot bullets next to my head. I didn't like that. And when this is done, I want out. Smuggling something periodically is one thing. Dying for it is another. Especially when it isn't my deal putting me under! So the way I see it is that if I'm gonna get it, then I might as well go enjoy myself somewhere until the time comes. If you want me to put myself in the line of fire again, then you gotta make it worth my while." Aug paused. "I want 30 percent of anything I recover, and some sort of guarantee that no one comes after me about it when this whole thing is done."

Mark was incensed. "You want a 30 percent finder's fee? That's like asking for someone to hunt you down even if they give you that. That's just asinine." He paused for a little bit. "If you want to live and get something out of this in the end, you gotta be reasonable. I don't think anyone would complain about . . . 5 percent."

Aug pushed. "To stand in the line of fire, I want more than five. I'm now the bait. Hell! I started off as the bait! I just didn't know it! That's worth more than 5 percent. I'd say that is worth at least . . . 20 percent."

Mark pushed back. "Aug, 20 percent is as good as saying I want a bullet from either side. How's about . . . how about 10 percent, and I talk to the powers that be about a better position for you. A change of scenery somewhere, maybe back up east? I think I can sell that."

There was silence as Aug thought about it. He extended a hand and then a look in the eye. "Ten percent . . . and a change of scenery. Deal." They shook on it.

Mark continued, "Now, what do you propose to be the next step?"

Aug's answer was "I go to Sandestin. I'll go meet with Jack Dough. Either his brother scammed him, or he is in on it. I think he was in on it and may have set the whole thing up. Either way, someone will come gunning for me. I'll plan to be ready for them. Somehow, I suspect that Jack has an idea of where everything is at anyway."

Mark asked, "Do you want me to go with you?"

Aug laughed at him. "You want to dodge bullets with me? Yeah. Right. I don't think so! Besides, I want the 10 percent for myself. I don't want to be splitting it with you." He stood up and stretched out some stiffness. "I'll . . . a . . . I'll get some things together and drive over there and see what I can find out. I'll be in touch." Aug extended his hand to Mark. "Goodbye, Uncle. Until we meet again." With that, he was off.

Aug stopped on the bridge to call Brad and tell him to meet him at the garage area. He looked north and south at the condos and hotels and buildings and cars and people. They all looked so South Florida to him. There was a cheesiness about it from the outside; so many humans in nondescript rectangles. There was heat and cement and pavement. Philly had been a different cement and pavement, and Michigan different still. The biggest wonder of all that Aug had was *Will I ever gaze upon these same buildings again?* Knowing that this could be the last time he stood there and soaked it in, he leaned against the metal fence over the bridge and wondered about what was and what shall never be.

Half an hour later, Aug met Bradley at his vehicle in the parking structure. Bradley was originally from the large Jewish community in Hollywood. They met years ago outside Zipperhead's on State Street in Philly. Brad was attending Penn while Aug attended Nova. The giant twenty-foot ants crawling up the side of the building were quite the conversation piece for drunks liquidating vehicles along the street at bar closing time. Brad convinced Aug to take a ride to the spic side of the Jungle to see what substances could be procured. It was safer than the black side and just as good as the Asian side. The Asians and the Hispanics wanted repeat customers, so they didn't rip people off. They wanted repeat business and kept their crazies under control. God only knows when you get that crazy black guy who cuts the white too much or comes running out, screaming narc and smashing taillights. Somehow, the blizzard experience made for bonding that lasted.

Aug approached Brad and said, "Bradley, so nice to see you again!" They shook. "I was just looking at the buildings up and down the road here. They aren't compact little houses in a mega mile 'hood, but it kinda seems like the Jungle all over again to me."

Brad laughed. He had a thicker voice, but not like a German. It was almost like his tongue was too big for his mouth, and it added a slow character to his speech pattern. "The Jungle! Now those were some good times! Almost as good as going to the Mint Liquor lounge."

Aug remembered the occasion. "The Mint, oh my god, I had forgotten about that."

They both laughed on that. One New Year's Eve when Aug and Laurie had just moved to Hollywood, Brad and Aug were supposed to meet a bunch of people at the City Park in Fort Lauderdale for a Pink Floyd laser show. They hadn't planned on twenty thousand people showing up. New Year's Eve was on a Sunday, and since they couldn't find any open bars, they drove all around to find a bar where they could ring in the New Year at. They wound up at a black strip club named the Mint where what they saw was what one would expect to see working a stage on New Year's Eve. The bottom of the barrel was working. It seemed like each individual bottom cheek that they saw shaking was larger than a barrel. The Count Choculas in attendance loved it. Brad and Aug did shots and drank in silent stunned amazement. The concept that blacks have strip clubs had never actually crossed their minds before they crossed that threshold. They would never have believed it if they had not seen it.

"That place was closed down last year," Brad informed him. "Good business opportunity for your future." They laughed further on that.

Aug went from there. "Yeah, well, I don't think that's the business opportunity I'm looking for."

Brad turned to his car. He said, "Hey, your looking pretty snazzy there. Nice eye, and did you, uh, have a little accident in your pants there?"

Aug laughed. "No, no. Those are just the results of more business opportunities that I really don't want anything to do with."

Brad opened the door of his '69 Corvette and pulled out a manila envelope. He undid the clasp and slid out a small box and handed it to Aug. "Is this the business opportunity you are looking for? Is that what you mean?"

Aug took a look inside the box. His grin was wry. "Well, kinda. Kinda yeah, kinda no." He closed the box and held it up. "Thanks for taking care of this for me. I appreciate that."

Brad smiled and said, "Anything for a paying customer." They laughed. Brad pointed at the box. "*A* is for Apple, *J* is for Jacks. That kinda has a nice ring to it, eh?"

Aug looked at the box and thought. He looked back to Brad. "Maybe it's *A* is for Amos, *J* is for Jandy."

Bradley pondered and countered, "Could be, or maybe it is *A* is for Alphonse, *J* is for Jastone."

Aug came back with "Howzabout *A* is for Antony, *J* is for J.Lo Patra!"

Brad laughed and spoke kinda Dice Clay—like. "Hey, I like that one." Brad continued, "Ya know, her booty ain't J.Lo sizin', but it's a very nice booty all the same. You must enjoy beating on that drum." Aug broadly smiled. Brad laughingly continued, "Maybe it's really *A* is for ass and *J* is for jizz?"

Aug cut him off. "All right, all right already. That's enough of that now!"

Brad opened the envelope again and slid out six passports. Aug was lost in thought, looking at the box. "You know, so much trouble for some diamonds. I was thinking about it, like, when I have gone hunting. When you are out there and you have that bow and that deer is twenty yards away and you're getting that jag about shooting it and killing that magnificent living animal and, well, like nothing there needs diamonds or jewels or money or anything. The birds don't need it. The trees don't need it. And they never do. All this money and everything, it's all stuff humans do. It's all a humans-only game. No other animal plays this game. It's all whatever we make it out to be. Just like the rules of the game are. The rules of investing in financial instruments or futures. It's all whatever we want the rules to be."

Brad was like "Whoa, check out Aug the Philosopher. You better watch yourself there. You're almost sounding religious-like." He paused. "Are you having a conversion? It's never too late for a bris, you know?" They laughed again.

Aug continued, "No no no, that's not what I mean. It's just that, years ago, all I wanted was a home and a family and some money and to have 'the good life.' And I thought I had it, and now it's all gone, and I have to start all over again, and it's like, 'Why?' I dunno, maybe it's time catching up with me." A pause. "Whaddaya got there? Are those the passports and IDs?"

Brad said, "Hey, of course, nothing like a good lawyer to get you taken care of. Besides, you paid for them." A pause. "Or did you? I don't recall getting any money from you." They laughed. Both knew full well that a hefty black market price had been paid.

Aug pushed the envelope back to Brad. "You hang on to those. I'll contact you if I need you or to get them. I don't have anywhere safe to keep them right now."

Brad replied, "Not a problem. I'll hang on to them—for a fee, of course." They laughed since they both knew no fee would be required.

Aug joked back, "Goddamn Jewboy, always looking to make a buck."

Bradley feigned pain at the remark. "Hey, hey, hey, no reason to get ethnic about it. You could stop at being a professional. I am lawyer you know. I did pass the bar, eventually. You could just call me a shyster and leave it at that."

Aug pulled out his wallet. He removed fifteen of the fifty or so c notes he had. "Here ya go, my friend. Go get yourself a body rub or go to the Booby Trap or something. Hell, for that kinda cash, you can do both!"

They hugged. Brad waved the envelope and said, "Goodbye, my friend. I'll be expecting to hear from you soon to pick these up. Besides, I wouldn't want to be involved in anything illegal. I am a lawyer, ya know." They both laughed, and they parted ways.

# PART II

## THE GULF COAST

# CHAPTER 16

## MR. SMOOTHIE

Crossing the Choctawhatchee Bay Bridge was like crossing into a new world. Even though it was getting late in the afternoon, it was like the dawning of a new era. The bridge spans nearly two miles of bay under blue sky and over blue water. So much of Florida is like a corporation that is up for sale: all blue sky.

Aug normally loved the blue sky and blue water, but somehow, this felt different. There was a serenity of smaller city and the road less traveled. It was a sojourn to another lifetime.

Aug's mind focused on the near future. He saw and did not see the cars surrounding him. He saw and did not see the boats in the water and landing area for fisherman that extended up the south side of the bridge. He heard and did not hear the news on the radio tell him that Discovery would be returning home and that the London bombing suspects were now held, that a Georgia fugitive had been captured the night before hiding beneath the Clyde Wells Bridge, and that a tropical depression had formed in the Gulf of Mexico.

His state of mind was like the state of Florida. Both states slowly evolved over time. Compared to other states of union, the development of Florida had been slower, but now the evolution was speeding. Developments speeded evolution. Air-conditioning and newer building materials and techniques as well as new land management techniques made the explosion of people in Florida possible.

The state was evolving like the evolution of a hot stock. New information rapidly transformed Florida from the *was* into the *now*.

Aug found happiness in his world and then his world evolved into something else. As he matured and experienced life, he learned new information about his past. He transformed from the *was* into the *now*. Both their landscapes had gone through human evolution.

The car had a dank smell to it from the water that had poured in the prior week. Aug opened the windows to let fresh air in. It was also time to change the soundscape of the stereo. The blah blah blah of talking heads gave way to "Interstate Love Song." He was "leaving on a southern train." He was watching the time go by. Aug cranked it up.

The car turned west onto Highway 98 heading toward Sandestin. Soon, he was heading into town. He passed the Sacred Heart Hospital, which demarked the entrance to the city. Up to that point, the drive was primarily a drive of trees, but for how much longer? Thirty years ago, there was so much less development. So many more trees right where he was. The waterfront areas had been developed by developers, but there was still more property to be evolved.

Who knew where the money to effect this transformation had come from? Many multi-million-dollar houses dotted areas hidden from this road in places where wetlands and trees had ruled for years. Other roads hid other manses. These residences and condos are hidden behind security. They had been built by a variety of contractual companies. Many different types of cash had flowed through. There was no one single source of cash. Some of the cash was public corporate cash, and some was private cash, but just because the cash came from a public corporation, did that make funding more legal than if the funding came from illegal drug money?

The development of Sandestin had been a money launderer's paradise. The area was away from the major cities. It was away from prying eyes. Paper currency shipped here and was miraculously transformed into houses or condos, golf courses, or businesses that became a different paper currency. Destin Dreams and the White Sands Bank had been very successful in this process. Nothing lasts forever. Unknown unknowns changed the situation.

Not all activity was ceased by Destin Dreams, but the usefulness of the company was just about spent. It should have been closed down a year ago, but at that point in time, it was not in the public's best interest. Public figures had private friends with too much interest to have the company and related activities immediately shut down. And just what does public interest really mean? Through the news media, Aug had seen time and again that someone's private interest money is what the public interest really is. This difference was that this time, he was living through it.

It would have already been closed down except for two final unknown unknowns. Jack Dough had come up with two final deals that were relatively so inexpensive to the capitalists that they couldn't pass it up. So activity was allowed to continue for just a little longer. Just long enough to squeeze out a few more millions in profit from laundering a little more cash that needed to go somewhere.

Aug turned left into the Market Shops on South Sandestin. As he walked to the offices of Destin Dreams, he passed such places with names like Barefoot Princess and Angels Cosmetics and Beyond the Grape Wine and LaBonboniere Ice Cream and the ubiquitous Starbucks. Flyers in the windows of the stores announced the opening of Poseidon's realm that Saturday at the beach below the Hilton. There would be free food for all at a public beach luau. Music was to be provided by Manchild, Denny Mclain and the Loansharks, and the Reverend Horton Heat. There would be a night of charity casino gambling. Table games would be set up, and the proceeds for the evening would be donated to local charities. Sand sculptures contests would be held. There would be entertainment from clowns and magicians. It was all to be topped off with a magnificent fireworks display.

Aug looked around him. Who the hell in this local area needed charity? The local AA? Had a local Catholic pedophile priest bankrupted a local parish?

The offices of Destin Dreams were very nondescript. Aug knew that this was the way Jack Dough liked them. The low-key approach kept out any visitors who didn't need to be there. And if you wanted to do business with Destin Dreams, then it wasn't going to be a splashy office that would make the difference. Very few people would ever know what transactions occurred behind the glass double doors that opened to a basic cubicle-lined venue behind a receptionist. The walls were plain wood paneling with maps of the area located on them. There were three offices at the back. One of the offices had the door closed.

Aug entered and approached the gum-chewing young receptionist. "Well, hello there! I am Mr. Holiday here to see Mr. Marshall."

She eyed him. "Do you have an appointment? Mr. Marshall has visitors at the moment."

Aug told her, "Please just tell him that Mr. Holiday is here."

The receptionist suspiciously eyed Aug. He listened with disinterest as she called in and heard Keith say "Who?" There was a pause followed by an "I'll be out in a minute."

The back door opened, and a very unhappy looking Curly Fine and John Candy exited the office. The look on their faces became unhappier upon seeing Augustus standing in the room. Keith was trailing behind the men, bearing a mien of concern. Fine and Candy were surprised to see that Mr. Holiday was actually Mr. Valentine. This surprise created a Floridian standoff. The big men slowly walked to the front of the room. Aug slowly circled to the back of the room. Aug could see the muscles tense up in the galoots. He spotted a Scotch tape dispenser on a desk and picked it up, holding the device in a threatening manner. Curly and John looked at each other with looks of curiosity and disgust on there faces. They nodded to each other and headed out the door.

Aug looked at Keith and the receptionist. They were looking at the Scotch tape dispenser he was still holding and then at him. "You never knew that a tape dispenser could be so threatening, did ya? Hey, I guess I should have brought ice cream to the social instead?"

Keith rolled his eyes. He was also rubbing his upper arm through his arrow-looking dress shirt. He looked at the receptionist and said, "Eileen, I'm going to take . . . Mr. Holiday here . . . out to look at some properties. I'll be back later."

They walked to the front of the office. Aug stopped and smiled at Eileen and poked his head down at her skirt. He was checking out her gams. They were pleasant to view. He smiled at her and turned to Keith and said, "Funny, looks like she has two legs to me."

Keith gave Aug a "shut up" and motioned Aug to the door. As Keith was walking out the door, he looked back at the confused female and said, "Eileen, I lean, one leg, get it now? He just wanted to check out your legs anyway."

Keith Marshall was an attractive man. He had perm curly hair and a perm curly beard. Both were coiffed at a respectable level. Keith had moved down south many years ago to be the eyes and hands of others to make sure events went smoothly. That was one of the reasons that he had the nickname of Mr. Smoothie. Other reasons were his tan and bedside manner as well as his customer schmoozability. In business, things will go wrong; but no matter how wrong they went, Keith could always schmooze the situation over.

Keith lit a death stick upon exiting the office. Their four eyes surveyed the stores and the parking lot as they walked through the shop promenade. They were looking for Curly Candy or whomever else they might see out of the ordinary. When they reached the parking lot, Keith bade Augustus to his Chrysler 300, but Aug begged off, stating that they would drive separately. They were off to Keith's house on Baytowne Avenue.

The cars exited the parking lot and crossed the highway. A black Cadillac with black windows followed them. They entered the Sandestin Golf and Beach Resort. Keith's vehicle passed the security guardhouse. He rolled down his window and told security to let Aug follow. The Cadillac slowly rolled by as the two men wove their cars through the complex of residences that dotted the four golf courses.

They worked their way around the Baytowne golf course. The golf course was undergoing renovation so no golfers were on the course. Aug felt the course should have been named the British Open Course as they passed St. Andrews Drive and Turnberry Court. They missed Troon Drive. When they turned on Baytowne, they passed Island Green Drive and pulled into a modest residence of ten thousand square feet and five bedrooms that Keith called home. The house was possibly the least expensive residence on the road.

They entered his house. The residence was quite spartan on the inside. There was not much furniture to be seen. It had all been moved out. A stale cigarette smell filled the air, and it was going to get thicker. Keith had another one ready to go. "Drink? How's about some Crown Royal."

Aug assented. There were some barstools, and he took a seat at one. His host retreated behind the bar. Keith threw some ice and glasses and poured them full of booze. He slid a glass toward Aug, and they clinked glasses in a toast. While they were drinking, Keith produced a revolver from under the bar. "Now where's my cargo, matey?"

Aug slowly stood up and walked about the room. The décor had been done in green. The walls were covered in light green paint. Green drapes hung down to a wooden floor. The bar opened into a living room area where there was a leather sofa and an entertainment center. One painting adorned the wall. The artwork was of Mount Fuji. Everything else was gone. The room looked way oversized. "I'd say your ex is the person who has all your cargo, wouldn't you?" Aug turned and looked at Keith and tasted some more bourbon. He noticed that Keith looked very tired; the eyes were baggy and black. "Now, why don't you put that toy away before something stupid happens with it? There's too many stories out there of people with guns who have them accidentally go off, and I don't want that to happen to me. Besides, you look like shit. You look like ten miles of bad road. Now I've had two other people actually shoot guns at me in the last week, but none of them scared me as much as you do now. Keith, buddy, think about it, you shoot me and it gets you nothing anyway. You need to get a grip."

Keith stared at Aug for a little, evaluating the situation. Eventually he downed his drink and put the gun on the bar top. He poured another glassful and fired up a Marly. He looked around the room and laughed disparagingly. "You ever hear the joke about how to stop having sex with a Jewish American princess? That the answer is to marry her? Well, don't laugh. It's true. I'm living proof of that." He paused a minute. "Maybe you're right. It's the stooge brothers. They got me nervous. They threatened to do some unpleasant things to me." He started rubbing his arm again. "They wanted to know what I knew about some gemstones. They seemed to think I might know something about some smuggling event. They also had a crazy story about some stunt you pulled last week. They thought that maybe I was somehow involved or responsible for that too. You wouldn't happen to be the reason that they have these crazy ideas, now would you?"

Aug acted surprised. "Me? Well, I suppose I could be somewhat responsible, but probably not. Your name has never come up in any conversation I have had with anyone about anything." A pause. "Maybe they just assume that there is some connection you know about. It's not like you haven't helped Jack on some dirty dealings before. I bet they think you know something, but the fact of the matter is that they're grasping at straws." Aug tasted some more Crown. "By the way, how is your arm? You keep rubbing it like something is wrong. Did they rough you up a little back there?"

Keith realized his involuntary massage work at that point. "I . . . ah . . . no . . . I had a tattoo started recently, kinda a tribute to Mom. It's a little sore, and that's where they decided to twist me a bit. It's just ore a bit, but it'll pass."

Aug laughed. "A tribute to Mom? What, in honor of being the last of the three amigos?"

Keith shot back. "That's not funny." He took a deep drag. "I'm sure my mom wouldn't appreciate that crack."

Aug apologized. "You're right. That is a tough crack." After a pause, he continued, "And how is your mother? It's gotta be hard on her to see her sons off to the grave."

Keith answered, "Mom died years ago. Thank God for that! I wouldn't want to have to explain things to her." More drink guzzling occurred. "Now give me my key and I'll pay you off."

Aug laughed at that. "Keith, I learned a little since I last talked to you. I learned a bit more about what that key is and what it is worth to you. Now considering the risk involved, it's worth a lot more than what we initially bargained for me to deliver it. You're gonna have to up the ante a bit. You didn't come clean with me about all the risks I was taking in helping you out. I want a bigger cut of the pie. I want, say, 10 percent of the total take. Seeing how your brothers are now dead and your split is now a lot more, I don't think that is too unreasonable."

Mr. Smoothie was not so smooth at the moment. "You dirty motherfucker." He put his butt out in the ashtray and slugged a gulp. "Here I come to you with a sweetheart deal. One grand to have a key delivered to your hotel room. And all ya gotta do is bring it back here to me. I'm not a bad guy. Why ya gotta play like this? Didn't I let you know they were planning to come fuck you over?"

Aug's reply was swift. "Hey, life's a bitch, ya know. Besides, you were in a jam, and there was no one else you could trust who would help you so easily." Aug drank some more. "And as for the information, well, while it made some things clearer, I already knew quite a bit of what was in the works anyway. Enough to know that what you told me didn't make that much of a difference.

An accusatory finger came his way. "Oh, so you already knew what was going on. And you just happened to be in Europe at just the time my brother dies, and you just happen to be available to help me out. That's a lot of 'just happen' for me to swallow. Maybe you knew what my brother was over there for, and maybe you were the one responsible for his death!"

The diplomat tone came out. "Swallow it or not, I didn't kill your brother. At that time, I had no idea what was going on from your end. And that key is useless to me without access to the location and code that go with it. I just happened to find out what you really wanted me to help you with. The same people who took out Zach want the same things that both of us have in our possession. And it's worth a hell of a lot more than one grand for the added risk to my life. Don't like it? Tough." Aug drank some more. "Face facts, Mr. Smoothie. Your brothers are dead, and someone knows what you guys did. You're gonna need some help to get the money anyway. Find yourself another partner if you like, but you still need your goods from me anyway. And it's already cost at least four people their lives. That's worth a lot more than a grand to me."

There was another pause before Keith spoke. "So just what do you propose?"

Aug paced the room a bit. "Well, the way I see the situation is this: we got big problems. I want what you got, and you want what I got, and it won't be long before the feds come and haul one or both of us away, at which point we are fucked anyway. Besides, how are you going to travel anyway? I bet your passport is no good, unless you have a fake one ready. And I don't know if you have the connections to take care of that, but I do. But if we disappear, that is it. There's no coming back here, and there's no going anywhere you won't be hunted." Aug smiled. "But we're both now hunted men regardless, right?"

Keith thought about it. "Let me get this straight. For 10 percent, you'll get me a passport and go to Europe with me, and we take care of business and then never see each other again? Is that what you are saying?"

Aug thought about it. "You're right. Ten percent is too little. Better make it twenty and I'll take care of your passport issues. We can leave next week. Assuming you can stay out of the pokey and stay alive that long. You may wantta disappear here and we meet up later."

Keith suspiciously eyeballed Aug. "How do I know I can trust you? And how do I know you actually have the key to the kingdom?"

Aug laughed. "Keith, I don't get shit unless I cash in with you, so why would I want to screw you? And the key is safe. I think you'd know if someone else had it or if the cops had turned it up in the hotel room in Paris. No, I have it all right."

Keith asked, "You have it on you?"

Aug laughed. "Ah, no. We'd have to go get it. But it's safe and warm." Aug laughed. "Safer than either you or I are." Aug paused. "But now the idea, my friend, my partner, is that we keep each other safe." Aug paused. "Tell you what. I'll come up with an exit strategy, and we can book out of Sandestin after the grand opening of Poseidon's. No one will do anything before that. We can plan to leave after that. Are you OK with that? That means come Sunday or Monday, you leave everything behind. Are you down with that?"

Keith nodded in reluctant agreement. *Leave everything behind,* he mused. *Like I haven't already left everything behind.*

Aug continued, "Good. It's settled. We have a deal." Aug approached Keith with his hand extended. They shook on it. "Now, I need you to call your boss and tell him that I have set up an eleven AM tee time for Burnt Pine tomorrow. I have a tee time for four people. I don't care who or if he brings anyone along. Just tell him that I know what he wants and for him to get it. He needs to play a round of golf with me tomorrow."

Keith looked at Aug quizzically. "Why would I do that? I mean, I'll make the call, but what makes you think he will agree to play?"

Aug answered, "Well, the reason that you need to do this is so that people who have seen me with you think we are talking about something else. And the reason that he will agree to meet is because I have something he wants. I have those diamonds the big boys were giving you grief about. You tell him that if he wants the jewels, he needs to meet tomorrow." Aug finished his drink. "And I'll see you at opening night."

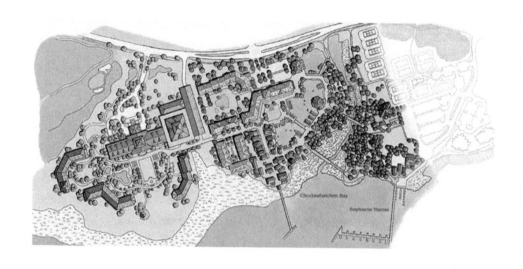

# Chapter 17

## Gizzards

The byline of Sandestin is "Off in our own little world," and this was so evident to Aug as he drove from Baytowne Avenue to the Village of Baytowne Wharf. He could only make out ten residences from the road as he drove through, but he knew more were hidden behind trees amongst the golf courses. There were many dream homes hidden behind even more security gates and security systems. Each residence was somewhat spectacular in its own right, costing how many million each? And this drive he was making covered maybe 5 percent of the grounds? Aug wondered how all these millions got here. He wondered how he got there.

His mind wandered to the trips he had made through the jungles of Philly or through the ghettos of Detroit. The Philly jungle has ancient housing built side by side and on top of each other with no privacy or insulation from any kind of element. The Detroit area has residences that used to be nice neighborhoods and lots but now looks like fires have raged through them and no one bothered to clean up. In either case, the value of one or two of these residences he was seeing were worth more than mega city blocks of tenement combined. And most of these residences were probably not even primary residences for their owners. Even with a good education, how in the world could someone go from those hell holes to living in this kind of luxury. Without crime, how could any of those people go from there to here in a lifetime?

He was off in a big little world. This secure community was big in capital and little in overall size. It was one of many pockets around the globe that function as such. He guessed that half the Sandestin residences had been built or purchased with fortunes that had been achieved through some sort of legal or illegal or ill-gotten gain in the lifetimes of the families there. An example, he thought, was the medical community. Sure, some medical company empires had been "legally" built. Sure, the overbilling of the government and the selling of pharmaceuticals that are of questionable value is construed as legal business practice, but is it any more right than defrauding a bank? Or maybe the question is, is defrauding a bank any more wrong than defrauding the public of money by pushing millions upon millions of doses of Celebrex and Vioxx to the public? Isn't that really the same as pushing pot and coke, except pot and coke dealers fill the prison system?

"Just say no!" Aug laughed to himself. Walk into a CVS or a Rite Aid or a Walgreens or any other storehouse of pharmacological delights and "just say no." "Just say no" is OK unless the individual will profit from the purchase of drugs. Then it is "Just say yes."

It's always good to rationalize to help one sleep soundly. Years ago, he had been a college student just looking to have a good time and forget his past and move on to happy and successful life. Then he had an opportunity, like his dad before him, to build a better life through crime. He rationalized it and accepted it. He rationalized it like children rationalize lies to their parents or executives rationalize ripping off the public.

If the meek are to inherit the earth, then how would the meek ever inherit Sandestin? They never would was the answer.

Aug was at the eye of a storm of schemes and schemers. He was like financial executives who cut their teeth as brokers getting the public to invest in IPOs and taking commissions on the sales. With time, the executives move up the corporate chain. The executives become involved in creating the inflated IPOs, thus making more money off the cons. Aug had started out taking a commission on the movement of goods. Now he had moved up in the chain, and his deal was bigger.

The Village of Baytowne is beautiful to see. There are over twenty stores offering clothes and frills and groceries and spirits. Another twenty restaurants and eateries are in the village, as well as seven more bars. The village caters to people who don't ever cook a meal. If one lives inside the gates, there is a level of expectation of epicurean expedition every day. If one is into it, it is a land of fishing at night. Number 6 was not at this village.

On a hot summer late afternoon or night, the area is a pickup artist's dream. Flock to the beach in the day and hit a score later. From what Aug knew of his dad, his father would have loved the place. Dad could continuously introduce himself to women, and sooner than later, one would say OK to a one-night stand. Aug was envious of the bliss of disavowment of the realities of other people's worlds that he observed as he walked through. The people themselves were not necessarily vacuous, and neither was their behavior, but observing their behavior left Aug feeling vacuous. It was a feeling he could not escape as he circled the village.

He did feel confident that he had escaped any tailing by anyone. He saw no followers as he walked and observed. It was time to see what the boys were up to. The cell phone was dialed. They were in the Graffiti and Funky Blues Shack, listening to some musician perform self-written tunes on Australian aboriginal instruments.

The Graffiti bar, like Rum Runners and the Marlin Grill and Jim 'n' Nick's, was packed. Mike and Steve were off to the side of the stage in a must-yell zone to be able to communicate. They had obviously thrown down some drafts as well as having gone shopping. The raiments worn were new. And considering their lack of inhibition in asking for some, they would do well here.

"Doggie! So nice to see you again!" More Coronas were quickly ordered as they reengaged in acquaintance conversations. They pointed out the instruments and music and chatted about the females frolicking. The band went to break, and their attention turned to more pressing matters. The menu was looked at. It was an appetizer night, and the spicy crawfish and eggplant were ordered, as well as crab cakes. The general consensus was "Tasty, but not as tasty as beer-battered gizzards."

"Gizzards, mmm, sounds good to me. Hey, Aug, you planning on heading up and going hunting this year?"

"Ha ha ha, that's rich. I dunno what I'm doing next week, let alone a couple months from now."

"Aw, man, it's just what you need—a break from the action. Hell, you could bring Jocelyn along. I bet she'd like sticking a round into a stag—and gutting him too!"

There was much laughter on that. "Bow hunting season isn't too far off. That rut'll be started soon, unlike little Auggie here who is already in heat." With that, the obligatory slap boxing began. It was like a cat rubbing it's head on something. They were scenting each other. When things calmed down a little, the brothers looked at each other and at Aug. He could tell something was up.

"OK, out with it," Aug said. "Something's bothering you. I can tell."

The brothers looked at each other and then down and then kind of grinned and looked at Aug. Mike spoke. "Well, it's funny you should ask that. We were talking about the . . . uh . . . 'device' and . . . ah . . . well, we think we may have miscalculated a little."

Aug was like "Miscalculated a little? Tell me, just what the hell does miscalculated a little actually mean?"

"Well," came the reply from Mike, "we may have used just a teensy bit too much . . . material . . . in the device. I think the casing is safe from accidental activation but . . . uh . . . I wouldn't want to be too close when it goes off. That might not be too wise."

Aug was surprised. "Get out."

Steve said, "Well, we were talking about it, and numbnuts here thinks it may be a lot more powerful than we were thinking." He paused a minute and looked at Mike and then at Aug. "We . . . uh . . . we went snooping around in Poseidon's, and we were looking at things, and now we are thinking—there's gonna be some major demolition if you blow that thing."

The look on Aug's face showed that he was clearly not thrilled with the new information.

Steve continued, "Don't get us wrong, it shouldn't arm itself unless you pull the trigger, but when it goes, well, it's gonna go."

Aug looked at Steve in disbelief. "I thought you guys knew what you were doing!"

Mike chimed in, "Hey, it's an inexact science, and we never said we were science majors. It's also not like we had anything to test it out on before rigging it. Or that we knew exactly what we were up against." Mike took a long chug of beer. "Anyway, it's too late to do anything about it now." Mike took another swig. "Oh, I can tell you that you can go 'fishing' for what yer looking for. I think you'll know what I mean when you get in there and look around."

Aug nodded and asked, "Do I still have my fifteen minutes?"

Mike nodded. "Affirmative, boss. We didn't screw that up!"

Aug nodded and pounded his Corona. He asked, "Do you guys have any other good news for me?"

Mike flipped two key sets over to Aug. "The first key is the Burnt Pine key you wanted. That'll getcha in the door, but I'm not sure what you can do about the alarm system. The second keys are for TOPS'L. You have number 116."

Aug continued, "And anything else? Like the location of some boxes? Hmmm?"

Mike and Steve looked at each other and then down. Steve sighed and said, "We don't know where they are. They lost our tail. I don't know what happened. I think we were spotted. They took everything up 1 headed toward Daytona, and then they killed the headlights and turned off on some roads and shook us. We never found them. They could be anywhere."

Aug thought about that and leaned forward, looking at them very intently. "You guys wouldn't be fibbing, would you? You're not holding out on me, trying to scam some of this for yourselves now, would you be?"

Mike and Steve both raised hands up on that accusation. "Scout's honor, Aug Man. We wouldn't do that to ya. You know us better than that. We wouldn't screw ya over. We just don't know where they ditched us."

Aug said, "Hell, I know I can trust you. And thanks again for getting me out of the water the other night. I think I'd have drowned if you hadn't a reeled me in."

Mike said, "Aug, that wasn't anything that you wouldn'ta done for either of us. Besides, we had to work with the navy during our army stint. Amphibious assaults and sea rescue were something we trained for." Mike paused and smiled. "That is, when we weren't too drunk to do training!" They all laughed.

Aug pocketed the keys that he had been fidgeting with. "There's a black Cadillac that followed me around earlier. There are two guys from Upper Terra who are probably inside. They didn't look too happy. You need to be on the lookout for them." The brothers nodded in understanding.

Mike asked, "So what's the game plan, boss?"

Aug thought about it. What was the game plan now? "Guys, whaddaya wanna do? Go for the gusto still? Or let the metals slide? Take the probable sure thing, or swing for the fences?"

The brothers looked at each other. They grinned. They looked at Aug. "The fences, of course. You know that we like fencing things anyway. You know us better than that."

Aug smiled. He did know them better than that. "OK then, well, since you guys got shaken on your tail, now I gotta come up with a new plan. I was figuring I'd wind things up with Jack on Sunday, snag Keith, and then we could raid the storage facility on the way outta Dodge. Maybe we can still do that. I just need to figure out a way to find out where he stored everything. Let me sleep on it. I'll call tomorrow." He stood up to leave. "But keep your eyes open. Ain't no one gonna wanna give up a portion of anything. And everyone wants to know where the jewels are hidden."

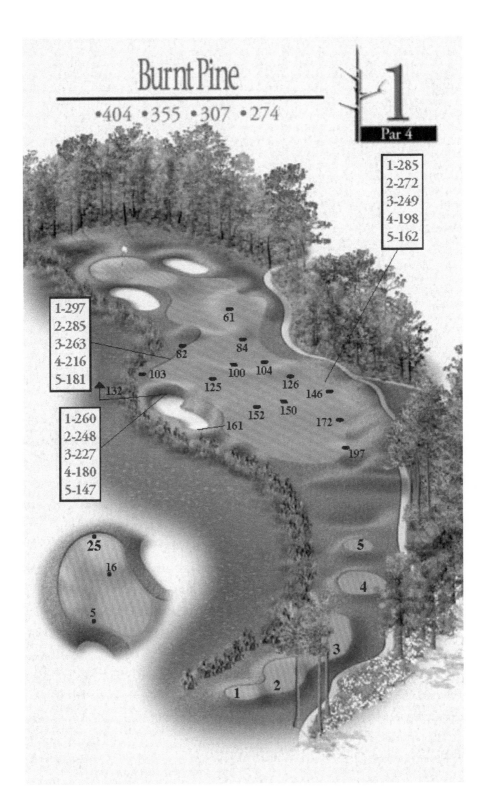

# Burnt Pine

•404 •355 •307 •274

## 1
### Par 4

1-285
2-272
3-249
4-198
5-162

1-297
2-285
3-263
4-216
5-181

1-260
2-248
3-227
4-180
5-147

61

82

84

103

100

104

125

126

146

132

152

150

172

161

197

25

16

5

5

4

3

1

2

# Chapter 18

## Tee Box

Aug had taken an executive suite at the top of the Sandestin Hilton. It was a lovely set of rooms that set him back about seven bills a night. The cost was no matter. He probably wouldn't be around to pay the credit card bill anyway.

His private balcony gave him a view of Poseidon's down on the beach below. There was activity down there to set up for the grand opening the next day. The sun was shining brightly, and there was no cloud to be seen. There was no breeze. The humid warmth rolled over him when he stepped outside. The humidity stayed on his body like clothing. It was close to eleven o'clock. It was easily over ninety degrees out. It was time to go meet his maker.

The drive to the course took about fifteen minutes. His car crossed the Emerald Way and reentered the security zone and curved around more dream homes. Aug wondered where Robin Leach and his camera crew were.

He arrived at the course about fifteen minutes late. The clubhouse at Burnt Pine was empty. The July temperature was too hot in the midday for anyone to be anywhere but the bar. Only an idiot would play golf in these conditions.

Aug parked and opened the trunk of the car. Before he could step to the back of the vehicle, a cart had already appeared. The man in the cart looked to be in his late thirties. He had thick black matted and curly hair and a thick black mustache. He also sported a set of guns that made obvious some sort of iron-pumping regimen. This complemented a well-built physique on a man standing just under six feet tall. His Greg Norman shirt was already showing signs of perspiration from the heat. "Augustus? Hi. I'm Chuck Hvala. I hope you don't mind, but Jack Dough invited me along to make the foursome."

They exchanged handshakes. Aug loaded his bag on the cart. "Pleased to meet you, Chuck. It's nice to have company around." Aug rotated his head. "I need to go pay, don't I?"

Chuck replied, "Oh no. Jack covered everything. And we need to get going. You're late, and we all are waiting. It looks like we'll have the course to ourselves today. It doesn't look like anyone is out here." He looked at his watch. It was a quarter past eleven. "Well, let's go." They drove off to the tee box.

The other cart was awaiting them at the tee. There were two gentlemen there. They were sitting in the cart, chatting with each other and pointing at various features of the golf course. As Chuck drove up, the gentlemen exited their cart and came together to exchange greetings. Both gentlemen were maybe five foot six and of wiry build. They had thick black hair showing under their sun visors, and they appeared to be older . . . maybe midfifties. Everyone had golf shorts and golf shirts on. The heat was already showing a bit on everyone. The greetings were exchanged. Chuck and Aug met Clayton Clakker and Jack Dough. They shook hands.

Jack spoke first to Aug. "It's nice to finally meet you. And it's nice of you to finally make it. We were getting worried. You know, this isn't too bright a time to set a tee time here in midsummer."

Aug replied, "Why, Jack, it is nice to finally meet you too. Sorry to keep you hanging around. But that's funny to hear you say that about the tee time. I thought you liked an eleven AM tee time."

Jack seemed surprised. "Whatever gave you that idea? It's roasting out here right now. We are going to be burnt to hell before this day is over!"

Aug replied, "Dunno. Just seems like I was talking golf with someone who had mentioned that midday was your favorite time to play." Aug looked at Clayton. "So, Clayton, what do you do? What brings you here today?"

Clayton replied, "Me? Me, I'm looking at investing in one of the properties here. I live over in Baton Rouge, and it's not too hard to get over here and enjoy time off, so I'm kinda scoping it out. And what about you? And what's up with that eye? That looks kinda nice there."

Aug answered, "Oh, my company shipped some goods to help Jack here open up his latest gift to Sandestin. A lot of the furnishings used at Poseidon's came from Europe, and my import company brought them in. I figured I had to come see the show. Yer all goin' tomorrow, aren't you?"

Chuck chimed in, "Yeah, I'm planning on going."

Clayton stated, "I will unfortunately miss it. I'm gonna have to take off tomorrow morning."

Aug was surprised by this. "Really? Too bad. It oughta be quite a show." Aug started loosening up with his driver. "And Chuck? What brings you here?"

Chuck answered, "Oh, I teach high school up in Iowa. But I had a nice lottery ticket come in, so I'm thinkin' about a vacation home, so I came down here to check out condos. And play a little golf." They were all swinging clubs around now. "And that eye of yours? What's the story behind that?"

"This?" Aug said. "This . . . this is now nothing. Hell, it'll be gone in a couple days. I pissed my girlfriend off, and she belted me one."

"Really?" Jack said.

Aug laughed. "No, not really. A bunch of Latino's work for me, and we were boxing around in the factory, and things got outta hand. I stepped back to wind up and land a roundhouse, and I slipped on a bar of soap laying around in the warehouse." He smiled at the playing partners. "Damn bars of soap! They always appear at the wrong place and the wrong time!" They all got a laugh out of that.

Chuck piped in, "That's a hell of a way to get a black eye! Anyway, gentlemen, shall we play a game while we are out here? Maybe a Skins game?"

Aug stated, "How about we play a game of Wolf? That way we don't have to worry about who has what handicap."

Clayton and Chuck looked at Aug. "Wolf? I don't know that one. How do you play?"

Aug explained, "Well, it's like this. We rotate who tees off. The person who tees off first is the wolf. Then the second player tees off. The wolf can decide to either partner with that person on the hole or pass and see what the next person does. If you pass on a partner, then you cannot go back and choose that person as a partner. After the fourth person has teed off, the wolf can either take that person as a partner or go at it alone. That is assuming that no partner has already been selected."

Aug continued, "We can play one of two ways or both. You can score your hole for the low score for the hole. The wolf and his partner get their lowest score. Everyone else gets their own score. Or we can do points. If the wolf has a partner, the winning team gets two points. If the wolf goes alone and wins, the wolf gets three points. If the wolf goes solo and loses, everyone else gets two points. No points for ties."

Chuck said, "I've never heard of that. I dunno. What would the stakes be?"

Aug offered, "Well, let's play points and do this. Twenty per person, or another way of saying it is sixty for the loser. What I mean is that the lowest point total has to pay everyone higher than him. So if you are lowest, you owe twenty to each of the other three. We can set the rotation by throwing a tee."

The men looked at each other and thought about it. Chuck offered, "What the hell? That sounds different. All right, I'll give it a go."

Jack said, "I'll buy in."

Clayton said, "I dunno, my game is not that good."

Jack berated him, "Oh, come on, Clayton! I covered your game of golf today, and that cost me a lot more than sixty bones. Don't be a weeny!"

Clayton eyed Jack with some dismay and disgust about being pushed into it. "Oh, all right," he said.

The men stood in a square, and Aug launched a tee. Jack would be wolf first. The remaining three triangled, and the second tee went to Aug. The tee launched again for the final two, and Chuck was third. Clayton looked at Aug and said, "Thanks a lot," rather sarcastically.

They shook hands on it. Clayton noticed the scar on Aug's left hand as he shook with it. "That's a nice scar you got there on yer hand."

Aug held up his hand. The palm exposed the remains of the knife gash that went from his fingers to the palm. "This? This is from where I got burned as a kid." He pulled his golf glove over the mark.

Clayton said, "That doesn't look like a scar from a burn."

Aug said, "I never said it was from a burn. I just said it was from where I got burned as a kid." He paused and looked out at the fairway thinking about it. "I suppose you could say it was from the first time I died. It was like I became the phoenix, and I ascended to heaven just like my body will do when I die. Maybe when I die, my body will rise up to heaven on a bright sunny day like today."

Clayton looked at him and started a soliloquy that baffled them all. "And how do you know that you will ascend to heaven when you die? Do you have some foresight as to such?"

Aug answered, "Sure, I know that I will ascend to heaven. I had a dream, a vision of it, just the other day. I soared to the sky and disappeared up above."

Clayton started a pacing motion periodically looking at the ground and then at the rest of the foursome and then back at the ground as he spoke. "You know, according to Catholic theology, your body won't actually ascend to heaven. Your soul will go, and you will be united with a glorified body. By a glorified body, I mean a body free from imperfections. Your glorified body, for example, probably won't have the scar that you bear on your hand. All of our . . ." Clayton paused, and his voice broke as he looked at heaven before he gathered himself. "All of our body will be reunited and will be glorified." He looked back at his playing partners. "But the physical act of ascension is only reserved for the holiest of holy figures."

Chuck spoke up. "Really? Uh, I don't remember my preacher talking about this from the Sunday pulpit."

Mr. Clakker continued, "Well, really. Ya know, preachers don't want to bore you on Sunday with excessive detail about what believing their religion means in detail. But back to my point, Jesus ascended into heaven, but Mother Mary did not. She is assumed to have been assumed into heaven, which means that something like the hand of God came down and pulled her up to heaven rather than her physically ascending into the sky. That is why it is called the Feast of the Assumption. You know, as an aside, depending on what one believes, the Jewish word for *virgin* actually means an unwed mother, so Mary could actually have conceived through the act of physical sex, but since she birthed the Son of Man, it would still be the Immaculate Conception even if it was through intercourse. And the Bible never states that Mary was assumed, but the pope said so in a decree of infallibility, so how could that idea be wrong since the pope is infallible in his decree? And no one knows what kind of day it was when Jesus ascended into heaven because the apostles did not provide a weather report."

Clayton sermonized more, "Isaiah is written to have ascended to the heavens and received the vision of Jesus's life, but then he descended and prophesized about it, and then he was subsequently physically sawed into two pieces. He prophesized, and then he spilled his guts. He literally spilled his guts. Elijah, he rode up to heaven in a blazing chariot, but that is not physically ascending as the horses took him up. Enoch, he walked with God and disappeared, but does that mean physical ascension? In Islam, the prophet Muhammad ascended into the heavens at the speed of light at which point he saw all past and history and had all knowledge revealed to him. So in Islam and Catholic beliefs, the only two beings who physically ascended into heaven were each of their greatest religious figures."

Clayton concluded, "Of course, how can we know if any of this is true? How can we know that any of the writings are not all pseudepigrapha? I will never know until my death, but you, my friend, you may want to think twice before comparing your ascension to that of Jesus or Muhammad."

There was silence as the other three stared at Clayton in disbelief. "Well, Father Clayton Clakker," Jack said. "Thank you for today's daily dose of religion that I am sure we all need in our lives. That was beautiful, but I don't have a damn idea what in the world you just said."

Clayton replied, "Ah, don't mind me. Every so often, I like to get up on a soapbox and sermonize a little and then I come back to reality." He looked at his golfing partners and said, "C'mon, let's tee off."

Jack went to tee off. He stared at a beautiful four-hundred-yard hole with a lake that ran up the length of the left fairway. He prepared to swing.

Aug went over to his cart, and he interrupted everyone before Jack could tee off. "Hey, everyone," he said, "I smuggled in a flask of some bourbon. Some Woodford Reserve. Feel free to have some, but you'll have to drink it neat. I didn't smuggle in any ice to the course today."

Jack gave him a rankled look. He regrouped and striped the ball down the center two hundred and fifty yards. He looked at the rest of the foursome and said, "I don't care what the rest of ya do. I'm goin' wolf alone!"

Aug teed off and went left into the lake. Clayton popped up his tee shot short down the right side. Chuck striped his down by Jack.

They gathered into the carts. Chuck was busy filling out the scorecard. Chuck asked, "Clayton, how do you spell your last name? Is it C-l-a-q-u-e-r?"

Clayton replied, "Noooo, you spell my last name C-l-a-k-k-e-r."

Chuck spelled the name back and asked, "Is that German? I thought that you being from Louisiana, your name would be more French in origin."

Clayton started off again, "You know, the assumption of race based upon region is so inanely prevalent. Look at blacks. I have friends from the Bahamas and Jamaica who are black, but no matter where they go in the USA, they are African Americans even though they aren't Americans and—"

An annoyed Jack cut him off, "Clayton! That's enough. I came here to play golf, not to listen to you get on a soapbox all day while the heat swelters around. C'mon, fellas, let's get this round in before dark! And before I melt!"

They started driving off. Chuck looked at Aug and said, "Do you know what a claquer is?"

Aug looked at Chuck and said, "A strange Louisianan who babbles off about a lot of nothing that anyone cares about?"

Chuck laughed and said, "Well, that may be. But a claquer is also a plant that a magician uses in the audience to help pull off a trick. I thought maybe you might like to know that."

Aug sat back in that cart. *Really?* His first thought as the cart drove off was *Now that is interesting.* His second unspoken thought was *At least my vocabulary didn't get belittled again.*

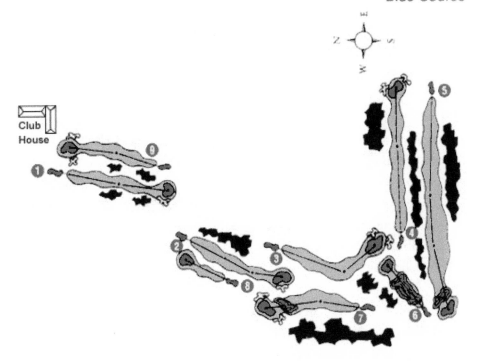

Blue Course

Club
House

# CHAPTER 19

## GARDEN HOSE

The sun was blazing above on the last day of June. The five of them made arrangements to play golf at Saskatoon on the way to Grand Haven. The tee time was eleven in the morning. If they knew everyone else was going to be out on the same course that day, they would have done things differently. Instead, it turned into what was going to be a six-hour round of golf. Every shot seemed like a fifteen-minute wait for the group in front to move.

The Stroh's was flowing. Lotion was applied all over the body. The carts had roofs, but the intense summer sun was burning. And more drinking was done.

The threesome in front of them could go nowhere. They were eighteen-year-olds who had nice Dutch Christian looks. One of the three was Bozo the Clown. Bozo clearly was using daddy's clubs and balls. He kept pulling brand-new Titleists out of box after box and losing them. Bozo would tee up and swing as hard as he could, and he would pull his head up. The woods and irons would barely hit the ball off the far end of the club. The brand-new Titleists he was using would roll twenty yards across the pine straw that layered the woods in between the pine trees. These pine trees created tree canyons for the holes on the course. And then Bozo would not go get the ball. He clearly had no concept of what he was doing on the course. He had no concept of the cost of the balls he was losing. That was why he was the single rider in his cart. His playing partners were annoyed to be seen on the course with him.

Eventually another swing would be taken, and eventually a good enough shot would be hit, allowing the threesome to move up and wait fifteen minutes. Tracy and Ginger would go and gather the free new golf ball and race the cart through the pines. There wasn't much else to do.

They had three carts. John Campbell and Robert Baumgardner rode in one cart. Their wives rode with the alcohol in another cart while Vitellius engaged the third cart. Valerie Valentine was picking up her brother Mark at Detroit Metro, and they would drive over to Grand Haven and meet everyone at Lake Michigan later that evening.

The slow play had been semiamusing for the first few holes of the white nine, but the novelty wore off as they realized, *We're screwed*. What could they do at that point? The options were to quit, play only nine, or gut out the full eighteen holes. Tracy and Ginger did not care. They were drinking and shedding clothes and copping a tan. They ran their cart all over the place, and they were happy to tease both the young boys in front of them or anyone else that they could. The miniskirts and bikini tops that barely adorned them allowed them to show a lot. They got a physical charge from public performance.

The men hemmed and hawed. Saskatoon was a beautiful golf course that they never played before and probably would never play again. It was just so goddamn slow out there on such a blistering hot day. But they really had no other plans than to head to the Tip a Few Tavern later, so what the hay? Plus summer only lasts so long in Michigan. They had learned to love the heat because it wouldn't be too long, and snow would be covering the same patch of land. They loaded up on more beer at the turn and hit the blue nine.

On the blue fifth hole, the fourteenth hole of the day, John and Robert duck-hooked their tee shots into the woods. Their lies were buried. No tree branch sound was heard. They might have cleared to the other fairway, but that was doubtful. Each hole was secluded by a good twenty yards of towering pines.

Vitellius took a shot of JD from the beer ladies and discreetly winked at Ginger. He teed the ball up high and hit the biggest slice he could. After an "oh shit," he went back to his cart and killed his beer, throwing the can in the tee box trash can and saying, "Beer me," as he drove off to find his balls. John and Robert took off in the other direction. The beer cart followed Vitellius.

John drove Robert slowly down the left side of the fairway under the trees. The course did have undulation to it, and they found themselves near where the threesome in front was waiting to hit. The hole was a 550-yard par 5 with a pond fronting the green, and there was a foursome finishing on the green with another waiting to approach and now two sets in the fairway. They parked, grabbed beers, found their tee shots, and went walking through the forest.

Robert the Ribbler was full of deep vocabularic thought. *Son of a Bitch, that shade feels good. Oh man, I need to take a leak.* Robert the Ribbler became Robert the Dribbler.

John pulled up and out alongside him. His flow was maxed. "Hey, Rob, looks like you're a little weak there, ol' buddy."

Rob relaxed and exerted his muscles a bit more and matched John's effort. "Naw, I've just been holding it in a few holes. It's kinda like everything receded up inside of me. It just needed a minute to get up to stream. Damn, that's a lot of beer to get rid of!"

John agreed, "I know. I'm gonna be so toast from this sun I'm gonna need a nap before we head out tonight. Damn, I can already feel the heat pouring off my skin." He sniffed the air. "Hell, I can already smell our piss evaporating!"

Rob said, "That's nice."

John said, "What, can't you? Don't be fibbin' now!"

Ribby laughed. "No, actually, I *can* smell it. The damn trees here are gonna love it! Those are two nice-sized lakes there, my friend!"

They finished and zipped up. There was still time to kill before the next shot. They putzed around looking for balls under the pine straw. John asked, "Hey, Robert . . . what's coming up on the horizon there?"

Robert was mindlessly wandering and said, "What do you mean? There's water in front of the green. I don't think we're doing anything but punching out and hopefully missing hitting a tree and going backward. That is, when we finally hit. We're pushin' three holes at this point. I don't know what kinda lie Vi is lookin' at over there, but I hope it's as shitty as ours. Son of a bitch, this is ridiculous! At least, the freaking squattles ain't buzzing all over us."

John laughed. "Ain't no water for the skeeters to breed in out here! But that isn't what I meant. I'm just wondering what the next deal or two might be. Daddy needs a new pair of shoes sometime, I'm just planning ahead. You know."

The Ribbler laughed. "What, do you wantta knock over a shoe store next? Is that what yer sayin'?"

John looked at him. "Hey, you know me. If the money's in it, I'll hit anything. Putting transmission cables in new cars is OK, but I always like to do better. I want to do better than that. I want to make bigger scores to get outta what I am doin' now."

"Sheeeeeeit, don't we all?" Robert paused and looked off. He pushed his club around the flora and thought. "Ya know, stagflation could be kinda good for us. There's been a few 'wink-wink' discussions I've had lately with some people who are looking to do anything they can to keep their lives afloat. I gotta watch how many of these we go after 'cuz I can't have too many customers having big insurance claims, but there are some nice deals I think can be had. People who gotta dump stuff just can't get what they want outta it. If we play it well, both of us could come out of this with very nice futures. How bad ya wanna go for it?"

John had a serious look on his face. "Make no mistake about it. I am very serious about this. Deadly serious. There are a few things I wanna go for real bad!"

Rob looked at John quizzically. "Really? It sounds like you got something in mind? Why do you need my help if you have some tasty deal on the hook?"

John posed on his club, staring at Rob. "Yeah, well, there may be one tasty deal that I know of." He pointed off to where Vitellius had gone. "It starts across the fairway."

Rob was confused. "What? What are you talking about?"

John solemnly spoke. "Robert, there's a price we have paid for marrying strippers. Sure, Father's Day we wake up to an incredible blow job, and that is a wonderful, nice experience while it lasts. But the flip side is, well, the flip side is I can probably guess what kinda lie Vitellius has with his balls right now."

Lake Vitellius was forcefully and frothingly forming in front of him. "MMMMM, Stroh's blows." He was drunkenly swaying while standing. He had a one-track mind at the moment, and it felt good.

A female hand came around on his snake. "Hey, big boy, need some help with that?" Ginger asked as she closed a hand around Vi's driver. She looked at Tracy and smiled, saying, "See? What did I tell you? Isn't this bad boy huge?"

Tracy was duly impressed. "Wow! No shit, you weren't lying. I kept wondering what I was looking at in those shorts." She joined Ginger in moving the warm beer tap from side to side. "Hey, this is fun! I can't do this with Robert!" The two women giggled. "Two hands and neither one of us is touching his head. I wish watering the garden was always this much fun."

Vitellius started massaging the women and made sure to say, "Ladies, this club is like the wood I just hit. It has a big head attached to stiff shaft!"

Ginger worked her hand. "I love it!" She looked at Tracy. "Feel that shaft getting harder? Damn, that feels good!"

Tracy looked at the beaming Vitellius whose ego was swelling with pride. "How the hell did you ever get a fifteen-year-old pregnant? I know when I was that young I wasn't swallowing this monster in my box! Good fucking god, I'm one kid down, and I still don't know if I could fit it in me!" She thought about it. "But I bet it feels good to try!" She looked at Vitellius. "How come you never came over to Trumpps when I was working there? We could have had a lot of fun."

Vi put his arms around both women and hugged them close while they worked him. He said, "Baby, we can still have a lot of fun. You just gotta let me know when."

Ginger tugged him away from the spreading canal. Her skirt was easy access, and she was ready to go. With a naughty smile, she said to Tracy, "Well, I know I can take it! You'll just have to wait your turn sometime. I'm not sharing today." She playfully slapped Tracy's hand away and told Vitellius, "C'mere, up against the tree. Tracy, keep an eye out for the guys, will ya?" With that, Ginger backed up against a pine tree, pulling Vitellius with her.

Ginger gave Vi a few more pleasing tugs, saying, "C'mon, c'mon, let's get rid of all that shake in there." Then with her one free hand, she hopped up her back against the fir and wrapped her legs around Vittelius's waist. "Ooooooohhh, that's soooooooo nice!" She spoke into his ear. "MMMM, drinking makes me sooooo horny!"

# 14
### Par 3

# Burnt Pine

•212 •193 •165 •118

31
28
20
18
13
14

118

165

193

212

# Chapter 20

## French Door

Twenty-six years later, John Campbell was Jack Dough, and he was still playing golf. The sun was still blazing, only this time it was almost the end of July. He was at the fourteenth hole again. It was once again Valentine's day, only this time it was with Augustus Valentine. It was once again blistering hot outside. He kept an eye out, but there were no shenanigans—or even a mulligan for that matter. They were running out of holes, but he suspected something would happen soon. This golf game wasn't for fun. The wolf was on the tee, and he did not disappoint.

The fourteenth hole was labeled as one ninety-three to the pin. It was all carry-over wetlands. To the right the Choctawhatchee Bay yawned. Across the bay, the Sandestin Hilton could be seen. Jack was surprised when Aug pulled out a driver. He had seen him hit driver farther than that earlier in the round. The ball was teed low to the ground. The address of the ball was fine—until the swing started. The body turned left. A scorching low-line drive was hit straight at the house short left of the green—Jack's house. The ball smashed glass on something.

Aug was laughing. He turned his head to his playing partners. "Oops, I guess I fell off a bit on that one!" He looked back at the house behind the tee box. "Ya know, I saw a thing yesterday that the Dow family is asking like eight mil for this place back here. Somehow I feel confident that whoever owns the place I just hit can afford the broken glass." He looked at the threesome. "I guess this wolf may need a partner."

The audacity of the remark stopped the other three in their tracks. Aug was bemused. He could see that all three knew who lived on the fourteenth. Clayton proceeded to tee off with a three iron—into the wetlands. Chuck proceeded to tee off with a five wood—into the wetlands.

Aug looked at Jack. "You're up. We are all in the drop area. Are you gonna put it on the green and give the wolf a partner?"

Jack mumbled a "You're an asshole" as he went to the tee. He looked at Aug before swinging. "I'll give the wolf a partner." He took dead aim with a three iron, dead aim at the porch of the house. He nailed it too. Something else was broken. Turning to Chuck and Clayton, he told them, "You two take my cart up to the drop area on the far side of the green. Mister driver and I will go see what the owner of the house has to say about this." And they were off.

Jack took a pitching wedge out of his bag and hopped into Aug's cart. Aug drove up the cart path and parked the club car in front of the residence. He removed an eight iron from his bag, and both men walked up to the house. They stepped up a couple of brick steps that bisected a three-foot brick wall.

The tee shots were quite incredible. The shots missed the wall. The balls flew over it. The patio furniture was a round glass table with a vase of roses on it. The tee shots missed the vase. Each tee shot had taken out a small pane of glass on a french door that fronted the porch. The balls were lying on the porch. They appeared to have rolled around, scraped themselves, possibly ricocheting between the house and wall.

Jack looked at Aug in dismay. "Well, ya gotta whatcha wanted. It took sending some golf balls into my house, but here I am." He turned his head to survey the damage. "It seems to me that if you wanted a place to talk, you could have just come by the place rather than wrecking it."

Aug lost it on that note. "Wrecking it? WRECKING IT?" He swung the eight iron at Jack's head, causing him to jump back to avoid being brained. Aug followed through with the swing of the club and took out some more door panes. "Are you calling me a home wrecker?"

## Swing, smash.

Aug screamed in anger, "You want home wrecker?"

## Swing, smash.

"I'll wreck your goddamn whole house!" With that, Aug shredded both the door and iron until there was nothing left of the club to be able to break anything with, throwing the shaft down on the porch. The french door was paneless.

Jack wasn't sure what his own emotions were. He gauged the situation. As much as he was furious over the door being trashed, he knew he deserved it. Besides, he would probably lose a fistfight at their respective ages, and a fight wouldn't get him what he wanted—the location of the gemstones. Still, he was pretty pissed off.

Jack asked rather snidely, "Well, well, well, if it isn't Mr. Mature. Are you all better now? What are ya gonna do for an encore? Kick the wall down?"

Aug took off his visor and wiped the sweat off his face and forehead with his shirt. He ran his fingers back through his hair. His breathing calmed down. An exhaling of air helped him regain his composure. "Maybe I have something better in mind. Maybe I'll just blow up the whole goddamn building with you inside. What do ya think of that plan?"

Jack wryly said, "I don't think a whole lot of that plan. I think a lot of people wouldn't like that plan. I think that maybe you need a better plan."

Aug asked him, "Oh? And I suppose that you just happen to have a better plan in mind? Tell me, just what do you have in mind?"

Jack replied, "Why don't you just tell me where you hid my gems? They aren't yours anyway. You stole them. They belong to someone else. You know there is no place you can go that someone won't find you. It would be better to just alleviate yourself of the problem you've created."

Aug laughed. "The problem that I've created? What makes you think I created this problem? You had your brother steal the gems from me, remember?" Aug pointed to the faded facial discoloration. "What, did you think I just bruised myself shaving? And how did these goods become *your gems* anyway? It's not like you personally put up the cash."

They eyeballed each other. Aug looked around at the house here, the house next door, the golf course, the buildings visible across the bay. "You're the guy who set this whole thing up. You set up the money laundering. You set up the platinum smuggling, the diamond smuggling—hell, you intended to set me up to take the fall for everything, didn't you? And now you've got a problem. You've got some diamonds, sapphires, and rubies—only they are phony—as phony as you are, as phony as your name is. What was your plan, Jack? How were you going to get away with stealing everything?"

There was a moment of silence. Aug smiled and continued, "Maybe I kinda like the situation we are in. Maybe I'm a dead man walking. But maybe we'll see who gets to the grave first."

Jack thought about it. This was not getting him the needed information. "Aug, be sensible, where ya gonna go with this? Ain't no one gonna just let you walk around with a bunch of other people's money. Do you have a death wish? Is that it? I mean, I can help, but you gotta help me first. There's buyers waiting to pay good money for the loot. I'll give you a cut of the action, but I can't liquidate anything I don't have."

"Liquidate things you don't have," mused Aug. "That's a good one. And if you don't deliver what you don't have, then who liquidates whom I wonder? Maybe I am not the only dead man walking? Hmmm? Jack, you're gonna have to work harder to close this deal than that. Why don't you tell me where you stashed those gold and platinum plates and goblets and maybe I'll consider letting you know where the ice is?" Aug bent down and picked up his golf ball. "Besides, didn't you hear the weather report? Hurricane Bill is now named and is targeted to hit Panama City in a couple days. You're gonna have to move everything again anyway to keep it safe from potential damage. I could help with that, so you don't have to drag anyone else in."

Jack told him, "Don't confuse issues here. The metals, that's none of your business. That's not your deal."

Aug told him, "You see, Jack, that's where you're wrong. You made it my business when you stole everything out of Trove and left me to be the fall guy.

Here I come, and I'm willing to work out a deal to split everything, and you want it all for yourself." A disapproving reproaching sound was made. "From where I stand, I think my loot is worth more than yours, so maybe I'll just keep my end for myself and see what happens."

Aug walked off the porch and up the path to the drop area. "You wanna see the ice? Give me a good reason and I'll take you to them." He looked back at the damage to the door. "You better get that door fixed soon. A storm is coming. It's time for you to return to your home."

# Chapter 21

## Greg Czarnacki

Greg Czarnacki hustled his body past the tall colonnades. It was dark out. Snow flakes swirled through the air. The snow wafted around in the wind and building lighting. Christmas was just around the corner.

He passed through a security check. He went to the north wing of the building. He went to second floor. He passed through the hall where the inauguration of Ulysses S. Grant occurred. Greg knew this was where the event took place due to his knowledge of the military. He marveled at the reconstructed Civil War motif and furniture. He had never been here before, and it was a far cry from his FinCEN office in Venice.

Greg's office was organized and had pictures of his wife and daughters on his desk and service photos and sheepskin on the walls. His computer files were organized, and he liked to keep a daily regimen of consistently orchestrated activity of family, career, and exercise. But here he was looking at cleanliness that only the highest levels of tax dollars can buy. This was the result of truly orchestrated activity.

Greg believed he was a pragmatic sort. His pragmatism problem was that he worked for Justice. The concept and fact of working for Justice were assuredly oxymoronic. The concept of working for Justice is black-and-white while the facts are a rainbow of colors. Greg owned the colorful title of regulatory enforcement specialist.

Age trumps youth in the category of understanding the environment that one lives in. Living long enough to make it to your midthirties means that along the way you made choices and you lived with the results of those choices. You are also impacted by the choices that others made. You develop a better understanding, a more complete model, of you perception of reality. The reality of existence and the existence of reality become clearer.

The realities of Greg's existence were about to become clearer to him. He was about to go upstairs to a much nicer office and have a chat about his more immediate future. He knew what the conversation was going to be about. He was uneasy about what was to occur.

The enrollment in the marines had been both about career and the love of country. Greg believed in the USA. Greg believed in his Catholic religion. Greg believed in the black-and-white difference between white and wrong. The problem was that he had been in Washington too long. His belief system was both shattered by the realities of his existence, and yet it was clearer than ever because of the existence of his realities.

He was thinking about a variety of those realities. He was thinking about how, behind the back of Justice, the Medicare administration recently negotiated a lenient settlement with HCA for defrauding the government. Sure, there were fines, but the deal was constructed to hurt some people while allowing the big money criminals to walk away in fine fettle from fraudulent financial finagling.

The Clintons made tons of money off friendly dealings. Greg chuckled to himself while he walked, remembering about the Rose Law Firm records that mysteriously appeared in the White House. The newspeople were so selective in their ability to put two and two together. Hillary was billing clients for all sorts of hours, at the same time she was executing massive amounts of trade to hyper profit from CBOT. How could someone performing hard work as a lawyer also fit in the time to make all the phone calls and perform all the research necessary to make all the necessary trades to turn one grand into one hundred grand in ninety days? Not while simultaneously performing work for clients. Certainly not in the pre-Internet age when there was no "click on the icon" method of trading.

Then there was Halliburton. There was another good one. The government blindly doled out money to the corporation because no other company is qualified to perform certain jobs. That is such a great argument used nowadays. Let's pay tons of money to crooks that run companies because there is no other company that knows so much of the business at hand and could be so well qualified. It is a self-serving argument to continue paying money to crooked individuals who are part of the game.

Greg saw the money trail everywhere around him in his daily life. He saw it in the halls he was walking through to reach the second-floor office that was his destination. His reality was that he could either accept an uncertain existence with his wife and kids, or he could join the gravy train.

There were so many other examples he had seen during his tenure. Some made the press, and some were never discovered. Well, anyway, it was 7:00 PM. It was time for him to arrive.

Mr. White's administrative assistant was there waiting for his arrival. She showed Greg into the office of Deputy Director Thomas White. She was then excused for the evening.

Greg looked around. The office was magnificent in its restored glory. He felt a personal thrill as he stood at attention in front of a Civil War—era chair. The wall murals and carpet and paintings were restored glory of America's past. He stared at a Civil War—era desk. There was a telephone on the desk as well as two large flat-screen monitors. There were also two files on the desk. Greg could see that one was his own employment file. The other file had no markings on it.

Mr. White stood up and walked around and shook his hand. Thomas White spoke. "Greg, thank you for meeting me at this time of day. I apologize for the late hour, but today was an exceptionally busy day. Please, please have a seat. Make yourself comfortable."

Greg replied, "The time is not a problem, sir. Thank you for the seat, sir."

Mr. White listened to what he heard. He saw what he saw. He liked it.

Thomas picked up the personnel file. "I was going over your record here. It is an impressive resume that you have been building. I see that you were on the front line in Desert Storm with the first wave of marines that went in. I also see that you have completed your law degree at American University. Your personnel file is filled with nothing but accolades for your work at FinCEN. I commend you on a job well done."

Greg replied, "Thank you, sir. Compliments coming from you are greatly appreciated."

Thomas eased back in his recliner and continued, "I gotta ask. What was it like being one of the first people sent to Iraq after the bombing? I mean, I'll never experience something like what happened. Few people in the world will ever go through something like that."

Greg told him, "Mr. White, sir, I can tell you that it was an unpleasant experience. But for my country, that was my job. And I may have gone through it in Iraq, but "—Greg looked around the room—" but you know, a lot of people died in the Civil War, and they were witness to gruesome things too. It's the nature of the business."

Mr. White smiled. "Nice answer. But I was curious what you saw firsthand."

Greg paused. "Well, sir, I don't think anyone can appreciate the experience without being there. When I grew up on the farm in Iowa, I did not imagine I would be fully garbed and be the first person to hop into bombed-out bunkers and see arms and legs and body bits all over. The stench of mass death in the desert is really incredible."

Mr. White said, "I'll bet."

Greg continued, "Oh yeah. That reminds me of this guy in my unit. There was this guy who went nutso on us. He decided he was gonna bring back a souvenir with him. Not a Hollywood souvenir. He was gonna bring back a severed arm with him. He put it in his tent and wouldn't let anyone near the tent. Well, after a couple of days in the hundred-degree heat, there was a really incredible stench. But this guy wouldn't let anyone into his tent to see what it was. We finally had to get the MPs to force open the tent, and then they found this rotting arm in there. That guy ended up in Leavenworth, sir." Greg shivered at the memory. He could not stop shivering for a minute.

Thomas noticed that. "I'm sorry. I didn't mean to bring back bad memories. Do you need a break? A glass of water or anything."

Greg told him, "No, no, I am OK, sir."

Thomas nodded. "I bet you gotta be glad to be away from all that! Back here in the USA in the land of plenty. Hopefully you can reap rewards for your sacrifice for your country."

Greg replied, "I hope so, sir."

Mr. White said, "Well, let me change the subject on you. Greg, the reason you are here is because of your involvement with certain suspicious activities reports that you have been working with. The White Sands SARs. I assume you know what I am talking about?"

Greg replied, "Yes, sir. Yes, I know what you are referring to, sir."

Thomas leaned back as best he could and said, "Greg, I'd like you to relax a bit while I tell you a story. And I'd like you to not feel that you have to call me *sir* with every sentence. I'd like you to consider me as a friend, maybe as a benefactor. Call me Thomas or Mr. White. Take your pick. But I'm not a drill commander here. Heck, it's nearly Christmas. Let's be of good cheer. You've got a nice family, and I understand that you've got another child on the way. Isn't that correct?"

Greg answered, "Yes, sir, that is correct. I have two daughters, and my wife just informed me today that we are expecting a son early next year."

Mr. White said, "HEY! A son! That has to be pretty exciting for you! Will you join me in a celebration drink?"

Greg replied, "Absolutely, s—." He caught himself. "Absolutely, Mr. White."

Thomas exclaimed, "Much better!" He opened a desk drawer and pulled out a sealed bottle of Rittenhouse Straight Rye Whiskey. Two glasses were also taken out of the desk. Stiff drinks were poured. "Cheers!" They clanked glasses.

Thomas let out the obligatory "ahhh" of tasteful satisfaction. He looked at his glass. "I love this stuff. It runs me a hundred fifty dollars a bottle, but I can't seem to get the taste for it out of my mouth." He took another taste and then turned and looked at Greg. "Greg, you joined FinCEN in the last couple years, but are you familiar with the Bank of New York incident maybe five, six years ago with some Russian activity?"

Greg looked at his glass. *Finally*, he thought, *we can actually get somewhere.*

"Well, Mr. White," he said, "what I know is that years ago, when the SAR's program was a lot younger, there were some incidents with the Bank of New York where they had activity that should have been reported via SARs but that the reports never actually were filed. That involved quite a few billion that went from the US to Russia. I don't know if that is what you are referring to."

Thomas said, "Ah! Very good. That *is* exactly what I am referring to. And I think if you check into it, you will find that the Bank of New York and the employees involved got off comparatively light in relation to what was going on. I mean, quite honestly, I happen to know for a fact that the people involved knew exactly what they were doing. Do you know how I know, Greg?"

Greg thought about it. "Because you worked on the case, sir?"

Thomas answered, "Exactly! It's why I am here today. In this office. In this building. Talking to you." Thomas had a broad smile on his face. He tasted some more alcohol. "God, I do love this stuff."

Greg was confused. He was not sure if he saw the light. "I'm not sure I follow you, sir."

"Well," Mr. White explained, "I was a few years younger, and I found myself with some decisions to make. I learned that the money was moving and how it was moving and where it was moving and who was moving it. Of course, the people moving the cash also found out about my knowledge. They had a little talk with me. They agreed to shut down what they were doing. Shut it down, that is, over a couple-year period. They wanted time to wind up activities and insulate themselves and set up a new route for what they were doing. They were very persuasive and, well, here you and I are in this fabulous Civil War office enjoying a holiday snort."

Mr. White pulled his chair up to the desk. He sat his glass down on the desk. He clasped his fingers together. "Now it just so happens that you have been building a case against White Sands. And I understand that. You are a good man, and you've done a good job, and your work is greatly appreciated by a variety of people. There are people who appreciate the sacrifice that you have made for your country. There are people who would like to see you continue up the ladder in your career. These people would like to, how shall I say, Bank of New York it? Does the meaning sink through to you?"

Greg sat silently. He looked into Mr. White's eyes. He thought about what had been said. Many things went through his head. His family. His career. The dead bodies he had seen. If he said no now, right here, today, then what would he do? Better yet, what could he do? Better yet, what would they do?

Greg replied, "I think I understand what you are saying, sir. What is it you would like me do, sir?"

Thomas said, "Very good. Now, what is needed is for someone to go to the area for a while and discreetly manage the situation. Of course, it will take some time to clean up things, and you'll have to work with a skeleton crew, and you will have to work under an alias. Eventually there will have to be a couple of successful prosecutions for the illegal activity that has occurred, but only after the time is right for such events to take place. In fact, some plea bargains would be much cleaner than any trial. Plea bargains are so much quieter and easier than a trial. Do you understand?"

Greg replied, "Yes, sir, I do. I do have one question for you, sir. When you say *a while*, how long are you thinking, sir?"

Thomas replied, "Well, maybe, a year and a half? I'd like to see this thing wound up maybe the end of next June or so."

Greg nodded his head. He understood. The good soldier would be away from his two- and four-year-old daughters for maybe eighteen months, and he would be lucky to see the birth of his son. This was the reward that Justice had in store for him for cleaning up the illegal yet profitable activities of wealthy, important people in the country he loved.

Thomas continued, "Of course, if you do a good job, I am confident that the right people will be impressed and that this will bid well for your future. Now, let's take a look at this folder here and go over some details. And don't forget to take this bottle with you as a Christmas present."

Greg and Thomas went over details. Chuck Hvala was born.

# CHAPTER 22

## DINNER AND DRINKS

Destin Commons is five miles east of Sandestin. The drive along the Emerald Way from Sandestin to Destin has become the home to many of the chains of stores that dot US cities. The stores cater to the cash offering fine entertainment value to all that can and can't afford it. The mall at the Commons is clean and well lit. It is a modern outdoor walk-around mall. There is never any snow or ice to plow around here. And at night, it is another pickup haven for bar patronry. Can you pay to play? Do you even want to pay to play?

Jack Dough and Chuck Hvala were eating dinner in a booth at the Bonefish Grill. Time had been taken to get cleaned up from a muggy round of golf, and now they were enjoying a table in the restaurant area of the eatery. The bar near the entrance was filled up this Friday. The local band the Schmucks was warming up on the deck area. The Schmucks were preparing to play all sorts of cover tunes for the combination of young and older adults here. Both older men and cougars were in abundance as well as the counterparts they sought.

Jack had been frightened by what it must be like to be a local band musician. To be someone who had never made it big-time. Someone who, thirty years later, was spending their evenings doing covers of songs that others made popular and watching drunks thirty years younger party it up until they were told to leave while others found partners for libidinous exploits. Years ago, he was afraid that a similar fate would befall him. That's why he became a criminal. He was smarter than the others. He was smart enough to go to college, but not smart enough to go to college. That didn't matter anyway.

The Enron folks and the WorldCom folks and the Adelphia folks and others had gone to college, but so what? Their fortunes and lavish lifestyles had been built on fraud. They were all con men when you got down to it. They were con men right down to their final church pleas for forgiveness. They had invoked the last-resort con of the "I'm so sorry I fell, please forgive me" con to try and minimize their damage. The con was played, and damage minimization meant a substantial financial contribution to the preacher absolving the sinner. Bill Clinton and Jesse Jackson offered free public seminars about how to play this con.

Jack also especially loved the "I have special knowledge" con. It is such a self-serving argument for white-collar criminals. The "I may be guilty, but I produce so much for society that you should let me go" con. Every year, millions of people graduate from colleges and the like, but they are all too stupid to capably replace the good deeds of those few who got nailed for ripping everyone off because the ones who got busted have special knowledge. The crooks had made their money, and they knew how to spend their capital to keep their positions.

Jack had special knowledge. He had knowledge of where the money came from. He knew how it filtered up. He had knowledge of how he washed it and what it had purchased. He also had education—or was it common sense? When the government told him that he was being shut down, he was educated enough to know that he had limited choices. Go to jail or go to jail for longer were two of the options. Jack didn't cotton to either one. He hadn't worked himself up to a life of luxury through a life of con, not to be pro and to end up a con. Besides, with the knowledge of bodies that he had, Jack wouldn't last long in the stir anyway.

What it meant was that a different and bigger con was required. Not the con of repentance. Not the con of special knowledge. There were too many cons to those cons to make them viable. He opted for the con he knew so well. He opted for the con of deceit.

Chuck had a leather zipper valise with him at the table. He held it up for Jack to see. "We typed up the recordings of your testimony so far for you to sign. Inside here are the transcripts implicating Donald Vitale and Antonio Rossini and

Mark Kledas, as well as others, of arranging shipments of unreported money for laundering as well as testimony implicating yourself and Augustus Valentine in both money laundering and smuggling. This is here for you to sign. Coupled with the signed testimonies of Arthur Marshall and Patrick See that we fortunately got before their untimely deaths, we have enough to proceed with the case. This assumes you don't contest the charges brought against you."

Chuck continued, "I can't tell the judge how to sentence you, but the recommendation that Justice is prepared to make is that if you go through with this and deliver the Philadelphia contacts that you have, we will recommend ten years with parole in five. If we go to court on all counts of money laundering and racketeering, you're looking at a minimum of twenty years. In either case, there will probably also be large a fine to be paid."

Jack slumped back in the booth. "There's really no way out, is there? You bastards pretty well have me by the balls, don't you?" He looked down and then spoke. "And my daughter? She walks away from this, right?"

Chuck answered, "If you agree to this deal, then we won't go after her as an accessory. If you don't agree, then I can't make any promises." He paused. "However, Justice would like to go higher up in the chain. You agree to go higher up in the chain, and the sentencing could possibly be reduced more."

Jack answered, "Justice? I think that is hardly 'justice'! That is called putting the squeeze on if you ask me! Justice would be seeing OJ in prison with me. Justice would be Ted Kennedy having to answer for Mary Jo Kopechne. Justice would be Dow Chemical executives having to answer for Bhopal. Justice would be Barry Bonds not being publicly lynched. That's what justice would be!" He paused and mused. "Justice. I'm willing to bet my testimony won't even be used for anything anyway. I'm not so stupid, you know. I know a setup when I see one."

The waitress came up. "Are you gentlemen all set? Do you see anything else you would like?"

Jack smiled and looked at her. He looked at Chuck and then looked back at her. "You've got a nice tableside manner there, miss. I certainly see many things I like, but this guy here wants me to go to prison instead, so I am afraid I can't partake."

The waitress looked at them both and laughed. She put her hand on Chuck's shoulder and looked at Jack. "Oh, I'm sure that this fine gentleman here wouldn't want to hurt you!" She looked at Chuck. "You wouldn't do such a thing now, would you?"

Jack said, "Sure, you're right. He's just a real pip. Anyway, we're all set here. Just bring us the bill."

"Sure," she said. "You're the boss!" She walked off.

Chuck said, "Well, well. Jack the Charmer. I may be a pip, but with other people, you're just a pimp!"

Jack said, "Hey, I am just expressing that I like what I see to the young lady. I have always had a soft spot for waitresses. Can't you see that I am just trying to enjoy my life on the outside a little longer?"

Chuck answered, "What you see is irrelevant. And besides, the longer you are outside, the greater the chance you end up like Art and Pat."

Jack was silent a moment. "Arthur and Patrick," he mused. "They didn't last long after they signed the papers, did they?" He thought a bit more. "Well, I'll miss Arthur, but Patrick isn't that great a loss."

Chuck laughed. "You sound very judgmental about him. Kinda like your preacher friend from the golf course today. Are you suggesting that he was the 'unholy See'?" Chuck continued, "Speaking of which, where did Clayton come from? He just happened to be around wanting to play a round of golf today?"

Jack answered, "He's just a potential Destin client. I do have to keep up the appearance of business, you know. I'm not quite in an orange jumpsuit yet." He looked around at the bar area and saw what he was looking for. He continued "Sooo the timing on this is Monday morning, right? I at least get to go through the grand opening of Poseidon's before you take it all away? My final coup de grace? The plan is that I go into the office on Monday morning and you shut down the bank and Destin Dreams and take me away?"

Chuck answered, "Well, technically nothing gets shut down. The bank and DD will still operate. It's just that there will be a new level of, how shall I say, management oversight?"

Jack continued, "And you'll guarantee both mine and Angel's safety throughout the testimony and trial?"

Chuck told him, "Jack, old pal, old buddy, do you think I am not a man of my word? I think I should have more suspicions of your intentions than you of mine."

"Let's not go there with that comment, OK?" Jack sighed, looking around aimlessly. His eyes espied Aug standing at the bar across the room, watching the two of them eat. "What the hell? What the hell is that asshole doing here?"

Chuck turned and saw Aug. "Well, well, well. If it isn't Mr. Tee Shot." He turned and looked at Jack. "You know, that was quite a scene that you and Mr. Valentine staged earlier. What was that all about? That's not too good for sales. I don't think your buddy the impromptu preacher man is going to be buying a condo after seeing that exhibition."

Jack was indignant. "What do you mean 'staged'? Goddamn bastard nearly took my head off with that iron of his. Didn't you see him trash my beautiful door? Now I gotta get someone in there to fix it before all hell from the storm breaks loose. Between opening day tomorrow and dealing with you, it's gonna be tough before the storm hits. Every handy man is going to be tied up shuttering houses all over the place. Ya know, it's not like replacement doors like I need are just waiting on store shelves here. It's gotta be ordered and yadda yadda." Jack paused. He leaned forward toward Chuck and continued, "Ya know, I'm tellin' ya, that guy is psycho. He's not stable. His parents died under strange circumstances, and he drove his wife to suicide. I'm sure it's no accident he's been in a fight and got that shiner. He accused me of setting up a robbery of the last batch of goods smuggled in. But you know what? He faked the robbery. He's trying to rip off the mob and make it look like I did it. The guy's a fucking time bomb waiting to explode. He and his uncle are the ones you need to be careful of. They're the ones who have all those jewels that were smuggled in."

Chuck looked at Aug and then back at Jack. "Really?"

Jack angelically replied, "Really. Scout's honor."

The bill came. Chuck told Jack, "Your treat."

Jack replied, "Gee, you're a peach." He paid in cash, and the waitress took it away. When she was gone, Jack continued, "Ya know, I learned earlier today from someone out there, they pulled a switch on the jewels. They've been planning this rip-off for a while, and they had a phony set of goods made. They had to pay a decent price for the fakes, and they had to have this in the works for a while to get the phonies made, but they have the goods." Jack leaned back. "That's a lot of dough out there waiting to be had."

Chuck thought about it for a little. "Just what are you saying there, Jack? Who told you this information?"

Jack looked at the envelope and then at Chuck. "You wanna talk? Let's talk, but not here."

Chuck replied to Jack, "C'mon, let's get outta here."

The bar crowd amused him. It was very casual preppy. It was pre- and postravelike. Preravelike in the regard that the younger adults were using this as a meeting place before clubbing the night away. Postravelike in that the adults who were too old to enjoy late-night clubbing anymore were there checking out the local fare to see what might be enjoyed. Even if the fare would not be taken home, it would still provide ample fantasy material from hand to revolver or other toys to enjoy. The special on the Bonefish menu was a flashing red light.

The lady in red was gathering attention. She had short curly hair, almost Shirley Temple-ish, which was blond with a reddish tint. The cherubic face had been made up with a strawberry tint. The strawberry blouse complimented her face. She had a long white skirt on. The heels weren't so high, and the straps were thick. Aug did enjoy eyeing her while he looked over at what was going on between Chuck and Jack. Eventually she broke away from her suitors and came over and asked him, "Excuse me, are you married?"

Aug held up his hands. "There's no ring on my fingers. So I guess, no, I am not married."

"Hmm" was the smirking reply. "Just because you don't currently have a ring on your finger doesn't mean that you aren't married!" She slid her hand into his. "Big hands, I like that. Not many calluses, although the nails could use some work." Her fingers tarried over his left hand. "Nice scar! So, Mr. 'I guess I am not married,' are you going to tell me what your name is?"

He laughed at her smile. "Sure. My name is Augustus. Augustus Valentine. Mr. Unmarried Augustus Valentine. And yours must be Angel?"

She looked at him very suspiciously. "That is my name!" Her eyes narrowed, and her head cocked. "How would you know that?"

"Oh," he answered, "it was just a guess." He pointed down at her ankle, which was adorned by a small angel tattoo. "Who else is going to have an angel tattoo but someone named Angel?"

"Oh. Well, you are right. My name is Angel." She rotated her hand in his to shake hands. "Pleased to meet you, Mr. Unmarried Augustus." She looked around and back at him. "I don't think I've seen you here before. Are you here for business or . . . ah . . . pleasure . . . maybe?" She gave him a nice smile. Like a horse breeder evaluating a filly, he noticed that dental work appeared to be well done and that teeth whitening was of prime importance.

He looked around the room. "Oh, I'm just . . . ah . . . hanging out for an evening."

She looked down at his dress pants and then back up at him, stating, "Yes, you are hanging out, just a bit."

The reply caused Aug to exhibit a surprised look on his face. "Tell me, Angel, are you always so forward with strange men that you meet in a bar? A girl could wind up in a lot of trouble that way, you know."

A cutesy smile appeared. "Maybe I'm just your guardian angel sent down from the heavens to watch over you." She looked over his face. "From the looks of your eye, I'd say that you need a guardian angel. What happened to you?"

There was only one answer for him to give. "What else? I slipped on a bar of soap and hit my head."

Angel gave him a disbelieving "Uh-huh. Yeah, riiiiggghhhhtttt. I dunno. Somehow, I smell a woman involved in that blow."

A surprised Aug asked, "Now, whatever could make you infer such an assertion?"

Her reply was sarcastic. "Ooohhh, 'infer such an assertion'? Such big words for such a big man! Well, maybe my inference is just based upon my woman's intuition. Maybe I have a keen sense of smell."

Aug looked over to the dinner table. He was dismayed. Chuck and Jack had left while he was distracted. Well, now he had time to see what Angel was up to. "So tell me, my guardian angel wannabe, are you from around here?"

"Not originally." A forced fake accent came out. "I'm originally from Nashville. Ya know, one of them Southern girls."

Aug gave her a bemused grunt. "Well, Ms.—or is it Mrs.?—Guardian Angel, can I buy you a beer or drink?"

She answered, "Howsabout a Bloody Mary? And no, I am not married." She held up her hand to show a ringless finger. "I am a *miss*. Ms. Angel to you, you *miss*ogynist!"

Aug laughed. "Oh, and I am Mr. Big Words? Well, Ms. Angel, if you don't mind waiting here for a couple, I'll go get us some drinks," he said. "It may take a minute, the line looks pretty long up there."

Aug made his way to the bar. It took a good five minutes of waiting, which meant checking out action around him and on the overhead TV screens while people were served. The band started up. He ordered a Bud and a Bloody Mary.

The bartendress asked, "Short, tall, or super? For the Bud, that is?" Looking behind the bar, he saw the option presented were twelve-, twenty-, and thirty-six-ounce sizes. A tall was ordered.

Angel had company when he returned with the drinks. A giant Hispanic-looking mountain of a man with a bald head was with Angel as well as an Italian-looking, shorter, big-schnozzed gentleman. The Mountain took the beer from Aug and spoke with a Latino accent, saying, "Gracias, señor." He drank the whole brew in one long draining.

Aug handed Angel the Bloody Mary and said, "Well, Angel, you didn't tell me it was old boyfriends night tonight! So tell me, who is the Mountain here that I just bought a beer for?"

She smiled back at him. "He's not mine. Although, I must admit that I do like the muscles." She ran her open hand over the biceps and chest. She looked at Aug. "But I figured Popeye here was one of your jealous old flames!"

Aug's reply to her was "The house isn't mine. And I don't think I like the muscles. That's way too manly for me. I like 'em when they have a soft belly and big breasts. And hair that is black, of course!"

Angel found the last quip insulting. "You know, all of a sudden, I think I'm liking Popeye here a lot more!"

The Nose spoke up. "C'mon, children, play nice. We're here to collect you both, so let's be nice for Daddy and make a nice quiet exit out of here." The Mountain grabbed both their wrists, and the Nose continued, "Bone snapping is a fun game for Canaan here, and there's no need to have him play here in front of all these people."

Aug piped up, "But I have to go the bathroom! Or does he enjoy holding on to that too?" He tried to take a step toward the back of the bar where the men's room was only to be pulled back the other way.

Canaan said, "Ah, señor, don't be like that. I don't snap that bone. If the situation calls for it, I cut that one off. Let's just leave nice and easy now." Canaan squeezed their wrists so it hurt them, causing Aug and Angel to each yelp a little. "Now."

Aug and Angel had the lead as they worked their way through the crowd to be able to approach the front exit. A body turned from the bar with two super beers in hand.

## SPLASH!

A collision occurred. The super beers passed behind Aug and Angel and poured all over Canaan and the Nose. A scene had been caused. People jumped back to avoid the beer spray in the air and the liquid pooling on the floor. The bouncers at the door started looking intently at the sudden commotion to figure out what was going on.

"Dude! Oh man! Oh, I am soooo sorry. Oh . . . here . . . let me get you some napkins and buy you a beer!" Steve Champion's rant went on as he separated Aug and Angel from their captors. They wasted little time getting out the door as the ruse worked to free them. A fast path was beat across the parking lot.

Aug grabbed Angel's arm. "C'mon, lets get outta here."

Angel balked. "Excuse me? I just met you, and that was no one I know back there. You got some crazy friends. Why would I want to go anywhere with you?"

Aug shrugged. "Suit yourself." He turned and started walking away.

## Whacked!

A shoe hit him in the back of the head, causing him to yell, "OW!"

"HEY! Don't you just walk away from me, Mr. Augustus Valentine!" Angel had taken her shoes off, and she had run up to him, and she had coshed him.

"Where do you think you're going?" Aug turned around to look at her, and he was caught by another shoe in the face.

"Goddammit!" was his exclamation as he grabbed his head "What the hell did you do that for?"

She swung at him again and again while he blocked her blows. "Because, you moron, you're supposed to try at least a little bit harder to get me to go somewhere with you!"

Aug tried grabbing her arms and was yelling, "STOP IT! STOP IT, will ya?" She quit swinging. "What the hell? I asked if you wanted a ride and you said no. OK. And now you wanna beat me up for saying no? Well, do you want a ride somewhere or what?" He looked at her and said, "Look, I don't know what Mountain Man is doing back there, but I don't want to wait and find out. Ya wanna have a drink somewhere else, then fine. Let's go for a ride. But I ain't hanging out here."

He hit the car unlocking light flashing sound chirping device on the key ring, and the DeVille spoke back. He looked back at her. "Ya coming?"

Angel marched by rather annoyingly and entered the passenger seat. When Aug entered, she hit him with a "You're not a very nice man, are you?" He found it exasperating. What had he done? She looked like Mount St. Helens ready to blow with her arms folded across her chest and a mean visage on her face. "So where are we going to have a drink?"

He drove out of the parking lot onto Danny Wuerffel Way and then onto the Emerald Coast Parkway. "I was thinking, maybe, Baytowne Village. It's not too far, and maybe the security will keep out the goon squad."

Angel smelled the air in the car. She rolled down a car window. "PU!" she said. "What have you been doing in here? God, don't you even know how to take care of a car?"

Aug wondered to himself. Should he tell Angel what he had done in here? "Well, well, don't you have a keen sense of smell," he said.

"I told you I actually do have an accelerated sense of smell" was her dry reply. "And I swear that you smell worse than this car does!" Aug laughed.

His cell phone rang. The Suicidal Tendencies ringtone told him who it was. The phone was answered. "Talk to me." There was a pause while he listened and then picked up the Caddy in the rearview mirror. "Got it. Whatareya thinkin'?" He listened. "South Sandestin . . . got it."

Angel asked, "What's at South Sandestin?" What's all that about?"

Aug slowed his speed down considerably and hung out in the right-hand lane. "Ya know, those shoes of yours kinda hurt. When you go to buy shoes, do you beat up the salespeople with them to see if you like the pair?" He kept his eyes on the rearview and the traffic up ahead. There were four golf courses and condo housing developments to be passed. The speed limit was forty-five, and he was slower than that, which pissed off the Friday-evening traffic.

"Don't you change the subject on me! What did you mean by South Sandestin? Who were you talking to?" She turned around and looked in the rearview. Cars were moving by rapidly on the left, but a Cadillac was trailing behind them. "Is that car following us? Are you in some sort of trouble? Is this some more of your 'friends'?"

"Want to be let out?" He stopped the car at an intersection. "Here ya go, here's your chance." Horns were honking behind as he held up traffic. He pointed to the street sign. "The road says it's Holiday. Here's your chance to take a holiday."

Angel pouted at him. "Oh, I'm supposed to hop out in the middle of nowhere? And then what am I supposed to do? Walk to my hotel?"

"You could walk, but"—he looked her up and down—"slit that skirt a little more and I'm sure you could earn some cab fare walking up and down the strip here." He made it counting to about finishing two one thousand before the fists started hitting his head and arms. He started driving while fending off her attack. "Hey, stop that. You're gonna cause an accident if you're not careful."

His eyes focused on the rearview mirror. The Caddy sped up with him. The center median disappeared at Casting Lake. Aug stayed in the right lane, speeding up and slowing down intermittently. The Caddy followed his driving patterns.

Angel informed him, "Your driving sucks. Just like your taste in women. Who taught you to drive, your grandfather?"

The light at Sandestin was approaching, and it was green. The street walkers were blinking; he slowed way down past Beach and then floored it as the light turned yellow. The Caddy took off with him. Aug ran the red light. Angel screamed. The Caddy ran the red light behind the Park Avenue, but an F350 came speeding out from Sandestin and T-boned the vehicle. It was a spectacularly loud crash that sent the car windows into pieces everywhere amongst bits of flying metal. Aug looked back and thought, *They really did buy a new toy!*

Aug took a quick right past the intersection into the TOPS'L complex. The TOPS'L complex was a nice tennis resort community rated as one of the top in the country. Aug reached into the glove box and removed a security pass for the complex.

Angel started, "What are we doing here? Are you crazy? What about that accident back there? I thought we were going to Baytowne? Where are you taking me? Why are we at TOPS'L? Where are we going?" The barrage of questions just kept coming.

He spoke his mind. "Will you please just SHUT UP! Goddamn! Must you be so annoying? All I ever said was that we're going to have a drink, remember?"

"Here? This isn't Baytowne?" She backed herself into the passenger door, facing him. "What are you up to, mister?"

"Relax, will ya? And drop the act." He exited the vehicle and looked back at her. "I know who your parents are." The car door was shut. He walked to the condo.

Angel stormed from the vehicle, snidely mimicking Aug. "I know who your parents are. Well, if it isn't Mr. Smarty Pants. If you know who my father is, then what are we doing here?"

"Well," he said as he opened the door, "I thought we might be able to have a drink. Maybe even an uninterrupted drink." They entered the condo. "Make yourself at home. Go ahead. Ransack the place all you want. Search for the jewels. That's what you're supposed to be here for anyway." He looked at her. "It is, isn't it?" He made his way to the kitchen area. "But you won't find them here."

Angel took him up on his offer. She poked around downstairs, in the couches and closets and anywhere she could think of where something might be hidden. When she was done, she headed upstairs.

There was an auto ice dispenser in the fridge and some cocktail glasses with golf ball designs in the cupboard. There was no mixer in the fridge except orange juice and Coca-Cola. He found a bottle of Grey Goose and Jack Daniel's in a cabinet next to a box of Grape-Nuts. He mixed up a Jack and Coke and a screwdriver.

Aug walked back into the living room. There was a ghetto blaster on a shelf there and some CDs lying around. He opened the back of the ghetto blaster where batteries are to be inserted, and he inserted a wadded-up roll of something in gauze. He shut the case and checked out the music selection. Some Billie Holiday was selected and played.

Upstairs, Angel poked around the place. She proceeded to the bedrooms. There was nothing in either one. There were no clothes. There was no suitcase. The beds had not been slept in. There were no toiletries. The sink, shower, and toilet looked clean. They looked unused since their last wash. This was no residence that anyone was staying at. What were they doing here? Why had Aug rented this place? Angel took the time to freshen up and check her face before she went back downstairs.

She returned downstairs to find Aug waiting with a couple of drinks. He asked her, "Screwdriver or Jack and Coke?"

She said, "Screwdriver." She raised the glass to her mouth and then looked at him suspiciously.

"No no no," he said. "There's nothing untoward in it. No GHB or whatever else people spike drinks with these days. I promise."

"Like a promise from you is worth anything," she said.

"Now, what makes you think I'm such a bad guy?" he asked her.

"Oh, let's see," she said. "Number one, you're a double-crosser as a smuggler. Number two, someone has obviously hit you up side the head. Number three, a big Mexican evidently wanted to beat the hell out of you tonight. Number four, you get us chased around by a Cadillac and nearly get us killed in a car accident. Gee! And you wonder why I think you are a bad guy?"

Aug guzzled his drink and said, "Ya know, I'm really not as bad as I may seem. Or maybe I am." He stuck a finger out and pulled her top forward a bit and peeked down. "Hmmm. Not too much of a chest and rather boring lingerie!"

# SLAP! ✋

Angel slapped his finger away and then slapped his face. "Yes, I think you are a bad guy! And you're also a pig too!"

Aug squealed like a pig and wandered off to the kitchen, singing to the song to be given a "pigfoot and a bottle of beer" and came back with a fresh new glassful. "C'mere, I want a dance," he said. "I wantta see how well you can dance."

He walked to her and took her hands. He forced her to dance close to him so he could study her face and eyes. It was a slow "Lover Man" dance. Angel did not like the song. It was too slow. It was too old-man-like. Aug was not impressed with style. Her movements were stiff. She could move her feet and her body, but it was not like bamboo trees bending in the wind. He told her, "You're not a very good dancer."

# SLAP! ✋

Angel was incensed, and she let him know with a slap across the cheek. "If you wanna dance, then we should at least have some real music to dance to!" She broke away from him and went over to the music box. A radio station was found. "If you wanna dance, then we need some dance music." She found what she was looking for. "Don't cha wantta dance with me?" She asked as she started in with the best moves her skirt would allow. To Aug, her movements, while much more fluid, were contrived and boring. He had no desire to join in her self-adulation as she danced around him. Angel chided him as she karaoke'd, "I thought you wanted to dance?"

He thought about Jocelyn. Where was she at this moment? He hadn't heard from her in the last day. His mind wandered as he saw double. Angel was physically there, but Jocelyn was ghost-dancing over her image. He shook his head to clear the cobwebs.

He walked over to the music factory and shut it off. "That's enough of that!" She gave a *Hmmph!* "C'mon, I'll give you a ride back to your car. You've seen what you came here to see, or actually, what you didn't come here to see. It's time to go."

They passed by the wreck being cleaned up on the way out. The car and the truck each had three quarters of their bodies intact and one quarter damaged extensively. They made a set of damaged goods.

The drive was silent with furtive glances back and forth and out the window. Each one was engaged in their own postgame analysis of the evening's events.

Angel suddenly had more questions than she had thought. They arrived back at her vehicle at Destin Commons. She exited the vehicle and leaned her face down into the open car window and asked him, "If you know who my dad is and you know that all I cared about was looking for the jewels, then why bother? Why did you pick me up if you weren't that interested anyway? It can't have been just to insult me."

Aug gave her a pleasant smile. "I was curious. I wanted to have a chance to meet you." He paused and looked forward. "You know, I don't know what you have been told about me. I'm supposed to be Jack's patsy and take the fall, and if I didn't steal the stones, I probably would be dead now. And I don't really want to be dead now." There was another pause, and he looked at her with a pained look in his eyes. "No one probably told you, but to answer your question from earlier, I was married—once. It didn't work out too well. You want to know what happened? Ask Jack Dough. Ask him what happened to Laurie. Ask him what happened to my parents. I betcha he won't want to answer those questions—at least not to you."

She paused and looked at him, thinking about what he said. "What will it take for you to tell me where the gems are?"

Aug answered, "What will it take for you to tell me where the platinum and gold are?" Angel looked at him with a "give me a break" look. "See, I didn't think so. You wanna know where the gems are? I need to know where the metals are. It's that simple." She stood up. He offered her on the way out, "And you can tell Jack to not bother searching my suite. Nothing is there either. And you watch yourself, Angel. Popeye is still out there somewhere. And he may want you more than he wants me."

Angel entered her car. She thought about what Aug said.

# Chapter 23

## Angel

Al Barlas was feeling good about himself. He was now down, so his ego was up. She had been down, and then she had received. It was the quiet before the pillow talk before leaving.

Angel felt less good about herself. She had once again performed her obligations on a man she believed she loved. Well, if nothing else, he was another man who had excited her at first but whom she never really found fulfilling no matter how hard she tried. That final spark was missing. The engine had once again misfired.

They originally met at Heartbeats. She thought he was a great dancer, and he seemed to be so nice. And he bought her flowers and chocolates and things and always had money, and he persistently called her. *I mean*, she thought, *that means love, doesn't it?*

Angel was an attractive petite female with a semi-Southern accent. The accent was semi-Southern because her father had moved to the Nashville area when she was very young. Her father was a Northerner, so his speech was very clear and direct. The surrogate women who helped in her rearing as well as her school life had all sorts of country sound. She developed a muttspeak accent. In some ways, it mirrored her life. Sometimes her words were Northern, and sometimes the words were Southern, but most of the time, it was a blend of both.

There were a few reasons for surrogate mothers, but the primary reason was that her mother had died before the move down South. Dad had some connections, and they moved south. Dad appeared to the public as an independent contractor, but the fact was that he managed some houses for people he knew. This meant that many surrogates appeared from time to time to help take care of the princess at George S. Patton Boulevard. Her father's burning through of adult partners in her formative years made her a somewhat reserved person. She found herself trusting her friends and her friend's families more than she trusted the family she was raised in.

In her teen years, her father informed her that he was moving to the Florida Panhandle for a new business opportunity. Angel's choice was to move to Florida or move in with her girlfriend Vanessa's family and complete high school with her classmates. Vanessa's family lived on an estate in Belle Meade. Belle Meade was a wonderful community where it was illegal for either men or women to go jogging topless in the community. But it was not the wealth of the community that made her decision. The decision was made because both a thirty-seven-year-old man and a thirteen-year-old girl knew that each of them would be happier apart from each other. She felt closer to her friend's parents than she was to her own father. Besides, there had been an insurance policy in her name from her mother, and there was some money that she would have control of upon coming of age. And Dad also kept her supplied with cash.

Since Angel did not have financial needs, she was able to travel. She could spring-break and summer-vacation wherever she wanted. Her path after high school was to get an undergraduate degree in information systems from Belmont. She purchased a new condo in Murfreesboro and moved in. She developed her IS skills working at AmSouth. The work was initially interesting, and the work ethic was there. But she really didn't need the cash, and the Dilbertness of the lower-level work world soon made the job seem like a chore.

Of course, there were boys. She had a steady in high school and a different one for college. Angel was an attractive young woman of some means, and that meant that there was no shortage of wolves to deal with. She watched her friends get married, and some of them rapidly divorce, and she saw them fight and argue with their spouses. Her girlfriends pontificated to her about how things have to be and what one is supposed to do with men. Angel's and her girlfriend's perspective of men and relationships were fed by one another and inputs such as *Cosmo* and TV. She felt a need for a relationship, but she had to have a male to say that she had one. This was very important, but it was also unfulfilling. Like this evening when she kind of enjoyed the sex, but she always felt more fulfilled by herself than with the men she tried to enjoy. It was all very unfulfilling.

And here she was with Al. He was a pharmaceutical salesperson, and he had to hit the road early tomorrow, so he would be leaving shortly. She was feeling old. She was twenty-five and going nowhere. She had done her duty, and she felt unsatisfied. The problem was that she just didn't know what to do about it.

He was clothed and ready to go. Angel put on a robe and followed Al downstairs. He hugged her. He smiled at her. He kissed her. He looked in her eyes and said, "I'm sorry I gotta go. I love you, baby. I'll call you from the road, but I gotta be in Memphis before noon tomorrow." He looked at his watch. "I mean today!" Al smiled at her. "It won't be long. I'll be back in a couple days, and we'll go out somewhere. OK?"

Angel smiled and said, "OK."

Al kissed her and said, "That's my girl. Now I gotta go. Kiss me once for the road." She did. Al opened the door to leave.

There was a tall brunette at the door. She had a look of fury on her face. She looked in his eye and coldly said, "You bastard!" She took a wedding ring off her finger and threw it in his face. The ring bounced off Al and rolled behind the door.

Al had a look of surprise on his face. It was the look of "How did I get caught?" Angel saw the look and knew that she was a sap. She was just a good time. Angel simultaneously felt empty, mad, and cheap. She had been used.

The brunette continued, "This is the last time. You're not getting in the house tonight! You can just stay here with your latest bitch, and you can get your divorce papers in the morning!" She stormed off to the parking lot.

Al forgot about Angel. He reached around the door and grabbed the ring and took off after the brunette. He was calling for her, "Suzette! Baby! Wait!" Suzette disappeared around a brick wall that led to the parking lot. Al ran after her. Angel stepped into the doorway to go see what would happen. Tears started to fill her eyes.

Al started to make the corner, and two large gentlemen appeared and grabbed his arms and hustled him to the wall. Al became angry. "Hey! What the fuck! Let me go! Who the hell do you think you are!"

Angel stepped out of the door to walk down and see what was happening. A third man came into Angel's view.

# POW! POW! POW!

The man wound up and delivered three powerful rights into Al's gut. The blows obviously hurt Al. A hand went up and grabbed Al's head. "Shut up, mister, and listen good. You're a married man, see?" There were a couple more powerful punches to the midsection. "That's supposed to mean something, see?" There were a couple more powerful punches to the midsection. "It means you don't stick your dick where it doesn't belong!" There were a couple more punches to the midsection and then one to the jaw. Al slumped down from the beating.

The man picked up Al's head and told him, "You stay away from this little girl from now on, ya here me? No calls, no contact, no anything. Ya got that? Yer dick don't belong here!" The director looked at the guy holding the left arm. The arm was rotated so that the hand was exposed. The director held up a wedding ring and said, "Here, we found your ring for ya. It's time you wore it."

The ring finger was exposed, and the ring was forced on. Then Angel watched in shock as the finger was bent backward as far as it would go. Al realized what was happening and started yelling, "NO! Please NO!" Angel felt she could hear the phalange bones snap as she watched them bend Al's finger all the way back until it snapped and the fingernail touched the back of the hand. Al screamed in pain with the break. The men proceeded to drag him away. It was the last Angel ever saw or heard of Al.

Angel staggered back to her condo. She shut the door and locked it. She was shaking from what she had just witnessed. She had no idea what was going on. She leaned back against the door and slowly sank down to the ground. She started crying. She was confused. She felt she should do something, but what was there to do?

After a while, she started to regain her composure. She started to stand up when she heard the voice say, "Now, now, are you feeling better, Angel?" She was startled, and her bare feet slipped on the wooden floor, and she crashed down on her bottom. She hit her head on the door. Her eyes looked around the room. Her father, Mr. John Campbell, was in the room.

"You bastard," she said. "I should have known. Those were your playthings out there, weren't they?" She stood up. "What are you doing here? What were they doing here? Is this your idea of a joke? Bringing Al's wife here?"

The tone of his voice came off as fatherly. It was compassionate and sad. "Is carrying on an affair with a married man your idea of a joke?"

"I didn't know he was married," she spat out.

"No," he said. He spoke both softly and sternly. "No, I know you didn't know he was married. And that's the saddest thing of all. It's sad that my daughter is spending her time being made a fool of by some guy just out to get his willie wet. I mean, really, it'd be one thing if it were the president of the United States or the president of AmSouth or, hell, the president of something worthwhile, but this guy? This guy had nothing going for him. With how many times he's cheated on his wife, he won't have anything left when divorce court is through. And you won't get anything out of it either."

She glared at her father. "Oh, what do you know! And since when do you really care who I spend my time with! I seem to recall there were quite a few women that you enjoyed when I was growing up! Don't even tell me that you never cheated on Mother when she was alive! You enjoyed your time with all those women a hell of a lot more than you enjoyed your time with me! What the hell gives you the right to come in here and tell me who to sleep with! Talk about nerve!"

John's face reflected sadness. "Ya know, you are oh so right," he said. "I do have a lot of nerve to come here and . . . and . . . and . . . well, try and lecture you. I'm sorry, and I'll be the first to admit that I have no right to come here and do that. But you are my daughter and . . . well . . . ya know . . . I turned fifty last year, and I started to ask myself things like what I regretted in life, and the thing I found I regretted the most is not having a real relationship with my daughter." He paused and then continued, "I'm sorry about that, and I'd like to make better of things. So in preparation of talking to you, I decided to discreetly find out what my daughter was up to. I found out that this guy was a multi-timing Romeo. And it bothered me to see this guy make a fool of you, so I made a decision that this would not continue."

Angel seethed, "YOU! You made a decision?" She laughed and walked around to a couch. She took a seat facing him. "I'm twenty-five, Daddy! Thank you for caring so much, but I am fully capable of taking care of myself and making my own decisions. Just like I have my whole life!"

John smiled at Angel. "I know you have, Angel, and you've made me very proud of you. I'm the one who's ashamed. I'm the one who has been the cad."

Angel sat in silence, thinking. She narrowed her eyes. "This isn't about Al at all, is it? You've got something else on your mind, don't you?"

"Yes, I do. You know me well," John replied. "What I've got on my mind is this: I want you to come to Florida and learn and eventually take over the family business. I want to make sure that my daughter has a pleasant life of her own and the freedom she deserves. I want my daughter to find real happiness in life."

Angel was very surprised by this statement. "Let me get this straight. You want me to learn to be a crook. Is that what you are saying?"

"Angel, dear," John said, "not everything I am involved in is illegal. Sure, there are some aspects of the business that are illicit, but there are many legitimate enterprises that we are now involved in down there. Heck, I haven't even run a cathouse in years!"

John continued, "You know what, Angel? I now have it made in life. I now have a decent amount of wealth and a mansion and . . . well, hell, I have goons at my disposal who can beat the tar out of creeps like Al. I've made it to a point where I have just about everything I want. I never had all of that before. The one thing I don't have is my family. The one thing I don't have is a positive relationship with my daughter. I regret that. I can't change the past, but I would like to change the future."

After a pause for reflection, John continued, "In many ways, you'd be your own boss. And wouldn't that be better than kissing butt at the bank here? I mean, how long do you plan on doing that? I'd like to offer you a life where you can choose your own destiny, to be your own person. I'd like an opportunity to patch up our relations and provide for you the things I never did. I'd like the opportunity to get to know my daughter. What do you say? Hmmm?"

Angel was suspicious. Her father never did anything without a plan. They talked about the possibility. They talked until the sun was rising. In the end, she agreed to move to a new destiny.

# CHAPTER 24

## NEVER TRUST ANYONE

Angel had a thoughtful drive back to Daddy's residence on Burnt Pine. The evening had not gone as planned. She had accomplished less than she had set out to do. Mr. Valentine seemed to be one step ahead of her. She was confused by what she had heard and seen. She was paranoid she was being followed.

The code was entered to open the gate to the driveway. She drove her Xterra along the house as the gate closed behind her. She parked outside the open garage next to the Taurus in the drive. There was company at the residence.

She walked past a Cadillac and entered through the house through a garage door. She came in past the wine room and then through the spacious kitchen. She passed into the den. It was a surprise to her to see the back porch smashed up. Glass was strewn about. What had happened here?

She walked down the hall to the study that doubled as Dad's office. The game room was passed along the way. Chuck and Father were in the office. She heard them discussing something about the shipments. They were both surprised to see Angel appear.

Jack asked, "Hello, Angel. What are you doing here?" He looked at his watch; he looked at his phone. He looked at Chuck. He looked at Angel.

"Hello, Chuck. Hello, Dad. Maybe I have nowhere else to go tonight?" she said. "Nice porch, Dad. Doing some redecorating?"

"Consider it a new method of hurricane preparation, Angel" was Jack's reply.

Chuck stood up and offered a "Hello, Angel."

Angel looked at him. "Hello, Chuck. What are you doing here? Did you come here to personally put my daddy in the slammer? You are such a pip, aren't you! Isn't it a little late in the evening for this sort of work? On a Friday night? You must be getting good overtime pay. W's gotta love the idea that his government employees are working oh so diligently! What's the matter? Can't wait a couple more days before hauling Dad away?" She looked at her father. "I'm sure he can't wait!"

Chuck offered a "Now, Angel. Be reasonable about this. Your father is. He's offering himself up so that nothing bad happens to you. And this is all being done very discreetly so there isn't any mud in the press or any issues there. Compared to what normally happens in cases like this, you're gonna hardly notice what happens!"

Angel dryly replied, "Rigggghhhhtttt. You are just oh so concerned about us that you are just doing everything in such a PC manner. Why, Chuck, I do declare! You are just such a gentleman! I never realized what a big heart you have!"

Chuck grabbed his valise and looked at Angel and Jack. "Jack, it's been a pleasant evening, but I think, on that note, I will take my leave. I can find my own way out." He walked to the doorway and turned. "Until we meet again."

Jack stood up and walked with Chuck to make sure that he left. Angel followed them out into the den area. She looked around the house at the Mediterranean motif. Somehow it looked more Médician than she remembered.

Jack came back. "Now will you tell me what the hell you're doing here? You're supposed to be up in Mr. Valentine's suite finding some missing gems. What, are you losing your charm? And what the hell was that all about insulting Chuck like that?"

Angel resignedly said, "You're right, Dad. I'm sure that spending Friday evening babbling with Mr. John Law is how you wanted to spend tonight. I thought you would appreciate my getting rid of him for you, especially knowing how busy the next couple days will be."

Jack smiled. "Angel, you're right. I owe you an apology on that one. Now tell me, dear, what happened with Mr. Valentine? Wasn't he interested in anything he saw?"

Angel said, "Well, I guess not. I guess he wasn't that interested in bedding me. And we didn't go to his suite. He's got a condo over at TOPS'L that we went to, although it looks like no one has stayed there. I went through that place, and there was nothing there, and he also said to tell you that the stones aren't in his hotel room either. I believe he was telling me the truth. Call it woman's intuition."

Jack was intrigued by this. "Really?"

She said, "Yes, and he also knew I was your daughter. And he told me to ask you about his wife and his parents. It was like I was expected. I felt like an idiot." She paused. "So you tell me. What am I supposed to be told about his wife and his parents?"

Jack thought about his answer. "He's full of shit. He' fishing, and he's trying to use you as bait."

Angel asked, "Really?" She thought about it. "I'm not really sure who is doing the fishing around here now."

"Angel!" Jack said in a surprised manner. "What is that supposed to mean?"

"What it means, Daddy-o, is that when I moved down here to learn the business, I didn't anticipate either you asking me to have sex with cronies for your benefit or that you would be getting busted," she explained. "Now? Now I'm not sure what to think."

"Angel," Jack said, "it's all part of the risk of being a crook. You never know when your time may come, and you have to be prepared and always keep ahead of things."

"Really?" she asked. "If that's true then how did you get caught?" She paused and thought about it. "Or did you get caught?" She walked over to the broken french door and played with it. She turned and looked at him and spoke. "I thought you told me the first rule of business is to never trust anyone. I don't seem to recall the exit-plan lesson coming in."

Jack was wondering where she was going with her train of thought. "I did tell you that the first order of business is to not trust anyone."

She looked at the smashed window. Angel mused, "Then maybe all that broken glass isn't broken dreams. Maybe the glass isn't broken after all. Maybe the panes of glass are still in the window. Maybe they are still here, and it's just me who can't see or feel them?" Angel ran her fingers over a jagged piece of glass still in the jamb. She turned and looked at him with narrowed eyes. "They are, aren't they?"

"Angel," he said, "I'm really tired tonight. It was a long hot day on the course today, and it has been a long night of negotiations, and you know as well as I do that the next two days are going to be exceptionally busy. We've both got a long night ahead of us tomorrow. I need to get some sleep, and I suggest that you do the same. We can talk about this later when we have more time. OK?"

"Sure, Daddy," she said. "Whatever you say." She looked at the broken door, and she swung it open and shut a few times. "We can always talk about this later."

# CHAPTER 25

## OOPS

Greg Czarnacki entered his office in a very good mood. The main deal was now cut. It was time to start his final phase of involvement. He had spoken with Thomas White, and Mr. White appeared to be pleased with the manner in which things were winding up.

Starting Monday, Greg and his staff could proceed with setting up arraignments and plea bargains and the like. He had set up his supplemental retirement fund. Soon he could get back to a life with his wife and children. There would be some delay because of the expected damage from the storm coming up the Gulf, but how bad could that affect things? It was the kind of morning that required a treat. Since he had to fill up with gas, he also picked up a cup of creamy cappuccino from the convenience store. It cost much less than a Starbucks, and it tasted better anyway.

He was meeting with his staff. There were four of them. Two accountants handled the bank side, and two lawyers handled the legal issues. The accountants were John Flack and Tom Welsh. The lawyers were Joe Wisz and Katrina Hartman.

He started, "Good news, everyone! We can move to the next phase of operations. Jack Dough has agreed to his plea agreement. We can organize the shutdown of the office of Destin Dreams and the White Sands Bank as well as the

Philly office of the Pseftikos Fund. It's going to take some heavy coordination the next couple of days. In case you've been working way too hard recently, something I highly doubt, you've undoubtedly heard that Hurricane Bill is projected to make landfall at Panama City in a few days. It looks like we've got maybe a couple days to secure the office here and documents before the storm hits."

The response to the announcement was underwhelming. The staff had an unenthused look. Greg was surprised. "Well, doesn't everyone get so excited about this. A hurricane is a big deal, but it's not the end of the world. It's been a long eighteen months since we started here."

The staff looked at each other and then at Greg. John Flack spoke up, "That's not it. The storm's not the issue. We've . . . ah . . . we've got a-another problem."

Greg was surprised to hear this. "Oh. OK, so we've got another problem. Would someone like to educate me as to the nature of this problem?"

The staff looked at each other and then back at Greg. He was starting to get a little concerned. This was unusual behavior. John spoke up again. "It looks like . . ." he sighed. "It looks like they looted the bank."

Greg spoke slowly. "They . . . looted . . . the . . . bank. Great. Now what the hell does that mean? Can one of you explain that to me? What the hell are you talking about?"

Tom Welsh chimed in, "They looted the White Sands Bank. There were a series of wire transfers of cash out of the country preset in a cascading manner that routed through a series of countries. We're still trying to track down what actually occurred, but it looks like a lot of cash was sent outside of White Sands and outside of the US, and we don't really know where it is. The bottom line is . . . the bank is probably teetering on insolvency."

Greg could not believe what he was hearing. "What do you mean there were a series of wire transfers set up? You guys were in the bank, weren't you? After See and Marshall died a couple weeks ago, you guys have been camping there. Hell. You've been monitoring bank activities for a year now." Greg leaned across his desk and looked at each person in the eyes. "Are you telling me that someone pulled a fast one right under your noses? Just who the hell is this, this *they* you keep mentioning?" Silence was the answer. Greg pounded his fist on his desk. "WELL? ANSWER ME!"

His staff all looked at each other. John spoke. "Uh . . . yeah . . . well . . . uh . . . it kinda looks like that is what happened. It looks like Patrick See and Arthur Marshall set this up before they died. The transfers seem to extend back a week ago. As senior executives at the bank, they don't have any direct authority to approve cash transfers to avoid something like this happening, but none of the staff there made the transfers. Neither did any customers. The transactions appear to have originated from the Marshall and See terminals. We're not exactly sure yet what happened. It's gonna take more time to figure this out. Someone planted a program that started wiping out records in the database. Once we started to trace transactions, it triggered the virus to destroy database records, so we had to stop what we were doing and engage in damage control. We've got some IS help on the way. We've got tracers going with the foreign banks, but this looks like embezzlement."

Greg was not pleased. "You're kidding me. And just what kind of embezzlement are we talking about? How much money is missing?"

Katrina spoke up, "Two, maybe three."

Greg answered, "Two, maybe three what? Million?"

Katrina replied, "Um . . . hundreds. Hundreds of millions."

Greg jumped up out of his chair. "HUNDREDS OF MILLIONS? Let me get this straight! You're telling me that the dead guys who ran the bank embezzled two to three hundred million from the bank right under your noses while you were there watching the candy store?" He closed his eyes in disbelief. "How the hell could this happen? What the hell were you doing? Where were your controls? Weren't you looking at the big transfers? Do you have any answers?"

Tom spoke. "Here's what we know. The transfers were from account holders' accounts and look like the account holder authorized them. But the account holders didn't make the transfers. In every situation we looked at, the IS system says the money is in the account, so the accounting looks correct, but the bank does not appear to have the cash. This is supposed to be impossible to happen. The authorization code system is isolated from the operational side. There is supposed to be constant account balancing. Someone had to breach the systems; this was coordinated by multiple people. This had to have been in the works for a while."

Greg spit out, "And you don't know the extent of the damage?"

John answered, "We're doing the forensic accounting now, but . . . uh . . . yeah . . . that's what it looks like right now. It only came to light now because it is the end of the month, and there is a close coming up. Whoever did this knew what they were doing. The accounting system looked like it was balancing fine, but once the month-end processing started in, the system started crashing, and a whole series of unseen transactions started appearing. Someone was very slick designing this. Once we started to request some queries and reports to be run against the database so that we could track transactions, the request for the queries and reports kicked off some dormant programs that had been planted that started eating data in both the primary and mirror systems. We had to shut the system down and now have to proceed very slowly or else we could lose even more data. We're looking at restoring files from hard data file storage, but that carries other headaches like accounting for what occurred since the backup was created. Whoever set this up envisioned a lot and hid a lot of bombs that somehow went undetected in the network."

Greg slumped back in his chair. "What you're telling me is that we've been played. That's it, isn't it?" He thought a minute. He moved his body back over the desk. "You said the bank is insolvent? Did I hear you right?"

Tom answered, "White Sands may be insolvent. We think so, but we really can't tell. I would recommend bringing in FDIC now, but that's not our call. The state regulating board will have to make that call unless creditors bring action first. Since no one really knows what we are looking at, then the business of paying creditors will probably be delayed a little while everyone tries to figure out what is real and what is not real. And while White Sands had quite a substantial cash reserve on the books and since no one really knows what is real, then it may survive this. But right now I am thinking . . . um . . . no."

Greg sat back and thought a while. His staff fidgeted and looked at each other. Greg spoke. "So let me see if this makes sense. Even though Justice was in the bank overseeing the wire transfers, the auditors will still take the fall because they are the ones who are supposed to ensure that proper bank controls are in place. Is that correct?"

The staff looked at each other. Joe Wisz spoke. "Well, that is a possibility. It's very hard to say how this will play out. The issue is that there are multiple government and nongovernment entities that were involved with the bank at the time of the fraud. There will be a lot of finger-pointing between entities to assign the blame for the failure in oversight, and this could take some time to unravel. It is hard to predict just how this will play out."

Joe continued, "My opinion is that there are two key factors that will determine how this plays out. The first factor is where does the evidentiary trail lead? What criminal acts can be determined to have been perpetuated by whom? The second factor is how long does this take to play out? There is little doubt in my mind that there will be a spate of very unpleasant press in the beginning. But the longer this drags out, the less ultimate pain in the end. Time heals a lot wounds, you know. I think that it is fair to assume that no parties involved are going to come out of this looking good."

Greg leaned back again and thought some more. He looked at his staff and spoke deliberately, "I want to make sure I got this straight. What you are telling me is two dead men who didn't have the authority to do so executed a whole series of cash transfers that sent an undetermined amount of cash out of White Sands. They did this under your noses, and they also beat bank regulators and auditors, also whatever other internal operational, audit, and IT controls were in place. And to make sure that things were harder to track, the dead men placed viruses that they probably weren't computer savvy enough to write. Is that what you are expecting me to swallow?"

His staff looked at each other and then back at Greg. Joe spoke. "We know. It doesn't seem either possible or plausible to us either. Yet right now, that is the best that we can determine what happened."

Greg eyed each staff member carefully. "No," he said. "No, it doesn't seem possible."

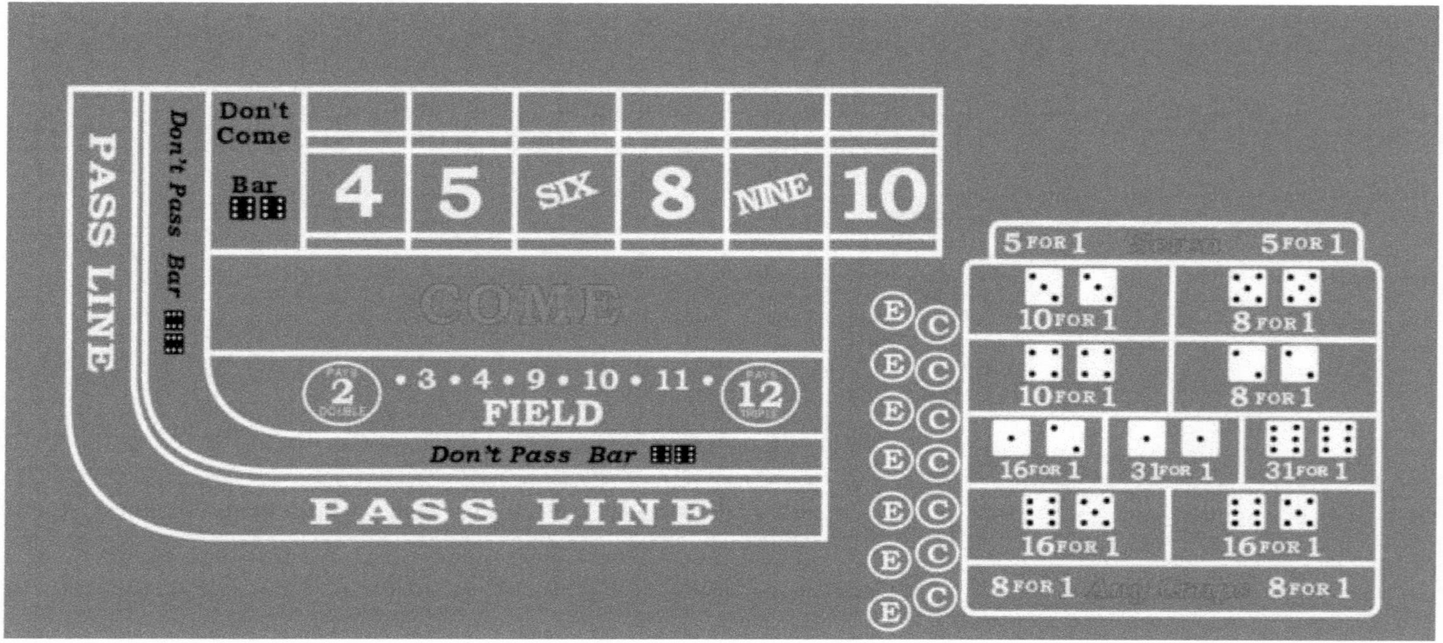
PASS LINE
Don't Pass Bar
Don't Come
Bar
4
5
SIX
8
NINE
10
COME
2
• 3 • 4 • 9 • 10 • 11 •
12
FIELD
Don't Pass Bar
PASS LINE
E
C
5 FOR 1
5 FOR 1
10 FOR 1
8 FOR 1
10 FOR 1
8 FOR 1
16 FOR 1
31 FOR 1
31 FOR 1
16 FOR 1
16 FOR 1
8 FOR 1
8 FOR 1

# CHAPTER 26

## SNAKE EYES

The condemned man always likes the finest of everything. Who cares what price there is to pay when you are already condemned? This feeling had driven Aug to let the presidential suite at the Hilton Sandestin. He didn't really need the full dining room to seat ten or the full kitchen. The giant bed was nice and so was the in-room spa. He just wished he had been given the real opportunity to enjoy it more.

The day was spent with e-mails and messages. He spoke to Jocelyn. She was on her way back to Florida. Her father would be OK. Aug told her he loved her and that he would contact her in a couple days when things calmed down. It would all be over soon. The spa looked very inviting after the call.

The view of the Gulf of Mexico was spectacular. From the sixteenth floor, he could see miles of turquoise water. Today he saw hundreds of boats. A smile crossed his face. There were boats and yachts from thirty to one hundred twenty feet in length. Ferries ran back and forth from the watercraft and a large staging party raft to the beach along a water-access corridor. PWCs were getting airborne off the waves. Children and parents and pets swam in the Gulf of Mexico. Various news agencies' cameras and crews reported on the scene.

The hundred yards of white sand covering the beach from the waterfront to wooden paths that access the parking lot were almost obliterated from Aug's view by the sea of humans covering them. Volleyball was being played. Footballs and Frisbees were thrown. Other beach games were played. Sand sculptures were being created. Parasols dotted the shore.

Stepping out on the balcony and tasting the sea air, he could hear the band playing below. A temporary stage had been erected, fronting the sands from which the musical entertainment flowed. Manchild was on stage. Their jazzy sound was melodic and soothing. The people on the boats were oblivious to realities of the world. Sure, most of them undoubtedly knew that a war is ongoing in Iraq, but who here really cared today? It was a day to have fun.

The Iraq war thought made Aug chuckle. The United States has hundreds of military bases around the globe in over fifty different countries, but no one in the United States protests any location around the globe except for one. The logic was funny to him. It's OK to have bases around the globe and have people in the military, just as long as they aren't in a place that is a combat zone. At that point, it is not OK. It's OK to be a soldier and have a job that entails the realities of the risk of death and dismemberment or other casualties such as separation from family, just as long as you never have to face those risks in a combat zone. That's the beauty of the USA. One can still say whatever you want without fear of a bayonet in the belly. Too bad the rest of the world isn't all so free of such combat. Well, Aug was heading for a combat zone. His combat zone just wasn't military in nature.

His mind came back to what he saw before him. Poseidon's was below him. If he had a sixteen-story playground slide, he could have slid right down to the roof of the building. Various coral reef displays, complete with reef dwellers, covered the four walls of the building. The reef formed the name of Poseidon on three sides of the building in three different scripts. The glass sky lighting rose from Poseidon's and sparkled like a diamond in the sun. He imagined that from the boats, it looked like a glittering jewel on the roof, reflecting sunlight. Periodically programmed colored light beams would project through, and the gem would change colors or go multicolored. The prism of Poseidon. Aug could envision how beautiful it would shine at nightfall when the coral reefs lit up.

The mind of Aug wandered again. It wandered back a year. He remembered Hurricanes Charlie, Frances, Ivan, and Jeanne. He looked at the jewel and thought about the shuttering job that lay ahead now that Hurricane Bill was building in the Gulf. The storm was projected to hit Panama City, and that was close enough to Sandestin to potentially cause major damage. There was no way building permits would have been issued without a shuttering plan, but there were so much angled glass and so many large glass panes that hurricane shuttering of Poseidon's must be a daylong project to accomplish.

It was opening day and night for Poseidon's, and all the stops had been pulled out. Golf carts ferried land participants back and forth from the parking areas under the watchful eyes of security. A daylong free full feast for everyone was set up. The sand sculpture competition themed around the concept of Poseidon was visible from his room. There were clown acts and magicians roving the beach, bringing joy to children and adults. Police and security patrolled the beach area. It was casino day and night inside Poseidon's. Tonight was to be topped off with a massive fireworks display. It was to be an incredible grand opening for all. It was a temporary magical mini-Atlantis for a day rising up against the ocean.

Augustus had been to Atlantis before. He had been at Atlantis on a Saturday night. The particular Atlantis in memory was the one located in Nassau in the Bahamas. It had been a year ago. The night he had been there was a magical night.

He had been dressed very nicely. He wore a fine Italian red silk shirt with tasteful ruffling that had set him back quite a few c's. His Brioni pants were tan and tapered. They fit his tall, slender frame perfectly. Jocelyn's outfit had cost him good coin. Her white deep-back Mugler dress centered on the waist with a beautiful diamond-fold design. When she bent over the table to roll the dice, she made sure to lean forward so that everyone would watch the tumble.

Jocelyn was magically rolling. Most times that they had gone to a craps table, they had blown a thousand or less but had enjoyed doing so, and they did not always lose. But their gambling was for entertainment. For Aug and Jocelyn, the cost may have been different, but the enjoyment was the same as the enjoyment of visiting a fine restaurant or the movies or theater or museum. It was an event to entertain. It was the enjoyment of both love and loving time with each other.

They didn't keep track except in their heads, but the times they had lost probably outweighed the times they had won. Well, that was why he had an investment in casino stocks anyway. In the end, the house will probably win.

Tonight was the night to get their money back and more. The dice had been in her hands for forty minutes, which meant a few different things. One thing it meant was that it now took five minutes or so for the table jockeys to pay off any roll. There were at least a hundred bets stacked all across the table. Another thing that this meant was that the locusts had flocked to the table. The table and the area around the table was packed, and the smoke was pouring from cigars and cigarettes. The booze was being poured into the patrons because the tips were good and the casino wanted happy drunks who would gamble back their winnings.

Jocy was at the end of the table, rolling the full length of the carpet. She had muscle, and the dice were thrown with force. There was no limp wrist in her body.

Aug looked around and saw that people were stacked three deep, trying to get a slot. Since everyone was sardined, there was little elbow room. This meant that Jocelyn had plenty of wiggle room. She was wiggling herself into Aug at every opportunity.

Many women scream and giggle at a craps table when any good number is rolled, but that was not Jocelyn's style upon rolling a good number. Jocelyn seductively smiled and rubbed her hands and body against her lover. She was pounding Zombies to his Woodford Reserve. At the start, she had given him a peck on the cheek for luck for every roll. Now she had graduated to a full mouth display. Aug was surprised that the table was not levitating off the ground from the men standing there.

Not everyone at the table was male. There were some couples in attendance. George and Gracie Burns were there. So were Golda Meir and Shimon Peres. At least the gamblers reminded Aug of those historical figures. Mixed in were some schoolkids who were there who had little to bet with and were embarrassing themselves amongst the rest of the money flowing. There were more singles and couples around the table who might normally be reserved, but tonight they were cheering with every roll. There were some happy Arabs and some emotional Arabs living and dying on each roll as they bet the farm, looking for a big kill. Edgar Allan Poe seemed to be at the table standing next to some big black guys who looked like they had been NFL linemen.

Everyone's eyes went from Jocelyn's cleavage to her hands to the roll as she bent over and rolled and rolled again. "Hard ten" was the call. "Fifty-five! The point is made! The lovely lady rolled a hard ten!" The table roared in approval. Jocelyn could not resist smiling into Aug's eyes and exclaiming quiet enough for only Aug to hear but loud enough for most of the table to hear, "MMMMMMMM, a hard ten, one of my favorite numbers"

Jocelyn was playing heavy on numbers and hardways. She had a two-hundred-dollar pass and max odds and a fifty-dollar hardway. Jocelyn pulled in twenty-five hundred, but he was so busy with his own bets and thoughts he couldn't really follow what she was doing.

Aug was in lust, so he was hard to think about his winnings, but he needed to. His tray was filled with black hundreds with a few purple fives. Both of them had been betting heavy tonight.

Aug played a come-bet strategy. The come bets were odds maxed at a fifty-dollar base with a century riding maxed on the pass line and another quarter each on the hardways. Jocelyn had been rolling hard number after hard number, and he had been pressing up against her. It had paid off well so far. Now he raked in a grand from his odds and another hundred from the pass, as well as another two and a quarter from the hardways.

He needed insurance on the come-out roll. It was time to go for a bigger kill. There was three hundred dollars of come bets to protect. He called his hardways off, left a hundred on the pass, hopped the sevens for fifty each, and laid a two-hundred-dollar horn. The table had seen him bet this strategy already tonight, and they were now comfortable with how to set up his bets.

Jocelyn kissed him and rolled a seven. The table erupted in cheers. Free money was continuing. This got him seven fifty plus a hundred on the pass, but he needed to spend three hundred to stay up on his bets plus another three hundred to stay up on his come bets. He netted two hundred and fifty. Aug kicked in another hundred and pressed up across the board against her. Jocelyn kissed him and rolled another seven. Another explosion of cheers came out.

The table workers had to lay out everything on the felt, not only for the camera to see, but also so that they could figure out what the payout was. His payout was fifteen hundred for the three-way seven plus another c for the pass.

It cost nine to stay up across the board. Aug kicked in the balance to press fully across the board. Jocelyn kissed him and rolled an eleven. The crowd around the table couldn't believe it. Delirium reigned.

The croupiers laid out the payoff again. Aug got three g's for the horn plus another hundred for the pass. It would cost twelve hundred to stay up. He was looking at a nineteen net. He looked at the smiling Jocelyn. She couldn't continue to do it, could she? It was destined to end at some point. The decision was painful. Shit, what to do! Aug figured, *What the hell? I'm here to gamble!* He pressed another hundred each on the sevens and on each of the horn numbers and trayed twelve hundred. The dice were passed to Jocelyn.

She turned and kissed him for luck. With her one free hand, she was somewhat indiscreetly rubbing him. "For good luck," she said, "this one's for you." It was good luck. She did roll for him. Boxcars came up.

Double sixes are a one-in-thirty-six possibility. The portion of Aug's horn bet relating to this roll paid thirty to one. This worked out to nine grand. Well, it was nine grand less the pass-line bet and horn balance and the hopped sevens. The pit bosses shook their heads in dismay. The croupiers were wowed by the action. The college students were bummed because their pass line lost, and they did not understand what was going on. The experienced crapsters who were watching the spectacle vociferously cheered. Some of them had also hit on horn bets. Aug's head was swimming. All he could manage was a stunned look at Jocelyn and a quiet "You did it!"

Her return smile slayed him. Her bets were on numbers, so the roll really didn't affect her, but she knew what Aug was betting. Jocelyn asked Aug, "What are you going to do, big boy?" She leaned her back against him, slinking her talents. "Are you going to ride me, or are you going to press me?" The accenting of the verbs with her physique left no question in his mind. Aug had to press.

It cost him nineteen to stay up. His boxcar take to the tray was seven grand. He pressed fourteen hundred of it in so that every number bet was at a neat five hundred. One-tenth as neat as the five thousand he had just picked up. His tray had colorful chips, and Jocelyn had *Brass In Pocket*.

The dice were issued. Jocelyn's kiss was issued. The chanting and cheering from the crowd descended into silence as the dice flowed from her fingers. The roll was ogled. The dice hit the back wall cushion. One die came up a three. The other die popped into the air. It popped out of the table and bounced off the crowd and under the table beyond. Fifty voices in unison sounded like a roaring gryphon, yelling, "SAME DICE!"

The die was eventually found, and it was returned to the table boss for examination. She slowly rolled it around in her fingers looking for a flaw. The boss looked at the crowd and said, "This die is fake. It is no good." The participants of the game screamed in anger with many outrageous comments. The pit boss laughed and placed the die back on the table. "Just kidding!" she loudly stated in a controlling voice. "I was just kidding, everyone! The lady is good to go!" She laughed to herself. Some of the gamblers looked like they had just peed in their clothing.

Many participants took the break time to drink a lot of alcohol. The dice were issued to Jocelyn. The kiss was issued to Aug. The deep lean over the table occurred. Lungs were filled with air. Jocelyn rolled, and one die came up a three. The second die spun on end. All eyes were intent. It spun like a top. The die seemed to take an eternity to stop turning. Eventually it did. The second die came up a four. Air-filled lungs were expelled with vehement exultation. Jocelyn had done it again.

For Aug, the value of the seven at fifteen to one for a five-hundred-dollar bet was seventy-five hundred. It would cost three grand to stay up plus another three hundred to pay for the come bets. His net was forty-two hundred plus the pass line hundred. It took a while for the pit crew to figure out what to do for the whole table and specifically for Aug's bets. There were too many unusual calculations for the croupiers to do it fast.

A heckler began complaining about the length of time it was taking to pay the bets. Various vociferous voices violently and virulently and venomously victimized the vagrants.

The booze in Aug and the excitement of the situation, as well as the tantalizing enjoyment Jocelyn provided, took over. He had an excellent vision of Jocelyn bending over the table and having a go for all to see. A euphoric god feeling filled him. He whispered in her ear, "Mmmmm, drinking makes me soooo horny." She let out a very delighted squeal.

He pressed up two hundred on each number so that every bet was at a neat seven hundred. He did the math. He had five thousand of bets on this roll, and it could all disappear in a second. This may not be a lot to either professional gamblers or whales, but it seemed to be a whale of a bet for Aug to be risking on a single roll of the dice. He did the math in his tray. He had already pocketed about eight thou on the come-out rolls. If he pulled his bets, he could have another five, and his take would be thirteen. He wondered what he was doing still betting. Jocelyn had hit five numbers for him in a row. It just couldn't continue. He should cut and run.

Aug looked at Jocelyn in glazed amazement and enjoyment. He knew then that if he cut and ran on her at this moment while she was rolling, with the dice in her hands, no matter how many material things he bought her with that five grand, Jocelyn would literally rip his dick off out of anger for his lack of trust in her. The dice were issued to Jocelyn. The kiss was issued to Aug. The deep lean over the table occurred. On drunken impulse, Aug grabbed a purple and two blacks from his tray and threw them on the table and exclaimed, "Press the sevens one each and the horn four," which was echoed back as "Seven three four horn pressure." Jocelyn's smile grew as she let go of the dice.

The dice caromed from left to right around the curve of the table toward the center croupier. One die hit a stack of chips behind the pass line at the far end of the table. That die came up a six. The second die kept tumbling around toward the center action and bounced into the tray of three alternate dice. The screams shook the foundation of Atlantis. Every other gaming table froze and looked over. It was a different form of shock and awe. The yells of "SAME DICE!" were heard, but which of the four was the same die?

The croupier rolled the dice together out on the table. Bedlam broke out as gamblers screamed in anger, but it was too late. The dice were mixed together. "DICE OUT" was yelled as the five dice were issued to Jocelyn for her to choose two from. Bettors frantically withdrew bets from the table in fear of the result. Aug was stuck with his bets. He knew something in his heart. Going forward there would be no going back on Jocelyn now.

Jocelyn kissed him. She selected two dice. The cheering started getting louder and louder. Jocelyn rolled. The table went silent. The spectators all leaned forward.

The dice crashed forward, hitting stacks of bets on numbers at the far end of the table. Chips were spewed everywhere. The first die came up a one. The second die ricocheted upward and came down rolling. It settled on a second one. Jocelyn rolled Snake Eyes. Aug was suddenly Doctor Octopus. His arms and legs and torso and everything about him squeezed Jocelyn tight. She was clearly thrilled and laughing joyously.

Aug's payout was an eight-hundred-dollar bet at thirty to one. The payout was twenty-four thousand dollars. He couldn't believe it. All the gambling winnings and losses in his life never added up to as much as he had won on that roll. The roll was like her pupils. They were small black snake eyes framed in emerald green. Her roll was the color of money.

The cost for Aug to stay up on his bets was forty-nine hundred. He trayed twenty grand. His original bet on the come-out roll had been three hundred and fifty dollars, and now six rolls later, he was up twenty-eight grand with another fifty-six hundred on the table. He pushed another fourteen hundred more of pressure on table. The dice were issued to Jocelyn. The kiss was issued to Aug. The deep lean over the table occurred. She rolled a seven. Aug netted another nine g's.

Aug pressed another fourteen. The dice were issued to Jocelyn. The kiss was issued to Aug. The deep lean over the table occurred. This time Jocelyn made a point. She rolled a six. It was a hard six. Aug lost over eight thousand on that roll, but he was up over thirty five thousand plus the thousands she had already won him on come bets.

The dice were issued to Jocelyn. The kiss was issued to Aug. The deep lean over the table occurred. This time Jocelyn sevened out right away. A clapping roar was heard throughout the casino. Jocelyn colored them both out. She tipped the table one thousand and took the rest of the money, telling Aug, "I'm going shopping. I'll be back soon. Why don't you be a good boy and go up to the room and wait for me, hmmm?" Aug was powerless to stop her. Aug didn't want to stop her.

Jocelyn was walking away out of the casino to the shopping areas. Aug was deep in fantasy land as he walked away from the table. His destination was a lavatory as the excitement and liquor had done their natural business.

He was standing at the stall, trying to calm down enough to take care of business. That was when the hand landed on his shoulder, and the business card was thrust in front of him. The business card indicated the gentleman worked for the US Treasury Department. "Augustus Valentine? My name is Greg Czarnacki. I'd like to have a little chat with you about some of your ... ah ... 'business dealings' at Trove. That is, when you are done with your other ... ahem ... business in hand at the moment. Can you come with me please?"

And so Aug's Atlantis descended into the sea. In one mighty moment, the magic was gone.

# Chapter 27

## Opening Day

The view from the suite was to the south. Everything was now heading south except for the sun. The sun was in the west, and it was setting. The big fireball cast an orange glow reflecting off all the yachts and the water and the buildings and the beach. The sand was still packed, and the night's entertainment was tuning up. The access from the parking lot to the beach was covered by wooden railings and platforms sided by other bars and shops with beach wares. A gazebo was in the center of it all behind the erected stage for the musical entertainment. The Reverend Horton Heat was preparing to preach to the choir.

Aug's life had turned south. He had been given options. Either perform long prison time or perform shorter prison time by turning into government evidence. But he had also been let in on other information. He was being set up to be the fall guy. Greg turned out to be dirty himself, but not so stupid. He didn't trust Jack Dough. Greg realized that if Jack wanted to stick it to Aug so bad, then here was his ally. This was Aug's tip to start making his plans for escape. Twelve months had come down to this last scramble.

He had learned so much in that time. He had learned much about his past and his parents' past. The legacy he had both created and inherited. For so many years, he had been in denial of his mother's role in setting up the death of his father. He refused to see the truth 'cuz it was *Mom*. He did not hate her for her actions. He was older now and had evolved a better understanding of the passages of life. She had been pregnant at fifteen. Was that her fault? Aug could never get a female that young pregnant. It was too unreal a concept for him. His father was a skirt chaser, but he evidently was a cradle robber too. Aug was the progeny of the union. Should he hold that union in contempt? If the union had not occurred, then he would not be. Wasn't that like "'Tis better to have been the offspring of illicit love than to not have been at all"?

What about Laurie's life and death? Had she died for no reason at all? In a sense, it did not matter. Aug couldn't go back. The dice had been rolled, and they came up snake eyes. Without snake eyes, he might still be in a grieving funk. He wiped the wetness from his eyes and got dressed. He put on his ruffled red shirt and black pants. It was time to head downstairs.

The condemned man gets a fine final meal. Well, it wouldn't be his last meal, maybe, probably, but it would be close enough. What to choose? Should he have some of the marlin? Maybe he should eat some of the pig roasting on the spit? The Reverend solved his dilemma by extolling the virtue of *Eat Steak,* and he settled on a big old steer. He saw a lot of cows to eat, and he was sure they went *moo.* He looked but did not see the eyeballs in a cup.

After eating, Aug went into Poseidon's to check the place out. It had wall-to-wall people. They were buzzing about, talking about how beautiful the place was and how Hurricane Bill was heading their way. "When and where would you be leaving to for escape?"

He turned his head around to admire the furnishings. This had to be fourteen thousand of the most expensive square feet in use that he had seen. The building was 120 square feet with a twenty-foot-long kitchen and a twenty-foot-long bar and an eighty-foot-long restaurant/dance floor. No wonder they wanted to be able to open the place and get it running so that it was not a total loss in the bust. It would be one thing to have the facility shut down halfway through construction and then try and sell the remnants at a severe loss. Now that it had been built, it could be sold off as a viable entity. The sale of the bar would be just more cashing out.

Aug entered the bar. The bar area had a series of flat screens angled down above the patrons' heads. A variety of boys of summer were hardly being noticed by the crowd on hand. Aug turned and looked out at the main floor. He saw a series of sixteen marble pillars that created two lines from front to back. They were adorned with celebrities reenvisioned as mermaids and mermen. Among them were the Robert Mitchum and Marilyn Monroe pillar. Someone had obviously liked Niagara Falls. There was a Richard Burton and Elizabeth Taylor pillar. Sophia Loren and Maurice Chevalier were among pillars he saw. Looking around, he picked out Gina Lollobrigida and Rock Hudson. The marble imagery was magnificent.

Lighting above was from chandeliers that looked like various elegant sea animals. There was a giant squid in the center with eight arms and two longer tentacles that curled upward into a chandelier. The suction cups were all lights that could vary in color and degrees of brightness. Other unique lighting fixtures were of smaller anemones and tube worms as well as manta rays.

Amongst the pillars, various casino tables had been set up for the evening. It was all for charity and was for one night only, so what do legal authorities care? Roulette wheels spun. Wheels of Guess the Denomination of the Dollar were spun. Blackjack was dealt. Craps were rolled. In the center of it was a large Hold 'Em game. The tables used in the game were the restaurant tables. The restaurant tables and dining furnishings had come in seven different sets. Each set was modeled after a different one of the septet of seas.

A huge mural of Poseidon and his realm was painted against the east wall. Poseidon was larger-than-life. He had a flowing red cape and held a massive trident that shot lightning bolts. Sea denizens bowed before him in a courtlike setting. Aug laughed as he looked harder at the mural. Vanity has its price, or was it that price allows a vanity? Poseidon's face was modeled after the visage of Jack Dough.

He wandered to the ocean side of the building. The ocean could be seen through three rows of thirteen panes of glass. Each pane of glass was eight feet wide and six feet high. This left a foot-high top and bottom frame and eight feet of block at each side of the glass. Revelers were seen regaling outside on the white sand; boats in the background and personal watercraft were still getting airborne off the waves. The sand castle contest entries were illuminated.

There was a large aquarium against the panes of glass on the west side of the building. The Reverend preached through multiple speaker sets. Two sets of speakers ran up the walls where the front of the building met the sides of the building. The cabinets formed a V that sent sounds out to meld with speaker sets that ran up the back of the east and west walls of the building. Coupled with other sets strategically placed below the lighting that adorned the tops of the pillars above the sculptures, the electronics set created a wall of sound that was magnificent.

Aug wandered around and checked out the various speaker sets. His wanderings led him to rest near one of the craps tables on the east side of the pillar sets. Jack Nicholson and Faye Dunaway looked down on him. He closed his eyes and listened to the sermon. The music sounded good. The song came through fine. Aug smiled. She had a *Bad Reputation*. She's the kind of girl he'd like to meet. Aug's smile grew.

His body was slightly bumped as he leaned against the pillar. The meditation was broken. A tastefully if not skimpily dressed very attractive brunette cocktail waitress had interrupted his thoughts. She hit his arm with her tray, and a drink went flying by him onto the ground. The drink just missed soaking Aug. He found her red lips captivating as she spoke.

"Oh, mister, please! Oh, I am so sorry! Did I spill anything on you?" Her hands rubbed over his shirt, looking for signs of liquid. "Oh, clumsy me. I'm sorry. I didn't see you there. Are you all right?"

Aug found his smile increasing. She looked thirtyish to him. In some sense, she physically seemed younger than that, but her personality came off as more mature. Her uniform looked tight, and he liked that. He held her wrist to stop her from rubbing him down. "I'm all right, miss. It's no big deal. See? I'm dry. You missed me completely."

She looked at him with a pout and said, "Are you sure you're all right?" She looked at the floor. "Damn!" She had napkins with her, and she proceeded to clean the floor up. When she had finished, she stood up with a tray full of wet napkins. She looked at him and laughed and said, "Well, I don't know about you, but I could use a drink!"

Aug laughed. "Yes, ma'am. Yes, I think I could use a drink."

She seductively smiled and asked, "What'll you have? Hmmm?"

He responded, "A Long Island iced tea please."

"Absolutely," she said. "One Long Island coming right up for the gentleman in the fancy shirt!"

When she left, he backed up a bit to lean against the nearest pillar, which afforded him a look at the craps-table action. The action was unprofessional. People who hardly knew how to operate a dice game tried to manage people who didn't know how to bet at a craps game. There were people all around the table, but there was little action on it. After watching for a while, the hostess came back with his drink.

She handed him the glass and said, "One Long Island for the very nice gentleman. On the house for my almost making a mess of you."

"Why, thank you! You are really way too kind!" he said.

"Not at all" was her reply. She took off to deliver more drinks.

Aug took his drink and leaned back against the pillar. He closed his eyes and thought about things to come.

The waitress came back and stood by his side. She watched him with curiosity. "So who's your favorite?" she asked him.

Aug was roused from his latest lost-in-space phase. "Excuse me?"

"Mermaid. Who's your favorite mermaid?" She pleasantly looked him over and then looked at the pillars. "You don't look like you're into the mermen. At least, I hope not!"

Aug thought about his reply. "Do you mean the ones on the pillars or the ones on the floor? The ones giving drinks away, I mean."

She stood back to give him the full view. "I meant the ones on the pillars." She gave Aug a wonderful smile. "But I'm glad you're noticing the ones serving drinks. Like the outfit?"

He mused a minute while he scoped her out. "I do, I do. I'm wondering who designed them. It's certainly not Gaultier, there's no breast plate. But there certainly is plenty of breast!"

"Well, you know, I'm not always in uniform," she replied.

Aug smiled at the thought that she implanted. He looked at the pillars. He noticed Ossie Davis and Ruby Dee as well as Salma Hayek and Antonio Banderas and Brigitte Lin and Leslie Cheung. He said, "Ya know, I guess I like the Duke and Maureen O'Hara best. Although no self respecting male would complain about the Sean Connery and Ursula Andress couple. They bond so well, you know."

"Hmmph!" the server said indignantly. "A redhead and a bimbo. You obviously have no taste in women. No self-respecting male would fail to pick out a brunette! You obviously are not self-respecting! In fact, I bet your girlfriend probably thinks you're not very respectful. I bet that is why she popped you in the eye!"

Aug was taken aback by the attack. "I was not popped in the eye by my girlfriend! I was . . ." He thought about what he was going to say and decided against it. "Well, never mind. It's a long story."

The server said, "Uh-huh. Riiigghhhttt."

Aug realized what she had said. "HEY! Ursula Andress was not a bimbo!"

She replied, "Bimbo? Did I say bimbo? I'm sorry. My tongue must have slipped. I meant blonde."

It was Aug's turn to reply, "Riiigghhhttt."

She turned to leave. She looked back and smiled and said, "It's a bad habit I have. My tongue sometimes likes to slip." She winked and walked away and left him with a very large smile. His eyes trained up and down. This one knew how to walk in heels. He started to lift the Long Island to his mouth.

Aug's arm was grabbed, and the drink was removed. Aug turned his head. He was confronted by Curly and Candy. They looked bad and mad. Curly's face had cuts all over it like shrapnel had pierced it in many places. Candy looked like he had broken his nose since the last time Aug had seen it.

"Well, hello, Curly," Aug said. "My, don't you look fine. Gee, fellas, I was just having a drink. Why don't you join me?"

Candy said, "I think I will." He downed the Long Island in one long guzzle.

Curly took Aug's hand and shook it with a grip that exerted an extreme amount of pressure. Aug had large powerful hands himself, but his hand was greatly hurting under the force applied. Curly leaned forward and spoke into Aug's ear. "My name isn't Curly. It's Pope. I'm also known as the Nut Crusher. You can guess why."

Aug's hand was released. He looked at Pope and said, "Geez! Nut Crusher, huh? Like, as in, the Crusher? Ya know, those were some great wrestling moves you had. You'da beat Bugs if you hadn'ta fallen for the ripped shorts routine!" Aug looked him up and down. "Or is crushing nuts how you got so big? Did your hand slip down or is your dick so small you also grabbed your balls when jacking off as a kid? Either way, you did a good job of creating the self-made eunuch!" He turned around and started to walk away.

The men came up behind Aug. Each man grabbed one of Aug's arms, and they somewhat discreetly threw him forward into the nearest pillar in front of him. They pinned his body up against the marble. He heard Candy say into his ear, "Ooohhh, funny guy! Ten thousand comedians outta work and we got da funny guy." Aug started to back up only to have a hand in his back press him against the pillar. "Funny guy, why don't you come with us and we can see how funny yer routine is."

Aug started to rotate his head to say something. His vision was drawn upward. Evidently, he wasn't the only person with a sense of humor. He smiled broadly. Vanity did have its price!

They locked his arms, and as discreetly as possible, they walked him forward through the crowd to the doors. Aug felt funny. He felt himself anatomically shrivel. He did not like the feeling. The doors were opened to exit.

"Augustus Valentine, how are you doing!" Jack Dough came entering the building accompanied by another tall gentleman and two uniformed police officers. "Hello, boys" was an acknowledgment to Curly and Candy. "Boys, I'd like you to meet my good friend Harold Bungro. Sheriff Harold Bungro. He's been looking for you guys to ask you some questions about a car accident yesterday or something." Aug was released. Jack smiled at Aug and put his arm around Aug's shoulder. "Aug, why don't you and I have a drink and talk some business." And they were off to the bar.

Aug said, "Well, Jack, thank you. And I never thought I would ever say thank you to you for anything in my life."

Jack replied, "Aug, there's an easier way to say thank you. Just tell me where my stones are."

Aug answered, "Stones? They're in your kidney waiting to pass, aren't they? That's why you normally have such a sour disposition, isn't it?"

Jack laughed as they approached the bar. "You're quite the comedian, aren't you? You know, I coulda left you back with Joe's boys back there. I think they wanted to ask you about the stones themselves." Jack paused in thought. "Ya know, I just saved you from some nice fireworks there. You should really stay around here tonight and enjoy the fireworks that I have staged to go off. Play some craps or something and enjoy yourself. Mine are much better than what the boys had planned for you. Hell, they better be. I spent two hundred grand on the explosives alone!" Jack faced Aug and put his hands on Aug's arms. "And speaking of explosives, whydja have ta tell Joe there was a hundred million in jewels? You and I both know that's not true. Now ya went and got him all pissed off at me. Ya know, I'm not too happy about that. Now c'mon, what're ya having?"

Aug said, "Hey, you know, at the time, it seemed like a fun thing to say. He was holding a piece to my head so what should I do? Besides, you're a nice guy. Why weren't you going to cut yer brother in on the deal? That's not very family oriented, ya know."

Jack eyed him up and down in thought. He thought about the past. "You think you know soooo much about family, don't you? I think that the fact of the matter is that you are just like a minister in some religion. You have so much faith in your beliefs that anything that challenges those beliefs only makes you so much more psychotic about your belief system. How terrible it is when someone realizes that they have wasted years of life believing untruths. The point when you realize and accept the fact that you wasted years of your life believing something that you now know cannot possibly be true. No wonder people die and new generations evolve. If the world were still full of people who believed in the infallibility of the pope, then where would we be?"

Aug stared at Jack. He replied, "The only thing that I believe is that your time is coming to an end."

Jack smiled. "You know what? You may be right in that belief. But Jack Dough is ready for death. Is Augustus Valentine ready for death?" Jack paused. "I believe that you believe in more than just my death. I also believe that while you may be ready for death, you are not ready to meet your maker!"

Aug seethed. He was staring at his maker. He was staring at the man who had killed his parents. He worked hard to contain his rage.

Heels came by. She looked at Aug and Jack and smiled back at Aug. "Good to see you are still here, big boy. I see you have found some company. I'm glad it's not of the female kind too!"

Aug smiled at her. "Oh, but I do have female companionship—now. And I'll have another Long Island, if you don't mind."

Jack looked at her and said, "You know, you have terrible taste in men." The waitress gave him quite the look on that remark. "And me? I'll have a martini made with the best vodka here—that is, if it is not too much trouble."

"Oh no, sir," she facetiously said. "Anything for you, Mr. Dough." She smiled at Aug and said, "Anything for you and your friends."

She turned and worked her way to the front of the bar ordering area. She knew the men were watching, so she put her legs together and raised up on her toes a bit for them while she was waiting for the drinks. Aug enjoyed the view for a while but then his eyes were drawn to the gold banister railing that was affixed to the bar that patrons were leaning on. It was inlayed with various forms of sea life. Aug knew this because it had been fashioned overseas, and the railing was imported through Trove.

It struck Aug that there was probably only one of these railings. If something marred it in some manner, a second would have to be made. Unless there were replacement sections in a back room somewhere. The lights went on at Poseidon's.

Legs came back with their drinks. "Compliments of the house!" She handed them the drinks. "And I'll leave you boys alone. Somehow, I think you have some mermaids to look at to keep yourselves busy!"

Aug stared at Jack. As much as he didn't want to, he had a small sense of admiration in his eyes. He raised his glass in a toast. "Skoal," he said. He prepared to drink as he said to Jack, "Now let's talk about our problem."

Suddenly Aug found his drink removed from his hand by a passing Chuck Hvala. "Hey, thanks for the drink!" Chuck said. Chuck proceeded to guzzle the drink and then pressed the drink against his head. "Damn, that was good, but it gives me a popsicle headache drinking like that!" He handed Aug back the empty glass. He looked at Aug and then Jack. "Speaking of headaches! Jack! I've been looking for you! I seem to have a bit of a big headache now. Something about some wire transfers. You wouldn't know anything about that now, would you?" Chuck put his arm around Jack's shoulder and said, "Could you please excuse us, Mr. Valentine? Mr. Dough and myself have some business to discuss." Chuck led Jack away.

Aug watched them walk away. Legs walked back. She looked at his drink with a suspicious eye. "You know, you better watch it. They're gonna need to roll you outta here if you keep slamming Long Islands." She smiled. "I may just have to take you home if you're not careful."

Aug smiled back. "In that case, you better bring me a couple Long Islands this time. But bring them in plastic please. I need to go get some fresh air and come back."

Legs gave Aug a pout. "Are you saying my air is stale? Well, you just make sure you come back and see me before you leave." She leaned forward to his ear. "You know, I've got some other cocktail outfits you may like better than this one!" She smiled and walked away to go get his drinks.

Aug stood by the Mae West and Cary Grant pillar while waiting. He felt the pillar was apt. No matter where he went nowadays, it seemed like the women he met were no angels.

Legs came back with his drinks. "Mae West, huh?" She held the drinks on her tray in her left hand. She held out her right hand and said, "Let me see your hand." Aug held out his right hand, and she said, "Nice. Very large yet very soft. Tell me, stranger, do you know what Mae West said about hands?"

He answered, "My name is Augustus Valentine. You can call me Aug. And no, I don't know what Mae West said about hands, miss . . . ?"

She handed him the drinks and said, "Well, Mr. Aug, my name is Dawn. You know, as in the dawn of a new era? Or if you like better, maybe the crack of dawn?" She seductively smiled. "Anyway, Mae said that good sex is like playing good bridge. If you don't have a good partner, you'd better have a good hand!"

Aug laughed as she handed him the drinks. "Compliments," she said.

"Of the house?" he asked.

"Yes," she said. "The house at 234 Pelican Place in Destin."

She turned to walk away and then turned her head back to look at him. She spoke with the proper accent. "Why don't you come on up and see me sometime!" And with a wink, she was gone. The Reverend sang of *Jezebel*.

Aug was impressed. His mind was on Dawn as he walked to the exit door. His head was craning backward as he was walking forward. He had full drinks in both hands when the doors opened and . . .

# SPLASH! 🌱

Aug was doused with not only his drinks but also four other huge beers. He had been bumped into by the Mountain and the Nose. They drenched him from head to toe.

The Mountain said, "Ah, señor, excusa por favor." With that, the Mountain started brushing the dripping booze upward so that it sprayed in Aug's face. Aug was actually very thirsty at this point. He tried lapping up any of the spray he could. He smacked his tongue at the taste he was presented with. Looking at the Mountain and Nose, he said, "You know, fellas, I dunno. I don't think Long Islands and beer will ever replace boilermakers."

The Nose spoke. "Let us help you with that." They grabbed his wet arms and started to lead him past the stage. The Reverend sermonized that Aug was *Cruisin' For A Bruisin'*. Aug felt that was the condition he was in.

The parking lot was on the far side of the stage. It was filled with vehicles, and there were golf carts and golf cart caddies ferrying groups of people to and from cars. Two golf cart caddies pulled up. The occupants were Keith Marshall accompanied by four of the security staff.

"Aug!" Keith said. "Why didn't you tell me you were going for a swim. You better come with me, and we'll get you out of those wet things before you catch a cold!"

Aug shook his arms free. "Thanks for the escort, boys. Next time, I'll have to make sure that the drinks aren't on me." With that, he hopped into the golf cart with Keith, and they were off. Aug looked around him. "This wouldn't happen to be the beer cart, would it?"

Keith laughed. "It looks like you've had a few too many already to me!"

They pulled up at Keith's 300. Aug asked, "Where are we going?"

Smoothie's reply was "Oh, I thought we would take a ride over to my place and talk about things."

Aug said, "Well, Keith, how about if I take my own car? I mean, I'm all wet, and I'd hate to get booze all over the front seat. I mean, if the cops pulled you over, they might think you'd been drinking or something."

Keith laughed. "Suit yourself. See ya over there." He looked at the security detail. "Boys, make sure that Mr. Valentine makes it to his vehicle, OK, will ya?" They nodded in approval.

Aug was dropped off at his Caddy. He entered the car and was dismayed. There was nothing to keep the car clean with. Jocelyn had removed her towels. He slowly squished onto the seat. The beer smell was quite overpowering. It went good with the stale water odor. Aug realized that his wallet was still dry, and he took it out and put it into the center console to keep it from getting wet. He left the windows down as he drove across the road to Keith's residence. It took about ten minutes to maneuver through the crowd, cars, and security to get over there.

The security guard at the booth stepped over to the open car window and eyed Aug suspiciously. "Mister, what is your business here? You always drive around covered in beer? You smell like you've had a few too many!"

Aug counseled the guard, "Relax there, chief. I'm just following Mr. Marshall on in. I'm expected. He just passed through here." He ran his hands over his clothes. "And this? This is just the latest French perfume I'm wearing. It's called eau de lager. You need to get outside of your box some more and go get you some. You never know, it might end up helping you get some anyway!" With that, he drove through.

Aug made his way to Keith's place. Keith was outside smoking with drinks already made up. He offered one to Aug, who declined. "Ah . . . no thanks," he said, flicking some more wet off. "I think I've had one too many already."

"Suit yourself," he said as he poured some down his throat. "It's a beautiful night out. God, I love this place. So peaceful, so rich. Summer almost twelve months of the year." Keith paused. "The fireworks outta be starting sometime soon. It should be a spectacular show. There really was no expense spared on this evening's entertainment."

"Yeah, well," Aug said looking around him, "you're gonna have to change your name from Marshall to Milton. It looks like you're gonna have to visit paradise lost to make it to paradise found. Are you ready to go?"

Keith looked at Aug. "Do you mean right now? Well, my things are packed. What's the plan? When do you give me my key?"

"You mean *our key*, don'tcha?" Aug smiled at Keith. "Ya know, I was going through some gossip today, and I heard a crazy story about a large embezzlement from the White Sands Bank. That's quite a haul you took in."

Keith smiled and then lost his smile. "Well, I don't know if the cost was worth it. It cost me the lives of my brothers, and I can't buy them back." He mournfully looked off and then looked back at Aug. "Is that worth it? If we'da known what was gonna happen, would we have done it? For all that money? I dunno . . . I guess I will never know. It's a choice that I can't go back and make again." There was silence. "So what's the plan there, partner."

Aug said, "The plan is this. I need to go for a walk for about an hour or two, and when I come back, I'll tell you where we are going and when. I need to set something up to get my associates taken care of. Let me take care of the timing of that, and I'll be back, and we can go over the details."

Keith told Aug, "Going for a walk, eh? Gee, I can imagine where you are going. And I can tell you now before you go, you won't find what you are looking for there." He took a drag on his smoke. "But I don't suppose you'll believe me. Suit yourself. Knock yourself out. Either way, I'll be back here ready to go."

Aug was surprised. "And what won't I find on my walk?"

Keith wryly laughed. "You won't find out what happened to the gold and platinum. That's what you won't find. But go ahead. You want to go anyway." Keith turned and went to the house. "I'm packed. I'm ready. Get going, and I'll be set when you get back."

Aug walked off to his car. He changed his shoes to a pair of jogging shoes that were in the car. He opened the door and removed a CD case from inside of it. He walked off to the road and started the twenty-minute traipse to Jack Dough's residence. He had made his way to the intersection of both Baytowne roads when a silver Lincoln came in his direction. It took him a minute to realize that the vehicle wasn't going to swerve. He moved to his left and the car followed him onto the grass. To Aug it appeared that the car was traveling thirty miles an hour or so.

# *SPLASH!* 💦

Aug dove into the lake that bordered the island green by the road to avoid being hit. The Lincoln continued on and turned down Keith's road.

"Son of a bitch!" He was soaked again, but this time with stinky pond water. He climbed out of the water. His shoes and socks were so wet he decided to take them off and abandon them. He decided to continue on foot. Panic set in, and he checked his pockets. The CD and his car keys were still with him. The journey was started again, but he stunk. The odor was now a combination of beer, Long Island, and algae. He was swamped with disgust. He picked up his pace in jogging.

Twenty minutes later, Jack's residence was made. He worked his way to the back golf course side entrance. Cardboard had been put over the broken glass of the door, but he could punch through and let himself in. The lights were off in this area of the house. He saw and heard no one.

As quietly and as dryly as he could, he made his way down the hall to the office area. Even now he still dripped liquid. He entered the room. He left the light off and took a seat in front of the PC on the far side of the desk. The power button on the computer was tripped. The CD case was accessed. A disc was inserted into the CD drive. The screen came up, asking for a supervisor login. Aug entered into the drive and called up a Web page. An FTP site was logged into. Programs on the CD drive were accessed. Program DATA was started. This program would send all the PC hard drive data to an FTP site. Program KEYSTROKE was started. This program accessed the keystroking sequence that had taken place on the keyboard. This data was sent to the FTP site. At that, he sat back and waited. This would take a while.

Boredom took over. A decision was made to explore the house. He went upstairs and started looking around. There were five bedrooms to choose from. He turned on the hall light and saw a back room had a suitcase on the floor and some clothes hanging in the closet. There were a half dozen of the boxes from Upper Terra in the room. They were not taped shut. He unfolded the lid of a box and pulled out a spectacular-looking platinum plate and goblet. He looked at their beauty. He mused to himself, *Is it live, or is it memorex?* Aug had no methodology to tell the difference.

He looked through the four other bedrooms. The master bedroom had a few clothes in it, but all in all, the place looked very empty. It didn't look lived in. The master bedroom bathroom door was shut. Aug tried slowly and quietly turning the handle. The door was locked. There was no light showing from under the door. Aug waited and listened for sounds he did not hear.

After waiting a while, he went back downstairs, making sure to flick the lights off on his way back down. Off the main door entrance from the garage was a wine cellar. Inside the room were maybe thirty bottles of wine, but there were racks for a few hundred more. He decided to grab some bottles to take with him. Noises were heard from the garage. Someone wicked this way comes.

Angel was prepared. She had staged the Upper Terra boxes in the garage just as Daddy requested. Now she had to wait for Chuck to show up and pick up his share. She came up the stairs and entered the house. She smelled stench. Her nose was piqued. The stench was disgusting; it smelled like . . . like the creature from the Black Lagoon had come in. Some wet spots were on the floor. *We are not alone* was her thought. She had better find a weapon. The kitchen would be the place to go. Angel went a couple steps toward the kitchen and realized she smelled Budweiser. This creature drank Bud.

Cautiously she made her way to the kitchen and procured both a carving and a butcher knife from the knife block. She started off out of the kitchen and then stopped. She opened a utensil drawer. She looked for something smaller she could stick in her pockets. Just in case. There was a wine bottle opener. It was a Playboy wine bottle opener. *How kitschy,* she thought. An ice pick was pulled out. She put that in a back jean pocket. She started off. She stopped. *What the hell?* she thought. The wine bottle opener went in the other back jean pocket. Angel was now armed to the cheeks.

Angel cautiously walked down the hall with the knives leading. The den was empty. She saw the cardboard ripped off the broken door. Farther down the hall was the game room. She thought, *Why didn't Dad buy the clapper?* Then she could just clap on the lights to see. Now she had to slowly enter the room and turn on the light. The pool table was there, but nothing else was. She looked at the floor. The trail did not lead there.

The office came next. Water drops did lead that way. PU! Whoever was in there reeked! The door was partially open. A deep breath was taken, and her nerves were steeled. The lights were out. Was she brave enough to enter? She decided yes. Angel stepped forward with the carving knife extended. There was someone behind the door.

Angel slammed her body into the door. An "OWW!" followed by a "GODDAMMIT" was heard. She swung around the door, leading with the butcher knife. Her arm was grabbed. She swung down with the carving knife. She found flesh. Another "OWW!" followed by a "GODDAMMIT" was heard. Her arm was released. She jabbed with the knife but got air. She felt a foot kick her crotch. It was one of the more unpleasant implements she had ever felt inserted into her crotch. Angel let out a scream of pain and anger. She stumbled backward. She lost her footing. She fell on her butt. The ice pick and the wine opener jabbed her gluteus maximus. They were two of the more unpleasant items she had ever felt on her butt cheeks. Angel let out another scream of pain and anger.

The lights came on. She saw a wet, smelly Aug in the room. He was holding his right arm. She had gashed it pretty decently, or so it looked. He was holding the arm, but some blood was flowing through his fingers. The recognition set in, and her anger grew. She rolled up to her feet, holding the blades in front of her. Her approach was menacing.

"YOU!" she yelled. "What the *hell* are *you* doing here?" She paused a second. "And why the *hell* do you stink so bad?"

Aug backed up from her approach. He was holding his arm. They started circling the desk that was in the room. He stopped and patted the palms of his hands on the desk as they circled while yelling, "Hey, hey, I'm bleeding here!" Blood ran from his left arm onto the desk.

Angel replied, "Like I care!"

Aug told her, That was supposed to be funny!"

She sneered. "Your humor is like your taste in women. It's very bad. And I'm not laughing."

Aug laughed at her. "Well, Angel, you're the one who said I stink, remember? Now put those knives down before you hurt something."

"HURT SOMETHING! I'll show you HURT SOMETHING!" Angel jabbed the blades across the desk at his crotch. "Kick me in my . . . in my . . . AHHHH!" Aug jumped back. "Come on, Mr. 'I can't dance!'" Angel swung the blades at his legs. "Let's see how good a dancer you are!" She continued swinging.

Aug was smarting from the gash in his arm as he backed around the desk. "Will you please calm down and cut that out?" he requested.

Angel was further enraged. "Cut that out? I'll cut that out all right! Kick me in the crotch, will ya?" She lunged violently at his privates.

Aug needed a weapon. He saw one of the wine bottles he had brought in by hand. He picked it up and smashed it on the desk to give himself a jagged glass edge to use. "Now calm down, will ya? I can't talk to you when you're angry like this."

"Angry? ANGRY? You want ANGRY? I'll give you angry, goddammit!" She lunged forward. He stepped aside and swung down with the broken bottle down on her wrist. She screamed as the bottle edge cut her wrist. The butcher knife was dropped. He swung a leg around and got it underneath her leg and tripped her. The carving knife flew out of her hands as she fell. Angel fell on her butt. The ice pick and the wine opener jabbed her cheeks. They were two of the more unpleasant items she had ever felt on her butt cheeks. Angel let out another scream of pain and anger.

Angel righted herself and angrily pulled the ice pick and bottle opener out of her pants and threw them down. Upon seeing what exited her pockets, Aug started laughing. "Angel! How'd you know I needed a wine bottle opener? Do you always walk around with a Playboy wine bottle opener in your pocket, or are you just happy to see me?" Angel picked up the carving knife and did a Norman Bates imitation at him. She was wildly swinging at Aug, back and forth. He was intently watching, waiting. After a right-to-left swing, she opened up, and he extended a quick but potent right jab. He caught her flush on the chin. Angel reacted the way many people who have never taken a shot to the jaw before react: she went down.

Angel wasn't out too long. It was long enough for Aug to procure kitchen towels to wrap their cuts with and also enough time for him to uncork the wine.

It was a red Coppola Reserve. He figured that since Coppola had made movies about criminals, this was an apropos choice. He committed a crime worse than stealing the bottle. He drank straight from the bottle. It was also long-enough time to pack up his CD from the computer and shut it down.

Angel awoke on the couch in the office. It took a minute for her sense to come back. She was in a particularly foul mood when she realized who and where she was. This led to her first statement: "You smell funny. You smell like you've been swimming in a swamp. You also smell like you're drunk. What, you need to go for a swim to get in the mood or something?" She looked at his feet. "And where are your shoes? God, you are a man in need of some serious psychiatric help!"

He told her, "I'm barefoot and wet 'cuz a goddamn Lincoln drove me into the lake on my way over here to see you!"

Angel sarcastically laughed at him. "Well, well, well, Mr. Charmer Man. You certainly have a knack for making friends, don't you? I take it back. You need Dale Carnegie's help as much as you need Dr. Phil's help!"

Aug pulled the office chair around the desk to look closer at her. "Whatever." His visage turned rather fatherly. "So, Angel, did you ask Jack about my wife? What did he tell you?"

Angel replied, "He said that you are full of shit and that he has no idea what you are talking about. That you were just fishing for information."

Aug sat back. "You know, I kinda expected that's about what he would tell you." Aug waited a moment. "What would you say if I told you that Jack offered to set his brother up in business in Cocoa after he got out of the stir if his brother would do him a favor." He held up his thumb and forefinger. "In his eyes, it was just one teensy, tiny, little favor."

Angel looked at Aug. "Does this story have a point somewhere?"

Aug guzzled some wine. "Yes. Yes, it does. You see, Jack had a score to settle that had been eating at him for twenty years. It was an itch he needed to scratch. He'd had a business dealing with my father that had gone sour many years ago. And Jack still wanted satisfaction out of it." Another guzzle occurred. Angel became a little surprised and a little scared. She could see emotion well up in his physique. The eyes became glassy. "But you know, my father was dead. He was beyond his reach. But his son was not beyond his reach. And so he cut a deal with his ne'er-do-well brother. He wanted the son's wife to be killed. That would be before he had the son killed. And for this favor, Jack's brother would get out of prison and have a nice little business to run in sunny Cocoa."

The voice haltingly spoke as Aug's teary gaze bore into her. "And so they did. I was sent out of town on a smuggling mission, and when I got back, I found that Laurie . . . my wife, Laurie . . . was dead. They hung her. It took time for her to die. It took time for the oxygen to be cut off from her body. They made it look like she committed suicide. They must have threatened her or me or something, and they convinced her to write a suicide note. And then they hung her in our house for me to find when I got back."

Aug guzzled some more wine and let out a heavy breath. Angel looked at him, wondering if this was a true story or not. "You're insane," she said. "You drove your wife to kill herself, and then you made up a fantasy that other people did it to justify your acts. You need help. Like shrink-type help."

Aug wryly laughed. "You know, Angel, you may be right about one. I may be insane." He guzzled some wine. "But you know what? You know who the only truly sane people are?"

She sarcastically replied, "No. Who are the only sane people?"

"The ones who have been let out of the insane asylum," he replied. "They're the only ones with a certificate to prove that they are sane!"

"Anyway," Aug continued, "well, her death was a few years ago, and if it weren't for a series of odd events and coincidences, I might never have been the wiser. It was hard for me to believe at first, but the more I learned, the more I realized what had happened. That's why I was set up to be a patsy. It was to be one of a couple last jabs at the Valentine family. Of course, I guess I really didn't expect for Jack to fess up the truth to you about that."

Angel had an incredulous look at him. "WHATEVER! You've really got a sick mind. You really should seek professional help."

Aug snorted, "Believe what you want."

"Anyway," she said. "That was a very enlightening story" was the sarcastic reply. "So what do you want from me?"

Aug looked at her very inquisitively. "You don't believe me, do you? Well, I suppose I can't blame you. There are many things in my life that I didn't want to believe when I was first confronted with them." He paused. "But let me leave you with this to think about. Why did Daddy despise you all these years and then suddenly become nice to you? Do you really think he had a religious conversion or something? You think about it. See where that gets ya."

Aug stood up and guzzled some more wine. "I'm going to take my leave now. You tell Jack that if he wants the jewels, he can come up to the suite at the Hilton tomorrow evening. Tell him to come around nine in the evening. And tell him to come alone. I'll be waiting for his visit."

Aug walked out of the room. He walked through the den and out onto the porch. The porch light was on, and he decided to stand there a second and get his composure back. He put the bottle to his lips and started another swig.

## CRASH!

The bottle exploded in his hand. He was sprayed with the half bottle of wine. The glass caused light cuts on his hand and cheek. His mind was somewhat blank as he tried to process the data.

## CRASH!

The vase of roses on the table exploded. Aug realized, *Someone is shooting at me! Someone with a silenced weapon is shooting at me!*

He hopped over the short porch and ran straight in the dark. He tripped facedown. He fell into the wetlands on the par 3. It was semidry. The base was mud. Aug found himself covered in mud. It covered his face and his clothes and squished in his toes. It was too much. He had had it. He rolled over on his back and let out a loud "ARRRRRGGGHHHH." When he was done, he could have sworn he heard some form of faint laughter on the breeze, but he wasn't sure.

What to do? Should he wait for a while, wallowing in the mud? Should he *oink* like a pig? His heart raced. Who in the world would be shooting at him? On the porch of Jack Dough's house? The more he thought about it, the more bizarre the scenario seemed. Well, bizarre or not, someone had taken some shots. And danger or not, he couldn't stay where he was. He was going to have to leave. Just then the fireworks started exploding in the distant night sky. The explosives went off across the bay and over the buildings that fronted the beach. It looked like a Disney event. Where was Tinkerbell flying in to strike the skyline? He lay there watching the show. He decided he had nothing better to do at the moment.

When the display ended, Aug got up to his knees. He looked out to the tee box, but he could not see it in the dark. He looked at the house and saw nothing. The outside porch light was now out. He ran to the house and sidled alongside of it. A flashback came through his head of being a child and playing either hide-and-seek or maybe ding dong ditch it. He made his way to the road. And then he started sprinting. After a couple minutes, he slowed to a jog like he was jogging to the park. It felt good. It burned off the adrenaline and slowed his heart rate down. He calmed down. The run gave him time to gather his thoughts.

There was no activity on the trot back. His plan was to get organized with Keith on putting the squeeze to Jack. Aug would take Jack to the jewels when no one was around. He would let Jack get the better of him, and then he would let Keith bail him out of the situation, and they could extract the info about the metals from Jack. It was a risky plan, but it made him nervous. He had better come up with a backup plan. He didn't know Keith well enough to trust him. But he did know that Keith would never get the key to the kingdom without Aug. So he had some leverage.

The approach to Keith's house was made. His DeVille was there. So was the Lincoln that had tried to run him down. What to do? Furtively he approached the residence. He circled the building. There was no sign of life. He couldn't see any lights on inside. Shit! What to do? Who had been in the Lincoln? What could he use as a weapon?

The back door was locked. Select windows were locked. The front door was unlocked. The carpet felt pleasant on his bare feet. His feet were very prunelike at this point.

The house was dark. Slowly he fumbled his way to the kitchen. He grabbed a butcher knife and a carving knife from the knife block. Should he grab anything else? He had a vision of Angel falling on her butt and hurting herself. He decided against it.

It took a slow fifteen minutes to circle through the downstairs as silently as possible. Nothing was found. The stairs up were attempted next. The hall presented options. Where to go? An assumption was made that a master bedroom was at the end of the hall. He went into it. It was hard to see anything in the darkness. His feet touched . . . clothing. He bent down to get a better feel. It appeared to be a shirt and a pair of pants. His eyes adjusted better, and he saw that the bed was still made.

There was a bathroom door at the far end of the room. Aug made his way to it. He made out shapes lying on the floor. He reached his arm out and found light switches to flick. He flicked them on. He nearly puked.

The shapes were bodies, and there was blood all over the bathroom. The blood came primarily from bullet holes to the heads of the bodies. The dead men had probably been caught by surprise, and their deaths had been quick. It looked like Curly and Candy had been torturing Keith, and they had been surprised by someone. Evidently, Curly hadn't lied. Keith had been stripped and bound at the legs and hands. Keith's nuts had been crushed. Curly must have squeezed them to get some answers.

Aug felt pain and uneasiness in his lower body. Only a real sadist could have enjoyed exerting that kind of torture. He felt nauseous again.

Fear then set in. Fear of the police arriving. Fear of his fingerprints everywhere. Fear of a bullet in the skull. Who had created this bloodbath? The same person who shot at him on the golf course? He did not want to hang out and find out.

Now what was he to do with the safe deposit box key that he possessed? He didn't know where it went. He did not know what bank. He did not know what country. He did not know what was in the box that the key opened. There were millions of dollars sitting in limbo that some rich bank would get to play with in perpetuity.

Poor Keith, he thought. The three Marshall brothers were all dead within a month. What would their mother have thought? Her tribute tattoo would never be finished. Aug looked at the tattoo. It was kind of a funny-looking tribute. It looked like Big Ben with a very large clock face. But the numbers on the clock made no sense.

There was one set of numbers in the twelve positions for the hours of the clock. The numbers on the face went this way:

7 5 1 0 1 1 0 5 1 16 10 40

Inside of those numbers and matching up position-wise were another set of hours that also appeared to be meaningless:

6 5 1 1 4 1 1 6 1 04 11 70

The clock face was large, and the tattoo looked incomplete. Aug was confused. Why would Keith lie about such a tattoo? Why would he have such a bizarre design? What would the design look like when it was finished? What did the design mean?

It was an hour later when Aug left. He wiped down every print of his he could imagine. He created a copy of the tattoo as best as his artistic capability could create. He took a bottle of Cointreau with him when he left and locked the door behind him. *Goodbye, Mr. Smoothie*, he thought, you deserved a better fate than you got.

# CHAPTER 28

## BOOM!

Tony Pizzano lay across the backseat of a Ford Taurus. He was trying to sleep, but the rising sun prevented it. He rose up from the back and got his senses together. His partner in the front was starting to doze. "Canaan. CANAAN!" he said as he pushed the big man's back. "Jesus Christ, man! You're supposed to be watching the place!"

Canaan had only recently dozed off. He was startled. He looked back at Tony and exhaled. "I-yi-yi, c'mon, man. Ain't nothin' happen' here." He looked at his watch. It was 6:30 AM. "The guy just got home an hour ago. He ain't goin' anywhere!"

Tony said, "That's not the point. And besides, ya never know who may show up." He opened the door and stood up. There was no one up yet this Sunday morning. He stepped to the back of the car for some relief.

Canaan rolled down a window and told Tony, "Yeah, well, if we would just go grab 'em, I wouldn't be nodding off here. This is just ridiculous."

After missing out on the opportunity to grab Aug, the men had been told by their boss to keep an eye on Jack Dough. They did. They followed Jack's Caddy here. Jack was busy at Poseidon's all night and arrived home at 5:30 AM. They had parked on the road outside the gate of the Dough residence.

Tony finished dewing the grass. He opened the front door of the car and sat in the passenger seat. "My goddamn sinuses are killing me," he said. "Anyway, whaddaya want from me? I'm just as bored as you are. I'd love to do something other than sit around and wait."

Canaan decided it was his turn to go. He stepped out and went to the back of the vehicle. It was still warm out. There was a slight breeze off the water that tasted good in the air.

Tony suddenly jumped up in his seat. He yelled to Canaan. "Hey! Look. The gate's opening. That's his car. C'mon. Fire this thing up. We gotta go."

Jack's Cadillac came out of the gated driveway. Canaan yelled to Tony, "You start the car! I'm in midstream here!"

Tony slid over and fired up the engine. He waited. The Cadillac disappeared down the road. Tony waited. Canaan finally reentered the Taurus. Tony looked at him and asked, "OK, Austin Powers, are you finally ready to go?" Canaan said, "AAAAAAAA, just doing my thing, ya know? What's your hurry, anyway? Where the hell can he be going now at this time of day? C'mon, let's go see what our boy is up to."

They slowly drove around the roads and caught sight of the car at the guardhouse. The guard was leaned over into the vehicle. Canaan told Tony, "Slow down. Let's see what he's doing."

Tony said, "Who the hell made you the captain of this ship? Whadja think I was going to do?"

Canaan asked, "Should we call the boss?"

Tony replied, "At this hour of the morning? Are you crazy? Let's see where he's going first."

They watched as the Caddy sat there. Tony asked, "What the hell? Is he trying to pick up the security guard or something? Jesus Christ! What the hell could they possibly have to gab about?"

## BOOM!

The car, the security guard, the security guardhouse all exploded from the force of the blast from the bomb inside the car. Tony and Canaan looked at each other stunned. Tony hit the quick dial on his cell phone. Mark Kledas answered, "Do you know what time it is? What the hell is so important?"

Tony said, "Boss, you ain't gonna believe this."

# CHAPTER 29

## DOORWAYS

The door was in front of him. The threshold was waiting to be crossed.

No matter how little or how much money anyone has, there is little that compares with the jag of having wads of hundred-dollar bills. And there were a lot of wads of hundred-dollar bills. Every box that was stacked three high on the skids in the semi was inner packed with hundred-dollar bills. The outer sides of the boxes were neatly packed with neatly packaged spare auto parts.

The crates were six-by-six-by-six cubes. The dollars were in wads of one thousand one hundreds per wad. There were twenty wads per row. There were five rows per layer, and the layers went six deep. Sixty million dollars were in each box, and there were twelve boxes. Seven hundred and twenty million dollars was there. His cut was a small but significant percentage to safely get the pony express shipped out of the USA and get it deposited in Costa Rica. Aug thought about what it all meant. How common sense it all was.

For legal drug companies hooking patients on Celebrex and Vioxx, the revenues are ten billion or more annually in the United States alone. Of course, the two million people who took Vioxx daily needed it. The evidence is common sense. Before Vioxx existed, people were dying left and right without the drug.

More common sense is demonstrated through the millions of war and nonwar wounded in the world that cannot exist today without Celebrex. These drugs are needed commodities that it is the legal right of corporations to hook society on daily doses of them. Besides, it increases the stock value, and that increases every shareholder's retirement fund, which makes it even more right to push these pills, these substances. There is also individualistic money that is pocketed from both legal drug use and abuse.

It's OK for individualistic corporations to make billions off legal drugs. There is no need to jail anyone for hooking millions of people on them. It is OK because Justice decided that those drugs are legal and because the sales bring in the money that drives the economy. Just like the money from supplements that the body does not digest help to drive the economy. It's all about sales, choice, responsibility, and the Benjamins. The choice is not only whether you personally ingest substances that others tell you that you need but also whether you have the responsibility necessary to walk away from the money that can be made being a pusher of any kind of substance abuse.

Recreational drugs are a choice that costs Benjamins. Common sense tells us that society would collapse in chaos if those drugs were decriminalized. Common sense tells us that there would be an explosion of death and addiction beyond what already is occurring. Common sense tells us that if the prison society that exists in the USA that is created by the use and sale of recreational drugs suddenly didn't exist, then there would be an explosion of anarchy. Common sense tells us that the near three quarters of a billion dollars in front of Aug being laundered in this shipment doesn't exist. The money being laundered can't exist because that means both responsible and irresponsible citizens in the USA are continuously spending billions on recreational drugs and that would conflict with common sense conclusions of the anarchy that must exist because common sense leads society to this conclusion. Society should have collapsed by now.

Of course, everyone knows that recreational drugs are the root of the evil in the corporate world. That is why so much money is spent drug-testing employees. Common sense tells us that it is only the drug users who defraud society by their greed for money. Common sense tells us that stock and financial instrument fraud only occurs due to recreational drug use. Common sense tells us that the bad management decisions made in the business world only occur due to recreational drug use. The Big Three and the Big Six drug test routinely for specific recreational drugs, yet the corporations have seen wide swings in profit due to bad management decisions. It could never be due to the incompetence of management built, fueled, and masked by the cons of unrealistic management theory. Could it?

Aug's train of thought compared this to his love's existence. It was drugs that kept Laurie alive. She should have died by now because of her faulty heart. She wasn't taking Vioxx or Celebrex or smoking grass or doing coke. She was taking powerful medications that physically and mentally toyed with her. There are millions of people out there who daily medicate themselves for either the enjoyment or the stupidity of it, and Laurie could not join in. She had to ingest powerful cocktails or die.

It was because of the illegal drugs that others ingest that Aug had a fortune in his possession. His job was to smuggle this batch of cash out of the USA. Many other people would want to have sex on the money or use the money to blow time in some hedonistic venture. Aug just wanted to be done with the deal and have his cut. His cut was more selfish than any prurient need. His cut, Laurie's cut, was hope.

Their cut would buy a good surrogate mother for a year to hopefully carry a child to life. They needed plenty of cash because the insurance wouldn't pay for a surrogate to live with them and take a pregnancy to term. Cash would have to be paid for the hospital birth and the battery of tests that would be required to determine if the child appeared to be a product of either intelligent or unintelligent design.

There was nearly three quarters of a billion dollars in front of him. It was enough for many men to buy a lifetime of women and drugs, and Aug could care less. He just wanted to have one child with his wife, his love, his Laurie. It was his impetus in life.

Aug wondered. Were the actions he was engaged in more morally wrong than the activities of a legal individualistic corporate criminal who pushed drugs or defrauded more individuals through financial fraud? He rationalized that his actions were not only more morally legitimate but also that he was less reprehensible as a human being.

It was an exciting and nerve-wracking journey on the boat and through customs in Costa Rica. They had split the shipments between the amusement game trick and the auto parts. Bribes were paid for government officials to look the other way. Bankers were paid to look the other way. The deposits were made.

The trip was over. He was surprised that his cell phone calls to Laurie hadn't been answered, but that was no big deal. She was blond, but she was not stupid. She could take care of herself. He was excited. Their dream could come true.

The door was in front of him. The threshold was waiting to be crossed. It was the door to their house. He opened the door.

A stench hit his nostrils. It was unlike anything he had ever smelled. It was septic in nature. It was powerful. Something was not right.

He called out Laurie's name. He walked through the living room. He walked into the kitchen. He walked into hell.

Laurie was hanging from the ceiling fan. Laurie was hanging with a noose around her neck.

The duration of Aug's insanity could not be quantified in terms of days or hours or seconds. Did it really start the moment he saw her hanging there? Her tongue was discolored and hanging out of her mouth. Her eyes were bugging and fluid filled. He crossed through another threshold in his life.

He cut her down and laid her on the table and held her. There was nothing else to do. There was nothing else that could be done. He had arrived in the morning. It was dark before he knew it. He called 911. He read her note.

> Dearest Aug, my Love
>
> It is time for me to leave you. I am tired from the daily pills and blackouts and not knowing where I will wake up or if I will wake up. I know now that we cannot have children, which I know you desire so greatly. It is better this way to leave you the chance to find a new life with someone who can give you what you need. Know that I love you and that at least I die not of a broken heart. Please forgive me, and go on to a better life.
>
> I love you,
> Laurie

It never made any sense to him. When he left for Costa Rica, their plan was to bring in the surrogate Laurie had lined up with the money from his end of the deal. Now he had been dealt this. What did she mean? What had she learned?

Why couldn't they try for a child? It didn't add up, but it didn't matter anyway. Laurie was not coming back.

It wasn't until Greg Czarnacki informed him that, for some reason, Jack Dough really wanted to stick it to Aug as part of the shutdown of Sandestin operations that Aug started to look into his past. Why would Jack care? Aug had never done anything to him. What axe was there to grind?

He turned over day-to-day TIE operations to Frank and started to explore his enemy. Who was he? He found out that Jack was originally from Michigan, from Detroit. He found out Jack's real name was John Campbell, and then pieces fell in place. He found out about Jack's brother being released from prison and being set up with a factory in Cocoa right at the time of Laurie's suicide. It was right when Aug needed to leave the country to take care of a deal that Jack set up. But he never put the pieces together.

He never put the pieces together until he took a trip to meet Rob Baumgardner. That's when he learned many more things.

Now there was another door in front of him. It was the door of his hotel room. He had heard the knocking. Aug figured it was Jack Dough a.k.a. John Campbell. Jack was way early, but it was time to settle the score once and for all.

He looked through the door portal. A visibly upset Angel was outside. Aug opened the door. *Oops*, he thought, *bad move*. Angel was not alone. The Mountain and the Nose were there.

Angel came at him with claws out toward his face. She was screaming. "You son of a bitch! You murderer!" Aug fell backward under the wrath of her attack. He didn't know what had set her off.

The Nose stepped in and wrested her off him. This was not an easy task as Angel vehemently wanted Aug. He was stunned by her onslaught. He stared at her, dumfounded.

The Mountain picked him up. What was happening didn't really click even when he heard a *tsk, tsk, tsk* sound. He turned his head and saw a fist heading to his temple. Now the *tsk* clicked. The vision that flashed through his head was Frank telling him that there are times that a boxer just needs to go down. There was also a second thought that went through his head as he eyeballed the fist. *Damn*, he thought. His black eye had just about cleared up. Here we go again.

"All the News That's Fit to Print"

# The New York Times

**Late Edition**

VOL. CXXXVII ... No. 47,288     NEW YORK, TUESDAY, OCTOBER 20, 1987     30 CENTS

## STOCKS PLUNGE 508 POINTS, A DROP OF 22.6%; 604 MILLION VOLUME NEARLY DOUBLES RECORD

**U.S. Ships Shell Iran Installation In Gulf Reprisal**

*Offshore Target Termed a Base for Gunboats*

### A Huge Blow to the Five-Year Bull Market

Dow's Record Fall

### WORLDWIDE IMPACT

**Frenzied Trading Raises Fears of Recession — Tape 2 Hours Late**

---

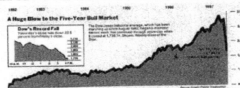

NOW OR NEVER — Cardinals face must-win situation. Page 1C

DOW'S DAY — Local effect. What's next? Pages 3A, 4C, 5C

ART APPEAL — Loves Park man heads art awards. Page 1B

## Rockford Register Star

## U.S. ships destroy Iran oil platforms

# Wall Street 'Armageddon'

**Tumble felt around the world**

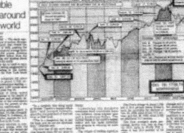

**Rockford bewildered but calm**

## Police made mistakes in Dismuke case, Logli says

**987-1409**

---

## The Philadelphia Inquirer

### Dow Dives 508.32 Points In Panic on Wall Street

*Billions lost in trading*

**Navy blasts Iran oil site in retaliation**

# Chicago Sun-Times

## Wall St. panic

## Los Angeles Times

### Bedlam on Wall St.

## The New York Times

STOCKS PLUNGE 508 POINTS, A DROP OF 22.6%; 604 MILLION VOLUME NEARLY DOUBLES RECORD

# NEW YORK POST

## CRASH

**Wall Street's blackest day rocks nation**

## DAILY NEWS

# PANIC

Dow drops through floor — 508.32

# CHAPTER 30

## BLACK MONDAY

Mark Kledas entered his office on Heather Road just off Conshohocken State Road. The Pseftikos Funds office was in a modest two-story office building that had been built in 1930. The office was nice if not overly modest. The furnishings of the office were hardly a concern to Mark.

For years, he had hustled investments. All the while, he tried to get in good with his wife's family. It took a long time to get the trust built to get in good. His family struggled to enjoy the life of the Joneses.

Eventually he had been set up in his own company to take care of some of his wife's family money. His charge was to make an adequate living at it. "Don't lose the money" was what he was told. "Show well, and then more responsibility can come your way." You can grow with the family like your family grows in life.

The "don't lose it" part was the catch. He had lost a lot of it. He had lost a couple million dollars investing in risky futures. He had invested in futures that were not his to invest in. The future would soon be the present.

Mark was like so many other money managers. He had information on ratios of stocks and financial statement ratios. He had beta data. He had quantitative mathematical models to predict stock values. He had information about management and products and product releases and industry maturity and more information than he could really digest. But he had never managed a company. He had no accounting degree. He had never created a financial statement. He took what information he gleaned and played poker with other people's money. He played poker against the same people as himself. Like a drug addict, the power of money seduced him. Like a drug addict in recovery, he was paying the price.

Now he had a busted nose and a swollen face. When he left Suzy's, he went by the residence of a friend of his that he knew would give him some shelter. He called Joan and lied that he had to go away for the night. He knew she did not believe him, but what else could he do? Then they did laundry to get rid of as much blood and urine as possible.

The brisk October Monday started off with an empty feeling. Donald knew. Donald knew about the falsified financial reports. He knew about the bets he had placed. He knew Mark was toast.

Mark called Rebecca and gave her the week off, so he was in all alone with Jim Beam. He had a .38 in a desk drawer, and he periodically pulled it out and looked at it. He could see his name on the bullet in the chamber. He figured it was either that or be hauled out to one of the outer Philadelphia estates and be fed to dogs or some other painful death.

The situation was so ironic to Mark because if he went to Atlantic City with friends, he could barely make a fifty-cent bet on a number at a roulette table. It was too risky. But bet millions on various market futures? Well, that was different. That was playing the market. That was just business. The irony was that the way things were playing out, he may have done better placing a million dollars on a roulette spin of thirteen and looking for that thirty-six to one payout. Certainly he could have split money and played corners and done better.

What was he to do? He had decided that he may as well go out with a bang. He sold short shares he didn't have at 5 percent less than current market value. He would have to complete the transaction at the end of the week. This was the only way he could possibly make enough money back before month end to save his skin. He sold five lots of one hundred thousand shares each of GE and Goodyear and IBM and CBS and Procter & Gamble. He placed a bet on fifty million dollars of stock he didn't own, hoping it would drop enough to recover the money he had lost. It was a stupid bet because even though the stocks had lost 5 percent in the last week, he still needed these blue-chip items to drop 10 percent more to just break even paying for all his past sins.

Mark didn't have the authority to place the bets, and most brokers wouldn't touch the bets. But there are always a couple gamblers willing to take the risk. These were people who knew that Mark may not be able to cover the bets but that the bets would be made good. Who cared if Mark died along the way?

So now he was drinking. There was nothing else he could do, and it helped ease the physical pain he had. The mental pain was something else that he struggled to deal with. He tried to sleep, but he could not. The phone started ringing quite a few times, but he ignored it. He did not want to speak with anyone. He dozed off on a couch in the room.

Around noon he jumped up. His nose was clogged, and when he blew it, blood started pouring out. He spent the next hour trying to stop the bleeding. He now had a wet, bloody shirt to lie around in. He didn't know what to do.

Desperation and depression drive people to depths of despair. In despair, Mark pulled the .38 out of the desk drawer. He had only fired a gun a couple times in his life, and it had made him nervous to do so. But staring at this pistol made him feel at ease. He could end it all and never have to worry about anything. It would be the easy way out, and Joan and the boys would be taken care of. Donald would see to that. He was the one who had screwed up. He stared and stared and stared at the gun. He started to raise it toward his mouth.

The phone rang, and Mark was startled from his drunken stupor. He dropped the revolver.

## BANG

A report occurred, and a bullet was sent into the wall beside him. The reality of what had just happened scared Mark. He stared at the ringing phone, and he stared at the revolver. He lay on the sofa and started crying.

He had to know what was happening with the stocks he had bet on. His office had a direct line to a brokerage so he could monitor the market. He turned on his computer, but he couldn't tell what was happening. The only thing he saw on his screen was

-**.99

It took a couple minutes for the meaning to filter through Mark's drunken fog. The asterisks meant that the market was collapsing. Mark did not know how much. He started making phone calls. No one in the world could tell where anything was. How many hundreds of points did that mean the market had fallen? How were individual stocks doing? No one in the world could tell. The programmers had never envisioned that the Dow could rise or fall more than one hundred points in a day, but it had. All of Mark's phone calls came back with the same answer. "I can't tell you what is happening."

Evening came around. He awoke again after having passed out from more and more whiskey. He crawled to a wastebasket. He filled it with foul-tasting liquid that came back up.

The phone rang. He looked at it. Was it Joan? Was it a friend? Was it a broker with information? Was it Donald? He was scared to answer. He took the receiver out of the cradle area. He croaked out, "Hello?"

Donald Vitale spoke. "Mark? Are you still there? Jesus Christ, man, are you trying to scare Joan and the kids? They're concerned for your well-being you know."

Mark tried to answer, but he only blew more bile and blood up. The smell only made it worse.

Donald could hear the noises over the phone. He spoke into the receiver, "Mark. MARK! Are you OK? What are you doing there?"

Mark spoke into the phone, "Nutting." His voice was all mouth. The nose was plugged.

Donald spoke. "Jesus Christ, man! You need to pull yourself together! You are the luckiest man alive today! Do you know what happened in the market today?"

Mark managed a "No."

Donald said, "Well, I will tell you what happened in the market today. The market lost over five hundred points! The market lost 25 percent of its value."

Mark tried to answer, but he only blew more bile and blood up. Donald relished what he was hearing over the end of the phone. He waited for a while.

Eventually Donald spoke. "If you're through puking, I'll give you some numbers. But for you, Mr. Lucky, everything you sold short went down over 25 percent." He waited a second before continuing. "Did you hear me? Everything you sold short went down over 25 percent."

Mark was so drunk he barely comprehended what Donald was telling him. The implications of the statements were lost. "What . . . whaddaya mean?"

This angered Donald. He could understand the depression, but Mark was a victim of his own actions. "Mark," he angrily asked, "are you drunk? Good God, man, how much have you had to drink today?"

Mark didn't know what to say. He tried to pull it together. "Yes, I am drunk. I am so fucking drunk I just puked my guts out, and I have a fucking broken nose that you gave me, and I still taste the fucking piss in my mouth that you washed my head in. Is that what you want to hear? Does that make you feel better? You're right. I fucked up. I fucked up royally, but I love Joan, and I love Joseph and Robert, and I am goddamn scared that I will never see them again. Is that what you want to hear? Does that make you feel better? Does it?"

Donald knew that Mark was ready to go off in drunken fury and despair. He did not have time for this. There were many other things he had to deal with at the moment. His voice snapped. "Mark . . . shut the fuck up! Listen to me! Grab something to write with. Do it. Now!"

Mark fumbled around on the desk and got pencil and paper. "I got a pencil."

Donald snapped, "Write the following down: GE, 41; Goodyear, 42; IBM, 103; CBS, 150; P&G, 61. Now did you get that?"

Mark wrote the figures down. "Yeah, I got it."

Donald continued, "*Now* pay attention. I am taking care of all your short deals. They are all good now. And I will take care of letting Joan and the kids know you are all right. And you are to do nothing but sleep it off. Do you hear me? You stay there and don't go anywhere, and I will take care of everything. Do you hear me?"

Mark's head was spinning. He was having a hard time staying conscious. He managed an "I hear you." He then hung up on Donald and fell out of his chair to the floor. Jim Beam had taken control.

A foot was kicking him. He could make out Donald's voice, yelling, "Mark, MARK. Get up! You don't want to be late for your own funeral, do ya?"

Mark made sense of what he was hearing. He slowly rolled around in something wet. The repulsive stench came through to him. In his stupor, he had knocked over the wastebasket, and he was wallowing in his own puke. He heard Donald telling him, "Get up!"

Mark crawled up to the couch. Donald handed him a piece of paper. It read,

| | SOLD SHORT AT | TOTAL SHORT | MORNING PRICE | TOTAL BUY | PROFIT |
|---|---|---|---|---|---|
| GE | $ 47.50 | $ 4,750,000 | $ 41.00 | $ 4,100,000 | $ 650,000 |
| P&G | $ 79.80 | $ 7,980,000 | $ 61.00 | $ 6,100,000 | $ 1,880,000 |
| CBS | $ 185.25 | $ 18,525,000 | $ 150.00 | $15,000,000 | $ 3,525,000 |
| IBM | $ 127.30 | $ 12,730,000 | $ 103.00 | $10,300,000 | $ 2,430,000 |
| GOODYEAR | $ 56.05 | $ 5,605,000 | $ 42.00 | $ 4,200,000 | $ 1,405,000 |
| | | | | | |
| TOTAL | | $ 49,590,000 | | $39,700,000 | $ 9,890,000 |

Mark was staring at the paper. Donald looked around at what he saw. He saw the handgun on the floor. He saw the near-empty fifth of Jim Beam. He saw the blood and vomit all over Mark. He saw a pistol hole in the wall. He smelled the vitriol. He loved it.

Donald bent down and picked up the gun. He checked the chamber to make sure there was a loaded bullet in it. He pointed the gun at Mark's head. Mark cringed in fear. He closed his eyes.

# BANG!

The bullet passed by Mark's skull and entered the wall. Donald spoke. "You are the luckiest man alive today. You are so lucky because you are going to stay alive. I don't know how but the market collapsed today just in time to save your ass. You just went from red to black. But, mister, you better remember this. If I *ever* find out you are pulling *anything* behind my back again, then the next bullet will be through your skull. You hear me? You ever *fuck* with me again and it's all over."

Mark was crying. He nodded his head. Donald continued, "Now pull your shit together. I'm buying you a cheap hotel room and some clothes and some food for the next couple days. I'll even get a maid in here to clean up this mess for you. I'll even smooth things over with Joan for you. But from now on, you *will* do exactly what I tell you!"

# CHAPTER 31

## CUE BALL

It was the ring of a cell phone that awoke Aug. He heard his uncle answer the call. "Mr. Donald! How are you doing?" There was a pause. "Oh, I am just fine. Peachy keen, in fact!" There was a pause. "No, no. He's here, with me." There was a pause. "His car exploded. Evidently someone planted a powerful bomb inside of it." There was a pause and then laughter. "Ah, no, I didn't do it. Yeah, I was thinking the same thing." There was a pause. "No, no. Robert and Joe have started their move to Hollywood. They've already taken over operations at TIE. I think they'll like the change of scenery." There was a pause. "Yeah, well, that doesn't make any sense to me at all." There was a pause. "No, well, ya know, I was told to make those deals happen, so I don't know what to say. I'm doing my best to find things, but I can't make any promises that I can't keep. Everyone knew the risk involved at this late in the game, but it was too sweetheart a deal not to do, so that decision was all out of my hands. I think I will find some things, and I am just getting ready to go to work on that with my house guest, but who can say?" There was a pause. "Yes, yes. I'll be in touch." There was a pause. Thank you, sir, you have a nice day yourself." There was a pause. "The storm? Oh, well, they are still projecting Panama City for landfall. There's an outside chance they say of a category 4 storm, but we should be all set. We're well prepared here. The house is shuttered, and we have food and supplies. It'll be like a major nor'easter

I'm sure." There was a pause. "OK, bye for now." Aug saw the cell phone shut off and inserted in Mark's shirt pocket.

During the call, Aug had been looking around. He could slightly lift his head and shoulders, but he seemed to be restrained. He was restrained. He could raise his head enough to see that he was tied down on a sheet of plastic that had been laid over on top of a full-length pool table. His wrists and legs were tightly tied to the center and end pockets with some kind of wire. His hands were also tied down on the table railing. Wire had been run at an angle through the middle pocket and four pool balls were pinned under each hand. This position laid his hands flat against the balls. He laid his head back down and thought, *Uh-oh, this could not be good.*

Mark realized that Aug was awake. He smiled as he came over. "Augustus! It is so nice to see my favorite nephew again!" He shook Aug's left leg. "How's it hangin'?"

Aug answered, "Hello, Uncle Mark. It's nice to see you again too. It's a . . . It's a hangin' all right. Let me think here a second. It's a . . . it's a hangin' left at the moment. I kinda have ta take a piss though. You know, that early-morning wake-up kind where ya gotta go real bad? Can you kindly help an old altar boy out here and let me go to the can? I'd really appreciate that."

Mark chuckled and smiled. "Ah, Aug, I wish I could . . . but I can't. We went to a lot of trouble to tie you down like this. It really took a lot of effort to get this done. Now it'd be a shame to go and waste all that work and start over again. I just don't think you appreciate how much work went into making you so comfortable. And besides, I know you were never an altar boy!" Mark resignedly sighed, "No . . . I'm afraid you're just going to have to wet yourself. But that's OK. That's why we put all this plastic down! Just to make cleaning up any mess easier."

Mark paused and walked over to a window ledge. It was then that Aug realized that the light was all internal. He could not tell if it was day or night. The window was shuttered. There was an ashtray at the sill. Mark picked up a partially smoked cigar from the ashtray and fired it up.

Aug asked Mark, "So your sons are moving down south, huh?"

Mark smiled at Aug. "Ah, so you did hear that call! I was just wondering about that. Yes. Yes, I'm afraid to tell you that you and Frank have been removed from

TIE and that Joe and Robert are taking over. They needed a new career anyway. It'll be a nice new way to break them into the biz. One of them might even buy that house of yours! I know that you sold it to an agent for a song. I'm sure that the broker is just itching to turn it over. The price outta be very reasonable."

Aug asked, "And my golden parachute?"

Mark came over to the table and pulled on the plastic. "This is your golden parachute."

Aug asked, "And Frank and the rest of my staff?"

Mark said, "You mean your *ex-staff*? Well, what can I say? One way or another, they are all being taken care of."

Aug asked, "So I guess this means that Labor Day at the Jersey Shore is out this year, huh?"

Mark smiled broadly at Aug. "You always were a fast learner. Yes, yes, I suspect that you will not be heading back to the shore ever again. Too bad. I really do wish things had not worked out this way, but ya know whaddaya gonna do?"

Mark stoked the stogie. "Ya know, Aug, since we are having this chat here, I'm gonna tell ya a little story of mine. There was a time when I thought that I would never see the Jersey Shore again. Or any shore for that matter. Ya see, I had screwed up. I was a loser. I was sure I was dead. Hell, I was so sure that I was going to die that I held a gun to my head in anticipation of it. It was while you were at Nova, on Black Monday. And then the strangest thing happened. God sent a miracle, and I was saved. I got a reprieve that maybe I didn't deserve, but I got it nonetheless. And I accepted my fate and made the most of it."

He continued, "I tell you this because maybe you don't deserve your fate, but ya know, Aug, the hand has been dealt. And you, nephew, you are just going to have to live with it. Just like the decisions that I made took me to where I am today and just like the decisions that my sister made took her to where she ended up, you have to face up to the fact that it is the decisions that you made that took you to where you are today."

Aug started laughing at Mark. Mark asked, "What? What's so funny about that?"

Aug said, "You are. You're so funny, Uncle. You're so full of sheeeeeeit! For all your talk about accepting responsibility for your actions, you seem to forget that you are the one who dealt me the hand that landed me here. That was a marked deck you dealt from! Hah! Considering the source, one could say that the deck was truly 'Mark'-ed! All I did was try and cheat the grim reaper just like you have for the last twenty years. Don't forget that I may not have been living at your house while I was in college, but I still remember when you hit it big. I also found out more in the last year about what really happened back then. What really happened is that you got lucky. You got lucky despite your own stupidity."

Aug continued, "You think you are so smart. It shows in how smug you are. You think that you will steal everything for yourself and that your bosses won't realize what happened because you will pin it on me. Hell! You're so obvious that even I know what you are thinking. Think Donald doesn't know what you are up to? Think Donald isn't playing you like you played me? The reality you need to face, Uncle, is that your borrowed time is just about up. One way or another, the reaper is waiting to finally collect from you."

Mark smoked his cigar and looked at Aug. He thought about what Aug was saying. "Really? Is that so?"

Aug said, "Don't take my word for it. I may not be alive to see it happen, but you'll find out soon enough!"

Mark smugly laughed at Aug. "Well, then we shall just have to see about that! Or maybe I should say, nephew, that I will see about that! I don't think you'll be around to know one way or another." Mark looked at Aug's scarred left hand. "Unless you wise up and be straight with me, your scar is going to have some company real soon."

He thoughtfully paused. "Tell you what, Aug. I'm going to ask you questions, and if I feel you give me straight answers, then I'll let you go, and you can take a carefree piss if you like. Deal?" Aug stared at him with grim determination. His uncle continued, "Now I figured out some things"—he stopped and pointed at Aug—"no thanks to you. But that's OK, I can forgive you some indiscretion."

There was puffing on the stogie. Mark smelled victory was in the air.

Aug blurted out, "Why did you have Laurie killed?"

Mark raised his eyebrows and looked at Aug. "Me? Oh, I had nothing to do with that. I only found out about what actually happened to her after you went and hung Joe Khan. I kinda liked that. That was a nice touch. That required some forethought and some help. When we are done here, we will see about addressing those buddies of yours. But it was still well done and required a lot of good timing. It may have been a bit out of character. It was certainly elaborate and extreme. But all in all, well done. I liked that."

Mark paused and continued, "But it made me wonder. It made me wonder why you would go to such an extreme. What was your purpose? So I had Canaan and Tony ask a few people why you would do that, and they got me the answers. And then I found out that maybe it wasn't so out of character after all." Some thoughtful cigar smoking occurred. "You know, I am actually real sorry about that. Laurie got a real shitty deal in life, what with her body betraying her and all. And hanging has gotta be such an ugly way to go." Mark shuddered. "It makes me shiver thinking about it. I wouldn't wanna die that way." Mark paused and then looked at Aug. "Laurie was a good woman and a fine person. Both of you have my sympathies for that."

Mark paused and puffed. He pointed a finger at Aug. "But here's what I don't understand. Why did you go back and kill Joe Kahn?"

Aug seethingly replied, "Because I wanted him to feel what Laurie must have felt. I wanted him to feel that rope choking off his breath while he hung there. Besides, I gave him more of a chance than Laurie ever had. His goon squad had time to cut him down. If they were too slow in cutting him down, then that was his problem. He should have hired better help. I gave him an opportunity to live." Aug paused. "Maybe his cronies just decided to let him die. From what I gather, Joe wasn't very well liked."

Mark got a quizzical look on his face. "Really? Hmmmmm. That is very interesting." Mark paused and looked down, thinking about something.

Mark continued, "OK. Next question. Now, how did you know you were going to be robbed that night at Trove? I mean, you didn't just shit a full set of fake jewels overnight. And how did you know about the metals being smuggled in? You didn't just have a hunch that all that gold and platinum was up at Upper Terra. You knew it was there. Your whole scheme took some planning. So tell me. Who tipped you off?"

Aug replied, "Just like I knew that my uncle was selling me down the river? Thanks a lot for your family help!"

Mark whimsically looked up and then back at Aug. "You know, Aug, I always kinda liked you. But the only reason I took you in was because you were my sister's kid and because my mother wanted my sister's kid, her grandchild, taken care of. So I did. But deep down, you were always Vittelius's son." Mark puffed away. "You know, that man couldn't keep his pecker in his pants." His anger grew, and Mark positioned himself on the pool table so he could get in Aug's face. "My sister was fifteen when he knocked her up. FIFTEEN! What kind of bastard who is twenty-five knocks up a fifteen-year-old and takes her miles away from her family. And then . . . then . . . then he abandons her family. Don't tell me you don't know that your *daddy* was fucking around on the side. I was too young to understand it when it all happened, but I tell you right now, I've got a fifteen-year-old daughter, and if some son of a bitch gets her pregnant now, I'll put a fucking bullet in his brain!"

Mark took a walk around for some more smoke and to regain his composure. He sat back down on the table and addressed Aug, "Now you didn't answer my question. Who tipped you off?"

Aug spoke slowly and angrily, "No one tipped me off." Smarmily he said, "I just figured it all out on my own." He paused a second. "Actually, honestly, I did have a little help."

Mark said, "Really? From whom?"

Aug said, "Madame Cleo. I called her, and she predicted the future." He thought a second and then continued, "Then I got a couple fortune cookies that told me what to expect."

Mark gave him a dejected look at that reply. "Really?"

Aug smiled at him and answered, "Really."

Mark got up from the table. "Suit yourself." He went to a railing to a staircase that went down somewhere that Aug could not see. Mark yelled down. "*Boys, could you come up here? It's time to go to work.*" Footsteps were heard, and the Mountain and the Nose appeared.

Mark looked at Aug and smiled. "Aug, let's play a game of pool. Now I'm gonna tell ya how we are going to play. I'm going to ask questions, and if I don't like your answers, then Canaan here"—he patted the shoulder of the Mountain—"Canaan here is going to take this cue ball"—he held up a cue ball—"and play pool with your hand and the balls underneath. Now, that's just the start. We can move on from there after that to other parts of your body." He raised his arm. "You know, a storm is coming, and people are evacuating the area. No one will bother us. We've got all the time in the world right now."

Mark handed the cue ball to the Mountain. The Mountain came closer to the left hand of Augustus. The Mountain smiled at Aug. His vision flitted from Aug's eyes to his hand.

Mark spoke. "Ya know, Aug, I wasn't quite sure what you had going on until I spied on Frank and saw him handing out Big Black Dick goods to the Trove staff. I knew when I saw that going on that those were the stolen Big Black Dick goods. But how could those goods be stolen and yet be handed out by Frank? If Frank had the skid, then you knew Frank had the skid, which meant that you knew something was up. Now who tipped you off?"

Aug answered, "I don't know what you are talking about."

Mark sighed and looked up the Mountain. Canaan focused in on Aug's left hand.

# BAM! BAM! BAM!

Aug had closed his eyes and averted his head so as to not watch. The three other men in the room started laughing. The cue ball had been brought down on the table rail.

Mark looked at the Nose and then at Aug. Mark said, "Aug! You weren't watching! We can't have that. Don't you know that in sports you always have to keep your eye on the ball? Here, why don't we let Tony help you with that!"

Tony came around and grabbed Aug's head. He held Aug's head toward the view of the left hand, and he pried open Aug's eyes with his thumbs and forefingers. Aug was forced to watch.

# BAM! BAM! BAM!

The cue ball was brought down three times in succession on the three sections of Aug's pinky. The phalange bones shattered. It was very painful to watch. It was more painful to experience. Aug screamed with the pain.

Mark spoke. "Now, Aug, Frank told us that you knew you were going to be robbed. It took a while. It took a painful while for him to tell us. But eventually he did." Mark looked at Canaan.

# BAM! BAM! BAM!

There went the ring finger. One of the tie wires popped from the beating. The knuckle collapsed under the blow. After Aug's screams subsided and enough tears cleaned out of his eyes, he saw that his finger was now shaped like the letter U. The knuckle had been above the gap of space between the spheres. Now it filled the gap.

Mark grinned and looked at the finger and then at Aug. "I hope you sold that wedding band that you used to have. I think it's gonna be a little hard to slip it on now!" He puffed on his cigar. "Now, you knew we were planning to rob you—at least of the jewels. That was the deal. The metals weren't supposed to be touched. But you knew that the jewels were going to be stolen, and you knew it far enough in advance to have a fake set made. Enough of a fake set to buy some time. Now, what I want to know is, who killed my men in the hotel room? They were the ones who were supposed to rob you, but someone took them out and did the dirty deed instead. Now, you tell me, who was your accomplice? Who let you know what was going on?"

Aug sputtered in speech. His body was shaking. "I . . . had . . . no . . . accomplice."

The Mountain didn't even look at Mark. He knew that was not a satisfactory answer.

# BAM! BAM! BAM!

The middle finger shattered in three places. Mark spoke. "Aug," he said in a drawn-out manner, "You're not doing very good here. You're three fingers down, and it won't get any easier." He puffed on his cigar a little. "Now let's try this one. Why'd you kill Jack Dough?"

This surprised Aug. "What are you talking about?" The Mountain raised the cue ball. Aug blurted out loudly, "I don't know what you're talking about!" The Mountain looked at Mark. Mark held up a staying hand.

Mark spoke. "The car bomb you planted last night when you visited his place, before you killed Keith Marshall and the goons that worked for Joe Kahn. The one that exploded and also killed the poor security guard at the security checkpoint at Sandestin. Why'dya do it?"

Aug replied, "I don't know what you're talking about." Mark looked at the Mountain. Canaan looked at Aug and then at his hand. He raised the cue ball, and Aug yelled, "HEY!" Canaan stopped his arm in the air and looked at Aug. Aug looked at him and asked, "What do a Mexican and a cue ball have in common?"

Canaan looked at the cue ball and looked at Aug and looked at Mark and Tony. They all shrugged, and Canaan said, "I don't know. What do a Mexican and a cue ball have in common?"

Aug haltingly laughed from the pain he was in and said, "The harder you hit 'em, the better English you get out of 'em." Aug started laughing harder.

Mark and Tony tried to keep from chuckling but could not keep it in. Canaan let out a "why you son of a—" and then he brought the cue ball down again.

## BAM! BAM! BAM!

There went the index finger. Another wire popped. Aug screamed in pain. Canaan angrily said, "I am a Colombian! I am not a goddamn Mexican!" Aug gasped out, "Yeah, well, y'all look the same to me."

## BAM! BAM! BAM!

Canaan was not amused. There went Aug's thumb.

Tony let go of Aug's head. Aug writhed and screamed in pain. The hand throbbed with every blood surge through it. The blood would rush to his head, and his head throbbed from the latest blow to it. He was covered in sweat from pain. Everything was pain. Aug was not painless.

Mark came over and looked at Aug's hand and then at Aug. "You know, I don't think yer gonna be doin' a good job of grabbing Jocelyn's titty anymore with that hand. Just think about that, Aug. That nice full young piece of flesh. Waiting for you. Ya know, I went looking for her. I wanted to bring her here. So you could see what fun we can have with that pretty young thing. But I couldn't find her. Too bad. It would have been such a nice reunion."

Mark smoked the cigar a little. "Well, anyway. It's time for a new game." The Nose surprised Aug from behind by putting a plastic rod in Aug's mouth to keep the jaw from closing. "It's time to play dentist. Let's have a look at your teeth. Nice! Nice and white. Good-lookin' choppers. Your dentist must be happy with you!" Mark looked at the Mountain. "Canaan, why don't you show Aug the utensil in your back pocket?" Canaan produced a long pair of pliers. "Now, Aug, the choice is yours. Tell me where the jewels are and you can keep your teeth. OK? Now where are my jewels? I know they ain't at your house 'cuz I trashed that place in the last week. I know they ain't at Trove 'cuz I also trashed that place . . . and I figure Frank would have known if they were there and would have told us before we killed him. They weren't in your room at the Hilton. They weren't at your place at TOPS'L. They weren't in your car. So where did you stash them?"

Aug haltingly managed a "Go . . . fuck . . . yourself." He gathered himself. "And the *pobrecito frito* banditos you brought with you!"

The three men looked at each other and then at Aug. Canaan spoke. "Ahhhhhhh, señor, there was no need for that. That was just wrong."

Aug could hear them discussing the teeth. He felt the pliers tapping at the enamel. Mark said, "That one there," and the Mountain affixed the pliers to the upper left front bicuspid. Canaan tugged and tugged and ripped the tooth out and held it for all to see before setting it on the rail. Aug screamed from the pain. Mark told Canaan, "Next to it. That one there," as he pointed. Aug felt the pliers on the tooth. The Mountain extracted the second bicuspid. Aug screamed from the pain. Aug could taste the blood going down his throat as well as feel the pain. He gurgled and spit up blood.

Mark puffed up a red ember on his cigar. "Aug! That's no good. We don't want you to drown in your own blood," he said, and he jammed the cigar into the wound, burning the gum area. Aug wrenched his head in pain. His mouth tasted of blood and ash.

Aug saw the three men grinning and laughing at his misery. Hate welled with the pain. Mark started up again. "Aug, it can all stop. Just tell me where the jew—huh?" There was some interruption. There was a look of surprise on the faces of the men.

# *BANG! BANG! BANG! BANG! BANG! BANG!*

Their heads and necks exploded in rapid succession as bullets tore through the torturers. Tony disappeared to the floor behind Aug. Mark and Canaan wobbled and then fell forward onto the pool table on top of Aug. There were a couple of last breaths and involuntary spasms that occurred. And then there was silence.

Aug was scared. He spit out the rod. He didn't know what was going on. Did the shooter leave? Were they going to come and torture him more for the location of the jewels? Were they here to free him? Nothing happened.

He was in serious pain. He was in tears. He waited. And waited. He saw the blood and skull innards oozing from the dead men. He tried to call out a "HELLO," but he choked on the fear and the blood in his mouth. He started crying. His head ached. His left hand was smashed, and two teeth were gone, and his mouth was burned, and there were dead bodies bleeding on him, and he didn't know if there was another sadist coming to torture him or a Samaritan coming to help him. What was going on? He craned his head to try and see, but there was no one there that he could see. It was silent.

After a fashion, he gained some composure back. He decided that whoever had shot Mark and the henchmen had decided to let him rot. God, he had fucked up. He had thought he was so smart and that he could figure out a way to outsmart everybody, and now he was a train wreck. Well, fuck it, he decided. He wasn't dead yet. What could he do? He thought about his options.

He tested the bonds with his right hand and his feet. They weren't going anywhere. He wasn't escaping without some utensils or some help. He couldn't use any utensils as he was in bondage. There was Mark's phone in his chest pocket on top of him. He could call for help, but how could he use the phone if he couldn't get free? And where would he tell someone he was located?

He looked at his left hand and wrist and arm. The hand was mangled and useless. The wrist and arm were functional, but moving them shot pain spiders throughout his body. His mouth throbbed and hurt and felt and tasted weird. His gums had blistered, and the cigar ash made him choke. He eyeballed the mangled hand. Wires that had held it in place had popped, and it also looked like the wires holding the wrist had also loosened.

He laid back and looked at the ceiling. He looked back at the mangled mess. He steeled himself. He took deep breaths and prepared to cry and scream. With every ounce of energy, he rocked his arm back and forth a bit, stomaching the pain until he had wiggled his wrist and hand a bit, and then he wrenched backward with his shoulder and arm as hard as he could to try and yank the hand free. The pain caused him to pass out.

---

He wasn't really sure how long he had passed out, but he was choking on blood. He spit it out on his chest. His body was wet with sweat. His gums felt sore and gushy soft like they were ready to burst with some yucky puslike substance. His arm had hardly moved a bit. But there had been slight movement, and by pressing down with his wrist, he might be able to pop one of the pool balls to the floor. He pressed down, crying with the pain. One ball went, dropping with a thud. One of the two pool balls near the fingers had pushed forward, and that had been knocked to the floor by the back ball pushing forward. Now he needed to work another ball out. He pressed down with his wrist and popped it out underneath what remained of his fingers. He disappeared from reality again.

---

He awoke choking again. He spit up more blood.

He tested his bonds. There was enough slack now. He could work the other balls loose and out. The hand was completely free, and the wrist was somewhat loose. He steeled himself and took deep breaths. This time he could pull back and rip his hand and wrist free. The pain surge was intense, but he could stand it this time without passing out.

Aug could now lean up. He now knew what a boxer who went the distance must feel like. It was the feeling of going on willpower. He needed to call someone. He needed to call . . . the Champions. They had to get the jewels.

Everything was gross and nauseating. The air smelled of sweat. The air smelled of blood. The air smelled of the insides of the corpses. They had released upon death. The air smelled of cigar. The smell of vomit was soon added to the unique mixture of aroma.

He leaned his elbow forward and elbowed Mark's body back enough so that he could elbow out the phone. Every single move with his claw arm was excruciating, and he could feel every pulse of his heart pump blood through the maiming. The endorphins were morphinelike. He was zombified in pain. Thank God he had long arms. Hallelujah! The phone came out, and it was not a flip-top design. But how was he to dial a number?

He had to slowly work the phone toward his head by dragging it with his elbow. Drool and blood and other substances were dripping from his mouth. It took some time and effort, but he got the phone toward his head. Now he had to work the pliers to his mouth and clamp down on the metal. Then he had to remember the number. He came up with it and slowly, painfully was able to punch the phone numbers with the pliers in his mouth. It was nearly impossible to do. He hit send, and the call went through. Voice mail never sounded so good and so long. It took forever for the generic "Leave a message after the tone" statement to cycle through. The Champions wouldn't pick up a call from Mark.

It was a struggle to speak; speaking hurt his mouth, and it had been so painful to make it this far. "Guys, it's me I . . . I . . . I fucked up. It's over. Get . . . get the loot as fast as you can after the storm before anyone gets back to town. It's over . . . I . . ." Aug never finished. He blacked out for one last time.

# CHAPTER 32

## LAURIE VALENTINE

He was in the hospital. She lay in the bed. He was beside her.

Laurie was having an ultrasound done at what was believed to be the eighteenth week of pregnancy. Augustus was there to provide support, just as he had done throughout the process. The process of getting here today had been difficult, and every day seemed even more difficult, but she had made the decision to move forward.

It all started shortly after their marriage and move to Hollywood. Their house was a two-story house. It was late afternoon. She was excited. Auggie would be home soon. Laurie felt fertile.

Dinner would be lobster newburg. Dessert would be strawberry cheesecake. She had procured a bottle of Marilyn Merlot for them to drink. Now was the time for Laurie to get (va-va-voom) dressed.

Their house had two levels. It had fifteen risers between the levels, although Laurie never counted them before. She always just walked up them. Maybe thirteen really was unlucky. When she hit thirteen, she hit the wall. Actually what she hit was the railing and the steps she had just finished walking up. But Laurie was not aware of that. She had blacked out.

In the beginning, there had been the "blackout count-o-meter" chronicling when and what happened when she blacked out. It scared her, and it scared her to think of it in the context of the phrase *scared her to death*. As time went on, she learned more as the blackouts continued. She realized that it was death calling her. As time went on and she learned more, there was no need for the count of how many times she blacked out because it didn't matter. There were just too many blackouts to care to count.

It scared her when she awoke and didn't know where she was or how she had gotten there. The first time, Augustus came home, and he found her at the base of the stairs. Like a dumb blonde, she was clueless as to what had happened, but she wasn't a dumb blonde, and she had a clue. This was not right. Something was wrong.

But you know, it's just one of those weird things that can be laughed off, right? Laurie was in her early twenties and was a very attractive healthy woman. She had a healthy-enough figure to model bathing suits, and she wasn't bulimic or anorexic. Aug could sense her fear, and he proposed a most sensible solution. He said, "Let's go shopping at Bal Harbor this weekend, and you can have whatever you want."

It was a busy weekend at the mall. Various celebrities were there, walking about. It was exciting because the shopping crowd was somewhat thick. They had started at Neiman and had been through Vera and Cartier and Tiffany and were at Saks when Laurie disappeared from reality again. In midspeech, while talking to some clerks and other shoppers. Just *pffft* and gone.

The next dose of reality was waking up somewhere, and Aug and people were around and staring at her and jabbering at her, and she wished they would all shut up and leave her alone. She felt tired. She felt anemic.

One life died and another began. The blackouts continued. The doctors didn't know what they were dealing with. Gourmandal gluttony; gone. The diet became whey. Only the blandest of bland so that the doctors could eliminate food as a possible event trigger. Eventually they figured out what it was. Laurie was the victim of hypertrophic cardiomyopathy. This meant that Laurie physically had a broken heart. The heart did not speed up when it was supposed to. Exertion caused blackouts due to a lack of oxygen brought on by a dearth of blood flow.

It caused some days to be unreal. Laurie would be almost unable to function. Her head would lay at ninety degrees on her shoulder, and the world seemed as if in a lazy dreamlike state. It would be so easy to let go and give in. But if you give in on one day, you give in on every day. So you fight to be productive.

Her marriage became transcendental. She blacked out during sex, causing Aug to freak out. Was she dead? Amorous physical contact was dealt with trepidation from that point forward. It was hardly the kind of emotion that people should have when engaging in libidinous passion, but they never knew when the next or last time was. Their physical relationship became very weird, and their love became true because the truth of love is that true love transcends physical contact.

Her old friends and her family were far away. They talked about moving back up north and decided not to. They would beat the illness. They would not let the illness defeat them.

Laurie's friends grew more distant. They couldn't relate. They were obsessed with men and clothes and children and parties and careers and money and pills and sex "and . . . and . . . and . . ." It was never-ending "anding." They talked about their illnesses and surgeries and implants and beauty treatments. They could go to "drugstores," and take all sorts of medications and preparations to help them with their daily lives. Laurie could not engage in these activities. She had potent pills that must be taken, and if she was lucky, she might complete a waking cycle with some sense of normalcy. Her friends were too possession oriented to really understand that. It didn't jibe with their concept of life. The concept of only just wanting a real day of life was beyond them. Her friends took life for granted.

It wasn't sin that had caused her disease. She had "Why me?" but no "Why me, God?" in her. The disease wasn't evil, and she wasn't a plaything in the realm of good and evil and God versus Satan. It was just a crappy genetic deal. Like a stray bullet hitting an innocent bystander in a drive-by shooting or in a war zone, Laurie was the victim of unintelligent design.

She found solace as a volunteer in the pediatric oncology ward at Joe Dimaggio's Children's Hospital. Her strength helped give strength to children who weren't as mature as she was, and their strength helped give Laurie strength. It was the strength to soldier on.

Some things did not change. She was still regular, and she made a decision that she wanted to have a child. The majority of people in her world said, "No, don't do it. You will kill either the fetus or yourself or both." But if she did not try, then why bother with life? If her life was not worth the possible life of her child's life, then what was the point anyway? Death was a sacrifice that she was prepared to make.

The miscarriages took their toll. So did the sudden deaths of her mother and her brother. Heart attacks claimed them. They were as devastating as her broken heart was. Laurie was the queen of broken hearts. She had multiple broken hearts, but enough time and people passed, and soon only those in the know knew. Her shell of resistance hardened.

And here she was with her love, Aug. They had made it to the eighteenth week, and they were at the hospital. There was a nervous, joyous anxiety as the nurse applied the gel to her belly. They smiled and glibly talked about nothings. Aug tickled her and kissed her. He chided her that for a person who disappeared from reality a lot, she sure had spent last night awake as they lay there together in bed. They held each other's hands. He ran his fingers through her long curly hair and told her how much he loved her and how wonderful their child would be.

The sonogram was started. Images appeared on screen. They looked at the images. The nurse was happy with what she saw. Aug was happy with what he saw. But Laurie was not. She was not a dumb blonde. She knew. And she had to ask:

"Nurse, where's my baby's head?"

She did not see a face. The face looked like the white theater masks of the happy face and the sad face. What passed for a head had a featureless smooth skin.

The nurse looked closely at the monitor. Then the nurse reached up and turned off the monitor. She said, "I have to go get the doctor."

Laurie knew it was over. She rolled over on her side, mouth open, breathing heavily. She felt Aug's hand in her hands, but she saw nothing. She had failed both of them. Again. With eyes wide open and tears streaming from them, she silently wept.

# CHAPTER 33

## LET GO

He was in the hospital. He lay in the bed. No one was beside him.

He had failed her in life, and he had failed her in death. It was all over now.

Greg Czarnacki and the feds somehow knew where he was. They stormed the house and brought Aug to the Sacred Heart Hospital. Whatever could be briefly done with his hand and mouth was addressed. The hand was in a soft cast. His wrists were handcuffed to the bed rail.

Premeditated murder was to be the charge. Six murder counts for the three people at Keith's and the three men at the pool table. Sure, it made no sense that a man tied to a pool table could have committed the murders, but there would be no problem charging Aug with the crime. Perhaps evidence would be fabricated. Perhaps not. Regardless, Aug was going nowhere.

Aug didn't care anymore. While he had never killed anyone, he was just as guilty as whoever had. And what difference did it make? Jack Dough was beyond his reach. Aug knew he wasn't dead. The car bomb had to be a ruse. Jack would get away with some of the loot. It would not be all of it, but it would be enough. The thought gave Aug no satisfaction because Jack would get away without ever having to answer for Laurie's murder. Aug was not mentally at Sacred Heart Hospital.

Hurricane Bill was coming. The storm was a day and a half away. The doctors and dentist patched him up somewhat and filled him with some sustenance and morphine. Now they were prepping him to be transferred to Tallahassee to weather the storm. The evacuation of the Destin/Sandestin area was underway. The hurricane routes were wall-to-wall with cars. Greg informed Aug that two of his agents would drive Aug there to Tallahassee to answer for his deeds. Greg was too busy with other hurricane-preparation tasks, but he would join them in a day for interrogation.

It was nighttime when they left. A resigned Aug was walked down to a transport van. He was left to his own thoughts as he lay handcuffed in the back of the van. The morphine was beginning to wear off, and he was somewhat able to think.

He thought of the irony of the situation. Laurie had wanted the blackouts to disappear, and right now he wanted a blackout to appear. He didn't want to feel the physical pain of his injuries and the mental pain of his failures. He wanted to sleep. He wanted to black out. But he could not.

The van slowly turned onto US 98 and drove in the opposite direction from the Emerald Parkway. He was leaving the Emerald City behind. Jocelyn's eyes were emerald green and her ring was emerald green, and he was leaving it all behind. There was no way he would ever see Jocelyn again from prison. He had lost Laurie and Jocelyn. He had lost his parents, and he had lost Angel. He had gambled in life, and he was a big-time loser. This time, the roll of snake eyes was worth nothing.

The highway was crawling. It was wall-to-wall with vehicles like a megalopolis traffic jam. Red taillights illuminated the night like slowly marching army ants. Laurie had spoken to Aug about the feeling of being alone in the crowd of people in the world. Aug felt alone in the line of evacuees. When the storm had passed, they could return and rebuild homes. There was to be no rebuilding for him. The self-pity wallow was eddying.

Aug thought about it, thought about the pain coming in his hands, the throbbing in his mouth, the comedown from the morphine. What the f—? Where the hell did he get off with self-pity? After the damn misery that Laurie went through, what right did he have feeling self-pity? He had toured the ward of child cancer patients with Laurie and seen what real devastation was like. Real devastation is when you never have a choice. His reality was due to choices he had made, and there will still be choices he could make. He needed a new plan; that is what he needed. He needed to find a way to take back control of the situation.

He sat up and started to think about his surroundings. It had taken nearly an hour and a half for the vehicle to reach the Clyde Wells Bridge. This was a trip that normally took ten to fifteen minutes. It was going to be a long drive to Tallahassee. What could he do before the vehicle arrived? Should he try bribing the drivers? He did know where a lot of cash equivalent of money in jewels was located.

He looked through the partition dividing the back of the van to the front and out the front window. They were just about to access the Choctawhatchee Bridge. He leaned forward and was about to make an offer when the vehicle suddenly turned to the right off the road. A man moved a barricade aside and the vehicle drove forward and under the bridge. They were at the fishing access area underneath the bridge. The van was shut off, and the lights were turned off. It was dark underneath the bridge. Drivers exiting over the bridge later said they saw flashes of light briefly illuminate the area below the bridge.

The door to the back of the van opened. In the dark, Aug could see Greg Czarnacki standing there with a flashlight in his hand.

Greg spoke. "Hello, Aug, nice to see you again. Surprised?" Greg entered the vehicle. In his hands were some of Aug's clothes taken from his luggage. The clothes were dropped. Greg undid the manacles. Aug stared at him in surprise. Greg told him, "You better change quickly. The faster we are outta here, the better."

Aug was not about to argue with the plan. He changed clothes as fast he could with a busted-up hand and exited the van. Greg was waiting for him. Aug walked up to the front of the van and looked at the bodies in the front. Tom Welsh and John Flack lay dead. There were entry wounds from bullets in their heads. Two Upper Terra boxes were in the front of the vehicle with them

There was another van there, and it had thirty-six Upper Terra boxes. Greg was taking Upper Terra boxes out of the one van and placing them in the vehicle with the dead men. A service vehicle that read Florida Emergency Vehicle was also present. Aug watched Greg's actions with curiosity. He walked over to the van he had been freed from and made a move toward one of the newly loaded boxes.

"DON'T," Greg said sternly. "Don't do that. There are some charges set inside, and I would hate for you to accidentally set anything off early from looking in the box." Greg finished loading six boxes in the back of the van. Three went down each side of the transport. When he was done, Greg shut the van doors and came over to where Aug was standing.

Greg removed a cigar from his pocket and offered it to Aug. He took another one out for himself. "You know, it's a shame. My staff was dirty. And they came here to meet your associates and pick up their cut. And your associates killed them and broke you out of jail. You'll now be wanted on eight murder charges." He paused and smiled. "Of course, I could run you on in now."

Aug shook his head. "Thanks, but no thanks. I'll take a pass on that."

Greg went on, "I thought you would say that." He flipped Aug a set of keys. "There's a vehicle there for you. You'll need an emergency vehicle to get around Sandestin."

Aug was confused. "What makes you think I'll go back to Sandestin?"

Greg replied, "Because I figure you have to. The jewels can't be anywhere else, or I or someone else would have found them. And I don't think you're going to leave them there for a hurricane to possibly take them away. Besides, I think you've still got a score to settle."

Aug held up the cigar. Greg offered him a light. Aug took a couple puffs. "You wouldn't, by chance, happen to have a few more of these, wouldja?"

Greg smiled and gave him a couple more stogies. "Here ya go. These are as much yours as mine anyway. It isn't Jocelyn's you-know-what, but you can blow a Big Black Dick or two tomorrow."

Aug continued, "You know where Jack is, don't cha?" Greg nodded. "And you're not coming with me?"

Greg shook his head. "I've got enough plunder for me," he said, looking at the Upper Terra boxes. "Besides, I can't just disappear for a while. I've still got a day job to deal with." He looked around. "Someone's gonna call to have this mess cleaned up. But I did leave ya with a full tank of gas!" He paused for a puff and an exhale. "Anyway, I imagine that once the storm is done, the area will be under martial law to prevent looting. I think I know where you're going and where to look to pick you up when the storm is done. You've only got a little time to square your debts. I don't see you being able to exit on the roads when this is done. I'll be looking for you."

Aug hopped into the emergency vehicle. He started the engine and pulled up to Greg on his way out. Aug rolled down the window and motioned Greg over. "Tell Jack to meet me at Poseidon's in another morning." He looked at the dash clock. The time was midnight. "Tell him eight AM on, what, that'd be Thursday, is it? My sense of days is messed up. Thirty-two hours from now."

Greg laughed. "Aug, you lost a day. We had you under for a full day. That would be Friday morning."

Aug said, "Really? Friday, huh? Well, then it will be a good Friday indeed."

Aug looked forward and then looked back to Greg and said, "Though I do have one more question for ya, and you don't have to answer it but . . ." Aug looked back at the car full of Upper Terra boxes. "What makes you so sure you got gold and platinum in those boxes? What makes you so sure that you don't have thirty boxes of silver instead?" With that, he floored it on out of there.

# PART III

## THE LANTERN OF DIOGENES

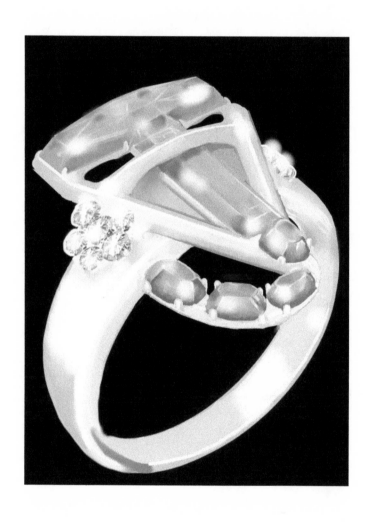

# CHAPTER 34

## HURRICANE BILL

When a hurricane is approaching, everyone holds their breaths on every wisp of wind. Is this the wind that will not stop blowing? One waits, holding one's breath. Then the wind stops, and you realize that your own anticipation got the better of you. For a moment, until the wind blows again, the anticipation process renews itself.

Eventually the wind starts and doesn't stop. The atmosphere always goes from dead calm to a slight constant and then slowly ratchets up in power during each passing hour.

The evolution of people is such that humans expand to new horizons. Humanity didn't build on the beach because the eventual storm would come and destroy what had been built. People with unintelligent design now build on the beach, perfecting the intelligent design that will withstand the storm. Humans test and probe new horizons with new building materials and new building methods just like nature tests and probes new species with evolutionary trials of unintelligent design until the acceptable improvement is made, and then there is intelligent design. What is either intelligent or unintelligent design always depends on the belief of the beholder.

Aug had a day to think and plan his intelligent design. His unintelligent design had got him this far. His dream home on the beach had been destroyed, yet he was determined to rebuild it. Like evolution, he couldn't know whether he had intelligent design until the time was ripe for the fruit to be plucked. He hoped that the plant made it far enough to bear fruit.

He drove that night from the bridge past the parade of cars. He was headed back to the Emerald Parkway. It was his yellow gold brick road. The thought bolstered his confidence. It was a sign, he thought. Like a sign from Sybil or Madame Cleo or Sydney Omarr or the Delphi Oracle or from a fortune cookie foretelling a positive future. The unseen stars were aligning in his favor.

He spent the day at TOPS'L inside a darkened residence. The residence was eerily dark because of the hurricane shutters that were in place. No light entered the condo. He was allowed into the complex because he had an emergency vehicle. Everyone else was evacuated.

Electrical power still existed at TOPS'L. It wouldn't last, but when would it go? Like the teasing wind, electrical power was a temporary wonder.

The place had been ransacked. When he entered, he eagerly went to the ghetto blaster. He opened the back of the case where the batteries go. The package he had hidden when Angel snooped around upstairs was still inside. The searchers had not accidentally found it. It was a gauze-wrapped package about four inches in length and had some depth. He needed to put it on his person. But where? He decided that he could wedge it hidden inside the wrist area of the hand cast. It caused pain to keep it there, but the pain was painless.

There was the box of Grape-Nuts in the cupboard and not much else to eat. Aug ate the dry cereal to get some nutrition. No matter how hard he tried to keep the meal on the right side of his mouth, there was no way to keep the granular substance from eventually grating against his puffy gums. It caused pain to eat, but the pain was painless. If this was to be his last meal, then it was a good supper.

He smoked his cigars as he thought about the murder raps on his head. The smoke added a nice taste to the wretched breath that he now had. The government would have a hard time proving guilt even with planted evidence. He might be guilty of leaving crime scenes, but proving murder in a court of law would be difficult. Still, proving smuggling and tax evasion probably would not be difficult. Augustus would have to evolve into a new animal. Fortunately, he had anticipated that, and his exit plan was underway.

*I have never murdered anyone*, he thought, *nor have I killed anyone*. The differentiation between killing and murder had never been so clear and so blurred in his mind. He was a carnivore. He did "eat steak." He had wanted to cut up and eat a big ol' steer. At a minimum, he had wanted to visit the slaughterhouse and throw an eyeball in a cup. He was now different from the Aug whom Laurie had married. He was now different from the man she had loved. Through intelligent design, he had evolved. It was his admission that he was the same as the rest of the lot of criminals.

The lot of them. Lot. The story of Lot. What Aug knew of the story of Lot was that Lot was a man of family and means who had it all wiped out through a bet between God and Satan, and then Lot got a replacement set back through his piety and belief. Kinda cool for Lot. Kinda. Kinda cool for the replacement family. Kinda not cool for the first family. They all died or were maimed and then died. It sucked to be them. They were like a footnote. Lot's children were wiped out, kinda like the kids who didn't survive the pediatric oncology ward and were wiped out. They became footnotes in someone's story of unintelligent design. Lot had evolved as had the story of Lot. It was the story of Lot that was the true embodiment of intelligent design.

Aug wasn't very pious, and he had no beliefs—at least not in the religious kind. So would his plans reward him with a new and happy life, with a new wife and children? At least, in a casino, he had liked casting lots.

*Geez*, he thought, *I really must be tired. That's some pretty weird stuff running through my head.* He tried to sleep and was somewhat successful. He was very concerned about crashing way too late, and he had no alarm clock. As the daytime grew into evening and late night, the wind started picking up. The sound of wind grew slowly, calling to Aug in a variety of voices that did not cease even for one second. When he moved his restless body with their calls, he shot pain through his injured body, but he was glad he didn't have any drugs to inhibit the pain. The pain made him feel alive, and the more the pain hurt, the less he felt it.

Eventually he got up and went out to the truck to check what time it was. The wind kept the door ajar a bit, but the gale was not too bad yet. The wind power of the storm had not rolled in yet. The truck dash told him it was three AM.

He decided he had taken enough rest. He opened the glove box and discovered a flashlight for emergency use. He took it and started off on a jog to the beach, using the torch to periodically illuminate the way.

It was a circuitous couple of miles to reach the beach area. At the beach, there was the gazebo pavilion near where the band stage had been. The geometric shape provided a bench and shelter from most of the increasing wind force, but the ever-present wind sound kept increasing. It was dark, and no one was around. His plan was to wait and surprise Jack upon Jack's arrival. He lay down on the bench. Despite the noise of the wind, his mental and physical exhaustion took full control. Aug blacked out.

Aug awoke and anxiously wondered what had happened and where he was. There was cloudy light in the air, and the wind was whipping violently. He oriented himself with his surroundings. He was still in the gazebo.

Rain had started falling. The tempo of the rain was moderate. It came down at a wind-blown forty-five-degree angle. The ever-persistent wail of wind was louder and would rise louder when stronger gusts blew. Then it would drop back to a range of force higher than what had been the lowest level the time before.

There was light, but not sunlight. It was "dark light." He turned his eyes to the beach and was stunned by what he saw. The last time he had been here, there had been seemingly thousands of boats and people in the water and on the land and sand castles of glory. There had been a hundred yards of pure white sand and beer tents and food tents and roasting pigs and warm revelry. Now there was a swelling angry sea. The beach was almost gone. The tidal surge had already come up to Poseidon's.

Jack Dough was standing outside of Poseidon's. His golf bag was against the door of the building, providing weight to keep the door from blowing open via the wind. Jack was scratching both his head with his hand and the sand with a club. Periodically Jack wiped the rain from his face and hands. He smoothed out a lie and dropped a ball, aiming east. He tagged a nice bunker shot into the breeze and watched the ball sail in the jet stream. A smile crossed his face. He appeared to be having fun.

Another ball was dropped. The position was manicured. The ball was teed up in the wet sand. The swing was made, and both the club and the ball went sailing. The ball sailed into the breeze, and the club sailed into the tidal surge. He thought Jack let out a "Goddammit," but he couldn't be sure. From the distance he was at, the wind championed all sound.

It was time for Aug to head down. First, he had to have his head down. The morning wake-up call was in his third leg. His stream never touched ground. The force of the wind was strong enough to gather it before it alit.

Aug looked at the palm trees that were near the beach. They were bending in the breeze. The branches angled a quarter of the way down and would snap back only to be thrust down again. Their fronds were blown mostly to the east side like a person in the wind having a bad hair day.

When Aug was empty, he made his way down to meet Jack. He could barely hear Jack's wave of hello that was shouted at him. The tropical storm winds were gale-ing, and the full force of the hurricane was not far off. When Aug made it down, Jack offered a hand in greeting; Aug just stared at him.

Jack shrugged. "Suit yourself," he yelled. "I was wondering when you would get here! I kept looking around and around, but I saw no sign. I thought maybe the cops nailed you again. You are many hours late. I thought you were more prompt than that! I've been killing time any way I can. Hell, we must be almost past the tropical force winds. I kinda wish I had an anemometer here." Jack looked at Poseidon's and laughed. "I spent millions on this place, and within one week of opening it, I'm already complaining about the little things I didn't buy.

Aug gave a dig. "Yeah, I'll bet. That mural with your face as Poseidon must have set you back a minimint by itself."

Jack replied, "Hey! That's just the Mel Brooks in me! 'It's good to be the king!' Or maybe I am just like Solomon, and I built the Temple Mount for capitalists to worship at." Jack paused a second. "I suppose that is a little strong, but no one knows the names of who actually funded the building of the temples of the Greek gods. And this temple is on the beach and not the mount, but who is to say if the building techniques available today weren't available back then, that they wouldn'ta built on the beach anyway."

He continued, "But regardless, that's what runnin' the show getsya. Ya get ta do things like that. Don't tell me that you have had that feeling at some point when running Trove. Now, now I guess that Marky Mark's boys will get that feeling, although somehow I think you both knew that was coming and that you won't miss it one day. That's kinda a definition of life, isn't it? Something's ya miss every day, and something's you're glad to have moved on from them."

Jack looked at the sky and sea and opened his arms up to them. He had an immense smile. "Goddamn, don'tcha just lovit?" Jack had to almost yell to be heard. He rotated his hips in a swivel around, looking at the world of nature. "This is just awesome! Much cooler than a blizzard, although much warmer at that. This wind will get a lot stronger than a blizzard does."

The wind was pushing them around. They were constantly reestablishing their position. The rain pellets stung a bit.

Aug offered back, "I'm more partial to an ice storm myself. The ice locks everything in time and space. The ice freezes the world the way it was. It's especially beautiful in the woods where the sound of the tree branches cracking is like gunshots going off."

Jack told him, "Ya know, that's kinda the difference between you and me. You like everything frozen in time. Hell, you want everything frozen in time. You want to go back in time! Me? Me, I'd just as soon keep movin' forward. Keep on evolving, maybe . . . keep on truckin' as it were."

Jack looked around at the rain and sand blowing everywhere. He looked at the tree trunks and branches bending deeper and deeper in the gusts while the two of them steadied themselves. He finished, "But wind, snow, ice, rain—it doesn't really matter much now, does it? Either way in any big storm, we all lose power, and then there's a big mess to clean up afterward."

An increase in wind force blew through. The two men couldn't hold themselves steady on the ground. It forced the two of them to stumble. They righted themselves.

Jack held up his golf club. "I'd offer you a swing," he said, pointing the club at Aug's hand. "But I heard about yer hand there. Too bad! You can really tag a five iron in this breeze! I've never before hit iron shots as far as Tiger can!" Another wind power increase nearly knocked them over. Jack looked around and said,

"Well, we better get inside while we can. It won't be long, and we won't be able to get the door shut."

The two men soldiered through the gale to the door. They moved the golf bag inside. They opened the unlatched door of the double door system. The wind took it from there, pushing the door open stiff. Aug stood outside and tried to wedge the door back with the weight of his body while Jack pulled on the door handle. They could not get the door shut. The wind was too powerful.

A metal link chain for chaining the locked doors at night was on the floor of the restaurant. They tied off an end of the chain against the closed door of the double doors and wrapped the chain through the open door handle. Like sailors hoisting a cannon, they pulled the chain link by link until they finally closed the door. Hastily they secured the locks and chained the doors. Both of them collapsed into chairs surrounding a four-person dining table. They looked at the door and were quite surprised and quietly concerned to see the glass in the door bubble inward and then recede back, but not all the way.

The building was eerily lit. Electrical power had gone down. The daytime dark extended through the ceiling glass and the beach glass front but only provided some illumination. The daytime dimly lighted the dining tables and chairs pushed against the wall and the pillars on the floor. There were a few tables placed around the pillars and bar area that had candles lit. Wafting wicks added a surreal glow. The mermen and mermaids had a menacing glean to their visages. The sound was way quieter inside, but the sound of the wind still moaned through. The candlelight flickered. The rain really started to come down heavily. The storm surge was climbing up the base of the building.

There was a reddish brown box on the table and a Coleman lantern. Jack lit the lantern. He picked up the box and pulled out a fancy-looking bottle of blended scotch whiskey. He tore off the plastic covering from the lid and opened the bottle. He offered the bottle to Aug. "I hope you aren't above joining me in a shnort of the creature. I brought this here especially for you. And since we are now stuck here until the storm passes and we are in a bar, we might as well drink." He noticed Aug trying to read the label in the light. "It's a thirty-eight-year Chivas Regal. They call it the Stone of Destiny brand, and I thought that, well, all things considered, the Stone of Destiny seemed apropos. Don't you?"

Aug took a belt from the bottle and handed it to Jack. "That is some excellent whiskey. My compliments to the chef." He watched as Jack took a blast.

Jack looked around and spoke. "Ya know, a couple of us die, and the whole world goes to hell. Plans were in place for this building to be shuttered up, but I guess people forgot what they were supposed to do. Good help *is* so hard to find these days." He took some more drink and passed the bottle back.

Aug replied, "Yeah, or maybe it's just another insurance scam of yours. Maybe it's just Jack John being ever the opportunist as always." Aug stood up and drank some more. He handed the bottle back.

Jack feigned surprise at Aug. "Aug! Now see? There ya go, trying to rile me up. Me? Insurance scam? Heaven forbid, no way. I've never done anything like that in my life." He took a belt and handed the bottle back.

"Yeah, right" was Aug's sarcastic retort. He threw a bit more down and took a few steps to the nearest pillar. It was a Raquel Welch and Marcello Mastroianni pillar. He held the bottle by the neck.

Jack smiled and watched his motions with interest. He pleaded innocence. "Honestly. Whatever gave you the idea that I pulled an insurance scam?"

Aug answered, "Because I chased down your old business partner and had a long conversation with him, and he told me about some of your past dealings. That's what gave me the idea." Aug paused and cocked his head and looked at Jack. "There was one scam in particular that I found interesting. It was a story about the insurance man being told that his wife was screwing around, which was true but not true with whom he was led to believe his wife was fooling around with. But not knowing any better and believing the untruth, the insurance man helped devise a scheme whereby one crook was set up to be framed for a robbery that wasn't a robbery and a drug deal that wasn't a drug deal. And the real paramour escaped all true indictment!" With that, Aug smashed the bottle on the pillar to get a jagged glass edge. He turned to swing the edge at Jack. He broke off his swing due to the sight of the revolver in Jack's hand.

"Tsk tsk tsk" was the belittling from Jack. "AUG! That was a huge waste! I spent damn near six hundred dollars on that whiskey for you, and you spill it all over the floor! Jesus Christ, man, we coulda at least finished more of the bottle before ya did that. I tell ya I'm more angry about the crime of wasting that fine whiskey than I am at the cost of the bottle! I thought you had more taste than that, more refinement. Instead, you're just like a bull in a china shop, smashing everything you see to get to your end." He motioned Aug to the front of the restaurant with menacing waves of the pistol. "Let's walk up front. Let's have at least a little light as long as we are going to shed light on the situation." They moved to the front. Their eyes saw that the large glass panes fronting the beach ballooned inward and back like a person starting to form a floating bubble by blowing through a ring and then stopping, causing the bubble start to fall back to the ring. The sight made both of them uneasy.

Jack started, "Look around you, Aug. What do you see? Do you see a beautiful house where people can come and have fun? I wanted to show you nice features of the place the other night, but sadly, you just couldn't stay still. Just like when you were a kid. You had to impetuously run off."

Jack continued, "Now, I built not only this building but also some nice fortunes for our friends up north. I took care of many problems for our friends up north. And what is it going to get me? They wanted me to fall on my sword for them. To go do hard time. While they enjoy life on the outside. I ask you, Aug, 'Who made them God to decide that I should lose years of my life?' If I had to die from this life to avoid the future designed for me, then so be it. I can move forward." Jack looked around. "And if Poseidon's crashes into the sea because of this hurricane, well then, so be it. What's my loss? It isn't my loss. It's my onetime benefactor's loss. The benefactors who relinquished belief in me. No insurance fraud. Just tit for tat. That's a concept that I believe you believe you know all about, don't you?"

Aug glared at him. Jack went on, "Speaking of retribution, ya know, I had some fun times with Vitellius. He was a good friend of mine. We made some good scores together, and we made some good money together. And honestly, he was always quite the ladies' man. Hell, look at your mother. When the situation arose, he was happy to take advantage of it. But there wasn't any woman that he wouldn't do. I'd always told him, 'Don't screw with me, and I won't screw with you.' Well, he screwed with me, and I screwed with him. He took away from me something that was *mine*! It was that simple."

"You are such a fucking hypocrite," Aug seethed.

"Oh fuck you, Aug," Jack snapped back. "If you hadn't been such a thuggy youth, then who knows what might have happened? Maybe you'd be inheriting everything down here in Sandestin that I built! Hell, if Vitellius would have just died in that El Dorado, it would have made everything so simple. We set him in that El Dorado. We set him up with the police. We even rigged an air bag in there to explode and make sure he died, but somehow, it just crushed his legs and spine."

Aug told him, "Sure. And that's why you had your wife killed with him!"

"SHE KILLED HER FUCKING SELF!" Jack's breathing was exceedingly rapid and heavy. "You have no fucking idea how close I came to calling the whole goddamn thing off. You think I wanted Ginger, my wife, Ginger, dead? You know a little bit about the pain of having your wife die, don't you? I loved Ginger! Goddammit, man, she wasn't even supposed to be in the fucking car! But nooooooooo, she had to come along! And then I stood in the house and watched and debated what to do. It had taken a long time to set everything up just right, and then she goes and throws a fucking wrench in everyone's plans. I was just about to call it off, and then I watched her go on up to the front seat and start jacking Vitellius off. While I'm inside supposedly robbing the house, she's out there giving him a goddamn hand job! I tried to give her every goddamn break, but she just wouldn't play nice with me! At that point, I decided, fuck it!"

There was pause while Jack and Aug listened to the howling gale. The storm was brewing big-time. Jack proceeded, "After the accident though, Vitellius didn't die, and the heroin we planted in the vehicle somehow was never found. So plan B was needed. So we came up with plan B. Some night when Vi was all alone, he would get paid. Your mother took you out to make sure there would be no interruption. She had asked that I take you in, and I said I would once things calmed down, and we got settled down, and your sibling was born, and we could be one happy family. But nooooooooooooooo, little Auggie couldn't just go to the movies that night. Val told me what happened when I took her to the hospital that night. Noooooooooo. Little Auggie had to come in and fuck with everyone's plans. *You* had to walk in before Vitellius could have everything squared up. If it weren't for *you*, we'd be one happy family! If it weren't for *you*, you'd have a sibling! If it weren't for *you*, your mother would still be *alive*!"

Aug lost it on that. He ran forward like a linebacker at Jack, screaming, "ARRRGHHHH."

## BANG! BANG!

Aug saw the flashes and heard the report, but he felt nothing. He caught Jack square in the midsection and carried him into tables and chairs, strewing them across the floor. They crashed into the wall mural. The head of Jack smacked into the image of Poseidon. The impact stunned him. He lost control of the gun. Aug started to swing wildly and punching at his head and abdomen with both fist and cast. Aug was oblivious to the physical pain as he poured out the emotional pain.

"*You* think I killed my mother? *You* killed her! *You* stuck the knife in her belly! *You* killed the baby! Just like *you* killed Laurie!" With that, he punched Jack so hard in the mouth that two teeth went flying. As best as he could with a hand and a cast, Aug grabbed Jack around the neck. "YOU KILLED LAURIE, AND YOU KILLED HER BABY! She had a surrogate mother lined up to carry an artificially inseminated child to birth. She wouldn't tell me who it was, but she said it was someone she trusted! *And you* killed her hope of life!" Aug choked and choked Jack, watching the blood pour from Jack's mouth. "You know what I am going to do? I'm going to take the life you wanted to have away from you. It's payback time." The pressure from the hurricane was making the mural paint wet, and the red cape of Poseidon was coming off onto Jack. It reminded Aug of the last time he had seen blood on a wall, and he choked even harder. "How does your last breath feel? How do you think Laurie's last breath felt? How does it feel to choke to death?"

## BANG! BANG!

Two shots rang out. A tinkling of broken glass was heard above the sound of the wind. A voice shouted out and said, "THAT'S ENOUGH!"

Aug let go, and Jack slumped to the floor, choking. He was choking for breath and choking on blood and pain from his new dental work.

Aug turned around and was confronted with Angel pointing a handgun at him. Aug sarcastically laughed. "Well, hello, my guardian angel. I was wondering when you would appear. Not sitting on a hill in a Windstar today?"

Angel was shaking with her own rage. She moved the gun to the left of Aug and squeezed off a round by his head and into the mural.

## BANG!

Angel told Aug, "Maybe I should put a bullet into your head, and then you'd know how it felt for Keith!"

Aug's retort was rapid. "If you think I killed Keith, then you're a bigger idiot than you even realize! Keith and I had a deal, and I wanted him alive, not dead. He was dead by the time I got there!"

Jack got up and walked to Angel. He was a bit annoyed. He looked up at the water starting to run down from the skylight glass that Angel had shot. He spit blood at the water. He took the gun from her as she coldly glared at Aug. "Jesus fucking Christ, Angel! Watch where you're shooting this thing. There's a fucking hurricane outside. You shoot out these panes of glass and the hurricane will then be inside! That's not a smart idea!" He took a deep breath to regain his composure. "Now, please be a dear and find me a towel from behind the bar so that I can stop bleeding all over." He thought about it. "And find a bottle of some real good booze also. Thank you!"

Jack walked over and retrieved his gun off the floor. He pointed the guns at Aug. "I trust now that maybe you've gotten some anger out of your system? Now that we've had a therapy session, can we get down to the business at hand?" He looked around the restaurant. "Aug, I assume that the jewels are somewhere in this building. I assume that you hid them somewhere in one of the last shipments that came in. Before I tear this place apart, why don't you tell me where you hid them?"

Aug said, "Why don't you go fuck yourself instead."

Angel came back with a wet hand towel and a larger dry towel and a bottle of Cointreau. Jack took the towels from Angel in exchange for one of the guns. He cleaned himself up as best he could. He tasted the orange.

"Aug, ya know, I thought you would say that." Jack took another taste. "Angel, be a dear and go get our present to Aug." Angel walked toward the back of the bar. She exited the main floor via swinging doors then entered the kitchen area. Jack pressed the dry towel up to his mouth to try and stop the bleeding. "Since you want to talk family, I figured that we should have a family reunion!"

The kitchen door swung open. A bound Jocelyn was led in by Angel. Rope bound her upper torso. Angel held a gun to her back. Angel told her, "Move it! Over by Jack and Aug. Let's go, sister!"

Jocelyn's face had eyeliner streaked over it, and she was whimpering in fear. Her hands were bound to her sides by rope. "Aug? Aug, baby. I'm so sorry." She looked around. "Who are these people? Where are we? What do they want?"

Aug looked at her. "Hey, baby, just remain calm. Everything will be all right. I won't let them hurt you. I love you, Jocy. Everything will be fine."

Angel led her to a nearby pillar and handed her gun to Jack. She had brought with her some rope, and with it, she tied Jocelyn to a pillar. She bound Jocelyn at the waist and feet, pulling the rope tight around her blue jeans and sweater. Sarcastically she mimicked them, "I love you, Jocy. PUH-LEASE. Could you two be more sappy?" She looked at Aug. "You want everything to be fine? Just tell us where the diamonds are at."

Aug replied, "Sorry, Angel. I just can't do that." Angel smirked at him.

When Angel was done, Jack inspected the binding and nodded to Angel. "Very good, you have learned well." Jack looked at Aug and said, "Now, Aug, are you gonna tell me where the jewels are, or am I gonna splatter Jocelyn's brains all over this place?" Jack pointed the gun to Jocelyn's head.

Jocelyn's eyes became huge. She started screaming at Aug, "TELL HIM! AUG! TELL HIM WHAT HE WANTS TO KNOW! MY GOD, AUG, HE'S GOING TO SHOOT ME!"

Angel curiously watched the byplay. Aug calmly spoke up, "Jocelyn, calm down. He's not going to shoot you. He's not going to shoot anybody."

Jack looked at Aug. "Do you think so, Aug? Do you think I won't shoot lover girl here?"

Aug looked at all three of them. "Go fuck yourself, Jack. You can stick that gun up your ass and blow your brains out for all I care."

Jack looked at Aug. "Really? Maybe I should do that. But maybe I have a better idea." Jack looked at Angel. "Angel, I've taught you a lot about the family business, and now I have something else for you to learn. Now, here's what I want you to do. I want you to put your gun to Jocelyn's pretty head, and if Aug won't tell us where he hid the jewels, I want you to blow her head off." Angel looked at Jack bewildered. She had fired a gun before, but she had never actually killed anyone before.

Angel took her pistol and held it near Jocelyn's head. Aug started speaking, looking at Angel. "ANGEL, DON'T DO IT!"

Jack chimed in. "You don't want her to pull the trigger, Aug? Where are the stones?"

The wind was roaring even louder now with an eerie whistle being heard from the holes in the skylight. The glow of the candles danced around everyone. They cycled through with all four of them yelling simultaneously a yes/no chorus. Jocelyn was screaming, "AUG! TELL THEM! FOR GOD'S SAKE! TELL THEM!"

Jack hit Aug with a "LAST CHANCE!"

Aug yelled, "ANGEL! NO!"

Jocelyn screamed as loud as she could.

Jack yelled, "DO IT NOW, ANGEL!" She wavered. Jack said, "THINK OF KEITH!

Aug yelled, "NO!"

Angel closed her eyes and pulled the trigger.

# *BANG!*

The report was heard. Then, except for the howling wind, the room was quiet. Angel opened her eyes. She was bewildered. She looked at the gun. She looked at Jack and Aug and Jocelyn and the gun. Jocelyn started laughing and tapping her boot on the ground. Tears of laughter started streaming from her eyes. Jack walked over to the stunned Angel and took the gun from her. He then popped her in the kisser. Angel ascended to heaven and crashed down to earth. She was dazed. Her eyes vacantly looked at all three of them. A thin red line slowly appeared and filled the gap between her swelling lips.

Aug started toward Angel, but Jack waved him off with the gun that had been in his hands. "Ah, no. Don't do that. This one has real bullets in it, and I won't hesitate to pop one of your kneecaps." Jack dropped Angel's revolver and undid Jocelyn's bonds while keeping the gun trained on Aug and Angel.

When he eventually freed her, Jocelyn reached up and gave him a hug and a kiss on the cheek. "Thank you, Daddy!" She walked on over to Jack's bag of golf clubs. She opened a pocket and pulled out a flashlight. Jocelyn walked back over to Angel and grabbed her by the hair and dragged her to the front of the pillar. Angel yowled as her tresses were tugged. Jocelyn stood Angel up and looked her in the eye. "Yes, silly little girl, Jack is *my* daddy, and he's not yours. And I want you to look at the present that Daddy gave his daughter." She yanked Angel's head back. She trained the torchlight on the marble.

Angel's eyes saw that the mermaid on the pillar was a life-size Jocelyn. Vanity had a price.

Jocelyn pushed Angel back against the pillar. She tied Angel's body to the stone. After she tied her legs, Jocelyn brought her face up eyeball to eyeball to a terrified Angel and said, "Don't worry, my dear. Bondage is painless!" Jocelyn gave Angel a kiss on the cheek.

Jocelyn then walked off behind the bar to where there was a large plate glass mirror. Using the torch, she crouched down in the dark behind the bar and found the purse that was stashed there. She fixed her hair and makeup as best she could by using the mirror behind the bar. She discreetly pulled out a small derringer from the purse and hid it in her clothing.

She turned her head and looked across the bar at her lover, yelling, "Aug, dear, aren't you happy to see me?" Aug did not reply. Jocelyn gave a *hmmph* and looked back at the mirror. When she finished, she walked around the bar to where everyone was at.

Aug had a combination sneer and grim resolve look for his mien. He asked her, "How was 'Daddy's' funeral, babe?"

Jocelyn laughed. "I imagine that, by now, you know that was a bullshit story. Neither of my daddies are dead. That was just a story so you wouldn't bother me while I took care of business!"

Aug's steely eyes bored into her emeralds. "Oh? And what kind of business would that be? You weren't tied up lining up another surrogate motherhood job, were you? Or do you have some other story in mind?"

Jocelyn snorted, "You're one to talk about stories." Her demeanor dipped a bit. She was saddened. "So you know about that, do you? Well, I must admit I'm not thrilled about how that turned out. I liked Laurie, and if I knew what was gonna happen then, well . . ." She paused and sighed. "But the deed was going to be done. There was nothing that I or anyone else could do about it. It was beyond our control. Sorry about that one."

She thought about it for a minute. "Butcha know what? Years ago, I made a deal to get out of the life that I had. I got out of a life that would have been nothing. Just like you made a deal to be a smuggler and to make more cash, to have a better life. So don't you judge me about what I did! Don't you be the pot calling the kettle black! Each of us had decisions to make that defined our lives." Aug and Jocelyn glared at each other. It suddenly sank into her head what he had said. She asked, "When did you know?"

Aug's gaze bore into Jocelyn. "I knew from the moment I met you. After her illness started, Laurie began keeping a diary that no one knew about, and after her death, I read it. It was one of the reasons that her death never made any sense to me. None of her entries were entries of a person struggling with the will to live. And when we lay in bed at night and made plans for our future, she never hinted at suicide. And then, in this diary, I read how she had met a woman who offered to carry the pregnancy to term for her. For a price, naturally. Someone she could trust. Someone she felt comfortable with. After her death, I expected this person to appear and ask what happened, but no one appeared. And as the weeks went on and no one showed, then I knew that whoever that person had been, she was a phony. But I also knew that someday this person would appear. One of the reasons I stayed single was because I knew. I knew that anyone else who took up with me would suffer a similar fate. So I waited and waited. And when I was out jogging that morning and you appeared, it just clicked, and I knew."

Jocelyn was surprised and stunned. "If you knew it was me, then why did you bother?"

Aug replied, "At first it was due to one of the oldest of all reasons. Keep your friends close and your enemies closer, right?" His glare softened. "But as time went on, well, I found myself . . . I found myself wanting to bother. It's just like you said. I realized that you were just a sucker. Just like I was a sucker. We are both the same bird in a storm of crooks. So don't tell me that I judged you harshly."

"Really?" Jocelyn retorted. "Is that why you gave me a phony wedding proposal? If you had actually cared enough to really propose marriage, then things could have been different. If you had trusted in me, then things could have been oh so different. But no. You had to give me a cock-and-bull story." She thought a second. "Hell, you did even better than that, didn't you? You gave me a no-cock-and-all-bull story, didn't you?"

Jocelyn's eyes narrowed and looked at Aug. His eyes also narrowed, and looks of suspicion soon replaced by emotional fury overtook both their expressions. Lightning bolts of anger were exchanged between each other's eyes. Jocelyn looked at Angel and started speaking again, "Well, none of that matters now because—"

Aug abruptly cut her off. "Doesn't it?"

Jocelyn looked back at Aug. Jack came toward Angel, laughing and clapping his hands. "Awww, you two are so cute together, ain'tcha? I must say that the two of you certainly can argue like a married couple!"

Jack made it to Angel. He grabbed her jaw and looked at her. There was anger in his voice. "You still don't get it, do ya? Well, let me make it simple for you. Vitellius Valentine took his salami and got your mother pregnant! Does that make it clear for you?"

Aug broke in, "And which girl is a year older, huh? You could conveniently ignore that, couldn't ya? It was so convenient to blame Angel's birth on my father when the truth is that you sired Jocelyn first! That's why your wife cheated on you with your partner. It was because you did it to her first!" Aug looked at Angel and spoke. "I told you I knew who your parents were! I guess maybe now I don't stink so bad, huh?"

## POW!

Jack walked over to Aug and belted him in the mouth right where the teeth were missing. "Fuck you, asshole."

Aug reeled back. Blood and liquids poured into his mouth, and he spat them out. Aug looked at Jocelyn. "Ya wanna know who the biggest bastard is of all?

It's 'Daddy' here! He left you in a family that half-wanted you." Aug pointed at Jack. "He knew that the man who reared you despised you because he knew you were not his daughter. Just like he always despised Angel as she grew up because she wasn't his daughter. But you know what he really is? In the end, he's death to everything that he touches. He was death to my father. He was death to my mother. He was death to his wife. He was death to Laurie. And in the end, he'll be death to you!" Aug looked at Jack. "You're one just evil son of a bitch!" he seethed.

# POW! Kick!

Jack punched Aug in the stomach this time. Aug went down. "You son of a bitch!" Jack kicked Aug in the gut. "You think you are so smart. You think you know so much. The fact of the matter is that you don't know anything. You talk to Rob Baumgardner one time, and you think you know everything about what happened back then. Well, I can tell you now that you don't know the whole story behind what happened. Hell, maybe we'd all be better off if you had died twenty-five years ago."

Jack walked over to Jocelyn and gave her his gun. He walked back over to Aug and grabbed him by his hair. "You think because both you and your dad had big dicks that you were father and son? You think they were your parents child just because Mommy and 'Daddy' lived together? You really are one stupid son of a bitch! You're pathetic. Did you ever think, *Gee, my mom was fifteen and pregnant in Philadelphia, and she ended up in Detroit*, and that didn't make any sense? You didn't, didja?" Jack spit blood in Aug's face. He stood up and walked away to the Cointreau and came back.

# Kick!

Jack kicked Aug in the midsection again and continued, "I'll tell you something's about your mom you didn't know. That very few people know. That your uncle never really knew. You see, when your mom got knocked up, she had a choice to make about being pregnant. The choice was 'leave Dodge, or die!' Not much of a choice, huh?" Jack drank some booze and wiped the drool from his mouth. Memories welled up inside him. "You see, your 'mommy' wasn't pregnant by just any family's son. Oh no! She was pregnant by like the son of a Kennedy clan. Only they didn't want you or her. They wanted her out of the way. They wanted to 'Chappaquidick' her, or maybe I should say 'Michael Skakel' her. But Val's mom, your grandmother, stepped in. She cut a deal. The deal was that Val could live and have her son, but that she was gone. Valerie had to disappear. That's how your mother ended up with Vitellius!"

Jack paused and drank some more. "There was money paid to keep her and Vitellius quiet. See, Vitellius knew the families involved from some of his criminal activity over the years. And also from some activity he had experienced with your grandmother years ago. Of course, you never wondered why Mommy and Daddy never worked a lot, did you? You stupid moron."

Aug was stunned. This couldn't be true, could it?

Jack gathered his composure. He threw down some more Cointreau. He went back to Jocelyn and retrieved the revolver. He pointed the gun at Aug and continued, "But right now, none of that matters because right now you're going to tell me where my jewels are!"

Aug answered, "I told you before, you can go fuck yourself!"

# SMACK!

The butt of the revolver struck Aug across the head. "No? Well, I thought you would be stubborn." Jack stepped back with the gun trained on Aug. "Jocelyn?"

Jocelyn proceeded to take her belt off. The belt had three catches positioned near the end of the belt. Jocelyn spoke as she released the buttoning mechanism. "Auggie, dear, you know what is funny? What's funny is that I bought this belt that night in Nassau when we hit it big at the craps table. Strangely enough, it was in one of the stores in the outdoor shopping area at Atlantis." She smiled at Aug. "If you hadn't suddenly weirded out that night, I might have let you use it on me!" The end of the belt opened into tendrils. It became a whip.

Jocelyn varied her look at Aug and Angel and continued, "I can't believe you really care that much for her. I mean, she's dull. She's got no taste. I mean, you said it yourself, she can't dance, she has no sense of style."

# Lash!

---

Jocelyn cracked her whip on the floor and continued, "Little Miss Princess always got to travel the globe and have whatever she wanted, and she never knew what she wanted because she is *boring*! B-B-B-B-ORING! Sooooooooo unimpulsive." She spied the handgun on the floor and picked it up and ran it along Angel's leg. Jocelyn strategically placed the gun and spoke to her. "You ever use a revolver to get off, honey? Ever run with the rabbit? Kiss the one-eyed monster? You ever enjoy it? Huh? No? And you know why? 'Cuz you can't let go of yourself! No wonder you've always been so frustrated!"

## BANG!

Angel's body jumped in fear with the report. Jocelyn got a big bang out that.

Jocelyn thought a second. She came eyeball to eyeball with Angel again. "Oh, and by the way, Aug didn't kill your lover boy, Keith. I did." Jocelyn laughed. "Actually, I did Keith a favor. Crusher had done a number on him, and he was gonna be eunuch boy from now on. It really was a gruesome sight to see. But I give him credit. I heard them torturing him when I entered the house, and he took it better than any man I know would have." She turned and looked at Aug. "And I do mean *any man*." She looked back in Angel's eyes. "By the time I got up there, he was so far gone he was asking to be put out of his misery." She looked back at Aug and then at Angel. "I did what he asked me to do!" Jocelyn thought a minute. She ran her glaring gaze between Aug and Angel. "I wanted Keith alive, and Keith would have lived if only Aug would have stayed at opening night at Poseidon's! But when he went to chase after you, I had a choice to make to see what he was up to or continue to watch Keith. If I'd been there, I'da spared him the crusher! But noooooooooo, Auggie couldn't be a good boy and play along—again!"

Jocelyn refocused on Angel. "But now? Now it's time for me to have some fun with you! Now, I'm gonna play with you! I'm gonna sing you a song!" Jocelyn stepped back. The brunette Blondie started singing,

"Your nose job is preatomic;

What it needs is Jocelyn's scar."

## Lash!

The whip came across and opened a breath-right strip cut on the bridge of Angel's nose as well as a line on the right cheek. Angel screamed. Her body shook.

"Your clothing is so platonic

It must have cost you a whole dol-lar"

## Lash! Lash!

Angel's top was ripped.

"You're so dull

I'm gonna whip you to shreds"

## Lash! Lash! Lash! Lash! Lash! Lash!

Jocelyn struck hard across various parts of Angel's anatomy. Angel shrieked with every whiplash. Her clothing was being cut open. Each flick either created welts or cuts.

"STOP IT!" Aug's shout froze everyone.

Jack said, "Jocelyn, that's enough fun." Jack took a swig and walked over to Angel and put the gun near her bloodied cheek. Angel was wide-eyed with fear. Jack looked at Aug and spoke. "You don't want me to blow her brains out, you tell me where the diamonds are!"

Thunder was heard above the wind. Shortly after a lightning strike illuminated the whole scene. Aug was struck by the surreality of the situation. The hurricane was furiously whipping outside. He knew the eye was close since the only lightning in a hurricane is near the eye wall. The noise of the wind inside was so loud that they were actually speaking very loudly to hear each other even though they were within ten feet of each other. He noticed the water in the building on the floor for the first time. It wasn't all from the holes in the skylight. Water had found some cracks and was coming in from below and above. The paint was bleeding from the mural on the wall. The storm had fomented the sea, and the water was at a couple feet height at the front windows. The candles flickered. Yet they were all oblivious to the storm outside. They were too caught up in their own internal storm to not see what was going on around them.

"All right." Aug spoke. "I'll give you what you want."

Jack spat back with years of pent-up rage, "You'll give me what I want? No! You'll give me what I earned!" Jack walked to the table by the door and picked up the lantern. He walked back to where Aug was standing and held the lantern so they could see each other's face and eyes. "Did you build not only this place but other business and residences in this area? NO. I DID! Did you set up the buys and make the smuggling and laundering possible? NO. I DID! No, all you did was get set up with a nice job for years to build a nice life with. You think that happened by accident? I had a hand in helping to set that up for you!"

Jack's storm raged. "You didn't do a goddamn thing except screw everything up for everyone. Do you think that if I hadn't set Greg up to tip you off, you wouldn't be dead by now? I tipped you off to start making your escape! I had to do it surreptitiously. I had to backdoor it. But if I hadn't, your uncle would have killed you! Just like you shoulda been dead twenty-five years ago. I didn't kill Vitellius. I didn't kill your mother, Valerie. NO! It was my brother you walked in on. I was outside in a car on the road keeping an eye out. And what do I see as I'm sitting there? Fucking Aug walking on in on the hit when you are supposed to be sitting at the fucking movies! By the time I got into the house, my brother had stabbed your mother, and he was getting ready to slice your unconscious throat. I saved your life because your mother wanted me to."

Jack's eye grew. "And who set you up with the info that my brother was hired to kill Laurie? I made that happen. I set you up so you could get your revenge. You just never knew it! You think Laurie's death was all about you! HAH! That's another good one! She died because of her family! You were just too tied up in your own self-pity to think to look in that direction. She was supposed to have been killed years ago. She was supposed to have died, very discreetly, from heart failure. It was no accident that she had a virus attack her heart. She was purposely infected. But somehow, she didn't die. Somehow, she cheated death for years. People kept waiting for her to drop, but she just wouldn't do it! She kept soldiering on until she had to be taken out. That's when they sprung my brother to take her out in as discreet a manner as possible."

"I sent Jocelyn in to help, but it was too late. There was nothing I could do. So I did something I thought was very nice for you. I set you up with Jocelyn! What the fuck more could you ask for? Why couldn't you just want to go have a happy life fucking your brains out with her? But noooooo, you couldn't just disappear and enjoy life with her! Nooooooo. That wouldn't be enough for you. You thought you were so slick. You thought you had everything figured out! The only thing you figured out is how to once again fuck up some beautiful plans I had for everyone!"

Aug said, "You lie!"

# BAM!

Jack wound up and hit Aug on the side of the head with the lantern as hard as possible. "Ya think so? Ya think I'm lying? Long ago, I suspected you would deny the truth when confronted with it. I knew that there would be almost no way I could convince you of the truth. Well, sonny boy, come here! Maybe this will convince you! Maybe my lantern will show you that I am an honest man!"

Jack and Aug walked to the back side of the pillar. Jack held the lantern up.

Aug stared at himself. He was married to Jocelyn in marble. His visage was the merman to her mermaid. He was speechless.

Jack spoke. "Do you really think I would have bothered if what I am telling you isn't true? I mean, tell me, Aug, what should I have done? Take you out to dinner and say, "Oh, by the way Aug, did you know it was my brother who sliced up your dad? And also, while I am at it, that Laurie's family is the reason she was killed? I tried to get you to stay at Poseidon's on opening night to explain things! I tried to get you to look at every pillar on opening night so that you would see what I had built! But nooooooooo, nooooooooo, you had to run off on your adventure and screw things up even more!"

Jack continued, "You never realized the truth of any of this, did you? And you know why you never realized it? It's all because of your beliefs. You're like those crazy Arabs who hold conferences about how the Holocaust never happened or a person who places the trust in their money in Wall Street or a corporation or a church. It's all what you believe in the face of facts. Your belief is painless delusion. Belief is abdication and absolution from responsibility!" Jack paused some suspenseful seconds, speaking sarcastically, showing sardonic smile. "Recidivism is ugly whether on a social or personal scale!"

Jack walked back to the other side of the pillar. He held the lantern up and pointed the gun back at Angel's terrified face. Jack pulled the hammer back on the gun. "But now, now I wash my hands of you, Augustus Valentine! And now I will tell you what I believe! I believe that if you don't tell me where those jewels are, I'll pull this trigger! Now don't think for a second that I won't splatter Angel's face and brains out all over this floor. And I'll still tear this place apart and find where you have stashed my goods! Or for once, you can be a good boy and play nice! NOW! For one last time! Where are my jewels?"

They stood in silence while the wind roared and the candles flickered. Aug spoke. "I need a club from your golf bag. Your five iron maybe. And I also need a chair."

Jack angrily said, "Fine! Go get yerself a five iron and a chair! Let's get this goddamn show on the road!"

Aug turned and walked to the front. Jack spoke to Angel when Aug left. "Sorry, 'daughter,'" he said as he smiled. "But remember what I told you when you first came down here?"

Angel slowly had a small sardonic smile appear on her face. Her blue eyes looked into Jack's gray-green eyes. She turned her head and looked into Jocelyn's emerald eyes. She turned her vision back into Jack's, and her smile became bigger. "Oh, I remember all right. Never trust anyone!" She then lost her smile, and her head slumped down toward her chest.

Jack looked at Angel and at Jocelyn. He lost his smile. He slowly backed away where he could see them both at the same time. Jocelyn was eyeing the two of them. Jack and Jocelyn were concerned by each other's concern.

Aug went to the golf bag and found a suitable iron. He carried the iron and a chair to the speaker set at the junction of the corner of the front of the building and the west wall. He was next to the aquarium. The day was lighter toward the front of Poseidon's as the light of the day that did exist came through the front windows. Aug noticed the aquarium. He noticed that there was no filter running and that the creatures inside seemed very agitated. They were drowning in the water that surrounded them. Aug set the chair in front of the speakers. Jack and Jocelyn followed. They intently watched his actions.

All their eyes were constantly shifting to and from the front windowpanes. The panes kept bowing inward farther and farther with the force of the wind. It concerned all of them. They expected the panes to break at any moment. The winds gusted and howled harder, and the panes bent in even more.

The speakers were actually a series of speakers stacked on top of each other, positioned to produce a wall-of-sound effect. Each speaker was four feet tall. Aug removed the speaker cover off the bottom speaker. He felt with his good hand up the lowest speaker. He was feeling for the pinholes that would tell him where the cabinet had been scored. They were not in this unit. He moved to the second speaker. He pulled the speaker cover off. At the base of the frame, he found what he was looking for. There were pinholes that a human couldn't see or wouldn't care about unless they knew what it was that they were looking for. A circle was scored on the back side that would allow the cabinet to be punctured with a blow.

Jack watched Aug take the club in his good hand and start strategically rapping against the cabinet with the head. Jack saw a circle the size of Aug's hand open up as a piece of the cabinet broke through.

Aug looked for a watch on his wrist, but he did not have one on. He reached in and found what he was looking for. Slowly, one by one, he pulled out the nine bags of dreams. There were three bags of diamonds. There were the three bags of sapphires. There were the three bags of rubies. He pulled the release. The clock was now ticking.

He handed the bags to Jack. Jack suspiciously eyed Aug and the bags.

Jack needed light. He procured a dining table and pulled it up to the front window. The bags were lain out on the table. Jack went and grabbed a couple of candles. A trip was made to his golf bag. Another flashlight was pulled out. Jack started to inspect each bag to see what he could see.

Aug watched Jack intently.

# Lash!

The whip came around Aug's legs and yanked him to floor. He fell with a splash as the water was now deep enough to cause a small liquid splattering. Aug rose to two knees, and then he found the whip was wrapped around his neck.

Jocelyn twisted the belt and pulled it tight around his throat. She was choking the life out of Aug.

Jocelyn spoke. "Good boy, Auggie! See how simple that was? If you had only been a good boy in the beginning, then none of this would have had to happen. But noooooooo, you had to set me up with phony goods. You had to fuck with us all."

The noose loosened so he could speak. Her emerald eyes raged at him. Was he looking at the lady and the tigress? Aug choked out, "I'd be dead by now if I hadn't done that."

Jocelyn's rage took over, and the lariat was tightened back up. "No! No, you wouldn't be dead! I'd have protected you! Just like I protected you from the beginning when I killed the guys who were coming to rob you in the first place! Just like I killed your Uncle Mark and his goons when they were torturing you! I told you that night at Sawgrass that we could run away and there would be enough for both of us to live happily ever after, but noooooooooo, noooooooooo, that wasn't good enough for you! You had to want to meet Angel. You had to want to have your revenge. You didn't trust *me*!" With that, she tightened the noose further.

Aug's choking scared her a bit, and she lessened her grip. He was able to speak out, "You've protected me all along, huh? Just like when you shot at me that night I was on Jack's porch?"

Jocelyn smiled and laughed on that one. "That? That was for fun! I wanted to see what you would do. Hell, I wanted to see if I could do that! Do you have any idea how fucking hard it is to hit the targets I hit in the dark? And then you jumped into the mud and got all so dirty! You looked so cute walking around in your nice Italian clothes barefoot and all covered in mud. God, how I wish I'da had my camera with me to take your picture! It would go perfect in my trophy room."

Aug choked out, "For fun, huh? Just like kicking me in the ass was for fun? Like whipping Angel was for fun?"

Jocelyn laughed and said, "It's all good! And it's all in good fun! But neither of you two know anything about finding some pleasure in pain. Do you? Hmmm? Besides, if you'da opened your mouth, you'da spared Angel that little whipping anyway, so don't even think of laying that on me!" She laughed further. Then she paused and bent down to him and put her face in his and said, "But the past is the past, and here we are now in the here and now. And the here and now is this: tell me now, Auggie dear, now that we have the jewels, and the platinum and the gold, after all the wonderful plans that I had for us that you fucked up, tell me why I shouldn't kill both you and your 'not half sister'? Hmmmm? Remember, 'I told you from the start just how this would end . . . when I get what I want . . . I never want it again!'"

Aug glared into her flashing eyes and spoke. "Sure. You could kill me now just as you could have killed me then. And I knew all along that you may end up putting a bullet in my brain and ending my life. And in the beginning, I was willing to accept that risk for the sake of revenge for my mother, my father, and for Laurie. I was willing to bother with you for their sake."

Aug raised his right leg so that he was on bended knee. He slowly reached his good hand into his cast to retrieve his gift. Jocelyn tightened the noose. She was suspicious of his intentions.

Aug continued, "But as time went on, I found that I wanted to bother for my sake. For our sake. And I was willing to accept that risk because I found that above all I else felt about everything, I found myself in love again. So you can kill me now, but is that what you really wanted to get in the end? Is that what will make you happy? Or would you rather 'live through this and be assured that I will die for you!'" Aug pulled out the gauze. Using his one good hand, he unwrapped the gauze to reveal a ring. He reached up to her left hand and removed it from the rope and slid the ring down her ring finger. "Jocelyn," he said, "will you marry me?"

It took time for Jocelyn's synapses to process the data. She had to retrieve the ball from left field.

She looked at the ring as best she could in the light. It was the most spectacular thing she had ever seen. Facing her was an emerald J. There was a center-top, baguette-cut emerald. There was another baguette emerald that formed the stem of the J followed by three more emeralds to make the tail of the J. The stones seemed to glow and speak to her like they had life. Framing the J was an inverted A. The A was made of gold. The cross bar of the A was a gold link to the emerald crossbar of the J. It was a union. A lightning strike occurred outside, which briefly illuminated the ring. In her mind, the ring had a glow of magical and mystical powers. The engagement ring was alive.

Jocelyn was speechless. She tightened the noose back around Aug's neck. Her gaze went back and forth from the ring to Aug and back again. Everything was silent except the hurricane swirling about. She finally looked at Aug and exclaimed, "Is this some kind of joke? Is this some more of your phony paste?"

Aug choked out, "For the price I paid, they better not be! And if it were or if I gave you something phony, then I expect that you would put a bullet in my skull anyway. But the ring is no phonier than my love for you. I want to marry you. I want to have a family life with you. And if you don't feel the same way, then you may as well kill me now and leave another John Doe in your wake."

Jocelyn was floored. She was endgamed. This was totally unexpected. She tensed her arms to pull the noose tighter. She couldn't do it.

They looked each other in the eyes. Their eyes flicked up and down rapidly as they stared at each other. Finally, she spoke. "How do I know you're not lying."

Aug replied, "If you trust me, you will know I am not lying. Either way, it's a decision you have to make that will define our lives."

Jocelyn was paralyzed. They were gazing in each other's eyes. For the first time, her impetuousness was gone. She did not know what to do. She was frozen in time.

Jack Dough had been watching the whole thing in stunned amazement. From his perspective, he couldn't believe it. His mind said, *SON OF A BITCH! The son of a bitch played her! Hell! The son of a bitch played me!* Jack was simultaneously annoyed, angry, irritated, and impressed. This was what his plan had been in the beginning but was not the way he had now planned things. His latest plan had been to get rid of Aug and Angel, and then Jack and Jocelyn could proceed from there. After all Aug had done, he had decided to be done with him. Could he know live with this turn of events? This called for a massive dose of booze.

Angel was stunned by the turn of events. There was nothing she could say. She watched with amused concern. Was this really what Aug had been up to all along?

Aug stood up and started walking Jocelyn backward to the nearest pillar. She completely loosened the grip on the noose. She repeatedly said, "Stop. Stop that. What are you doing?"

He pressed her against the Bridgette Bardot mermaid. Jocelyn was still aimlessly babbling, "What . . . what are you doing? Stop that." Aug pressed her against the pillar and passionately kissed Jocelyn. He pythoned her body. His bloody mouth mixed with her mouth. She could taste and feel his injuries. As they kissed, she could feel a whole lot more. Every epidermal cell exploded, exclaiming and exalting euphoria. The wind was howling, and she could feel the water running down the pillar all over her body washing her.

## Crack! BOOM!

There was a lightning strike nearby that sent their bodies even closer together. She could tell that this was real. Jocelyn could tell that Aug was real.

Jack had seen enough. He now knew what Aug had meant about taking his life away from him. Aug had meant he was going to take Jocelyn away from him. He started to walk toward them.

Jocelyn sensed the splashing of Jack's feet above the tempest. She opened her eyes and saw him coming toward them. Hurriedly she removed the derringer she had stashed in her clothing. She pointed the gun at Jack with disapproving sound. "Don't fuck with me, Daddy," she said. "Not now, not this time."

Jack stopped. What could he do? He walked back to his table. His eyes looked out over the Gulf of Mexico. The waves were crashing against the arced glass panes. Large pieces of natural and man-made debris were flying through the air outdoors. There were pieces of buildings flying. There were pieces of foliage and tree branches flying. There were two large boats that had broken loose from moorings that were seen outside the window heading inland.

Jocelyn looked in Aug's eyes. Her every feature was smiling. "So just what exactly are you proposing, Mr. Valentine?"

Aug answered, "Well, Mrs. Valentine. Let's you and I go. Just like you said we should do." He nodded his head over to Jack. "We can leave him the lion's share of everything and disappear with enough to live comfortable off on."

Jocelyn liked the idea. "And Angel?" she asked.

Aug sighed. "Does she really need to die? Does she really deserve to die? Hasn't she been through enough? Isn't there enough for everyone? I can now let the past go. What's done is done."

Jocelyn cocked her beaming face back and looked at him suspiciously. She then pulled him close and spoke in his ear, "You know, wedding proposals make me very horny!"

Aug laughed and kissed her. "Let's go have a drink to celebrate. There has to be some champagne in this building somewhere." He put his arm around Jocelyn. They walked over to the table that Jack was at. Aug reached down and slowly grabbed two of the jewelry bags under Jack's watchful eyes. He handed one bag to Jocelyn and he put one bag in his pants pocket. "Consider it a dowry, *Daddy*," he said. Jocelyn smiled at her father. The two of them walked off to the bar.

Jack glared at them as they walked away, and he went back to inspection duty. It was just so damn hard to see what he had in the poor light. Never trust anyone. Where were the flaws?

Jocelyn and Aug reached the bar. She set her whip down on the counter and proceeded to ogle her ring. Aug stepped behind the bar. "This calls for champagne. There has to be some here somewhere." He looked for some champagne. He became caught up in the moment. Jocelyn had accepted his proposal.

"Stay right here," he told her. "Don't move. I'll go in the back and find some champagne." Jocelyn distractedly nodded. She was checking out the ring. She was looking at the detailing, and she was wondering, *What is it worth, and oh, the emeralds look so brilliant, and they match my eyes, and the design is so cool, and it is so romantic that Aug designed this, and I can't believe he did this, and I can't believe that after everything, he did propose to me, and I can't believe this is real, and it's so romantic with the hurricane for a setting and . . .* her mind raced on.

Aug found her flashlight, and he went into the kitchen area. His mind was racing. He had to find champagne, but what is champagne for a wedding proposal without flutes? And then there needs to be a tray to carry things, and there must be some cake here somewhere to bring everything out on—and on his mind went. He was in love. He was caught up in the moment, and it was hard to do everything with one arm. It took him a while to find and gather up his plunder.

The tray was set: champagne, flutes, cheesecake, forks. The door was in front of him. The threshold was waiting to be crossed.

Jocelyn was looking at her ring. The lighting was not good. She couldn't admire the ring like she needed to. The best lighting available in the building was at the front window. She floated through the water puddle on the bar floor to get up there to have the best view possible of the reflection of light in the emeralds. She beamed broadly. The persistent, howling gale and raging storm only made the occasion that much more special. It would make it more memorable as time went on. It would be an engagement story that would rival that of any other female she ever talked to. He had proposed to her during the eye of a major hurricane.

Jack eyed Jocelyn. He eyed the door to the kitchen area. Aug couldn't have some sort of weapon in there, could he? He couldn't have planned that far in advance, could he? Just what had Angel meant? Jack's spidey sense was on high alert. He put the bags of jewels in his pants pockets. He eyed the revolver on the table.

Angel was still silently tied up against the Jocelyn pillar. She felt betrayed, but she was not completely surprised. It sounded as if she would be released. She decided to wait until Aug returned before saying anything.

Aug passed through the door. He crossed the threshold to hell. It wasn't the hell of fire and brimstone. It was the hell of wind and watery death. Life became a series of seemingly slow-motion events.

Aug came through the door. He looked for Jocelyn where he had told her to stay. Jocelyn was not there. He looked around and saw her at the front window. He set the tray on the bar and started running forward. He yelled "NO. JOCELYN AWAY FROM THERE. COME HERE NOW!"

She couldn't understand him through the wind in the building. The distance was too great. She saw him running at her frantically. It made no sense to her.

Jack saw Aug's display. He couldn't hear over the wind what Aug was yelling, but he could tell something was up. He looked at Jocelyn and saw the speaker behind her against the wall. Jack suddenly knew where Aug's play had been. Frantically he started to run away. He got about one step forward.

**BOOM!**

The bomb exploded. The splatter grenades ejected round metal pellets designed to stun. Some pellets blasted Jocelyn. She was knocked downward to the floor by the blast. Jack was blown sideways to the mural. Aug was blown backward toward the bar. The aquarium exploded, and the sea creatures inside flew out onto the floor. More pellets put bullet-style holes in the glass of the front windows, causing the panes to develop spiderweb cracks.

The Champions were right. They had used too much explosive. A six-foot section of concrete wall was gone. Hurricane Bill had now entered and was unleashing his force. The decibel level of the wind deafened.

A dazed and stunned Jocelyn stood up. She heard strange sounds behind her, and she turned to look out the windows. The glass concaved and convexed in the hurricane-force winds. It was as if the panes were breathing. Jocelyn was hypnotized by the motion of the glass. The pellets that had hit her in the skull had addled her. Then she realized what she was seeing. She screamed as all the glass windows shattered inward over her. The front windowpanes exploded. Jocelyn's hands went up to cover her eyes. At the same time, the diamond skylight windows above blew upward.

Poseidon's was paneless.

Jocelyn turned and looked at Aug from across the building. He was still down on the floor, but he made eye contact with her. Her face and body were impaled with bloodied glass shards. A large piece of window was impaled in her right cheek. Other large pieces had impaled her legs through her blue jeans and her arms and torso through her sweater. The palms of her hands were stigmatalike. She inhaled as if to scream, but then the tornadic gale of winds in excess of one hundred and twenty miles per hour established a funnel rushing through Poseidon's. The path went from the front of Poseidon's through the skylight. The gale grabbed hold of Jocelyn like a hand from the sky, and she rose, spinning and tumbling into the heavens and disappeared from his sight. His bird had flown. Jocelyn ascended into heaven.

Chairs, tables, bottles, cigarette ashtrays jetted about the room. The storm surge pushed in through the opening left by the windows. The ocean poured into the building from the hole in the front of it. The wounded and weakened building started creaking and making all sorts of noises. The chandeliers broke loose and began flying about.

Aug's body blew backward toward the bar. He stuck his good hand out and caught something flying in the air. He caught Jocelyn's belt. He locked his left arm around the gold banister at the bar rail. With his right hand and arm, he draped the belt around the rail and lashed his left arm to the railing. His body buffeted about like a kite in the wind and a boat on rough seas. The Gulf rapidly filled the bar.

Jack saw the bloodied and battered Jocelyn. Then he saw the bloodied and battered Jocelyn twirl into heaven. Suddenly, he was swimming with the tide and the creatures in the water covering the floor. He screamed as loud as he could, but he could not hear his own voice above the wind. The waves and wind bashed him against his mural. Then the surge took him out toward the center of the building. Jack tried to grab on to anything he could, but there was nothing he could anchor himself to. The water level came up four feet, five feet. The wave action was higher. He was pelted with debris as he tried to tread water. He raised his head, and the flying green lantern bashed into his skull.

Angel had been privy to a clear view of it all. The vision of Jocelyn flying upward filled her with a horror she had never imagined. In one second, her mind was thankful that she was tied down and would not suffer a similar fate. Then she realized she could not move as chairs and tables and glass and chandeliers flying about the room came at her. Her last conscious thought was the view of a glass anemone coming at her head. The anemone crashed into both the pillar and her skull, and she lost consciousness amidst the chaos.

More ocean water poured in. The seawater furiously rose with cascading waves going in all directions. The chest-high water bashed Aug against the bar and then took him back and then bashed him again. This was while airborne projectiles hit him. The flat-screen TV above his head broke and came straight down at Aug. He thought he was dead for sure, but the wind blew it behind him, and it crashed onto the bar top. Aug's mouth was full of seawater. He spit salt and then was buffeted upward again.

Aug did not know how long he was bashed about when he heard a strange wind sound. The gale was so loud that he could not hear his own screams, yet it sounded like a cross between a harpy and a gryphon and a banshee let out wails or roars unlike any noise he had ever heard.

# Crack! *BOOM!*

A lightning bolt flashed close above the skylight and struck nearby. Aug could see the detail of the bolt as it crackled past the skylight hole. His eyes were drawn forward to where Jack was furiously treading water. Aug's numbed mind was such that he wanted to ask Jack if Jack had just seen that.

A lightning bolt flashed down and struck Poseidon's where the bomb had exploded. The side of the building exploded in a white blast of electrical charge. Cement pieces joined the jet-borne debris. The noise of the lightning blast was terrifying to Aug as it overrode the sound of the storm. His eyes were blinded by the flash, but they came back to functioning. Aug looked toward the blown hole in the front of the building. Jack Dough had disappeared.

Through the skylight came a third lightning bolt. The pillar of Jocelyn/Aug was struck, and they split. The top of the pillar shattered. Aug saw a piece of Jocelyn's eye come flying toward him. He tried to raise an arm to shield himself from her, but the eye struck him. That was all he knew.

Aug was only out for a short period. He awoke spitting salty seawater as it had risen up toward his head. The wind and water were still buffeting his body. His left shoulder finally broke from being jerked around. Aug started mindlessly praying for the terror to end while he tried to keep his head above the water

# Crack! Crack! Crack!

The cement building blocks started cracking from the damage done. The building began speaking in a terrible voice as the wind continued pouring in. The roof started to peel away from front to back to where the skylight had been. Mega hundred pounds of concrete peeled off into the wind, exposing the sky. More concrete chunks careened toward Aug. His eyes bugged out as he saw that the line a boulder was on would brain him. The wind and waves blew him aside just enough to avoid a direct hit on his skull. The force of the blow knocked Aug out.

It was now dark out. The winds were still high at tropical force. The winds still howled loudly, but the overpowering roar had lessened. The sea surge was abating and was down to below-the-bar level. The smell of ocean was pervasive. Aug was surprised he was alive. Hurricane-speed wind was still roaring in his ears. His body was motionless, and yet he was in motion at the same time like he had just steeped off a boat after a long boat ride. The pain in his hand and arm and mouth and body suddenly surged through him like an electric shock, causing him to scream in agony.

Angel. He remembered Angel. Where was Angel? Was she still there? Was she alive? Had she too been blown away? He unlashed his arm, intermittently screaming in agony the whole time as electric pain tendrils cascaded through his nervous system. Instinctively he stuffed the belt in his pants pocket. He felt something. Whatever bag of gems he had grabbed was still there.

Aug sloshed his way through the wind and water from next pillar to next pillar. He could barely see, and he had no idea which pillar had been Angel's home. He was disoriented.

He found her. She was still bound to the Jocelyn pillar. He swam to the front and searched for signs of life. There was breathing. Aug wanted to free her, but how? One arm was useless. The rope was wet and wouldn't give. He could not untie her. He had nothing to cut the rope with. He cried in frustration as he made his way back to the bar. It was useless. There was nothing he could do. He had failed Laurie. He had failed Jocelyn. Now he had failed Angel.

# CHAPTER 35

## OPERATION RECOVERY

The brothers had received Aug's phone message. The call meant that the creation of a plan was in order. They immediately set about creating the plan of Operation Recovery.

They were going to have to take the Sea Bass up the Gulf in the wake of the storm. They would need to pilot by compass. No GPS or stars would be available. One of them would have to get ashore in rough seas. Who would go, and who would stay with the boat? A decision was required, which meant one thing—rock, scissors, paper. Mike threw rock; Steve threw scissors.

They set about the task of securing a Boston Whaler to the back of their boat. They also secured plenty of fuel for the journey up and back. They also brought along anything they figured they might possibly need for Steve to use to enter the shuttered building.

The Sea Bass rode up the Gulf in dangerous choppy waters. They didn't want to wait until the hurricane was completely gone before retrieving their loot. Forty million dollars worth of gems will make people take risks that are insane and incredible. They wanted to beat any emergency services into the area.

Eventually they figured they were near where they should be. The boat lurched in the water as they looked through night-vision goggles at the shore. What they saw blew them away. They saw Poseidon's pillars extending in the air and a shell of a building and not much more. Poseidon's had been blown away. The Temple Mount, the Temple Beach, was destroyed. They saw Sounion in ruin.

They decided to take a risk on grounding the boat and got as close to the shore as possible. Steve lowered the smaller boat in the water and fired up the motor. He had a dim hope of finding speakers intact somewhere. The tidal surge was still high enough that he could pilot the small craft into the carnage. He saw Angel tied to a pillar.

Steve produced a knife and cut her bonds. She was still alive, but she was unresponsive. He managed to get her into the dinghy. Above the lowered wind sound, he heard noises. He killed the motor and moored the boat to the pillar. Steve sloshed through to the bar area. He found Aug laid out on the bar.

Steve yelled, "Aug!" to get a response. Aug numbly opened his eyes. Steve distinctly yelled at him, "Where are the diamonds?" Aug reached in his pocket and handed Steve the one bag that he had. Steve yelled back, "Is that it? Where are the others?" Aug shook his head. Steve pulled him off the bar. "C'mon, let's go!"

They made their way back to the craft. Steve helped Aug into the boat, and then he climbed in. He untied the rope, and they started to pull away. Aug saw a flashlight in the dinghy. He lunged for it. He nearly caused them to tip, but he had to see. He had to take one final look. He aimed the torch up top at Jocelyn's face.

The head was cracked. One quarter of it was gone. He saw an eye and a smile, and that was it. She was still smiling at him. *I praise to you*, Aug thought. *Nothing ever goes away.*

Steve recognized the face. He felt creepy. He saw a union in ruin. He fired the motor back up and drove out of there as fast as he could.

It was a perilous journey with both the bodies with the Whaler getting airborne and crashing back down along the ride. Water filled the bottom of the boat in a short period. Steve feared that the craft would sink from the water that they took on.

Mike saw the boat approaching, and he threw on every light he could to make the approach easier. He was momentarily stopped by the thought that he heard a bloodcurdling scream from somewhere, but he saw and heard nothing else. Steve piloted close enough for Mike to get them a rope and help reel them in. They hoisted Angel in the boat. With Mike and Steve's help, Aug was able to manage to crawl up the boat steps. Steve hopped on and cut the Whaler loose to let it go its own way.

Steve and Mike hustled Angel down below. Steve stayed down to provide medical attention. Mike came up to get the boat out of there as fast as possible.

Aug stayed topside. He pulled the belt from his pocket. It was his only remnant of Jocelyn. He made his way to the front of the deck and used the whip to lash himself to the boat railing. He lay on the deck. The rain poured down on him as he stared at the sky. He was painless from the physical pain that he felt. The mental pain overrode everything. Hurricane-speed wind roared through his ears.

Had Jack been true with his statements? Had Jack actually been a benefactor all these years? Had he actually believed many things that were not true? Was Laurie's family really responsible for her death? Or was everything a conniving mix of half-lies and half-truths like a politician or a preacher or a businessman spinning in the press to confuse the public about the crimes and bad decisions that they really committed? Like the plates and goblets he had seen in Jack's house, what method could be used to determine what was real and fake?

He did not know, and now he would never know because they were gone. They were gone because he triggered the bomb. He could have warned them, or he could have attempted to deactivate the device. He had not done so because of his individualistic belief. He had to accept responsibility for his actions. He was beyond being a believer in a moment of crisis. He was lost in disbelief. His prideful disambiguation was complete. He was now a "relinquisher."

He looked for Laurie in the sky, but he could not see her. She had passed beyond his sight. What Aug now saw in the sky was Jocelyn. His whole life with Jocelyn played across the skies. He saw her ascend into heaven.

Aug knew it was over. He rolled over on his side, mouth open, breathing heavily. He had failed them all. Again. With eyes wide open and tears streaming from them, he silently wept.

# EPILOGUE

---

The Painless love of Laurie and Augustus Valentine had ended. But the pursuit of the purloined plunder continues in:

# BLINDLESS

CPSIA information can be obtained
at www.ICGtesting.com
Printed in the USA
LVHW03*1018070918
589381LV00001B/4/P